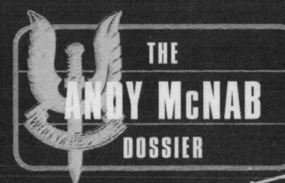

THE ANDY McNAB DOSSIER

CONFIDENTIAL

D0928246

ANDY McN

➲ In 1984 he was 'badged' as a member of 22 SAS Regiment.

➲ Over the course of the next nine years he was at the centre of covert operations on five continents.

➲ During the first Gulf War he commanded Bravo Two Zero, a patrol that, in the words of his commanding officer, 'will remain in regimental history for ever'.

➲ Awarded both the Distinguished Conduct Medal (DCM) and Military Medal (MM) during his military career.

➲ McNab was the British Army's most highly decorated serving soldier when he finally left the SAS in February 1993.

➲ He is a patron of the *Help for Heroes* campaign.

➲ He is now the author of twelve bestselling thrillers, as well as two Quick Read novels, *The Grey Man* and *Last Night Another Soldier*. He has also edited *Spoken from the Front*, an oral history of the conflict in Afghanistan.

NMLIRF

'A richly detailed picture of life in the SAS'
Sunday Telegraph

BRAVO TWO ZERO

In January 1991, eight members of the SAS regiment, under the command of Sergeant Andy McNab, embarked upon a top secret mission in Iraq to infiltrate them deep behind enemy lines. Their call sign: 'Bravo Two Zero'.

IMMEDIATE ACTION

The no–holds–barred account of an extraordinary life, from the day McNab as a baby was found in a carrier bag on the steps of Guy's Hospital to the day he went to fight in the Gulf War. As a delinquent youth he kicked against society. As a young soldier he waged war against the IRA in the streets and fields of South Armagh.

SEVEN TROOP

Andy McNab's gripping story of the time he served in the company of a remarkable band of brothers. The things they saw and did during that time would take them all to breaking point – and some beyond – in the years that followed. He who dares doesn't always win . . .

Nick Stone titles

Nick Stone, ex–SAS trooper, now gun–for–hire working on deniable ops for the British government, is the perfect man for the dirtiest of jobs, doing whatever it takes by whatever means necessary…

REMOTE CONTROL
✠ **Dateline: Washington DC, USA**

Stone is drawn into the bloody killing of an ex–SAS officer and his family and soon finds himself on the run with the one survivor who can identify the killer – a seven-year-old girl.

'Proceeds with a testosterone surge' *Daily Telegraph*

CRISIS FOUR
✠ **Dateline: North Carolina, USA**

In the backwoods of the American South, Stone has to keep alive the beautiful young woman who holds the key to unlock a chilling conspiracy that will threaten world peace.

'When it comes to thrills, he's Forsyth class' *Mail on Sunday*

FIREWALL
✠ **Dateline: Finland**

The kidnapping of a Russian Mafia warlord takes Stone into the heart of the global espionage world and into conflict with some of the most dangerous killers around.

'Other thriller writers do their research, but McNab has actually been there' *Sunday Times*

LAST LIGHT
✛ Dateline: Panama

Stone finds himself at the centre of a lethal conspiracy involving ruthless Colombian mercenaries, the US government and Chinese big business. It's an uncomfortable place to be . . .

'A heart thumping read' *Mail on Sunday*

LIBERATION DAY
✛ Dateline: Cannes, France

Behind its glamorous exterior, the city's seething underworld is the battleground for a very dirty drugs war and Stone must reach deep within himself to fight it on their terms.

'McNab's great asset is that the heart of his fiction is non–fiction' *Sunday Times*

DARK WINTER
✛ Dateline: Malaysia

A straightforward action on behalf of the War on Terror turns into a race to escape his past for Stone if he is to save himself and those closest to him.

'Addictive . . . Packed with wild action and revealing tradecraft' *Daily Telegraph*

DEEP BLACK
✛ Dateline: Bosnia

All too late Stone realizes that he is being used as bait to lure into the open a man whom the darker forces of the West will stop at nothing to destroy.

'One of the UK's top thriller writers' *Daily Express*

AGGRESSOR
⊕ Dateline: Georgia, former Soviet Union

A longstanding debt of friendship to an SAS comrade takes Stone on a journey where he will have to risk everything to repay what he owes, even his life ...

'A terrific novelist' *Mail on Sunday*

RECOIL
⊕ Dateline: The Congo, Africa

What starts out as a personal quest for a missing woman quickly becomes a headlong rush from his own past for Stone.

'Stunning ... A first class action thriller' *The Sun*

CROSSFIRE
⊕ Dateline: Kabul

Nick Stone enters the modern day wild west that is Afghanistan in search of a kidnapped reporter.

'Authentic to the core ... McNab at his electrifying best' *Daily Express*

BRUTE FORCE
⊕ Dateline: Tripoli

An undercover operation is about to have deadly long term consequences...

'Violent and gripping, this is classic McNab' *News of the World*

EXIT WOUND
⊕ Dateline: Dubai

Nick Stone embarks on a quest to track down the killer of two ex-SAS comrades.

'Could hardly be more topical... all the elements of a McNab novel are here'
Mail on Sunday

ZERO HOUR
⊕ Dateline: Amsterdam

A code that will jam every item of military hardware from Kabul to Washington. A terrorist group who nearly have it in their hands. And a soldier who wants to go down fighting...

'Like his creator, the ex-SAS soldier turned uber-agent is unstoppable'
Daily Mirror

Andy McNab and Kym Jordan's new series of novels traces the interwoven stories of one platoon's experience of warfare in the twenty-first century. Packed with the searing danger and high-octane excitement of modern combat, it also explores the impact of its aftershocks upon the soldiers themselves, and upon those who love them. It will take you straight into the heat of battle and the hearts of those who are burned by it.

WAR TORN

Two tours of Iraq under his belt, Sergeant Dave Henley has seen something of how modern battles are fought. But nothing can prepare him for the posting to Forward Operating Base Senzhiri, Helmand Province, Afghanistan. This is a warzone like even he's never seen before.

'Andy McNab's books get better and better. *War Torn* brilliantly portrays the lives of a platoon embarking on a tour of duty in Helmand province' *Daily Express*

ANDY McNAB
CROSSFIRE

CORGI BOOKS

TRANSWORLD PUBLISHERS
61–63 Uxbridge Road, London W5 5SA
A Random House Group Company
www.transworldbooks.co.uk

CROSSFIRE
A CORGI BOOK: 9780552163620

First published in Great Britain
in 2007 by Bantam Press
an imprint of Transworld Publishers
Corgi edition published 2008
Corgi edition reissued 2011

Addresses for Random House Group Ltd companies outside the UK
can be found at: www.randomhouse.co.uk
The Random House Group Ltd Reg. No. 954009

The Random House Group Limited supports The Forest Stewardship
Council (FSC®), the leading international forest certification organisation.
Our books carrying the FSC label are printed on FSC® certified paper. FSC is
the only forest certification scheme endorsed by the leading environmental
organisations, including Greenpeace. Our paper procurement policy can be
found at www.randomhouse.co.uk/environment

Typeset in Palatino by Falcon Oast Graphic Art Ltd.
Printed and bound by CPI Group (UK) Ltd, Croydon, CR0 4YY.

6 8 10 9 7 5

Dedication

This book is dedicated to the men of 2 Rifles and 2 Lancs, for their bravery and endurance. I was privileged to spend time in Iraq with both of these battalions, and without doubt they are some of the most professional soldiers our country has ever seen.

2nd Battalion the Rifles

Rifleman Daniel Lee Coffey, aged twenty-one, from Exeter, died as a result of injuries sustained in Basra City on 27 February 2007.

Rifleman Aaron Lincoln, aged eighteen, from Durham, died as a result of injuries sustained in Basra City on 2 April 2007.

Rifleman Paul Donnachie, aged eighteen, from Reading, was killed in a small-arms fire attack in Basra City on 29 April 2007.

2nd Battalion the Duke of Lancaster's Regiment

Kingsman Jamie Lee Hancock, aged nineteen, from Wigan, died as a result of injuries sustained during small-arms fire against a coalition forces base in Basra on 6 November 2006.

Sergeant Graham Hesketh, aged thirty-five, from Liverpool, was killed during a patrol in Basra City on 28 December 2006.

Kingsman Alexander William Green, aged twenty-one, from Warrington, died as a result of injuries sustained in Basra City on 13 January 2007.

Second Lieutenant Jonathan Bracho-Cooke, aged twenty-four, from Hove, died as a result of injuries sustained by an improvised explosive device (IED) attack on 5 February 2007.

Kingsman Danny John Wilson, aged twenty-eight, from Workington, died as a result of injuries sustained in Basra City on 1 April 2007.

Kingsman Adam James Smith, aged nineteen, from the Isle of Man, died as a result of injuries sustained by an IED attack on 5 April 2007.

Second Lieutenant Joanna Yorke Dyer, aged twenty-four, from Yeovil, died as a result of injuries sustained by an IED attack on 5 April 2007.

Kingsman Alan Joseph Jones, aged twenty, from Liverpool, was killed when his Warrior armoured fighting vehicle came under small-arms fire on 23 April 2007.

Prologue

60 miles west of Jalalabad, Afghanistan
17 June 1986
Last light

I didn't know the name of the village, though we'd been through there many times. It was just a collection of mud huts on a plateau, three-quarters of the way down a mountain, in a snow-capped range halfway between Kabul and the Khyber Pass.

We had to be out again by first light, when the Hinds would be back to hand out the early-morning news. If they spotted us, the gunships would annihilate the place, and anyone inside. That was how they did things.

We were in-country because the Ivans were in-country, and the West didn't want them to be. It wasn't the invasion they objected to. It was Soviet troops massed so close to the oil-rich Gulf.

The sheiks were flapping, so the bad boys had to be persuaded to fuck off back to the land of vodka.

The mujahideen – *soldiers of Allah* – had only put up weak resistance to start with. Fragmented, and armed with no more than rifles and pistols, all they had going for them was their lifelong knowledge of the terrain and an unshakeable faith in their God.

That was when dickheads like me were told to get the maps out and see where the fuck Afghanistan was, then get our arses over from Hereford and help. We came, we saw, we dropped bridges, attacked police stations, built IEDs, and blew up armoured convoys. I wasn't wild about living in a cave, but other than that, I'd been having the time of my life.

'See that?'

'What, Nick?'

'Over there, in the alleyway. Looks like a body.'

'It will just be a girl,' Ahmad grunted. He wore the kind of expression you use when someone's just pointed out the shit on your shoe. 'We go on, Nick. We need food.'

My new best mujahideen mate cut away and gestured to the others to sort themselves out before the long tab back to our holes in the rock above the snowline.

The girl's body was lying between two mud-walled shacks. At least somebody had had the decency to drape the charred remains of her clothes over what was left of her. Going by the scorchmarks on the ground, it looked like she'd set herself on fire in plain view. When the flames died down, the villagers had probably just dragged her here out of the way and got on with their lives.

I nearly hadn't come over. I'd seen it all too many times before. But this one was different – even in the fading light, I thought I'd seen movement. And, besides, the girl with the cheeky grin lived in one of these huts. I always looked out for her when we came this way. The landscape might be cold, harsh and unforgiving, but somhow her smile always made me think that what we were doing was worthwhile.

The people who scratched a living in these mountains didn't have enough even to feed themselves, but that didn't stop them sharing it with us. I'd never spoken to the girl with the cheeky grin. It would have been taboo. But she'd run up a couple of times and handed me a sliver of watermelon or a cup of water. She couldn't have been more than fourteen.

Not so long ago, the cheeky grin had disappeared, as if someone had thrown a switch. 'Yes,' Ahmad had said. 'Now she have husband.' Apparently he was nearly three times her age and from another band of muj. Ahmad seemed to think her husband was having trouble teaching her respect.

She'd looked a little more desperate each time I saw her after that. The last couple of times, I'd noticed the bruises.

I squatted down by the heap of blackened material. There was a terrible stench of singed hair, burnt meat and kerosene, like the smell that hung in the air after the gunships had called.

I laid my AK on a rock and took off my Bergen. I lifted the charred clothes away from her head and gagged. The scorched skin was peeling from her face and neck. Blisters were still forming. The skin round her mouth stretched back to expose her teeth in a hideous parody of her cheeky grin. It wasn't how I wanted to remember her.

She opened her eyes just a fraction, and when she saw me she murmured softly. There'd be no screaming out in pain for her. That stage was well gone. Her burns were so severe that even the nerve endings had evaporated.

Like Ahmad and his boys, I was in full Gunga Din gear and cowpat hat. I took off my waistcoat and tucked it gently under the back of her head to protect it from the rocks.

She had an hour at the most. There wasn't even a field clinic or a nurse up here. The nearest hospital was in Jalalabad, a couple of days away on foot, and the roads round the city were teeming with hammers and sickles.

I doubted she even had someone who cared enough to bury her. Treated like a slave, not only by the husband but also the rest of his family, I guessed she'd just had enough. Most of the women stuck at these shit marriages because that was the way things were. By tradition, every Afghan girl or woman had to be attached to some man – her father, husband, brother, son, uncle – and for all too many of them the kerosene trick was the only way out.

Boots scrambled towards me. 'Nick! We have hut – come.'

I looked up. Ahmad's beard was longer than mine, and he was proud of it. He hadn't shaved these last seven years, ever since the Russians had arrived to 'liberate' his country. He was a hard fucker, like the rest of the muj, a good Muslim, a good fighter, a good man. I enjoyed working with them, but I could never understand why they were total arseholes to their women. They treated them like shit.

He didn't even bother to glance at the girl. She might as well not have been there. 'Come, leave it. We're cooking.'

'Go on, mate, you get stuck in. But maybe bring me something, will you?'

I knew there was fuck-all I could do for her, but there'd been enough killing up on the mountain. It seemed such a waste of a young life for her to have done it to herself.

She'd probably been sold into her marriage. Some of the muj I knew had sold their own daughters when they were twelve or thirteen. They even claimed a bride price as payback for raising the poor little fuckers in the first place. Others gave them away to repay bets or settle arguments.

After the girls got palmed off and married, they were raped continuously. If they complained, they might find themselves flung into prison. The ones that could afford it took overdoses. The poorer ones cut their wrists, hanged themselves or chucked themselves into the nearest river. But this one, she'd had spirit. She wasn't going out with a whimper.

I pictured her sitting there, tipping the kerosene over her head and striking a match. But she'd fucked up. Maybe she couldn't afford a full can. Now she was lying in the dust, waiting to die.

Ahmad came back with half a big green watermelon. 'Nick, please, you not be long. The meat, he nearly gone . . .'

'Thanks, mate.' I took the melon off him. I couldn't understand why these guys didn't care. 'She hasn't got long. But I can't leave her, can I?'

He eyed me as if I was a lunatic. 'They say her name is Farah.' He turned to leave, then stopped. 'Of course you can leave her, Nick. This her choice. This what she want.'

He walked away.

I looked down at her. What she want? No, not really.

I pulled my AK bayonet from my belt and cut into the melon. The juice flowed down my fingers, which were black with weeks of grime.

'Farah, here . . .' I touched a sliver of the fruit to what was left of her lips.

She sucked it in. Her eyes flickered open again and I thought I could see something resembling a smile in them. She tried her best to swallow as the juice ran down the side of her ravaged face. Painfully slowly, she shifted her eyes towards me. She began to weep gently, but no tears fell.

I cut another slice of melon. I didn't know what else to do.

The late-afternoon sun bathed her face for a moment, then disappeared. As darkness fell, we both waited for her to die.

PART ONE

1

Tuesday, 27 February 2007
0015 hrs
North-west of Basra

The noise and heat, gloom and sheer fucking claustrophobia in the back of the Warrior were oppressive enough, but now the armour was suddenly clanging three times a second like the world's strongest madman was using it for sledgehammer practice. We were taking rounds. It could only mean we were closing in on target.

The engine roared and the tracks screeched over the rock.

The front end dipped hard.

'Fuck!' the Scouse driver screamed over the radio net, as he stood on the anchors. 'There's a fuck'n' bastard tank!'

The commander yelled back so loud I had to

lift the PRR pad from my ear. 'Go right, you cunt
– you'll hit the fucker!' Until a few years ago, the
only way troops could communicate with each
other was by shouting or hand signals, but every
man and his dog now wore a personal role radio.
It had revolutionized the infantry. Just four
inches by six, with a headset consisting of an ear
pad, Velcro strap and little boom mike, PRR acted
effectively as a secure chat net between troops.

The Challenger's thundering growl had come
from our left. The tracks squealed and we gripped
whatever we could get hold of to stop ourselves
being flung from our seats. We took more small-
arms fire into the hull, and then there was a much
louder bang two feet away from my shoulder.

'RPG!'

Rocket-propelled grenades could punch holes
in concrete walls. I knew it would just bounce off
the skirt of bar armour surrounding us, but I still
felt like I was trapped in a locked safe while
people on the outside were fucking about with
blowtorches and gelignite.

It wasn't simply that I couldn't see what was
happening. It was having no control that
bothered me. I was at the mercy of the driver, the
gunner and the commander in the turret. He was
a platoon sergeant called Rhett or Red – I didn't
catch it when we met, and then we got past the
point where I could ask again.

Our Warrior was part of the battle group's

recce platoon. Dom, Pete and I were embedded. 'Entombed, more like,' Pete said. He'd been a tankie himself once upon a time, and even he didn't like the lid coming down. We were jammed shoulder to shoulder in the eerie red glow of the night-lights. Rhett's scuffed and dusty desert boots were level with my face. The gunner was up there on his left, frantically feeding rounds into the 30mm cannon.

The wagon took one final hard right and came to a jarring, gut-wrenching halt. The stern reared up under the momentum, then crashed down like a breaking wave.

'Dismount! Dismount!'

Rhett's shout was drowned by the cannon kicking off above us.

Dom got a punch from one of the Kingsmen and hit the button above his head. The rear-door hydraulics whined. I could see stars, hear the roar of gunfire and heavy machinery.

The four recce guys tumbled out into the inky blackness. Pete shoved a hand over his lens and we followed.

My Timberlands slid and twisted on the rubble as I ducked down against the bar armour, gulping fresh but dust-laden air. Oil wells blazed out of control on the horizon. Gases and crude were being forced out of the ground under phenomenal pressure, shooting flames a hundred feet into the air.

The night was filled with the thunder of 30mm cannon kicking off across the dried-up wadi bed that separated us from our target – the buildings no more than a hundred away. It had prevented the drivers going right up to the front doors.

I was hungry for more air. My nostrils filled with sand, but I didn't care. I had my feet on the ground and I was in control of them. And, thanks to the mortar platoon, I could see what was happening. Their 81mm tubes had filled the sky with illume. Balls of blazing magnesium hung in the air above the town before beginning their descent, casting shadows left and right as they swung under their parachutes, silhouetting the two massive Challengers rumbling left and right of us.

Bright muzzle flashes from four or five AKs sparked up from the line of houses that edged the built-up area.

Our gunner switched from the 30mm Rarden cannon to the 7.62mm Hughes Helicopter Chain Gun to dish out a different edition of the same good news.

Two Warriors lurched to a halt alongside us, throwing up a plume of dust. My nose was totally clogged now. Guys spilled out of the back doors with bayonets fixed.

Pete adjusted the oversized Batman utility belt round his waist where he stuffed his lenses and shit, and raised his infrared camera to his face.

He was like a kid in a sweetshop as the mass of armour surrounding the town spewed infantry into the sand.

Dom got ready to do his Jeremy Bowen bit to camera. He rehearsed a few soundbites to himself as Pete sorted the sound check.

'The Kingsmen of the Duke of Lancaster's Regiment are halfway through their six-month tour. They have been shot at twenty-four/seven by small arms, RPGs and mortars, but ask any one of them and they'll tell you it's what they signed up to do.'

Tonight they were about to kick the shit out of the insurgents who were within spitting distance of taking over Al Gurnan and starting to claim the ground as their own. They had to be broken. An insurgent stronghold soon became another link in the supply chain from Iran, just ten clicks away.

The Kingsmen's mission was to do the breaking, and ours was to report it. Dom talked, Pete filmed him, and I had to make sure the two didn't get shot, snatched or run over by a set of tracks sent screaming across the desert by a bunch of jabbering Scousers.

It wasn't easy. When Dom started playing newsman, he seemed to think there was a magic six-foot forcefield standing between him and any incoming fire. Sometimes he thought he didn't even need to wear a helmet. But in this war the enemy didn't give a shit whether you were a journalist or a soldier. If you were a foreigner they wanted you out, preferably in a body-bag. If they could get you alive, so much the better: you'd be the new star of *The Al Jazeera Show*, and all you could do was hope your next appearance wouldn't end with them slicing off your head online.

The chain gun ceased fire. The Kingsmen swarmed down into the wadi.

Dom made to follow, but I grabbed him and pulled him on to his knees. Another flurry of illume kicked off over the town and the cannon opened up again. I had to scream into his ear: 'They said not to go forward until they call us! Wait. Let them get on with it.'

The Kingsmen vanished for a few seconds in the dead ground of the riverbed, before re-appearing on the far bank, screaming and shouting all sorts of Scouse shit they probably didn't even understand themselves.

They kicked their way through a series of old wooden doors and into whatever chaos lay the other side.

2

The sun had risen enough to chuck out a bit of heat, but not enough to coax me out of the over-sized fleece I had on over my body armour. I ran my tongue over my furred-up teeth and gave my greasy, stubbled face a rub.

Dom and Pete sat among steel ammo boxes, day sacks and general wagon shit the other side of the idling Warrior. Pete fucked about on his Mac laptop, editing the bulletin Dom had made during the attack. He wasn't one of those bunker journos who gave their action-packed report from the safety of a Green Zone balcony. And that was my big problem. I spent every waking hour either pulling him down or away from someone or something that could kill him.

Paul, one of the recce platoon, was top cover

29

with a Minimi; he had to stand between us with his head and shoulders sticking out through the open mortar hatch. Sand and all sorts showered down each time he moved.

I brushed some desert off my fleece. It got cold out here at night and I was a bit of a lizard. I liked to keep warm, even if it meant wearing something Pete described as the colour of shite after a bad vindaloo. I hadn't got it from an outdoors store; I always ended up throwing my kit away every few weeks because it got so minging, so I'd treated myself to a trip to Oxfam. Three and a half quid as opposed to thirty; a bargain whatever the colour.

Last night had produced an insurgent body count of eighteen, at a cost of two wounded Kingsmen. Now a Challenger and our three recce-platoon Warriors had been tasked with setting up a vehicle checkpoint on the eastern road out of town to see what got caught in the net.

Looking out of the open rear door, I could see the wadi the guys had run through during last night's attack. It was littered with carrier-bags, dog shit, drinks cans, water-bottles; all kinds of trash that wouldn't be washed downstream until next year when the rains came.

A pack of scabby old dogs were kept at bay by the heat blasting from the grilles of the Challenger's massive turbo-charged diesel engine. Like the Warriors', its hull and tracks were caked with mud and dust. No call for spit and polish here: they were fighting a war. The bar armour surrounding the lower hull and tracks looked like a series of buckled and scorched farm gates. That was because it was doing its job, deflecting RPGs.

Now it was light, I couldn't see too much flame from the blazing oil wells, just thick black pillars of smoke on the horizon. It was going to be a long time before this place was stable enough for the conglomerates to come and start sucking out black gold.

The Challenger pointed its big fuck-off barrel at the town like it was giving the locals the finger. *Come and have a go, if you think you're hard enough.* It wouldn't take a genius to get the message.

A helmet jutted from its turret. Tank crews wore dark green covers to blend in with their vehicles; light desert camouflage would make a perfect target for a sniper or any half-decent shot who'd bothered to zero his weapon.

The Kingsmen had five VCPs covering all the roads in and out of town. After last night's attack they dominated the area. At first light they'd started searching and questioning every male of fighting age. Notionally that was fourteen to sixty. The reality was that if you could lift a weapon you could fire it, so the guys had massaged the age bands. Terrorists, insurgents, whatever the government had decided to call them this week, to the Kingsmen it was academic. Out here on the ground, politics meant nothing. Even kids and old men were firing AKs and RPGs at them, and they were firing back.

There was never any doubt who was in command. I could hear Rhett right now, out on the VCP, giving shit to the platoon.

It was easy to tell the guys at the sharp end from the rest of the army, even though they wore the same uniform. They were in shit state. Their boots were hammered and fell apart before they ever got a clean. Their uniforms were dirty and ragged, their camouflaged helmet covers and body armour so worn and ripped it was hard to see the pattern.

The Challenger wasn't the only one with its engine running. All three Warriors had theirs idling so the big square boiling vessels inside could heat water.

I pushed the button at the bottom of our BV and made three brews.

'Here, mate.'

Pete took his white, no sugar. Fuck knows why, but this lot called it a Shirley Temple. I passed the mug to him round Paul's legs.

He took it without looking up and settled it on the steel floor beside him, pausing only to blow sand off his keyboard.

The Kingsmen thought Pete was weird for not

taking sugar. 'He worried about his figure or something?'

Dom took sugar, but as far as they were concerned he was still from a completely different planet, not because he was a Pole but because he drank only three brews a day.

To make up the shortfall, I threw Pete a Yorkie bar from the ration packs. He glanced at the wrapper and gave a little chuckle. Where it normally read 'It's Not For Girls', the army ration pack version had 'It's Not For Civvies'. Now that he'd been let in on the joke, it never ceased to amuse him.

Paul's brew was next. Like the whole of recce platoon he took it NATO standard: white, two sugars. Me too. Not because I liked it that way any more but so I could join the others taking the piss out of Pete for being a girl.

I tugged at his trousers and a leather-gloved hand whisked the plastic mug on to the roof.

'Cheers, la'.' Pete's accent would always be more Bermondsey than Scouse, but he needed to level the score.

Paul muttered something back and Pete laughed. The banter had been ricocheting between them for the last two days.

Paul's tone changed suddenly. 'I got movement ... in the wadi ... three fifty. *They're carrying ...*'

Radios crackled and another Warrior from

a VCP south of us opened up with its cannon.

I watched through the rear doors as the ground round the bodies erupted in clouds of dust. The small figures scattered.

Dom grabbed Pete's camera and almost fell out of the wagon. He was nearest the door and Pete still had his iBook on his lap.

Paul got a lead on one of the runners. He kicked off a short burst and the empty cases cascaded on to Pete's head as he hunched over his screen.

Then Rhett yelled, 'Check fire, check fire!'

Paul froze.

'It's kids!'

3

The radio net went ballistic as everyone was told to stop firing.

Rhett paced angrily as the net commanded a call sign to go and check if any of them had been hit. 'Little shites!'

Then he shouted into the camera, a finger jabbing at the lens with every word as Dom kept it stable on his shoulder. 'The little bastards shove a black sock over a water-bottle, put it on the end of a stick and play RPGs. It might be the only game they know, but it's going to get them killed. Or one of my guys, while he's trying to work out what the fuck's being aimed at him. It pisses me off. Why don't their parents grip the little shites?'

He stormed away to give someone else a bollocking. Our driver walked past the open rear door with an SA80 in one hand and a big wheel wrench in the other. Our Warrior had had two wheels blown off a fortnight ago by an improvised explosive device dug into the side of the road. Now the nuts on one always seemed to be coming loose, and the driver liked to tighten them at every opportunity.

''Ere, Paul . . .' Pete gestured towards the driver '. . . you Scousers, you're always at it – your mate's nicking the wheels off your own fucking wagon . . .'

The mouthful he was about to get back was interrupted as the net reported no bodies in the contact area.

'Thank fuck for that.' In helmet, padded gloves and body armour, Paul was the next best thing to the Terminator. His ballistic glasses looked like untinted Oakleys. Like the leather gloves, they were worn to protect against fragmentation from RPGs and upblast from IEDs. The original issue had been ski goggles, but nobody wanted to wear them. Maybe it was the curvature or the Perspex, but they gave a weird perspective when you took aim. These ballistic gigs gave superior vision and far more protection.

His Osprey body armour had two big plates front and rear, and a big collar that came right up to his ears to protect against upblast. I particularly liked the bat-wings – Kevlar pads extending from the shoulder to the elbow to give extra protection when he stuck his top half out of the mortar hatch, ready to back the three lads with his Minimi 5.56 machine-gun if things kicked off.

I just wished Pete, Dom and I had the same protection, instead of the blue baby armour the media always minced about in. The theory was that we stood out from the military, but through the iron sights of an AK we'd be the only blue things in the desert.

A contact kicked off in the distance, probably at a VCP on the other side of town. Tracer rounds bounced into the sky.

The VCP set-up was simple. Two Warriors parked about fifty metres apart, on opposite sides of the road and angled at forty-five degrees to it, forming a chicane. One had its 30mm cannon facing out-of-town traffic, the other facing traffic coming in. Every vehicle, even donkeys and carts, was stopped by whichever Warrior it came to first and fed through into the safe area to be searched. The rest of the platoon was spread out in fire positions as all-round defence.

We'd had a big rush out of town to start with, as the locals tried to leg it, but then it died down when they realized no one was going to escape with their hauls of weapons, explosives and drugs.

The problem was, no vehicles meant no locals the insurgents had to worry about killing by mistake, so we were an unprotected target. 'Open season,' Pete muttered.

Dom climbed back in and the two of them got back to work.

I sat down with my brew near the open doorway and watched as a battered 4x4 crept into the VCP.

4

Many of the vehicles I'd seen looked brand-new. Some had Kuwait or Dubai numberplates. All flew a white flag. This one was a Land Cruiser, and its best days were behind it. Paul's feet shifted as he shadowed it with his Minimi. I watched as it moved into the safe ground. A white pillowcase hung from its aerial.

Five males of fighting age got out with their hands in the air. They knew the drill; they'd been doing it for nearly four years now.

I stretched my legs along the seat. Pete tapped away at the keyboard, preparing to send TVZ 24 the latest report from its star correspondent.

It was Poland's first twenty-four-hour news channel. I'd watched a few of Dom's pieces. It looked like Sky, News 24 or CNN with additional gobbledegook; they were all the same format, lots of primary colours, rousing music, girls with big hair and white teeth. Their headquarters were in Krakow, but TVZ 24 didn't only beam out to Poland: plumbers and builders all over Europe were regular viewers on satellite or cable. Dom and Pete worked out of the Dublin office. There were better tax breaks in the Republic than in the UK.

It wasn't only the Poles who knew our hero. Dominik Condratowicz was a bit of a celeb in reporting circles, the golden boy of war journalism with platinum-plated bollocks. He was one of those people who believed he would never get shot or damaged, the sort, Pete said, who walked into nothing but good. He wore a memory stick on a chain round his neck. Maybe it was to ward off evil spirits.

He was tall and annoyingly good-looking, even when a thick layer of dust had given him a horror-film face. His *Top Gun*-style dark brown hair, blindingly white teeth and firm jawline were featured most weeks next to his wife's in Poland's answer to *Hello!*. As far as I knew, he lived in Dublin with Siobhan, his Irish wife, and her son. He kept things close to his chest, did Platinum Bollocks.

Pete was getting pissed off with the dust billowing off Dom's jacket. 'Here, Dracula, you going to take your fucking cloak off or what?' Dom's mother was from Transylvania. When he'd found out Pete obviously thought he'd died

40

and gone to heaven. He was laughing so much he had to close his iBook to stop his own dust getting on the keys.

Dom cocked an ear as Pete went back to his edit. 'Talking of creatures of the night . . .' His English had an accent, but it was a whole lot better than mine. This guy had education behind him.

An unmanned aerial vehicle – the battle group's eyes – buzzed overhead in the brilliantly clear sky. Like a large model plane with a huge wingspan and a couple of cameras in the body, the UAV was flown by remote control from one of the Warriors.

Pete took the final bite of his Yorkie, pulled a can of compressed air from his Bat-belt and gave the laptop keys a few bursts. As he treated himself to a blast down the front of his shirt, I spotted a memory stick like Dom's round his neck. I hadn't realized superstition was so rife in this business.

Bosnia, Sudan, Afghanistan, Iraq. They'd been there, seen it, done it together, and Pete had filmed Dom wearing the T-shirt. He never lost an opportunity to remind Dom it was his camerawork that had won them all their awards. They'd picked up an Emmy last year for a documentary on women's rights in Afghanistan – almost non-existent under the Taliban, and not much improved, apparently, under new management.

5

A couple of cars and trucks were still being held at either end of the chicane, waiting to be fed into the safe ground.

Pete was about to upload the report. He joined Paul in the mortar hatch and plonked his sat phone on a flat stretch of hull. The BGAN Explorer 500 looked more like a George Foreman grill than a mobile. Lying on its side with the lid open, it was pointing straight at Paul.

'Mind the old family jewels, mate.' Pete grinned from ear to ear. 'You know what they say about them microwaves . . .'

Pete used a little inbuilt button compass to point it towards the satellite, then ran the USB lead back down through the hatch and into his iBook. The power lead was plugged into the vehicle supply.

'All set?' Dom closed his eyes and tried to get comfortable.

Pete tapped away. 'On its way.'

A shaft of early-morning light shone through the mortar hatch and on to my face.

'Back in your coffin, Drac.' Pete wasn't missing a trick this morning.

Dom kept his eyes shut but couldn't stop a grin.

'What now, Pete?' I shifted a day sack out of the way. 'You going to go and talk tanks with your new mates?'

He shook his head. 'Had enough of that shit when I was in. I never liked the fucking things even then. Besides, Tallulah wants me to give Ruby a virtual bollocking.'

Pete logged on to BT at least once a day and checked his emails. The ones he got from seven-year-old Ruby and her step-mum Tallulah always raised a smile with him. They did with me, too, but only because Ruby and Tallulah sounded more like a *Eurovision Song Contest* entry than real people.

Emails were OK, but no one out here was allowed to use a mobile phone to call home. The insurgents had infiltrated the phone companies, and if a soldier was allowed to waffle to his family they could triangulate the signal, get a fix on his location and an early warning of any troop movement across the desert. Which meant they could scatter – or they could attack.

Pete was in his late forties, and had been a squaddy himself for four or five years when he was younger. Hussars, dragoons, lancers – some tank regiment, I'd never understood who was what. I liked him a lot, and it wasn't just because of his accent. The moment I'd heard it at Amman airport, I'd known we had a lot more in common than an army past.

What we didn't share was his almost obsessive-compulsive approach to organization. Pete had to be the most fastidious man on the planet. Maybe that wasn't so surprising, after being cooped up for the whole of his army career with a crew who farted every five minutes and pissed in empty plastic bottles. He washed his socks and underwear every night, even though he had a fortnight's worth in his bag, and spent so long with the Colgate and floss I thought he was going to wear his teeth out.

''Ere, Nick . . . You want to get online before the Prince of Darkness here hogs the fucking thing?' He looked across at Dom and the smile evaporated.

Dom seemed to spend longer on the phone and email than a lovestruck teenager, and it never seemed to be to his wife. His hours online were to Moira, his producer back in Dublin.

'The price of fame.' I raised an eyebrow.

'Rather him than me,' Pete said. 'She's an arse-hole.'

It was true. The only decent person I'd spoken to in the whole office was Kate, her PA.

He went back to his laptop. It still felt strange to me that they were able to maintain contact with the outside world and conduct their lives almost normally while sitting in the back of one of these things in the middle of a war zone. It wasn't just the technology that amazed me. It was sustaining the relationship.

An RPG kicked off somewhere in the city. A 30mm fired up and gave it a few rounds back.

Dom opened his eyes and reached for a bottle of water. He took a few swigs and offered it to Pete, who looked at him in disgust. 'After you've had your fangs round it?'

Dom finished it off. I could almost hear his mind ticking over as he drank. 'Did the two of you see the trackmarks on their arms last night?'

We'd got called forward at dark o'clock to check out the aftermath of one of the house attacks. There were four dead, all in their twenties. Two had had AKs, the others RPG launchers.

Pete gave me a here-we-go-again look. 'I keep telling you, Drac. There's loads of these fuckers on the gear. It's even worse than at home.'

Dom dropped the empty bottle on the floor. 'I understand that, Peter, but the ones at the bottom of the food chain, why do they fight? Ideology, or just to earn their next fix? Iran is supplying them with heroin, along with the weapons and ammunition they fight with.'

Pete gave me another glance. We'd been over this ground many times. Dom had obsessed about the heroin trade ever since we'd got here, and Pete was worried.

'Listen, Drac, Iran has the worst drug problem in the world. Two million of the fuckers are hooked. It's the law of averages that the locals are on the gear. You can spit at the border from here.'

Pete punched Dom on the arm and gave him a 500-watt grin. 'I bet even that little git Ahmadinejad shoots up. Probably what stunted his growth . . .'

Dom couldn't raise a smile. 'Those young guys last night, and these . . .' He pointed at Paul's legs. 'Guys like this are fighting a war while people make fortunes trafficking heroin. Using the very wars they're fighting as cover.' He turned to me. 'What if we could prove there are people in Afghanistan and Iraq who are using the wars to move heroin into Europe and who knows where else? Tell me that isn't a story.'

Pete rolled his eyes. 'He won't leave this shit alone, Nick. You just watch when we get back to base. He'll be into the FCO mob like a rat up a drainpipe, trying to get them to pay attention.

And for what? Whatever they say, you ain't getting me running round filming a bunch of junkies.'

Pete slapped the back of his hand against Paul's legs. 'Oi, you're supposed to be a mate. If you treat a mate like that, I'm glad we're going back to Basra tomorrow. Leave you fuckers out here in the world's biggest ashtray.'

Paul cut him off. He yelled to the three in the VCP: 'Vehicle . . . I don't like it. The fucker's not slowing . . .'

Rhett charged past the rear of our wagon. 'Hold your fire . . . On my command . . .'

Pete picked up the camera.

Dom shot me a glance. 'Suicide-bomber?'

Pete was already out and running. Dom and I followed. Fuck the helmets. If the wagon was packed with high explosive, they weren't going to be much help.

6

The lead Warrior was still parked at forty-five degrees to the road.

Rhett assessed as we took cover behind. He rattled a commentary into his PRR as he scoped it through binos. 'One-up, looking young. Still closing, maybe a hundred away.'

I stuck my head out. It was an old Toyota Hilux, dark blue or black. A white rag fluttered on a length of wood behind the cab. A green tarpaulin over the tail-bed flapped in the slipstream.

'Wait, wait, wait . . .' Rhett had to make sure it wasn't some dickhead tuning the radio instead of watching the road. Could be. It had been known.

Pete had strayed out into the road as he filmed. I grabbed his body armour and hauled him back into cover. Dom was tight in behind me.

Rhett stepped out when the Hilux was just

fifty metres away. He tried to wave him down. 'Keep that fucking cannon on him.'

The driver's grim-set face filled the windscreen. This was no dickhead surfing the channels for Radio Basra.

The Hilux accelerated.

'Hit it, hit it, *hit it!*'

Rhett's voice was lost in the hail of 30mm as he dived for cover next to us. Rounds punched into the Hilux and kicked up chunks of tarmac around it. The windscreen disintegrated. The wagon was taking so many hits, I couldn't believe the whole thing didn't fall apart.

Everybody in the all-round protection cordon hit the ground, braced for the inevitable.

Pete had disappeared. Dom got up off his knees and was about to follow. I lunged for his body armour and grabbed him as the Hilux screamed past, pulling him to the ground. 'No fucking way!'

Paul gave him a long burst. The high-velocity rounds made my ears ring. I jumped on top of Dom to keep the fucker on the ground as Paul stopped firing and dropped down into the Warrior.

The Hilux slammed straight into the bar armour at the front of our wagon. There was a loud bang and bits of metal and glass showered down on us. Then there was a deathly silence.

I peered round. The Hilux had been no contest

for twenty-five tonnes of armoured vehicle. The whole left side of its engine compartment looked like it had gone through a crusher. Steam hissed from broken pipes. Oil smoked on hot metal.

Paul's head appeared through the hatch. He was straight back on the Minimi and resumed firing, directly into the cab. The body behind the wheel jerked and danced as the rounds thumped home.

Rhett was up on his feet and running. He was joined by two of the platoon. They stood and emptied their magazines into the cab until he finally raised his arm. 'Stop! Stop! Check firing!'

He took the last couple of steps, jumped up on the bar armour and peered through the smashed glass. 'We can't make the cunt any more dead.'

Pete appeared, camera up, and filmed the three Kingsmen at the driver's door.

I let go of Dom and helped him to his feet.

Rhett wrenched the door open. The body rolled out on to the sand-covered tarmac. The only sound was the steady rumble of the Warriors' engines, and the hiss of steam.

Rhett beckoned us forward. He pointed to a car battery in the footwell. The negative terminal was already connected to one of the two-core cables running out of the passenger door and under the green tarpaulin at the back. The second strand lay loose, ready to be touched to the positive.

'The battery first, Peter. Then whatever the Kingsmen do next.' Dom glanced down at what was left of the body. 'No, wait – see the track-marks?' He pointed at the body's bloodsoaked arms. 'I need a close-up.'

I gripped the back of Pete's body armour to steady him. Left to his own devices, he'd have climbed into the cab to get a better picture and ended up kicking the loose wire on to the battery terminal.

He got the shots Dom had asked for, then zoomed in on a corporal as he ripped the wire from the battery.

Dom called us to the rear of the Hilux as a couple of Kingsmen lifted the green tarpaulin carefully from the flatbed to expose what looked like a pile of hardened mashed potato.

I tapped Pete's arm. 'Plastic explosive.' It was moulded over a cluster of six mortar bombs that had been gaffer-taped together. 'Eighty-one millimetre. Mint condition. See that? Even the brass around the percussion cap is still shiny. Look at the base of the rounds, mate. Can you get the stamps?'

Pete zoomed in. '"Lot 16 2006". They Brit or Yank?'

'Neither.'

The fact that it was written in English didn't mean they'd been factory-made in an English-speaking country, or that Islamic fundamentalists were knocking up 81mm mortar rounds in a shed behind Bolton railway station. All exported munitions carry English ID. It's the language of war and Iranian mortars. Rhett eased the detonator from the pile of mash and looked at the body on the ground. 'Fucking useless twat, doped to the eyeballs – couldn't even kill himself properly, could he?'

Dom took the two steps to me and kept his voice low so the Kingsmen couldn't hear. 'You see what I mean, Nick? These mortar rounds are coming into the country in the same shipments as the heroin. This guy's not a militant, he's a victim, just like these soldiers. They're all just pawns, Nick.' He pointed at the trackmarks, trembling with anger. 'It's not just happening here.'

He stared into the distance and his voice cracked. I thought he might be about to cry. 'Dublin. London. They're all lining their pockets. We have to do something about it. We can't just stand by and do nothing.'

7

Wednesday, 28 February
2043 hrs
Basra Airport

'Say what you like about Saddam Hussein,' the Media Ops guy said, 'but he didn't mess around when it came to ordering up the gold leaf and sculpted marble.'

We were sitting in a Portakabin at the COB (Contingency Operating Base), getting increasingly bored by the Royal Artillery captain's tour-guide spiel. We weren't the new kids on the block. All we'd needed was a brief on the situation, a timetable for the embed, and a helicopter ride out to where the action was. Personally, I wasn't that interested in hearing about the fifty-six windows on the front façade, the eighteen giant reception rooms, twelve balconies, five grand staircases and eight spacious toilets with gold taps Saddam had knocked up on a commandeered public park in 1990 while his subjects scratched a squalid living around him.

Nor was Pete, by the look of him. He was trying hard not to yawn.

'And that's just one of fifteen buildings in the same complex,' the captain went on. 'Little did he know his palace would become a fortified British camp. The grounds are now home to 2 Rifles.'

I knew the second battalion of the British Army's new rifle regiment had been formed a week or two earlier from the Light Infantry, Green Jackets and Gloucesters, but only because the Scousers had been moaning about it. This amalgamation business was all the rage. The Duke of Lancs had been the King's Regiment until five minutes ago.

The captain shrugged. 'Or maybe he did. In the end, he never came here, not even for the weekend.' He laughed at his own joke.

I felt sorry for the fucker. He would probably have much preferred to be out there doing some proper soldiering instead of fronting the army's PR machine. That said, it was my job to protect Dom and Pete, and not just from bombs and ricochets. I put up my hand. 'Is there really a Pizza Hut here? If so, can we order?'

When we'd landed from Jordan on the only

civilian flight serving the city, we'd seen the rows of tents and vehicles stretching away to the horizon. To most soldiers out there, 'COB' was just another way of saying 'in the rear with the gear'. Word had it they even had two Indian guys running round on mopeds delivering American Hots with extra pepperoni.

The captain looked at his watch. 'No time, I'm afraid. Your carriage awaits.'

Even at night, which was the only time it wasn't too dangerous to fly into the compound, the pilot had to keep the rear tailgate down so the gunner had a good arc of fire. It gave us a spectacular view of the Shatt-Al-Arab waterway, glinting in the moonlight as it snaked through a series of mansions. They were flanked by palm trees and what had probably once been exotic gardens. Now they were just tank parks for 2 Rifles' armour, and as the Merlin dropped closer to the ground it looked as if every square metre had been rotavated by IDF (indirect fire).

The heli touched down just long enough for the loadmaster to kick us out and then it was airborne again. As briefed, we ran towards the torchlight that flickered on the edge of the pad, sweating in our Osprey body armour and helmets. Things were going to be different in the city. Our baby armour would have been as much protection here as an extra pullover.

A total blackout was in force. Fuck knows who held the torch, but he came from Essex. 'You can expect at least three or four mortar or rocket attacks a day while you're here.'

We followed him past wall upon wall of HESCOs, massive defences made from circular bins of galvanized steel mesh and polypropylene, filled with whatever was to hand. 'Sand's the material of choice around here,' our guy quipped, loving the chance to showboat a little. 'But it stops shrapnel all the same.'

We soon reached a building. Moonlight shone on huge marble pillars supporting a stone portico.

'Fuck me.' Pete craned his neck. 'That's Tallulah straight off to B&Q when I send her the pics.'

We went through a pair of five-metre-tall doors, and into a marble-floored hall. The guy with the torch had to be the army's oldest corporal.

Pete surveyed the empty room. 'Couldn't he afford any furniture, then?'

'Looters had it away before the Royal Marines arrived during the war.' The corporal nodded at a door to the left. 'Just a few gold taps left in the bogs. Fancy a brew?'

There was a loud thud out in the compound, then another.

'Katyushas.' The corporal poured hot water

into white styrofoam cups. 'Hundred-and-seven-millimetre. All brand-new stock. Everyone knows it can't be local. No heavy-calibre munitions have been made in Iraq since 2003.'

Pete asked the obvious question: 'So where is it being made, then?'

He handed Pete a steaming cup. 'Iran, mate. The border's just ten K away.'

8

Thursday, 1 March
1829 hrs
Basra Palace

'I'd be lying if I said I wasn't worried about him.'
Pete sipped his brew, trying not to burn his lips
and fingers.

We were sitting at the back of one of Saddam's
old state rooms as we listened to the CSM's con-
firmatory orders. Dom had disappeared to a
different part of the palace complex to have
another go at the FCO. I'd offered to escort him,
but he insisted he was fine.

'I mean, there's more chance of being struck by
lightning than getting an interview with the
spooks and the Foreign Office lot. Drac knows
that, but he's gone back for more. I don't like
the way they treat him. Particularly since he

comes straight back and takes it out on me.'

I tried to make light of it. 'Maybe that's what pisses him off. Somebody actually refusing to be interviewed by Platinum Bollocks.'

Pete leant over to talk quietly in my ear. The CSM didn't take kindly to people chatting in his Orders, even if they weren't on his payroll. 'He's been really off, this last three or four weeks.'

'You want me to have a word? It's my job – I'm supposed to look after you. Whatever's bugging him could affect his safety.'

He thought about it for a second. 'Nah, I've been trying to work out what goes on in that head of his for years.' He shrugged. 'I just have a laugh with the bit of Dom I know.'

I looked around me. We were sitting just a few feet from the famous toilet that every newspaper in the world seemed to have printed a picture of. Sculptures of men and women with stern faces and square jaws were carved into the marble walls, pointing heroically skyward. They were a bit less heroic now they had dark glasses, moustaches and teeth, courtesy of a string of bored squaddies with marker pens.

The marble floors were cracked and scraped after years of abuse from boots, chairs and desks. Gaffer-taped cables snaked underfoot and up the walls. The rooms were subdivided into offices and briefing areas by sheets of 3x3-metre plywood. The partition doors, also made of plywood, were pulled shut by a two-litre water-bottle suspended on a length of paracord running through a hole in the frame.

Phones rang incessantly. Kettles boiled 24/7 alongside ration packs of brew kit.

'Any questions?' The CSM's voice boomed round the room. He had some sort of northern accent, but at least it wasn't Scouse. Even though he spoke at a million miles an hour, I could understand him. He may have been plain Dave to his wife and other civvies, but he was 'sir' to anyone in uniform below the rank of major, and he had everyone's complete attention. It wasn't just because the army insisted on it: piled on the floor to my left were the remains of some mortar rounds and rockets that had thumped into the compound over the months of their tour – we were in serious country.

The twenty or so team commanders for tonight's strike operation, all NCOs, had had their formal orders earlier in the day, followed by full tabletop rehearsals. Dom had been present for those. Dave was now doing the final run-through.

'No? Good. OK, the house we're going to hit . . .' He glanced at the huge wall map of the city behind him. Satellite photos and int briefs lined its sides. 'The spooks over in the west wing have strong reason to believe it's part of the supply chain between Iran and local insurgents. Weapons, ordnance, explosives – they think we'll find the lot. No need to remind you, this affects us all. We've lost enough good people.'

He tapped the satellite photography with his steel pointer. 'Take a lot of care. Look again at the junctions either side, look at the buildings all around. Before we move out, make sure your people are aware of where they need to be, what they need to do, where everyone else is and what they're doing. There will be no fuck-ups.'

B Company's target, in the Gazaya district of the city, the main stronghold of Muqtada Al-Sadr's Mahdi Army, was a small two-storey building surrounded by a concrete-block wall with a steel door on to the street.

The strike was phase two of the operation to kill and disperse the insurgents in the Brits' area of operations. They had also been gathering in Gazaya over the past two weeks, and their numbers would have kicked up a notch if any had managed to escape the Kingsmen's attacks out in the sandpit.

It was obvious from the photos there hadn't been any town planners around when Gazaya went up. Houses and apartment blocks up to four storeys high seemed to have been piled on top of each other with a warren of alleyways and wasteground between them.

Dave gobbed away about the outlying areas, the other houses that were going to be hit by the other rifle companies, where they'd had contacts in the past, where their guys had been shot. The team commanders nodded; so did the two female RMPs (Royal Miltary Police) and a medic. None of them could have been over twenty-five. Some things don't change. I'd been a corporal in this very battalion when I was nineteen.

By comparison Dave was an old man. He must have been about forty; either he was using hair dye, or he was so laid-back he was almost horizontal. There wasn't a grey hair in sight, and his face was almost completely unlined, except for a thin scar that ran from the edge of his top lip up the side of his cheek.

'Number one on the door is Rifleman Duggan.' He turned to his lads and stabbed a finger at them, more out of pride than aggression. He was the CSM, this was his rifle company, and the respect between them was so solid you could reach out and touch it. 'You lot make sure you big him up before tonight. It's a big deal for him. It's a big deal for anyone.' He paused to make sure it sank in. 'He leads us in and we take on whoever's there. We lift the targets, then the film crew come in to do their thing and make you all famous.'

A ripple of laughter spread round the room. They knew a couple of the young lads would be taking up fire positions a little more dramatically than usual if Pete and his camera were nearby.

'And then we stay and fight. But remember, this is a hard-arsed area. They like to keep all their mortars and explosives to themselves. We've never left there without a contact.'

There was a loud thud out in the compound. We jerked down to tighten our body armour and get our helmets from under our seats. Nobody went anywhere without them.

Then, maybe fifty metres away, a second rocket exploded. We were being IDFd by 107mm Katyushas.

'Remember.' Dave scanned the room as the third and fourth rockets slammed into the compound. 'The house is probably holding the guys who killed the Marines last Remembrance Day. That's why the media are coming with B Company. We're going to show some payback.'

He jerked a thumb at the vehicle-group commander, a Fijian corporal with a head the size of a watermelon and hands that made his notebook look like a postage stamp. 'If they start firing, you hit them with everything you've got, you understand me? I want all our lads out of there alive – and that's an order.'

This was a really tight company. You could feel it. Even if I'd told them I was from the Green Jackets and later the Regiment it wouldn't have counted for anything. They were fighting a war together and didn't give a shit about anyone else.

Dave was still going nineteen to the dozen; maybe he had his eye on another brew. 'Once we're in there, we're staying. We'll wait for the fuckers to try it on and see what happens. Corporal Barney,' he pointed to the sniper commander, who looked up from his notes, 'you tell your lot to get a few drops of that Optrex stuff down their eyes. I don't want them missing anyone coming our way.

'If it kicks off, don't worry, I've got more brass in my wagon to resupply your lot than they had at the Alamo. We might need it. C Company were in there last week. Five fucking hours that contact lasted.'

His jaw tightened as there was another explosion in the compound. 'Remember the two lads killed last week, and the poor fucker sent back to the UK with half his guts hanging out after one of those fucking things landed on him. Just make sure you look after your people and keep them alive, OK?'

There was a murmur as everyone stood. We headed for the brew area. Nobody was going anywhere until the attack had stopped and the munitions guys had got out there to clear the compound.

9

Pete stood up with his empty cup still in his hand and his helmet at a jaunty angle. He didn't wear one of the black Wehrmacht-style helmets like the rest of the media. He said the lip at the front got in the way when he filmed. Instead, he'd got hold of an old British steel helmet on eBay, and ground down the front of the rim.

He wore it tipped back and to the left, with a square of shammy leather underneath so it stayed at the same angle and didn't slide about on his bald head. With the corners of the shammy hanging down over his ears, all he needed was a Capstan Full Strength glued to his bottom lip and he'd have been a ringer for old Tommy Atkins in the trenches.

I tapped his arm. 'Finish your emails, Bermondsey Boy, I'll see to these.'

'Thanks.' He passed his cup. 'That's if the sat phone ain't shot to bits.'

Pete went to the other side of the room, where his iBook was rigged up to a BGAN wire running out through the window. The BGAN itself was sitting on top of one of the HESCOs outside.

Yet another rocket landed with a dull crump. It was the fourth attack we'd had that day. The last one had been mortars and had taken out two of the quartermaster's steel freight containers. No one was killed or injured, so I could just imagine the QM rubbing his hands as he prepared to compile a list of bomb-damaged goods long enough to fill two ships, let alone two containers.

When I got back to Pete with his Shirley Temple, he was sitting cross-legged on the floor, back against the wall, his iBook on his lap. The memory stick he normally wore round his neck was jutting out of the USB port.

He wore a big smile under the helmet.

'Family stuff?' I laughed. 'So that's what you keep on those things. I thought you boys had 'em as some sort of good-luck charm. Fucking Dom walks round like he's immune to everything except green kryptonite.'

'Don't I know it, mate. It's a worry. Here you are . . .' He shifted the screen so I could share. 'Last year's birthday party. Six years old and bright as a button.'

A tall woman in a bikini with long wavy

blonde hair was doing her best to keep control of half a dozen kids in armbands and goggles. The camera panned to take in more of the background.

I did a double-take. 'Fuck me, Brockwell Park lido! That takes me back a bit.'

'Done a few laps in your time, have you?'

'We used to go and mess about there as kids.' I watched his grin widen. 'We'd get out at Brixton and go to the market first, see what we could nick. We usually landed up with a couple of tomatoes or some green thing we didn't even know the name of, but it still made a nice picnic. Then we'd doss by the pool until we got thrown out for divebombing the grown-ups.'

Pete had been nodding along. He gave a burst of laughter louder than a 30mm. 'I got chucked out too! Wrongly accused of being the previous owner of a turd they found floating in the deep end. Wasn't you, was it? Too much exotic veg?'

I pointed at the screen. 'That Tallulah?'

'Yes.' He beamed. 'And that's the birthday girl.' His finger touched the screen and lingered as she blew out the candles on her cake. He was lost in his own world for a bit. 'I've missed every one of the last three . . .' He looked up suddenly. 'But do you know what, Nick? I'm not fucking missing her seventh, in three weeks' time. Or any of the others after that. I'm jacking it in, mate.

Local news and quality family time, that's me from now on.'

I wasn't sure if he was serious. 'But you'd miss all this.' I waved my arm to embrace the chaos.

'Miss what? A reporter on a personal crusade he won't let me in on, crap tea – no offence – and an arse full of sand?' He tapped the screen again. 'No contest, mate.'

I understood the tea and sand bit. 'Crusade?'

He blew out his cheeks. 'He's always been hungry for it. *Passionate*, you know? I used to be up there with him, righting wrongs, changing the world. But I just don't have the appetite for it any more. It's partly the fact that all we're producing here is tomorrow's chip paper. Disposable news – nobody gives a fuck.' His eyes roamed back to the birthday party. 'Partly that other things, like spending time with Tallulah and watching Ruby grow up, are a whole lot more important to me now.' He shrugged. 'Don't get me wrong, the awards we got for the Kabul doc mean something because they were recognition for exposing the fucking nightmare out there, but I just ... I just don't share Dom's passion any more.'

'And the new passion is drugs? That's the crusade?'

He leant forward to get his face closer to mine. 'He's so fixated he even had me secret-filming in Dublin a couple of weeks ago ...' He slumped back and stared up at the ornate ceiling. 'But I'm

68

checking out now. Maybe I'll do the odd wildlife documentary. Just as long as I can know what my schedule is far enough in advance not to risk missing another of Ruby's birthdays . . .' His eyes narrowed. 'You got family, Nick?'

'I did have, once.' I got a sudden rush of pins and needles in my legs, a sensation I hadn't experienced for a long, long time. 'A little girl who was a lot like your Ruby, as a matter of fact. Her parents were killed, I was her guardian.' I was vaguely aware that sweat was now leaking more heavily down my face and tried to wipe it away. 'I never really got the birthday thing right . . . In the end I had to ask someone more reliable to take over.'

My memory stick was set to locked, and that was the way I liked it. Somebody once told me I lived life with the lid on, and I guessed they were right. It was the way it had to be. How was I supposed to function if I spent all my time clicking thumbnails of a teenager dead on a King's Cross bed? The image I tried to cling to was of her bright and sparkly at the one birthday I did manage to get right, at the replica of the Golden Hind on the Thames.

I was spared having to go there, and poor Pete was spared having to listen. One of the rifle-company lads appeared and stood next to me, but it was Pete he was after. He had a blue Helly Hansen T-shirt on under his armour, and a brand-new tattoo of barbed wire curling round his right arm. Here and there a few scabs still clung to the ink – but not as many as there were on the zits he'd popped on his face.

Pete looked up at him with a big smile. 'Hello, mate. What can I do you for?'

The young lad smiled back. 'I heard you was a tankie. My dad was, too – Jim Duggan, you know him?'

Pete moved his head from side to side in thought mode. 'No, mate, sorry, don't ring any bells. He still in?'

The lad was Welsh, and flushed with pride for his dad. 'No, he's here, in Iraq, working for one of the security companies.'

Duggan . . . The name suddenly rang a bell with me. He was the boy who needed bigging up. I held out a hand. 'I'm Nick, that's Pete. You number one on the door tonight?'

He got even prouder. 'Terry. Yeah, first time. The platoon swaps round the entry teams.'

'Good luck, mate. You know, until about four years ago only special forces would be doing that shit.'

His eyes widened and he kept shaking my hand, and Pete just kept looking at him, deep in thought.

'Yeah?'

'That's right, mate. Big day. Good luck.'

One of the RMP girls walked past and Terry's

70

eyes swivelled. Pete laid down his iBook, stood up and wrapped a fatherly arm round him. 'You do good tonight, my son, and she'll be all over you like a rash.'

Terry might have been about to get the party gear on and make entry into a house packed with guys wanting to kill him, but he was maybe nineteen at a push. The RMP would have had him soft-boiled for breakfast.

Pete gestured at the iBook. 'If that old man of yours is on email, you want to drop him a line? Tell him you're OK?'

Pete and I exchanged a glance. He knew as well as I did that if tonight went to rat shit this might be the last time he ever made contact.

Terry was even more made up as he sat and started tapping away.

Pete stepped over to me, looking pleased with himself. 'You know what? There *would* be stuff I'd miss. Mostly the camaraderie. The brotherhood. It's a bit like being a squaddy, what we do. Even when you're up to your neck in shit, you're surrounded by mates.' He smiled. 'We were in Kabul when Ruby's mum fucked off to Spain with the bloke who built our extension. It was Dom and all the other guys who kept me afloat.'

He slapped my arm. 'Sorry, mate, too much information. If you do ever get there, though, the Gandamack Lodge is the place to drown your sorrows. Great bar. The city's not exactly awash with them. All the news crews stay there, and it's the circuit's watering-hole. Plenty of company.'

The shout went up that the attack was over, but we stayed where we were. The area still had to be cleared before anyone could move.

'Talking of keeping afloat . . .' he hit my arm again . . . 'when Tel's finished, why don't you go online to Sad Fucks Reunited, see if you can hunt down the old diving team?'

10

The tank park
2340 hrs

'Where the fuck is Peter with those drinks?'

It was the first time I'd heard Dom swear. Things obviously weren't too hunky-dory on Planet Platinum Bollocks. He'd come back fuming from his session at the FCO building. Pete and I had tried to draw him out, but he stayed tight-lipped.

It was H-hour minus twenty, and we were choking on the exhaust from B Company's nine Bulldogs. Their back doors were open. In the dull red glow from the interiors I could see a mass of last-minute checks going on. I watched Terry as he tugged his chest harness over his Osprey body armour and positioned the pouches to make sure his mags, frag and smoke grenades were secure.

Once he was sorted, he couldn't resist having another quick squeeze of a zit.

All I had to check was the field dressing in the left map pocket of my cargos, same place everyone kept one. That way we knew where to grab it if someone took a hit and started leaking.

The ear pad of my PRR crackled as guys blew into their mikes to test their radios were working and on the right channel.

Dom turned to me. The guys were around us so he kept his voice low. 'They are so young.'

I pointed to Terry, now pulling on his gloves – maybe to stop himself attacking his face. 'That little fucker there's first through the door tonight.'

Dom moved a few steps to check he really was seeing teenage spots on the man leading the attack.

'That's how it is.' I shrugged. 'They're infantry, they're all young fuckers.'

Dom was still brooding as Terry clambered into the back of his Bulldog. Maybe he was thinking how lucky that stepson of his was in comparison. I guessed he'd be tucked away in a nice warm university bed right now, probably not his own. Good for him. I always wished I'd had the chance of college instead of running round like Terry, with a tin hat on, getting shot at.

Pete returned with three white cups and caught the fag end of the conversation. 'That kid who's first through the door tonight is only nineteen.'

I took my brew but Dom shook his head.

'Take it, you'll like this one. I got us some real coffee. I told 'em vampires can't drink tea, it kills them. Go on, it'll calm you down. You shouldn't go chasing after those fuckers. It winds you up too much.'

I took a sip of the strong, milky brew as Dave came on the PRR. 'All call signs. Ten minutes.'

Around us, working parts were cocked.

''Ere, Drac, you get any one of those spooks to interview yet? We got a busy day tomorrow?'

Dom's mobile rang before he got the chance to answer. 'Baz! You sure?' He jammed a finger in his other ear and shouted: 'Is that better? I said, are you sure it's him? That's great news. When did you find out?'

He closed down and put the phone back in his pocket. He looked at Pete. 'I've got a lead.'

'Want me to come with you?'

'No, I'll go first thing – should only be a few days. Just get lots of footage. You know, the boys emailing home, that sort of thing. Bread-and-butter stuff. Cover for me with Moira. You know how much she hates me doing my stuff on her dime.'

Pete was frowning. 'What are you—'

There was an explosion two hundred away, followed closely by another.

'Take cover!'

As if anyone needed telling. Cups dropped to the tarmac as we legged it into our Bulldog.

Pete grabbed my arm. 'Something's wrong, Nick. This is about more than an interview.'

'Personal?'

'Very.'

Dave was already on the net. 'Soon as all call signs are complete, we're mobile.'

Thirty seconds later, the company rolled out of the tank park in their nine wagons, just as another Katyusha piled into the compound. The explosion sounded much closer this time. Yet another whooshed over the open mortar hatches, its rocket even louder than the wagon's engines and tracks.

The Bulldog was essentially the old APC (armoured personnel carrier) that had been rumbling over the Westphalian plains of Germany for thirty or forty years as part of the BAOR and during the Cold War. I'd spent two years in them myself as mechanized infantry, and remembered them as slow and sluggish. But this lot had been geared up with a brand-new power pack so they could scream along at fifty m.p.h., keeping pace with the Challengers and Warriors. They also had brand-new armour all round, including bar armour to keep the RPGs at bay, and a turret with a GPMG had been mounted where the wagon's commander would normally sit and poke his head out to watch thousands of Russian tanks screaming towards him.

Ours was the command vehicle, at the rear of the column. Dom, Pete and I were crammed into the back, along with Dave, two medics, the company commander and his signaller.

The company commander, a major, was on the net to another rifle company, Chindit, to tell them we were leaving early. Chindit were from 2 Lancs, who were defending the OSB (Old State Building) in the centre of the city.

They'd be backing us once the contacts started. The plan was to let the militants run and drive into the contact area and take us on. As soon as that happened, Chindit Company, reinforced by three extra Warriors from Rhett and his recce platoon, would scream out of the OSB in their Warriors and cordon them off. With so many Warriors on the ground, the militants would have nowhere to run. It was then the job of both companies to dispose of as many insurgents as they could in the killing ground they had created.

This was just one of the four strike ops that would be going in tonight. The other companies from 2 Rifles would be doing the same in other areas, also with 2 Lancs backing them in their Warriors. It was going to be one fuck of a party.

I bent my five-inch plastic IR cyalume stick so that the glass inside broke, mixing the chemicals that made the thing glow, though only when viewed through NVAs.

Everyone else was doing the same, then attaching them to the back of their helmet or Osprey. In the confusion of contact it was a good way of knowing where your mates were before you decided to take a shot through your night sight at a moving body.

11

It was just as suffocating inside the Bulldog as it was in the Warrior, even with the mortar hatches open. Dust and exhaust fumes blasted in as we roared towards the compound exit.

Dave sat next to the door handle and pointed out where all the wagon's shit was located. 'Behind the boss there, morphine and tourniquets. Spare ammo is here.' He kicked the metal boxes below his seat with his heel.

Another rocket went off in the compound. He waved a finger under the table that held all the computer and signals kit the company commander was gobbing off into. 'Pass 'em about, will you?'

I leant over and lifted the lid of a battered plastic picnic cooler. It was packed with 500ml bottles. Drinking water wasn't in short supply in the compound. There were pallets of the stuff people could just help themselves to, and almost as many squirty bottles of hand cleanser. Out here, soldiers had to wash their hands every time they ate, had a dump or simply had nothing else to do. Sickness and diarrhoea could affect anyone; get a couple of guys with a bug and soon the whole company's out of action.

I threw him the bottle and passed a couple more round. I reached behind the company commander and tapped the scabby boots of the gunner. He reached down from his turret and grabbed it. Next thing I saw, he was pouring the contents away and preparing to take a piss into the empty bottle.

The company commander pressed a series of buttons on the control panel in front of him to switch between the different nets he was listening to and waffling on. His laptop showed the positions of all call signs in the city.

Dom and Pete were squashed up on my left. Sonia, one of the medics, was by the door. The other medic, sitting next to Dave, was dressed in full party gear – body armour, bingo wings, ballistic glasses, leather gloves. At a nudge from the CSM he stood up through the hatch and stuck his SA80 out into the gloom. The GPMG turret swung right as we passed through Saddam's majestic gates. We were out of the compound.

Nobody said a word. Through a haze of dust piling in through the mortar hatch, I'd caught the occasional glimpse of clear starlit night. Now I began to see bulbs. They dangled across the streets like strings of big party lights, and led off to concrete-block houses at either side. Normal street-lighting had been fucked years ago.

Faded billboards advertised Marlboro and Nescafé, and gave a message in Arabic that I guessed said Gillette was the best a man could get. The newest ones advertised Iraqna, the country's mobile-phone network.

Washing hung from balconies above closed-up shop fronts. Kids' Teletubby T-shirts and football shirts were soon filthy again from the dustcloud we kicked up. From this angle, I could have been in the back streets of Naples.

The wagon came to a sudden halt. Dave pushed down the lever on the big metal door and let it swing open. No hydraulics on these old things. He grabbed the top cover to tell him to jump out with him.

Dom was confused. 'We there already?'

Through the open door, I could see the top cover was already taking a fire position by a wrecked car.

'Not yet.' Dave kept the door open and yelled to Pete to jump out with his IR camera. 'There's time to film if you want. One of the locations saw where the rockets came from and called in a fire mission. We can't go any further until it's done.'

Sonia eased her feet out of the way so

Pete could dismount, and Dom was close behind.

I followed, glad to be out of the wagon even after such a short time. 'How long we got?'

'Just enough to make sure the fuckers don't hit us as well as the firing points – it's only about a K away.'

Dave pushed the door shut and Sonia locked it from the inside.

'Who's firing?'

'The artillery. We've got a 105 from the COB on the case. That's why we stay well back. Can't trust them to shoot straight.' Dave chortled away to himself.

I made sure Dom and Pete were in cover, then sheltered in a doorway. Lights went out all round us. I pictured kids and grannies being jammed under tables for a bit of protection. The locals knew as well as we did that shit was on its way. If the Brits were static, they were a target.

12

The whole company was shaken out in all-round defence along the road. My PRR was alive with guys making sure all the arcs were covered.

Pete started filming as Riflemen pulled down the night-viewing aids attached to their helmets over their non-aiming eye. The NVAs on their weapons were already switched on, ready to take aim if they saw a target. A lot of them had chosen to wear their normal dark green camouflage smocks. Some had also covered their helmets with dark green covers. It was a matter of personal choice. They were fighting at night in a town, not in a sandpit.

Nothing could be heard above the rumble of the Bulldogs and the now much calmer chat on the net. I'd just taken a couple of steps out of my doorway to get closer to Dom when a loud whoosh overhead was followed by an explosion as a 105mm artillery shell slammed into the city ahead of us.

Dave ran over to me as another whistled over our heads. He crouched against a Datsun that looked like it was held together with gaffer-tape. 'I bet they don't tell you about any of this shit back home, eh? Can you imagine what the papers would say?' He ran his hand along an imaginary headline in the air. 'British Artillery Shells Basra.'

A third 105 round landed, and seconds later an AK opened up just ahead. Two Bulldog guns and six or seven SA80s returned fire.

Two more AKs opened up. The PRRs were jumping and the CSM got on the net. 'Leave 'em, we've got things to do. Let's go, mount up.'

The Bulldogs' guns kept up the rates as guys jumped back in. I grabbed hold of Dom and Pete. Dave and the medic kept their covering positions as Sonia held open the door. We scrambled in and the others followed.

Dave seized the door handle and pointed at Pete and Dom. 'Make sure you look after those two. If they can lift you, they will. They're always after a squaddy. One of you guys would be even better. Bigger ransom.'

Pete turned to Sonia. 'And they'd be able to understand what we were saying. He'd be no good on Al Jazeera.'

Dave waited on the PRR for confirmation that

everybody was back inside their wagons. Finally he leant across and thumped the company commander on the leg before giving him the thumbs-up.

As the tracks squealed again, we took three or four rounds of AK into the side. The GPMG rattled off a reply.

The wagon jerked and there was a loud scrape of metal on metal. The whole right side of the Bulldog lifted and the scraping continued.

Pete grinned. 'Someone won't be driving to work in the morning.'

Dave thumbed the medic to get his arse back on top cover, and it wasn't long before he was signalling Pete to join them with his camera.

Dom wanted to follow but Sonia grabbed him. She sounded like she should have been on *EastEnders*. 'It's just where the rocket launcher was, innit? Stay here, love, it's safer.'

Pete came back down. He opened the side screen of the camera and pressed play. We crowded round. It was fantastic quality, black-and-white IR, none of that hazy green stuff I was used to seeing on TV. The 105s had wreaked devastation. The remains of a six-barrel rocket launcher lay mangled on the back of a truck. Pete had homed in on what was left of a body. The image shook as the Bulldog bounced about, but he looked to be in his teens. The shredded clothing was still smouldering. An arm was missing, and a big chunk of the launcher stuck out of his back.

'We got one of the fuckers, anyway.' Sonia's East London tones even drowned the engine noise.

My nostrils twitched. I could smell shit. I looked at Sonia and raised an eyebrow.

'Not me.' She smiled. 'We're nearly there. Their sewers are fucked.'

Dave got on to his PRR. 'Front vehicle, count us in. Everyone, listen in.'

The company commander's head was buried in his laptop. Signals popped up on the screen every few seconds like messages in a chatroom. He talked non-stop on the net. The signaller worked frantically beside him. It was almost like watching a movie.

The Fijian's voice filled the net, very slow, very laid back, speaking as if he couldn't smell a whiff of shit. 'We're turning on to the target street now. Four hundred to go. Street is lit, house lights going out.'

13

The PRRs fell silent as the Fijian counted us in. Serious faces looked up and out at the buildings that hemmed us in on both sides.

'Fifteen . . . twenty . . .'

Dave pushed down the locking bar of the rear door and held it closed.

I checked my Osprey collar was up and the Velcro fastening in the front was secure enough to keep it that way.

'On target – stop, stop, stop!'

The wagon tipped forward. Dave hurled the door open before it had even finished rocking. He and the second medic both jumped out and disappeared towards the front of the wagon. He had to organize the strike and the protection, and relay everything back to the company commander. Sonia stayed in the wagon to receive any casualties.

Pete tumbled out. He had a job to do as well. He had to keep as close as he could to the entry team without getting killed.

Dom and I were close behind. All the Bulldog commanders were ripping down the cables overhead. Bulbs shattered on the ground. Lights went out along the rows of buildings as the area closed down and got ready for a nightmare. Petrified kids screamed at each other inside the buildings all round us.

Pete had reached the door in the outer wall of the target. The strike team was forming up each side. Terry checked it wasn't unlocked before the battering ram was swung into action. The bang of steel on steel mixed with the rumble of the wagon power packs, smashing glass and the screams of revved-up soldiers and terrified civilians.

Dom filmed with the IR camera in front of him as we moved along the line of Bulldogs. I gripped the back of his Osprey to steady him and keep him out of the team's way as he concentrated on the small digital screen.

The ladder crews ran across our path from left to right, heading for the rear of the building. Others legged it to the far side of the street. They needed to get Barney and his snipers up on vantage-points both sides of the road, soon as. Guys with Minimis followed to give all-round defence.

There was an almighty crash as the battering ram slammed into the steel door for the fifth time. Its top hinge ripped apart and the door fell halfway to the ground but held.

Pete's stills camera flashed on multidrive. The strobe effect made the entry team's movements look like something out of the Keystone Kops.

Snipers raced up ladders and on to walls.

The entry team formed up on the front door, half a dozen each side. Terry already had his weapon in the shoulder, facing in. His zit-covered face glistened with sweat. His mate behind held him by his Osprey, as if he was restraining a hyped-up greyhound.

'Get that fucking door in!' The yell echoed above the Bulldogs' engines.

The battering ram crashed against the steel door again and again. Pete did his paparazzo thing, triggering so many bursts of flashlight it seemed like there were a dozen cameras, not just one.

The steel door came off its hinges and crashed to the ground.

'Get in there! *Now!*' Dave somehow managed to make himself heard above the din of engines, shouts and screams from what seemed like every building in the street.

Terry yelled at the top of his voice as he was released, and disappeared through the open door. The number two followed. The entry team with their battering ram were next, and I heard the first thud as they pounded against the wooden front door of the house just two metres inside the wall.

Dom arrived at the breach and stood trying to get some film of the guys inside. Most of the strike team hadn't been able to get into the confined space between the wall and the door.

'It's blocked inside! It's blocked!'

'Fucking hit it! Hit it!'

Pete got up on the tips of his toes. He stretched his arm and aimed the camera over the wall, then hit the multidrive.

Dom strained forward, trying to get into the tiny courtyard with the team. He really thought that forcefield of his would make him bulletproof.

I hauled him back, doing my job. Even Terry was holding back from the door frame until it was time to move.

I shouted into Dom's ear, 'Just let them get on with it, mate.'

There was fire from inside the house. I pulled Dom further back. He fell. Good. I wanted him on the ground anyway. I wanted him anywhere out of the line of fire as Riflemen collapsed against the wall each side of the door as it erupted in a cloud of splinters. Another burst headed the Riflemen's way. The rounds hit the outer wall. Pete, now on the ground streetside, was showered with concrete dust.

'Gunner! Gunner!'

A Rifleman ran to the door and fired his Minimi from the hip. As he moved from the side of the door to directly in front of it, his body rocked back and his helmet rattled with the recoil of a good thirty-round burst.

The echoes bounced round the street, drowning out all other noise. I hauled Dom up so he could film. Pete saw us move and jumped up to get his camera back over the wall.

It's not enough just to be able to carry one of these machine-guns. You need to have the attitude to use the fucking thing. This lad had it. He kicked off a twenty-round burst, standing not even a metre from the door. Gun oil smoked on its red-hot barrel.

The wagon commanders chucked rocks at the last few lights that couldn't be reached any other way. Cyalume sticks glowed on the roofs and walls around us to indicate the location of the snipers. When the shit hit the fan, the GPMG gunners on the Bulldogs would know to aim at anything but blue.

The Minimi stopped. The air was thick with cordite. The gunner jumped out of the way as the door collapsed and Terry and the strike team surged through. Their shouts were mixed with screams from terrified women and children.

Dom moved through the gateway as a burst of AK came from inside followed by four or five quick rounds of 5.56.

It was pitch dark now. No more flashes from Pete, and the last of the street-lights had been killed.

Pete pushed his way inside. 'Hope Tel's OK, eh?'

I let go of Dom, only for him to get knocked aside by the RMPs as they barged their way through. One had a full Royal Mail post sack over her shoulder.

The air was thick with sweet, flowery incense to hide the smell of shit from the open sewers, but it couldn't hide the cordite. There were just three small, dimly lit rooms on the ground floor. An external stairway curled up to the second floor. The Minimi had disintegrated the wall opposite. It was now rubble spread across the floor.

Riflemen dominated every room.

14

One of the Rifles was an Arab from Birmingham. He yelled at a man kneeling on the threadbare carpet in a narrow room to our right. The prisoner was young twenties, definitely of fighting age. Cushions lined one wall. His hands had been plasticuffed in front of him. He was still begging the interpreter as a pair of ski goggles blacked out with gaffer-tape was pulled over his eyes.

One of the RMPs went ballistic, screaming questions for the Arab to translate. 'Name? What's your name? Any more men in the house?'

She checked her picture cards of Basra's most wanted as she went. He looked up, his hands pleading as desperately as his mouth.

'Shut the fuck up!' She bent down until she was inches from his face. 'Name! ID card! Where's your ID?'

Dom carried on filming. Riflemen drenched in

sweat shouted at each other as they controlled the rooms.

Screams came from the middle room. Dom swung round. He got some footage through the half-closed door as women, young and old, huddled on the floor with the children. The other RMP jabbered away in Arabic, trying to calm them as she opened the mailbag and handed the kids little day sacks. Bad cop, good cop.

The Rifleman guarding the door pointed at Dom's camera. 'Not here, mate. Just let her do her stuff. Leave the women alone and they'll tell you more than these cunts.'

Flashes from Pete's camera bounced into the hallway from the third room. I went with Dom to see the body of another man of fighting age, a bit older than the last, stretched out on the floor. His blood soaked the carpet and had splattered over a pile of what looked like mud bricks wrapped in heavy polythene in front of the TV. Tom and Jerry kicked the shit out of each other on screen. An AK lay in the corner. There was a pistol tucked under the waistband of his jeans. Muqtada Al-Sadr, sun-beams radiating from behind his head, gazed down at him from a massive poster on the wall.

Terry stood over him, waiting to see who he'd dropped.

A corporal with a set of picture cards was down on his knees, inspecting his handiwork. 'Yep, you got him. One of the bombers.'

Dom was examining the pile of brown blocks. 'And what looks like half Afghanistan's heroin output for a month.'

The lad's face lit up as he took slaps on the back from the lads.

Pete did the same. 'Well done, mate – and still alive to tell your old man the tale. Good news.'

Our PRRs sparked up. 'One dead, one lifted,' the company commander said. 'They've confirmed, we've got them both.'

A mobile phone rang the Nokia tune and its display flashed in the dead man's jeans.

Dom and Pete filmed the AK and the polythene blocks of heroin being placed in clear-plastic evidence bags. Kingsmen took digital pictures of notebooks, photographs and anything else evidential before it, too, was bagged up and taken away.

Terry nodded down at the body. The mobile was still ringing. 'Wonder if it's his mates warning him there's a patrol.'

Pete smiled back. 'Nah, it's the neighbours telling him to turn the fucking noise down.'

Our PRRs sparked up once more as Dave now took control from the street. 'OK, listen in. Barney, your snipers set?'

'Set.'

'Wagon commanders, set?'

'Yeah, all set.' The Fijian sounded as if he was ordering pizza.

'Strike team, crack on and finish the search. I want this done quickly before we're taking incoming.'

They lifted books from their shelves, flicked through all the pages, and pulled drawers from an antique sideboard that might have been looted from Basra Palace.

We moved back into the other room. Dom filmed the live body again. The guy was still on his knees, but his plasticuffed hands were now covered with a clear-plastic bag to preserve any explosive or weapon residue on his skin. He also had a set of defenders over his ears, and a white markerboard hung round his neck on a loop of paracord upon which the name SADIQ had been written in marker pen. A yellow cyalume stick was taped to the board to help with ID in the confusion and darkness. The interrogator stood over him, taking digital pictures.

Dave came into the building and got on his PRR. 'All call signs, stand to. They'll be here soon.'

He grabbed a squaddy in body armour moving past him. 'Where are the women and kids?'

He was directed to the middle room. He knocked on the door. 'OK, girls, let's get them out.'

The kids were playing with colouring books, plastic toys, the sort of stuff they hand out on long-haul flights. The women were totally covered. Evidence bags containing three mobile phones and a couple of notebooks lay by their feet. The RMPs were scribbling details.

The search teams had unearthed more weapons. A couple of AKs, some pistols and ammunition were being bagged up, together with some DVDs. According to the crude photocopies on the covers, they were of Western hostages being decapitated, Algerian soldiers having their throats slit, and IED attacks on American Humvees. Dom filmed it all with the IR.

The RMPs and a couple of Riflemen escorted the women and kids to a Bulldog. They would sit out the next couple of hours in cover while the rest of us waited for the inevitable.

The search team entered the newly vacated room and started to rip it apart.

As if on cue, two shots rang out from the snipers above us. Barney's voice barked over the net: 'That's one down. I'm claiming it.'

15

'Tel, mate, look over 'ere . . .'

Pete kept snapping away as Terry and the strike teams prepared to surge out of the house and back on to the street. Dave was sharp with him. 'No more flash – you'll make yourself a target.'

Pete's tin helmet was tilted back so he could get the camera to his right eye. He looked ridiculous. Even the Riflemen laughed at him as they ran past. He packed his stills camera away in his Batman utility belt and took over with the IR handheld, changing batteries like Riflemen change magazines. Always have a full weapon.

I leant against one of the interior walls near the door and watched the guys look mega-warlike for the camera as they waited their turn to move out. I felt a pang of jealousy. At least they were in control. It always felt good to be able to fire back.

A Manchester lad of eighteen or nineteen did a last check of the link on his Minimi before moving out with his team. He was about as tall as his weapon – and with the collapsible butt folded down, that wasn't much bigger than a ketchup bottle. Sweat poured down his face and dripped off his nose.

His lance corporal eyeballed him. 'You OK?'

The lad nodded.

Dom moved away and rolled up the dead man's sleeves. I could see the trackmarks even from where I was standing. He looked up at the lad. 'They're high as kites. Be careful.'

It was nearly the Rifleman's turn to leg it out of the building. He nodded at me. 'Where the fuck's he from?' Manchester, by the sound of it.

'He's Polish. He's the Polish Jeremy Bowen.'

He glanced back at me blankly as he got the go from his corporal. 'Who the fuck's Jeremy Bowen?' He legged it out on to the street before I could answer.

The rest of the team followed. The PRRs were full of chatter but soon cut it when the first burst of AK rattled down the street.

Dave appeared next to me. 'Here we go.' He jerked a thumb as the last man disappeared through the hole in the wall and into the street. 'It's up to you what you lot do. Stay in the house, go back to the wagon, or get out there. Just don't get in the lads' way, OK?'

Pete shouted over at Dom: 'We going, Drac, or what?'

The AK kicked off again and six or seven SA80s gave some back. All of a sudden it seemed the whole street was alive with gunfire. AK rounds bounced off the wagons and into walls.

The Riflemen gave it back in spades.

I caught Pete's eye. 'You all right?' It seemed the thing to say when this sort of shit was happening.

'Don't be fucking stupid. I'm shitting myself.'

The air filled with the roar of engines and the squeal of tracks as the wagons moved out to make better use of their guns.

Dave called for sit reps from the roof snipers. It was pointless Pete asking Dom what he wanted to do. We both knew.

'Wait here.' I left the building and stuck my head through the gap in the wall where there'd once been a door. Most of the Bulldogs were on the move, taking both ends of the street and covering the corners with their GPMGs. One, the rear command vehicle, stayed static. Its top cover cracked off rounds in all directions. Every dog and human in the neighbourhood was going berserk.

Pete was behind me, camera up. Dom was redundant until he could get his report in, but he was tucked in behind him.

We legged it to the command Bulldog and

moved along its flank to a Rifleman at the front-corner bar armour.

Briefly, a bright burst of muzzle fire lit the dark. Weapon reports echoed along the street, making it hard to work out where they had originated. The Rifleman loosed off six or seven shots in reply.

I held Pete by his body armour to steady and control him as he filmed. 'Follow the road up on the left, about a hundred. There's an alleyway. That's where they're firing from.'

Suddenly the Rifleman stopped firing and jumped back. I yanked Pete so the guy could get into cover. Pro that he was, Pete filmed the lad as he hit his release catch and the mag fell to the ground. He slammed in a fresh one, hit the release catch for the working parts to go forward, and swung back into position. Pete moved behind him, filming over his shoulder.

Dom tugged at my arm. 'Let's go.'

Another bright burst of AK lit the alley mouth and thudded into the command wagon. Pete turned back to Dom. 'Go forward? You got a death wish, Drac, or what? We'll get enough good gear here.'

Before he'd even finished, all hell let loose on the PRR. The snipers had seen more Iraqis moving in.

16

Dave didn't want to know about the dramas, he just wanted a body count.

Barney got on the air. 'Five. But we got groups of two or three moving all over the arc.'

'Wait out. Boss – Chindit?'

You could have heard a pin drop on the net. Nobody was going to talk over the top of those two.

'Chindit now mobile.'

It was hard to see exactly what was happening in the dark now the street-lighting was dead. Riflemen ran all over the place. Contacts could be heard left and right, as well as beyond the buildings on both sides of the street. Shouts and screams of command filled the short lulls when the Bulldog guns weren't firing. I didn't try to work out what was going on. It's always best just to get on with your own stuff.

An eight-strong Rifleman patrol came up behind us, panting and sweating, just as the wagon's gunner aimed a long burst at the end of the road. My ears rang. Empty cases tumbled off the hull and clinked on to the crumbling tarmac.

The patrol's NCO yelled at the gunner. 'We're moving into the alley, crossing your front!'

The last thing they wanted was a blue on blue.

Pete filmed them as they hunched behind the Bulldog, waiting for the gun to stop. 'All right, Tel?'

Pete had the handheld up to his eye. He couldn't use the hinged screen like a tourist because of the telltale glow.

Dom got into reporter mode. 'Can you tell me what's happening?'

The NCO didn't bother looking at him or the camera as he replied. His eyes switched between the road and the gunner, who was still firing. He had to force the words out as he tried to regain his breath. 'We're going to go down the alley and bomb-burst out the other side of the building. We got movement in cover over there and the snipers can't get 'em – so we're going to flush 'em out.'

Pete put the camera on Terry, but only for a second before our gun stopped and the NCO legged it. The patrol followed. I watched the last man, the little Manchester lad, as he ran across the street and veered right, up towards the alley mouth. Blue cyalumes hung off buildings either side.

There was no need for discussion. Dom was already on his feet and about to follow.

I restrained him as another long burst came from the other side of the buildings, and checked he and Pete still had IR cyalumes gaffered to the backs of their helmets. 'You've definitely bent those things?'

They nodded. I kept low and followed the patrol, who were well ahead of us now. An RPG kicked off to our right and flew straight down the middle of the road. It slammed into a building fifty metres further on and exploded. Lumps of concrete rained down on us. When I looked up again, the last man was disappearing into the alley.

'Come on, quick!' We needed to get there before they were swallowed into the darkness.

I stopped at the intersection.

A dull glow shone along the alley from the street a couple of hundred beyond it. It was about two metres wide. Rusty metal doors and barred windows lined both sides. The ground was strewn with litter, rubble, puddles, dog shit. The patrol was nowhere to be seen. They had already bomb-burst out the other end.

We crunched our way towards it. Dom needed

controlling. He'd switched on his forcefield again and was surging ahead.

'No one goes any further than the end, OK? We've got snipers above us and we don't know what the fuck's going on out there.'

Pete snorted. 'You won't have to tell me twice, mate.'

Dom got there first. He was scoping up and down as I joined him. Out there somewhere was the distant rumble of Chindit Company's Warrior tracks. Immediately ahead, across about thirty metres of sewage-covered wasteground, lay a rabbit warren of side-streets, ramshackle buildings and bomb-blasted sewers. That was where the patrol must have gone.

I gripped Dom, the stench of shit burning deep into my sinuses. 'This is as far as we go, all right?'

He pointed frantically to a fallen wall about fifteen away. 'There, Peter, look!'

A body lay motionless in the half-light, face down on the wasteground.

Pete started filming. With his camera's night-viewing capability he could see better than we could. 'He's got one round through the nut and there's an AK next to him.'

Dom spotted another body sprawled on the road further on, just before the warren where the patrol must be. The snipers couldn't have missed the fuckers at that range.

SA80s stuttered behind us back in the street.

Pete arranged Dom at the edge of the alley so he had the body in the background. Dom started gobbing off to camera in hushed and dramatic Polish.

Above us, another sniper added to the sound-track. It was going to be award-winning footage.

17

Pete was still filming as a burst of AK screamed out of the warren. The rounds zinged over our heads and into the walls behind us.

Pete jerked the camera away from Dom. 'Tel!'

I turned to see a body staggering out of a half-demolished building and into the wasteground.

It was a Rifleman – the dome of his helmet was silhouetted against the distant glow. He stumbled a few steps more and fell.

Pete pushed the camera into Dom's hands and legged it across the wasteground.

'Pete, stop!'

Either he couldn't hear me or he didn't want to. I shoved Dom back against the wall. 'Stay here!'

I tried to gain ground and catch up with him but it wasn't long before my boots were sinking into calf-deep puddles of sewage.

The Rifleman lay prone on the ground. Sniper fire cracked off above us. The rest of the patrol was now engaged in a contact inside the warren. As long as they kept the fire going I could get Pete and the Rifleman – if he was still alive – back into cover.

Pete was bent over the body. I fell on my knees next to him. Sewage splashed up my Osprey.

Pete must have spotted Terry through the viewfinder. The boy groaned.

'Pete, he's OK, he's alive. Come on, let's get him up.'

Terry had taken a couple of rounds into his front plate. The force would have knocked him to the ground, but he wasn't injured, just bruised. He lay there in shock at still being alive. 'Fuck . . . fuck . . .'

For Pete it was relief.

'Get up, both of you. Come on!'

I grabbed Pete as a scream from the snipers told us to get out of the killing ground. They cracked a couple of rounds over our heads.

I looked up towards the warren as a body dropped just metres away. His AK hit the ground before he did.

More bodies poured from the darkness. They weren't firing.

'Run! They're going to lift us!'

Pete and Terry were on their feet. I pushed

them on through the stinking mud as the snipers tried to cover us.

It was too late.

An arm appeared from behind me. Then I felt hot breath on my neck and a head against my shoulders. He tightened the armlock, and the world was full of grunts and stale tobacco. His weight was dragging me down. The Velcro of my PRR ear pad ripped away and fell to the ground.

Other bodies swarmed over Pete and Terry but they were going down fighting. There was nothing I could do for them until I was free.

The screams, gunfire and Warrior engines receded into the background as I jerked left and right, pushing my head back to nut him, anything to get the fucker off me.

My knees buckled. I fell to the ground and he collapsed on top of me. I kicked, pushed, punched, anything to get him off so Barney – anyone – could take a shot.

I kicked out but this boy was massive and he kept hold. Wet with shit, his hair slapped against my face. We tumbled into a shallow ditch. I made a grab for his head and tried to butt him.

We rolled over and over in the shit puddles. I saw the stars, and the next thing I knew my face was in the mud. I tried to keep my mouth shut, but I had to breathe. It was like holding your mouth and nose as a kid after taking a deep breath, then carrying on until it becomes unbearable and keeping on going a few seconds past that.

I felt a stabbing pain in my eyes and ears. I felt pressure in my chest and throat. I thrashed and bucked, but only succeeded in burrowing my head further into the slime.

My body was telling me to breathe, but it wouldn't let me inhale water. I jerked and convulsed like a madman. After ten or fifteen seconds more I felt like I was in a vice that was being gradually tightened across my breastbone and spinal column. Water seeped into my lungs, my body was a mass of pain and I knew I was dying.

I didn't even sense the other body appearing above us, or jumping down into the ditch, or the boot that must have come in fast and hard and smacked against the Iraqi's head. All I heard was a bone-crunching thud, then the man crushing me spasmed and relaxed. Next thing I knew, his weight was pulled off me. My lungs roared as I filled them with air.

Another kick barrelled into my assailant as I gulped and coughed.

The boot was Pete's. I could see him through the blur of mud and shit that covered my face. And then I heard the loud bang as he followed up with just one round from Terry's weapon into the Iraqi's head.

'Staying down there all night, mate?'

His free hand was outstretched. He hauled me to my feet.

Sniper rounds whistled overhead, thudding into the warren. I fought for breath and spat shit from my mouth.

A few metres away, Terry was kicking another dead body off him. He scrambled to his feet and stepped over the one Pete must have dropped.

'Man on! Man on!' The screams came from the snipers.

I spun round to see more bodies closing fast.

Pete didn't miss a beat. Terry's SA80 went straight into the shoulder. 'Go, go!'

I turned and ran, pushing the boy ahead of me. Pete put down a series of short sharp bursts that punctuated the stream of sniper fire above me.

I stopped halfway and turned back, letting Terry go on. AK muzzle flashes strobed in the darkness as Pete kept firing.

'Enough, Pete. Come on!'

My body jerked as if somebody had swung a pickaxe handle into my chest. I was hurled back. My hands were flung into the air and I fell, pain searing my arm. The force spun me round and I crumpled, face down.

I lay there, a bundle of pain, fear and disbelief. Like Dom with his invisible forcefield, I'd thought I'd never get shot again.

I didn't have as much as a nanosecond to start crawling before Pete caught up with me. He managed one short burst before he ran out of rounds.

He dropped the SA80 into the shit next to me and his bony hands grabbed my good arm and pulled. His grunts sounded louder than the gunfire.

Bodies surged from the warren; the patrol was taking on the insurgents as they moved back towards the alley.

The Manc lad stood his ground in the middle of the wasteground, his shoulder rocking back with the recoil from his weapon. The moment we were in the alley, Terry helped get me over Pete's shoulder in a fireman's lift.

'You're all right, Nick. Sonia'll sort you. See you later, Tel.'

He turned towards the Bulldogs and legged it.

My forearm jolted with pain each time his feet hit the ground. I looked down. The skin was punctured big-time, but it wasn't flapping about. Maybe the round that had hit me hadn't smashed the bone. I couldn't tell.

Sonia had the back of the wagon open and ready. Pete threw rather than loaded me in. Rounds from both sides of the street smashed against the armour. The GPMGs returned fire. The gunner above me gave it max.

Sonia jabbed an autojet of morphine into my arse and tore at my T-shirt with scissors. She pulled a face. 'I might let off the odd fart, but I don't bloody shit myself!'

I could hear Pete laughing with sheer relief as he and Dom jumped in for cover. 'Fuck me, mate. You're supposed to be looking after us!'

Another burst slammed against the armour plating of the wagon and I heard two Warriors scream up alongside us.

18

Somebody leant over me, high collar and bat-wings silhouetted against the red light. His hand was in the air. His fingers were gripped round a plastic bottle. A tube ran down from it and into my good arm.

A cannon kicked off a few rounds. Everything jerked as we moved off again. The guy holding the saline cursed as he tried to keep his balance.

I could see Warrior seats. I must be on the floor, between the two benches.

We lurched off again and my head rolled to the right.

Dom and Pete looked down at me. Pete was filming.

'You'll thank me for this later, mate. One for the family get-together . . .'

I sort of saw a smile behind the lens.

My head bumped on the steel floor and I

realized I didn't have my helmet on. I couldn't remember it being taken off. Not that it mattered. My head didn't hurt. Morphine rules.

One minute, two minutes, five minutes, an hour later, for all I knew, the wagon stopped and the door was pulled open. Scouse voices echoed in the darkness.

'Get them out of there! I'm not fucking waiting out here all day, you cunts – get them out!'

The guy with the saline shouted back, 'This one first!'

Hands gripped me and floated me on to a stretcher. Red night-lights and dark shadows had been replaced by shot-to-fuck HESCOs and a sky speckled with stars.

My new best friend with the drip stayed alongside the stretcher as I jerked up and down. Dom and Pete were nowhere to be seen. Boots crunched over a stretch of rubble-strewn ground. Seconds later I was blinking under blindingly white light.

White tiles, white floors. Maybe six or seven others lying on stretchers, bound up with awesomely white dressings over filthy combats and body armour.

A medic with rubber gloves on swam across my vision. He was Ospreyed up and helmeted. Wherever I was, they must be taking incoming as well.

It had to be OSB. The place was permanently

under siege from indirect fire, small arms and RPGs. One of their sangars held the record for having the most contacts in the whole of Iraq. The Chindits had even built earth ramps up to the HESCO walls so their Warriors' 30mm cannon could join in the firefights.

My stretcher was lowered on to a table. Within seconds somebody was cutting off Sonia's field dressing.

'It's OK, mate. It didn't hit a bone. Just a meaty hole, that's all.'

A mortar landed close by and I must have flinched. The guy doing the cutting was a Jock. 'It's OK. They'll get bored in a minute.'

Automatic fire kicked off from somewhere above me. Maybe it was that record-breaking sangar.

Through the blur, I could see Dom and Pete in the room.

The Jock was cleaning my left hand now. The liquid stank.

'Pete!'

They were busy talking to the guys, pointing at me.

'Pete!'

A burst of Scouse came from behind me. 'You'll be OK, la'!'

Rhett came into vision. He inspected the wound as Dom and Pete stepped up beside him.

116

Pete pointed at my Osprey. 'You copped this, mate.'

I looked down like a drunk to see a blurred couple of strike marks, almost indents in the front plate. I couldn't see the ripped material because it was covered with shit and mud.

Pete brought his camera up as Dom eased off my body armour and one of the medics cut along the inseam of my cargoes with a pair of scissors.

'Nick, they're going to clean you up here. As soon as the attack stops Rhett's taking you back to the COB with the other casualties. We'll see you there after they've sorted you out.'

'You'll soon be sound as a fuck'n' pound.' Pete's bad Scouse echoed off the tiles.

I tried to reach out to him with my good hand and was told to stay exactly where I was. 'Pete . . . thanks, mate . . .'

'Oh, fuck off.' He laughed. 'It's only 'cos I need you.'

I must have frowned.

'You're a witness in the case of the floating turd!'

I heard him laugh again, loud and long, and then the world grew gradually calmer.

The morphine took effect.

I felt myself floating.

My world became a drowsy haze of dim red light.

19

I felt numb and dumb, like a drunk bouncing off the furniture in some badly lit nightclub.

It was Dom, I was sure of it, shaking me, talking close to my ear. He was panicky, out of breath. Scared.

'Pete's gone . . .' He said it over and over. 'Pete's gone . . . It's all my fault . . . I'm so sorry, Nick. I've got to go . . . I've got to go . . .'

Was he crying? 'What the fuck you on about?'

'I've got to go . . .'

He was a blur, but it was definitely Dom. He sobbed something I couldn't quite hear. 'What you on about, mate?' I tried to push myself up but he stuck out an arm, told me to rest.

His head moved closer to mine. 'Nick, no matter what you're told, it wasn't me, OK? It – was – not – me . . .'

I felt him grip my hand. I tried to make sense of what the fuck he was on about. My head was still full of whatever shit had been mixed with the morphine.

'Wasn't what? Wasn't you who what?'

He squeezed my hand. 'You'll know soon, when the drugs have worn off. They'll tell you. Remember – it wasn't me. Say it, Nick.'

'It wasn't me . . .'

He let go of my hand and I tried to stay awake.

20

Friday, 2 March
1126 hrs

'Nick, it's me. Wake up, lad.'

'Dom?' I turned over in a semi-daze. 'What you on about? Pete's done what?' My arm was throbbing. I eased open one eye. My arm was covered with a clean dressing. It felt newly sewn up.

'You're going to be right as rain, lad. The doctor said you'll be up and walking today.' The Scouse was thick as soup.

'Rhett?' I tried to open both eyes.

'Course it is, you soft twat.'

He was sitting on a plastic chair beside me. He had fresh combats and body armour on, and sweat ran down his shiny clean-shaven face. He cradled his helmet under his arm.

We were in a huge marquee. The plastic roof was twenty metres above me, stretched over an aluminium frame. The area had been partitioned into cubicles with 3x3-metre plywood. My head hurt, and I smelt of Dettol, or whatever had been thrown over me when I'd been washed and sorted out. It was hot and muggy. Shouldn't a hospital or whatever this was have air-conditioning?

'I feel like shit. Where am I?'

He tried to laugh, but couldn't manage it. 'COB.'

My eyelids drooped. They wanted to stay glued together. I was thirsty, but my mouth felt too furred-up ever to let anything through again. As I lay on my back and tried to get my fingers working, I heard Land Rovers speed past. I'd have recognized that engine note anywhere. The odd Brit shout penetrated the marquee walls. I eventually opened my eyes again. It was still a bit blurry but that felt like tiredness rather than drugs.

All my kit from the palace was on a bench in the corner. There wasn't much of it, but I didn't care. Out here, whatever you had would be in shit state within seconds.

I took a breath and forced myself to sit up.

'I got bad news, Nick. It's Pete . . .' Rhett was grim-faced. 'He's dead, mate.'

I couldn't have heard him right.

'He got shot about four hours ago. Sorry, mate, he was a good lad.'

Pete's gone . . . I've got to go . . . I've got to go . . .

'Where's Dom?'

'Dunno. Probably well shook up. He saw it happen. Media Ops asked me to break the news. It's a fucker.'

I pointed over to my kit. 'Can you pass my mobile? It's in one of the side pouches.'

I was fully awake now. I was thinking about Tallulah, Ruby and those birthdays he was determined not to miss.

I sparked up the phone. Iraqna had treated me to a three-bar signal.

I called Dom. The default Vodafone Ireland message kicked in immediately.

'It's Nick. Rhett's just told me. Call me back soon as, mate. I need to know you're OK.'

I sat cradling the phone in my lap. 'What the fuck happened?'

He placed his helmet carefully on the plywood floor. 'Fucking nightmare.' He shook his head. 'We brought both of them back here from OSB. You were out of it, so Dom said they'd decided to go outside the wire to film the Merlins flying low into the city. Some fucker must have been waiting. Pete took two rounds. There's always some of those shites hanging around looking for a target. Dom ran and got help, but it was useless.

He'd have died instantly. What can I say? Fucking crying shame . . .'

'What about the shooters?'

'The QRF [quick reaction force] were out like a bunch of fucking whippets, but they'd legged it.'

'Where's Dom?'

'His kit's gone. He's fucked off.'

I willed the phone to ring. A cameraman had died on my watch, and now the reporter was missing.

I looked up. 'Help me get dressed, mate.'

21

I did it as fast as I could, one-handed and with a bit of help from Rhett. My jeans and T-shirt were on my Bergen, but my boots had probably been burnt along with the rest of last night's shit-covered, infected gear. I dug out my trainers.

'You know where they keep the bodies?'

Rhett was in awkward mode. 'No, it's not the sort of place we want to go near.'

I held out my good hand and we shook. 'Thanks, Rhett. If you want to come with me and have a last look, you can.'

'Nah, I want to remember him as a gobby shite.'

He left and I finished dressing. A mirror hung on a bit of string from a section of frame by the side of the bench, and I saw what was left of a large black M that had been written on my fore-head in permanent marker. At some stage I would have had a label attached to me too, to make doubly sure everybody further down the chain knew I'd been administered morphine. It affects other treatments.

With greasy, sticking-up hair and already sweating, I pushed aside the green nylon sheet that acted as a door, turned left and walked down a corridor of cubicle walls towards the sound of music. I passed air-conditioning ducts, but they weren't working.

There was another cubicle at the end of the corridor. This one was an office. Two guys in white coats sat on plastic chairs, watching MTV. They had their backs to me but I could see the mugs of brew and a packet of Rich Tea.

'Lads, where's the morgue? I think one of my mates is there – you know, the cameraman who got shot.'

They both looked round, and then at each other. It was hard to interpret their expressions. Either I wasn't allowed access, or neither of them wanted to miss Beyoncé shaking her tits on MTV.

The blond one stood up. 'Next door.' He picked up his armour and helmet. 'Where's yours?'

'Don't know, mate.'

I followed him out into the blinding sunshine. I almost had to close my eyes. We turned right in the sand and headed for a concrete-block building. The guy turned back to me as we walked. 'You ever seen a dead body before, mate?'

I nodded.

Entering the building was like stepping into a fridge. This was where all the air-conditioning lived. Beyond sheets of thick plastic hanging from the ceiling lay five stone slabs like kitchen worktops.

A body lay on one, covered with a sheet. Two clear evidence bags lay on the floor next to him. One was smeared on the inside with wet blood that must have rubbed off his clothes. The other, much smaller, contained his personal effects. His wallet, his watch, his wedding ring. And his precious memory stick.

The guy went over and pulled the sheet back, then stood aside and leant against the next slab along.

Pete's couple of days' stubble would keep growing for a bit longer, but he'd been cleaned up pretty well. I realized this was the first time I'd seen him without a smile on his face.

He had two strike marks in his chest. They'd dried up and looked like big scabs. The rest of his skin was pale.

'What's going to happen now? How's he going to get home?'

'I guess we'll fly him back to Brize. That's what normally happens.'

I looked at Pete again. Something about those

strike marks wasn't right.

I walked all the way round him, looking for more strikes, more marks. 'Why wasn't he wearing armour?'

The guy was getting bored now. He'd done his bit. Beyoncé beckoned. 'Don't know, mate. He just got shot and brought here. That's it.'

I lifted Pete's right arm, then pulled it up a bit more until his shoulder lifted and I could see the exit wounds in his back. They were large, as they always are when the rounds are allowed to exit the body. I put his arm down where it belonged.

'I'm going to see you all right, mate . . .' I said quietly.

The medic came towards me with the sheet. 'No need to worry about that.'

'I wasn't talking to you.'

I picked up Pete's personal stuff and left him to it. I walked back out into the sun. Dom and I would take his gear to his family. The least we could do was make sure the stuff that was most important to him got back to the people who were most important to him. Small things in big firms always tended to go missing.

Why wasn't he wearing Osprey? Everyone had to wear it even to go for a dump. Pete was so careful. He would have had it on. Even if those two rounds had pierced his body armour by some sort of miracle, they wouldn't have exited like they did. When a high-velocity round enters the body, it creates a vortex behind it like the wake after a boat. As it leaves, the pressure equalizes. There's a small air explosion that rips the exit wound open. It's what high-velocity rounds are designed to do.

22

My arm hurt like fuck as it swung and I had to cradle it against my chest.

Screwing up my eyes, I turned right, headed past the morgue and into the dining tent. People were coming and going with mugs of brew. The entrance was full of people in body armour and helmets washing their hands in cleansing liquid so's not to waste water. They looked at me like I was an alien. 'I know, I haven't got any. Anybody know where Media Ops are?'

I was pointed beyond the cookhouse. I turned left by the showers and half walked, half ran, asking for directions along the way. Most people knew their own areas and that was it.

Eventually I found myself outside two Portakabins with huge air-conditioning condenser boxes. I knew where I was now. This was where we'd had our briefings.

There was movement inside the second Portakabin. I went in and the place was almost as cold as the mortuary tent. The Royal Artillery captain who'd done the meet and greet was behind a desk. I couldn't remember his name – I'd just nodded and agreed as he gave his talk, not expecting to see him again. But I did remember he was in the Territorials, and had volunteered to come out here. In the real world, he was responsible for Plymouth Council's CCTV cameras.

He seemed shocked to see me. 'Nick, how are you? I was coming round later. I wanted you to rest first.' He looked uncomfortable. He stood up and took a breath to give me the bad news.

I put up a hand. 'I know Pete's dead. The recce sergeant's already seen me.'

He sat down, relieved not to be the one. I was a civvy. I might want to cry on his shoulder and have a hug.

'Why didn't he have any body armour on?'

'I don't know. We told you lot to wear it all the time – and a helmet. It was part of the briefing. Dom told us they were getting some shots of the Merlins flying low. They didn't have permission. They didn't inform anyone of what they were doing. We cannot take responsibility for these actions. They should have informed me that they—'

This was bollocks. 'Where's Dom now?'

'He's left. I don't know where or how. His kit's gone and he hasn't even signed out.'

'Signed out? How the fuck's he going to get out of here? Call a minicab?'

'He must be taking the two o'clock. It's thoroughly irresponsible behaviour – it doesn't help the media's call for closer liaison.'

'Shut up, for fuck's sake, and give me a lift to the terminal.'

I followed him back out into the heat. The Media Ops company car was a dust-covered Discovery that knocked out air-conditioning, but not enough. I shielded my eyes from the glare as we came out of one compound and went into another. We bounced over dusty tracks, working our way up to the metalled road that paralleled the runway.

'What's going to happen to Pete?'

'The TV station has notified his wife. They're arranging for her to receive him at Brize Norton. After that? Well . . .'

I held up the plastic bag. 'I'll take this back to her.'

We hit the tarmac. The terminal was about two clicks further up. It looked like another of Saddam's palaces. Lots of marble and towers, but surrounded by barbed wire and HESCOs. Squaddies zoomed up and down the road in stripped-down Land Rovers with .50-cal machine-guns on the back.

The Brits had used the terminal as their temporary HQ after the war until the COB was built. It had since been handed back to the civilian authorities, and catered for just one flight a day. No airline except Jordanian was willing to take the risk.

We parked outside the building. I didn't care if the media guy stayed or not. I just ran into the cavernous empty terminal.

There were about four people in civvies, but none was Dom. All the rest, about ten of them, were RMPs with dogs and SA80s.

Another marble quarry must have been gutted to build this place. The roof had to be at least seventy metres high. The walls still had gaffer-tape marks from where the Brits had run cables.

The check-in area was a line of about forty desks along the far wall. All had digital displays behind them. None was working. None of the belts was moving.

One solitary guy sat behind one of the desks. His eyes widened as I ran towards him. The flight wasn't for at least another hour and a half and it wasn't as if there were masses of people gagging to get aboard.

'This for the Jordanian flight? The Amman flight?'

'Yes, yes.'

'Has Dominik Condratowicz checked in yet?'

He looked at me blankly.

I took a breath and slowed down. 'Mr Dom-in-ik Con-drat-o-wicz.'

He checked his manifests and I leant forward to help him. I couldn't see the name. 'Do we buy tickets here? This desk?'

'Yes, yes.'

'Has he bought a ticket?'

'No.'

Dom hadn't checked in so he certainly hadn't gone airside – if there was an airside. I didn't know how it worked in this place.

Fuck it, I'd stay right here until the flight left and see if he turned up.

I moved off and sat on one of the millions of vacant chairs, waiting for him to show.

Flicking through Pete's gear, I found nothing that gave me any clues about what had happened. There was just the normal stuff in his wallet. Two Lloyds debit cards, organ-donor card, that sort of thing, with about sixty dollars.

Filming helicopters, my arse.

I got out my mobile.

'It's Nick Stone in Basra. I need to talk to Moira Foley. It's important.'

I was waiting for Kate to answer, then go to find Moira, but the boss herself came straight on. 'Hello, Nick. It's Moira, how are you? I've been so worried . . .'

I knew she hadn't so she didn't have to sound so concerned. 'Pete . . . you know?'

'God, it's fucking awful. They called me at home and—'

'Where's Dom? You know where he is?'

'With you. He filed with Pete, then called me after Pete was shot. He said he'd told you what happened.'

I held the mobile away from me and checked the display for messages. The thing was always on silent as it was a big no-no to have a mobile go off in the field.

'Nick, hello? Hello?'

I didn't need to move it back to my ear to hear her.

'I need him to call me back soon, Nick. Tell him we need a report to go with the film. It's great footage and we really need to—'

I cut her off, sat back and waited.

PART TWO

23

Guy's Hospital, London
Monday, 5 March
1538 hrs

My arse was numb. I'd been parked on a hard plastic chair in A and E for the best part of four hours and still hadn't been called to see a doctor. Maybe I shouldn't have told the triage nurse I'd gouged my arm at work with a chisel. I should have been more upfront about being brassed up by a 7.62 short. At least it was getting a rest in the foam sling they'd given me in the land of Pizza Hut delivery.

The only entertainment left after *London Lite* and a couple of Sunday supplements people had dropped under the chairs was the flat-screen TV on the wall above the reception desk. It played without sound, and there's only so much BBC 24 tickertape reading you can take. Besides, I didn't like what I'd been seeing.

Two Polish builders were sitting next to me, one with half a finger hanging off and the other making more noise than if it was his injury and he'd lost a whole hand. Two teenage girls with huge earrings and their hair scraped back went on much too loudly about who was having who on their estate, and who'd had whose kid.

I stared down at the Bergen between my feet, getting even more angry with Dom as I thought about Pete's few possessions stuffed into my side pouch. It hadn't been an attack while filming, and it couldn't have been an ND (negligent discharge). The rumour mill would have exposed it by now.

But I'd find out who had done it and why, and Dom was going to tell me the truth if it was the last thing he did. But the fucker had evaporated.

The Big Mac and fries I'd blocked my arteries with at the on-site McDonald's an hour ago were making me thirsty. A kid came in with a blood-stained T-shirt wrapped round his hand. Within minutes, he was called to the only free cubicle. There was time to go and get a drink.

I checked the dressing wasn't leaking as I'd ripped the wound open on the way back to the UK. My Bergen strap had scraped down my arm as I took it off and its weight had ripped the stitches from the skin.

Trolleys lined both sides of the corridor, loaded with old people coughing up shit. I couldn't tell if they were waiting for A and E or were just overspill from the wards.

The two Poles got very excited about something on the TV. I looked up to see, for maybe the tenth time since I'd been sitting there, the crystal-clear, black-and-white images of me tumbling into the sewage and Pete being my hero. Of course, the part where he'd killed people had been cut. Cameramen don't do things like that.

It was being played over and over again, not only because it was great bang-bang but also because it was being pushed out as a tribute to Pete – and to Platinum Bollocks, of course, for filming it. As for me, being security, thankfully I didn't get a mention. I was just 'a member of the crew'. No TV company wants it known that they have protection. It isn't good for the image.

I watched as I got hit and dropped like a bag of shit. The Poles were loving it. Real live bang-bang, filmed by a real live Polish hero.

I'd booked myself on to the next day's two p.m. Royal Jordanian to Amman. The flight had had the world's most obvious sky marshal sitting in the galley by the cockpit door. Kitted out in a very sharp suit and some of Russia's finest steel sticking out of his holster, he was even scaring the flight attendants.

We landed at three thirty, but there were no useful connecting flights till the morning. I'd spent last night on an airport bench because I wanted to be sure of a ticket for the nine a.m. BA to Heathrow the moment the desk opened – only to discover when it did that the airline will put you up in a hotel if you're waiting overnight for a connecting flight.

It had been last night that I fucked up my arm again. I sort of let them think I was a wounded soldier and they upgraded me to business all the way through to London.

I'd taken the fast train to Paddington, jumped into a cab and got the driver to take me to Guy's. I could have walked round the corner to St Mary's, but south London was more my stamping ground. Going to Guy's was a trip down Memory Lane.

Besides, it was closer to Brockwell Park.

24

I tried Dom's mobile for the fifth time since landing. Still only voicemail.

I rang Moira again. 'Has he called in yet?'

'No. Have you heard anything?'

'Nothing. I'm in London.'

There was a long pause. Something not very good was about to happen.

'Listen, Nick, with Pete gone and Dom missing, there isn't any reason to keep you on. That's it, I'm afraid. Send me an invoice for the days worked and I'll get our accounts department to sort it out.'

She wasn't one to mess about, was she?

'Nick, I have to go.'

So, that was it, then. No more pay cheques from TVZ 24.

A very pissed-off voice paged a doctor on the Tannoy. They might have installed CCTV since the 1970s, but some things about the place hadn't changed. The woman's voice sounded exactly the same as the reception staff had when I'd been there as a nine-year-old leaking red stuff.

I lived on the Tabard Estate, a few streets away, in a block of council flats thrown up after the war. They'd been built on a newly vacant site. Demolition had been cheap, courtesy of the Luftwaffe.

All the houses were given names associated with Chaucer's *Canterbury Tales*. Apparently the pilgrimage had started from the Tabard Inn or somewhere. We ended up in Eastwell House: Eastwell was one of the stops along the pilgrims' route, they'd said. I'd never read the *Canterbury Tales*. I'd thumbed through the *Canterbury Messenger* once while waiting for a train back to Shorncliff barracks when I was a boy soldier, but that probably didn't count.

I went to a primary school near the chocolate factory, which for some reason us kids thought was owned by Bob Monkhouse. Another rumour flying round was that the sweet shop in Kirby Grove had a shed behind it stacked with Coca-Cola and R. White's lemonade. One dinner-time, a gang of us set off to scale the wall. Like a dick-head, I volunteered to be first up. I hadn't taken account of the broken glass set into the concrete along the top. I fucked myself up big-time. Blood poured from my lacerated hand, but I knew Guy's was just a couple of minutes away. I ran all the way there. They did their stuff, and told me to go home. I didn't argue. After that I was forever grazing my knees and elbows and taking myself off to Guy's, then home for the rest of the day.

All I needed now were a few new sutures and some more antibiotics to counter any infection in the wound and the shit I must have swallowed. They'd do it, no trouble. This was south London. It wasn't like they didn't know how to treat gunshot wounds. Once they'd sewn me up and handed out some more antibiotics and painkillers, I'd be looking for Dom, and my first stop would be Tallulah and Ruby's. They were the real casualties. My arm would heal.

I stuck it out for another twenty minutes as old people vomited into plastic containers and called for their forty-something children, who were wandering round, trying to find out why their parents had been abandoned in the corridors.

It depressed the shit out of me, and reinforced my own plans for old age. I wasn't going to hang about. Once I started pissing in my pants, it was time to drop myself.

I got to my feet, picked up all my worldly goods in my Bergen, and asked the Polish builders to keep my seat for me.

At the coffee machine, I scrabbled in my pocket for change with my free hand, when a gravel-voiced Ulsterman piped up behind me: 'It's all right, boy, I'll get that.'

I didn't turn. I knew who it was. I could feel his roll-up tobacco breath against my ear. My heart sank.

'Shirley Temple, if I remember right?' A worn brown leather-covered arm brushed past my face and a big freckled hand threw a quid into the slot and punched 'white no sugar' with a nicotine-stained forefinger.

25

Sundance saw the expression on my face. 'Don't worry, boy, we're not carrying. We're not going to hurt you.'

We? Where there was Sundance, you also got Trainers. I looked round and, sure enough, he was sitting a little further down the corridor. He was there to block a getaway, but he seemed more intent on checking out the nurses, cleaners, female patients, anyone with a pair of tits. His forearms rippled below his short-sleeved shirt as he worked a roll-up. His Red Hand of Ulster tattoo had just been lasered off last time I saw him, and all traces of it had now disappeared.

I didn't care what Sundance said. I was fucking concerned. They had kicked the shit out of me once before just because the Yes Man, the arsehole they worked for, felt in that kind of mood. He'd given me a brief to kill a kid, which would send a warning to his father. I hadn't complied, so Sundance and Trainers had introduced me to the Yes Man's alternative brief: go to Panama and kill the father. If not, Kelly, a child who was my last remaining link with the human race, would die.

I'd nicknamed him Sundance because of his thick, blond, side-parted hair and Robert Redford looks, back in the days when Bob was young enough to play Paul Newman's mate. The years hadn't been kind. His face had dropped an inch or two, and the parting had widened to take in much of the top of his nut.

And Trainers? He'd got his name because he wore them all the time and they were the first thing I'd seen of him when they were kicking me to shit.

They'd obviously kept hitting the weights since their days in the H Blocks, but still looked bulked-up rather than honed. With their broken noses and big barrel chests they wouldn't have been out of place outside a nightclub in ill-fitting dinner jackets and Dr Martens. But they were in the Good Lads' Club now, and worked for the Firm.

Sundance nodded down at my arm as the cup dropped on to the tray. 'Had a bit of a rough time there, eh? I saw it on the news. Hit a bone?'

I shook my head. He glanced up again as the cup filled. 'Fucking chaos out there, eh?'

As if he'd know. Guys like him were just muscle, not two brain cells to rub together. They stayed local, within the M25. These days, they were probably used to fight the new enemy – anyone with a towel on their heads. They probably went round intimidating young Muslim men, trying to turn them into sources in the mosques.

'It has its moments,' I said. 'So, what the fuck are you after?'

Sundance lifted the steaming coffee from the machine and presented it to me. 'The boss wants to see you at the office.'

I took the plastic rim with my thumb and forefinger, but I'd gone off the idea. In fact, I suddenly felt sicker than I had when I came into this fucking place. 'When?'

'Eight thirty tonight.' He reached into his jacket and pulled out a white envelope. 'Here.' He slapped it against my chest. The end had been ripped open and I could see cash.

'It's for being a good boy and agreeing to see the boss. Extension two seven double eight. There's a taxi waiting outside. It'll take you to Harley Street and get that arm of yours sorted.' Sundance pushed his fist harder into me. 'You'll die waiting for these fuckers to take a look at you, and you've got an appointment this evening.'

I took the envelope and he backed off.

'See you later, boy.'

'Don't hold your breath. There's somewhere I've got to go first.'

Sundance's head leapt towards mine. His face was just inches away. 'The boss said half eight, so be there.'

It would have been stupid to get big-time with those two, but I was sorely tempted.

He shifted so his eyes drilled into mine. 'If you're one second late we'll be seeing you again, only without the smile. You understand, boy?'

Yes, I knew exactly what he meant. 'What's he want to see me for?'

He pointed to the screen. The tribute to Pete was coming to an end. 'To do with that pal of yours.'

They lumbered off down the corridor, thighs rubbing against each other. I didn't breathe again until the two brick shithouses had disappeared through the door.

I opened the envelope and counted eight hundred pounds in fifties. The Harley Street address was written on the back. The wad had started out as a grand, for sure. They'd deducted a few expenses. I headed outside. The cab could take me to Pete's – or, rather, Tallulah and Ruby's – instead. I'd have to get my arse in gear if I was going to make it to the Yes Man on time.

I usually got dragged in because they had a job no one else in their right mind would take. But I'd have put good money on that not being the case today. I would be there on time, and for reasons that had nothing to do with those two reading me my horoscope.

26

It was about four miles dead south from the hospital, a journey that would have taken ten minutes in the middle of the night. I'd been sitting in the cab for the best part of half an hour, and we probably had another mile to go. I had to be back up with the Yes Man at Vauxhall in an hour and a half, and I didn't want to be late. My arm hurt enough as it was.

I leant forward to the dividing window. 'Mate, can you wait when we get there? I'll be half-hour, max.'

'No problem for me, son. It's your clock.'

One of the Firm's alias-business-cover accounts would be picking up the tab. There were hundreds of ABCs dotted round the world. They financed operations, provided cover jobs, and generally acted as conduits for cash the Firm needed to move into various foreign pockets.

ABCs spared government ever having to know what was done in its name. Politicians like to hear about results, not how the Firm achieves them.

The area hadn't changed much, apart from a one-way system and traffic-lights every few yards. We headed round the edge of the park and turned into Croxted Road. Pete was definitely local-boy-done-good. The Victorian three-storey terraced houses came complete with bay windows and shiny door brasses and must have been going for at least half a million.

'Just drop us here, mate. There's a parking spot to the right.'

I got out and took a couple of big breaths. I wanted to be sure I said the right thing. These people were grieving. I couldn't fuck up.

I hit the doorbell.

A few seconds later there was a voice the other side. 'Is that you, Nick?'

I'd called earlier to check she was in.

The door opened. Tallulah was tall, a good foot taller than Pete. She was wearing a baggy red jumper. Her feet were bare. The shock of long, wavy, hippie-girl hair I'd seen in the photo-graphs and movie clips was tied at the nape of her neck.

She shook my hand blankly. 'Come on in . . .'

I followed her past a sitting room and stairs, then down a couple of steps towards a new-looking kitchen-conservatory. She steered me into a room just before it on the right. Maybe she didn't want me to comment on how nice the extension was and ask for the builder's name.

It was a family room, with a sofa, TV, toys, a beaten-up computer. A window gave out on to a small but perfect garden. Pete's seven-year-old was playing on a swing.

'Ruby?'

There was no doubting whose block she was a chip off.

Tallulah stood a couple of steps away from me, arms folded. She smiled. 'I told her Daddy's gone to heaven. You know what she said? "Is he making a film about God?"'

On the wall behind her were pictures of Pete doing camera stuff, and the three of them on holiday, all the normal gear. A couple of cut-glass cameras stood on the first shelf above his desk; awards he'd won for doing the job he loved.

She offered me tea but, fuck it, I had no time for that.

I didn't sit down but Tallulah did, expectantly.

I unzipped the side pouch of my Bergen and handed her the bag containing Pete's belongings.

'Thank you so much for doing this, Nick. You don't know what it means to me.'

She lifted out his things one by one, laying them on the lid of a pink mini-piano at her feet. She almost caressed each item.

She took out his wedding ring and the tears came. I just stood there, thinking maybe tea would have been a good idea. 'The station's looking after you, I hope?' I said.

Tallulah closed her fingers round the gold band. She looked up and sort of nodded.

I didn't understand.

She pointed at the shelf. An opened envelope stood between the two glass cameras. 'They cremated him in Basra.' Tallulah reached for a fistful of Kleenex.

'Oh . . .' I thought about the donor card I'd seen amongst his stuff at Basra airport. 'I thought . . .'

'I know, it doesn't make sense. He always wanted the bits that still worked to go to some one who needed them.'

Her head dropped.

'Do you mind if I have a read?'

She took the memory stick from the bag and plugged it into the PC. As she sat down in front of the screen I took out the single sheet of A4 and unfolded it. The embossed FCO crest was top centre. There was no extension under the main Whitehall number. The signature block belonged to David Morlands, but there was no departmental accreditation.

I stood behind her and read the six stark, sterile lines that had been sent to a grieving wife. 'I don't understand, Tallulah,' I lied. 'Maybe there was a mix-up and they thought he was a soldier.'

I was glad she couldn't see me. I was trying to sound compassionate, but really I wanted to scream at the top of my voice that this was bollocks. There wasn't going to be a David Morlands anywhere in the FCO.

Tallulah stroked some strands of hair away from her mouth. 'But they bring soldiers home in coffins, don't they? I wouldn't have expected them to drape him in a flag or any of that, but they should have got my permission for cremation, surely.'

The screen filled with the pictures of Ruby that Pete had shown me.

What was I going to do? Tell her my suspicions? What was the point in making these two's lives even more complicated, especially when I had no proof? 'Have you heard from Dom?'

'You're the first to come. The station's been sorting out for me to go to Brize Norton to collect the urn. But I don't really care about that, Nick. I just wish he'd been brought home the way he wanted.'

She clicked on a movie clip I hadn't seen. Pete was in the garden in a pair of orange Hawaiian shorts I could only hope he'd been ashamed of, trying to push Ruby's ice-cream cone on to her nose.

'Me, too. Maybe if Dom calls you could ask him to get in touch. Maybe tell you where he is.'

Her shoulders lifted again as she fought back a new wave of grief.

'You know, Tallulah, I think Pete and Dom might have had a fall-out these past couple of weeks. Maybe that's why he hasn't called – you know, feeling a bit guilty.'

She bit her bottom lip as she stared out of the window. 'He said Dom had become withdrawn. They used to be so open with each other. It was depressing the hell out of Pete. He said Dom had got one-tracked about some drug story. He made a joke about him being more addicted to the story than the junkies were to the heroin.'

'That sounds like Pete . . .'

She tilted her head. 'He was always shielding me like that. A few weeks ago Dom had him filming dirty old men in Dublin. They supplied young guys with drugs, then had sex with them. God knows what was really going on.' She smiled bravely, but she couldn't stop the tears. 'He was going to ask the station about changing jobs. He wanted to spend more time . . .'

It was all too much. I reached for the box of tissues.

'Tally! Tally!' Ruby ran into the room. She froze as she spotted the stranger.

'Ruby, this is Nick. He's a friend of Daddy's.'

'Hello, Ruby.' I crouched down and held out my hand. A small and grubby one reached out, very shyly, and clung to it.

'I knew a little girl just like you once. She used to play on her swing, kicking her legs so she got really high. But not as high as you. You were really good.'

Ruby's hand fell from mine. She shifted from one foot to the other. 'What's her name?'

'Kelly.'

I got up slowly.

'My daddy's with God. He's shooting.'

She was proud of the jargon her dad had taught her. As she craned her neck to peer up at me I saw Pete craning his to look in the columns outside Basra Palace. She was his spitting image. His legacy was going to be hanging about for another few decades for sure.

'I know. Your daddy's so good at what he does that God wanted him on his team.'

She folded her arms and tilted her head. 'Are you a reporter?'

'No.'

'Well, I'm going to be a producer.'

'I see. Like Moira?'

'Yes. Daddy says she's a richid producer.' She paused. 'Does that mean she's very rich?'

'Richid?' I looked at Tallulah for help.

She couldn't help smiling. 'He may have said wretched . . .'

I smiled back. 'Not Pete's favourite person, I think. He said that, as far as she was concerned, news was more about the bottom line than the front line.'

And then something clicked.

Pete was freelance. If he'd filmed in Dublin, he'd have been paid. He would have raised an invoice. Even if it was for cash, he was so methodical he'd have kept a record.

'Tallulah, do you mind if I ask you something? The cremation . . . Dom acting strange . . . There are some things that don't quite make sense. I don't know what I'm looking for, but maybe there's a file or something . . . Maybe the station had them filming stuff they didn't want to do. Maybe they were playing silly buggers. You know what a stickler Pete was. He would have minded about stuff like that. Did he have an office? Maybe I could . . .'

She wiped away a tear and gave me a big smile. 'Oh, Nick, you are sweet.' She tried to laugh. 'You're going to look for porn or his mistress's love letters and spirit them away, aren't you?'

'Got it in one. Look, I know he didn't get on with the producer, maybe there's—'

'Nick, please, do – it's a lovely idea. But leave the porn where it is. I may as well take the bad with the good. It's the first on the right at the top of the stairs. I'll go and put the kettle on.'

I sat at Pete's desk, feeling sad and angry in just about equal proportions. The three of them had

had it all in front of them. Whoever had killed Pete had also gunned down a lot of dreams.

The desk faced the window and looked down on the garden. Ruby was back outside, playing on her swing. She sang a little song to herself. I watched her for a while, but my mind was elsewhere. I had a perfect mental picture of Kelly doing exactly the same thing. It was no time at all before she hadn't wanted to play on swings any more. It would happen to Ruby, too, in a year or two . . .

Fuck it. Time to cut away from that shit.

It was an uncluttered office, as I'd expected. There was a desk, the swivel chair I was sitting in, a filing cabinet, shelves containing hundreds of labelled video-cassettes and DVDs. Sudan, Darfur, Baghdad. Anywhere that had seen conflict, Pete had shot some film.

Family pictures were Blu-Tacked to the walls. A framed portrait of Dom and Pete in black tie stood on the desk. Between them they held an Emmy aloft like it was the FA Cup. Both wore huge grins as they basked in the moment, partners in crime.

I could smell perfume. Tallulah had been here very recently . . . as if sitting in his chair, in his room, might somehow bring him back.

Pete had said he'd miss the camaraderie if he gave up the front line, and then he'd laughed. Now I realized why. He was already a member of a much stronger unit. I wondered what it must be like.

I got up and looked along the spines of the VHS and DVD cases. All were neatly and precisely labelled, including several for Kabul 2006, but none said Dublin. There wasn't anything dated this year.

The Mac was on screen-saver. I hit a key and had a look at the desktop. It was packed with folder icons. I did a search for Dublin. Nothing. Then anything with D as a first letter. I got a QuickTime film of Dubai: Pete mucking about with Ruby in a water park. I even searched for Dirty Old Men. Nothing. Not even any porn.

Ruby's song floated up from the garden as I pulled open P–Z, the bottom of the three drawers. I opened a folder marked VAT. Pete had done himself proud. All the returns were in date order, but there weren't any receipts or invoices.

Dublin with a D.

I pulled open the top drawer, A–J. There was nothing labelled Dublin, but there was a hanging folder labelled 'Invoices'. As I opened it, Ruby was drowned by a jet lining up on Heathrow.

The folder was stuffed with receipts, ready for Pete to process. A sheet of A4 was addressed to TVZ in Dublin: '2 DAYS FILMING – DUBLIN.'

His rate was £200 a day, plus hotel, flight and van hire. The invoice was for the attention of Moira Foley, Head of News, but it had been returned. Scrawled across the bottom in thick felt tip was: 'WHAT JOB? DON'T TRY TO PULL THE FUCKING WOOL OVER MY EYES – YOU'RE NOT SMART ENOUGH.'

A yellow Post-it note was stuck next to Moira's kind words. On it, in neat biro, was: *Sorry about the misunderstanding – here's the cheque – All best, Dom.*

'Here we go.' Tallulah came in with a mug in each hand.

I closed the file and replaced it. 'Tallulah, I'm sorry, I've just realized the time.' I tapped my arm. 'Hospital appointment. I didn't find anything, but I will. I promise you.'

She put the mugs on the desk and a couple of fresh tears rolled down her cheeks as she gave me a hug. Her face burnt. Her gorgeous green eyes were puffy and swollen.

'Who's Kelly, Nick? Your daughter?'

'No, I was a bit like you, really. I sort of landed up looking after her.'

'Was? You mean you're not looking after her any more? She's grown-up now?'

'She got to be sixteen, then went to show God how to use a swing.'

I left her to it and saw myself out. My arm was throbbing, and so was my head.

27

Vauxhall Bridge
2017 hrs

The evening was still warm when the cab dropped me at Vauxhall station. Even the daffs were pushing up here and there. I crossed to a traffic island, leather bomber over my right arm, the other in a sling.

It wasn't just the weather that had changed since the last time I was here. The roads were plastered with big red Cs to show the start of the congestion zone, while CCTV and number-plate-recognition cameras had sprouted everywhere.

The railway arches were no longer the shabby tyre warehouses and dodgy MOT centres I remembered from four or five years ago. They'd been turned into trendy wine merchants and bathroom stores. There was even a gay club and sauna, and a wine bar with little aluminium tables and chairs outside trying to keep the office workers there all night with happy-hour wine deals and free dips. The sauna lights flashed enticingly.

MI6, the Secret Intelligence Service, the Firm, the Office: everybody had a different name for it. Some insiders had even called it Caesar's Palace when it first went up, and it wasn't hard to see why. It was a beige and black pyramid with its top cut off, and large towers at either side. There was even a terrace bar overlooking the river. It only needed a few swirls of neon and you'd swear you were in Las Vegas. Maybe it would become a super-casino when it had had its time.

I'd always preferred Century House myself, the old SIS building near Waterloo station. It might have been 1960s square minging architecture with droopy net curtains and antennae all over the roof but it was a lot handier for the bus and tube, and much more homely. And the old guy who ran the greasy spoon on the corner had served real food – dead animals and snacks with so many E numbers they glowed in the dark.

Even at this time of night, the multiple lanes of city traffic rumbled along like a slow-motion explosion. I crossed at the lights. I'd never expected to come face to face with the Yes Man again, but it wasn't like I had a whole lot of choice. The Firm had known where to find me within hours of my landing at Heathrow. Maybe it was the flight manifest, maybe face-recognition cameras at the airport. Whatever, if I tried to run they'd lift me before I got a mile down the road. Then they'd do more than ask for their envelope back.

This wasn't the Women's Institute, and it wasn't just a cake-baking session I'd be refusing to attend. The people who worked in the building in front of me killed for a living. It was pointless running: I'd just die knackered and out of breath. I didn't want to be a body pulled from a car crash just for saying no to a meeting. Besides, I wanted to find out what job he had in mind. I was pretty sure that the reappearance of the Yes Man at this precise moment in my life was no coincidence.

And, anyway, I'd just got the sack. There might be cash involved. When you live at the bottom of the food chain you have to take a bite of the shit sandwich when it's shoved in your face. Maybe that was why I'd never found it hard to get on with Africans, Arabs, squaddies, whoever. They soon discovered I was like them – waist deep in the shit-pit and happy to get my head up enough to take a few breaths occasionally before I got pushed back down.

I followed a couple of suits along the pavement. They must have been the night shift. They disappeared behind the steel fencing of 85 Albert Embankment and into the pyramid. I followed.

28

I wondered how an arsehole like the Yes Man fitted in with life behind the triple-glazed windows, these days. I'd heard the Firm's new leadership matched the new building: younger, meaner, more aggressive. If the Yes Man was still the boss of deniable operators, the Ks, it could only mean he'd slipped off the greasy pole. Good. Fuck him and the boils on his neck.

The physical threat had increased since 9/11 and the Firm had obviously been given a big wad of cash to boost its security. I entered via a single metal door and got funnelled towards six perspex security cubicles that looked like giant test-tubes. A small queue of suits had formed. They placed their bags on an X-ray machine and waited in line to swipe their card and enter their PIN. If they got accepted, the perspex door opened and they stepped inside. A pressure pad on the floor made the door close behind them again, trapping them in the capsule.

All sorts of tests would be carried out during the next couple of seconds. For starters, the air would be analysed for traces of weapons or explosives. If the electronics were happy, the door in front would open, releasing them into the inner sanctum.

A perspex cylinder wasn't for the likes of me. I had to go to the visitors' desk, where a woman in her forties with thick-rimmed glasses sat behind a bulletproof screen. She looked at me a bit sadly. The words 'disappointing' and 'divorce settlement' were written all over her.

I put my mouth close to the microphone. 'I have an appointment. Extension two seven double eight.'

'You need to fill this in.' She pushed a ledger under the glass. 'Do you know the name?'

'No, sorry. Can't remember.'

She picked up a phone and checked a monitor to her left that must have held the internal-numbers list. 'Do you have a picture ID?'

I fished out my passport and held it open on the photo page. 'He's expecting me at eight thirty. What's his name again?'

She gave me another of her sad looks as she hit some keys. I signed in the two marked boxes in the ledger and passed it back under the window.

With the phone still to her ear, she tore my signed strip from the ledger and folded it into a small plastic holder with a blue ribbon to go round my neck. She pushed it under the glass. The badge was blue too, and said, 'Escorted Everywhere'.

She put down the receiver. 'Wait over there. Someone will be along to collect you.'

I tried to get a smile out of her and held up the pass at the window. 'That's good. I'd only get lost.'

It wasn't going to happen. I wandered over to a backless black leather settee with chrome legs.

The doors of the security pods opened and closed as they chomped their way through the queue. A young clerk appeared, dressed in a black suit, checked shirt and a tie with a knot that was far too big for the collar. He had the kind of madly enthusiastic smile they normally only teach you at estate-agent school. He held out a hand. 'Mr Stone?'

I stood up and followed suit.

'If you'd like to go through that glass door to your right, I'll meet you on the other side.'

I nodded at the X-ray machine and held up my bomber. 'You want this in there?'

'No, the room will detect anything.'

A female guard buzzed the door open. A sign on the wall opposite told me to stand still until instructed to move. I couldn't hear any machinery or sucking sounds as the atmosphere was extracted to check for weapons or explosives residue, but I was sure it was happening.

The clerk appeared at the other side of the glass exit. The door clicked open.

The walk to the lifts took us over ivory marble floors, past grey slate walls. No wonder the building had come in at twice the estimate.

We whooshed upwards.

'Which floor we going to?'

'Fifth.'

It would have been pointless asking him more. Even if he'd known the answers he wouldn't have told me.

We stepped out into a world of grey carpet tiles and white-emulsioned walls. I felt conned, like when a hotel invests in a big makeover down in Reception but as soon as you get upstairs it's all shite – and tough, you've already checked in.

We set off down a bare corridor. There were no names on the doors, only acronyms I didn't understand. The armed services are fanatical about the fucking things, and the Firm had fallen into step. Even when I was in the Regiment and working here, I'd only been able to remember up to the three-letter ones.

Vauxhall Cross was a category-A post, which meant that, like Beijing, Moscow and other major stations abroad, it had an HPT (high potential threat) from terrorism and sophisticated HIS (hostile intelligence services). Operatives from the TSD (technical services department) in Milton Keynes ensured that the building was protected from HTA (high-tech attack).

The triple glazing didn't have anything to do with the government's new green policy. It was a safeguard against laser and radio-frequency flooding techniques as every HIS and his dog tried to hear what you were talking about. There were even techniques now to read the radiation from computer and photocopying machines, so every bit of machinery in the building was specially shielded. If anyone got on a boat and spent the day bobbing up and down on the Thames pointing technical stuff at the decapitated pyramid, they'd be wasting their fare.

The corridor opened up left and right into open-plan offices. Men and women bent over computer screens, processing information, collating, whatever the fuck they did to support the five hundred officers running round overseas. There was little noise apart from the air-conditioning and the rustle of deli bags as people weakened.

We came to an office at the far end. No acronym on this door. The clerk took me straight in without knocking. 'He'll be with you soon.'

I walked into what looked like a solicitor's office. There was a round, beech-veneer IKEA table, with a telephone in the middle, and matching chairs with leatherette seats.

At the far side of the large room was a desk. I wandered over to have a look at the framed pictures among the files by the PC monitor. They were of the Yes Man and his loving family, all smiles, and, judging by the ages of the kids and the generosity of his hair, the pictures were a few years old.

I looked out of his large window, almost the length of the room, at the bright lights of the railway-arch shops the other side of the road. Headlights moved noiselessly in both directions. The motorbike shop was still there. I really wanted to get a new one. I missed riding.

The Yes Man hadn't been given an office with a river view, but at least he got catering. A full cafetière and a small mountain of shortbread fingers sat on a nearby tray.

Maybe things weren't as bad as I'd thought.

29

The door opened. The Yes Man had two buff folders in his hand. He was exactly as I remembered him: five foot six, florid complexion.

'How was Harley Street?'

I held up my arm a little, as if he could see through the dressing. 'Haven't been yet. In the morning.'

He wore a dark business suit, with a white shirt and a scarlet tie. On his left hand he still wore a wedding ring.

I pointed through the window. 'Changed a bit since I was here last.'

He was busy pulling a chair from under the table. 'My new office?'

I joined him at the long table but kept a three-chair distance. 'New shops. The gay place. You lot get corporate membership?'

He stared at me across the table, not enjoying

my joke. I smiled even more broadly. 'It says it's got a sauna.'

The Yes Man pushed one of the folders across the table and started to pour the coffee. Even upside-down, I could read the stencil UK EYES ALPHA, which meant it was for the eyes of MI5, MI6, Special Forces, GCHQ and Whitehall only, and never to be read by a non-British citizen. There was no yellow card paperclipped to the cover. This was still an unaccountable document, a mere draft or proposal. That normally meant they hadn't found anyone stupid enough for the job.

The cover sheet was stamped with various acronyms, like O2G2/OPS and IO/GN, all meaningless to me. They'd have been senior officers, though, who'd signed it off as read. Like every organization, the Firm liked to cover its arse.

The best part of any MI6 file, as far as I was concerned, had always been the title, and this one said simply: 'The Need to Locate Dominik Condratowicz, Polish TV Journalist'.

The reports themselves might be full of gobbledegook, but the titles were always bang on the money. The best one I'd ever seen was: 'The Need to Assassinate President Milosevic of Serbia'. There hadn't been a yellow card on it, though, which was probably the reason he'd ended up in the dock at The Hague instead of dead in a Belgrade gutter.

I opened the folder to find just two printed pages of A4. The document might have been stamped by whoever had had to read it, but the signature page on the inside flap was missing.

The two pages included a digital photograph, probably from his passport application. It was definitely Dom.

I looked up. 'Locate? Don't the Firm know where he is? I assumed you—'

'He's disappeared. Nobody's heard from him.'

I ran a thumb over my stubble. 'He was pretty shaken after what happened, by all accounts. I left messages for him, and made arrangements for Media Ops to look after him when he turned up. It was all I could do before I flew out. I had some other stuff to see to here. Then I was going to make some calls. You sure he isn't just off on some story?'

'I don't believe so.' The Yes Man reached for the coffee and nudged a full cup my way. 'I'm still trying to sift through what I can rule in and what I can rule out. Did he mention anything out of the ordinary while you were there? Anything about his home life, family, Dublin, that sort of thing? Anything that might give us any indication of his whereabouts or plans?'

'Nothing. He just got on with his job, really. I'm not exactly a bosom buddy.'

The Yes Man sat forward and took one of the

shortbreads. 'Did he say anything about his work, perhaps?'

I had to give him something or he'd know I was fucking him about. Which would mean Sundance and Trainers being told to fuck *me* about. 'Nothing much. I know he was fixated on the heroin trade, but on the whole Dom kept things close to his chest.'

The Yes Man sat back with his brew, deep in thought.

'You don't think he's been lifted, do you?'

He pursed his lips. 'It's a scenario, Nick.'

I frowned, and not just because of what he'd called me. If Dom was being held, the decision whether or not even to try to rescue him would be made very high up. It all boiled down to PR. What was the propaganda value of a rescue? Would it actually be better for the government if the fucker died? Would a nice beheading online get the public sparked up? Chances were, the Regiment had only gone in for that charity worker Norman Kember because somebody had done their sums and worked out there was more mileage in a recovery than a beheading. I could just hear the discussion. 'He's already done the interviews to camera. We've seen him making his statements online. Public opinion has already reached the height of shock and horror. There's nothing to be gained by letting him be killed. He's old, he's a peace worker. Let's see if we can get him back before his head rolls.'

Would the Yes Man help make the risk assessment? If the danger of SAS casualties was too high, the troopers would stay in their tents. The PR gain wouldn't be worth the pain, especially if the hostage got killed in the attempt. Maybe that was what this was about. They were going to send in Ks. It was a matter of economics as much as anything else. It cost the taxpayer three or four million pounds a time to train an SAS trooper. All I'd cost was the price of a cremation.

I scrolled down the page. Dom had read English literature at Krakow University and found a job straight away on a Polish national newspaper. The rest was platinum-plated history.

Now was the time to ask. 'He's not a British national. What do you want him back for?'

The Yes Man sighed and pushed the second folder across the table. 'Because Dominik Condratowicz is not just a journalist, Nick. He's an asset.'

30

People paid by Her Majesty's Government to provide information or 'keep their eyes open' are known as 'assistants', 'onside' – or 'assets'. Journalists have perfect cover because it's their job to investigate and be nosy. The Firm pays them, but only just enough to establish the contract. Money isn't the issue. They usually become assets for reasons of ideology, or simply to get themselves the inside track on any good leaks.

Frontline reporters aren't the only ones approached and asked if they'd like to 'do something interesting' for HMG. Newspaper editors are sometimes onside, though they're unlikely to be recruited directly. The Firm needs permission from the foreign secretary for that level of stuff, and they hate asking a politician for anything. They wouldn't like to be refused. On the other hand, if journalists are recruited early in their careers, it can eventually mean high-ranking assets in most news and media organizations. Whatever, reporters are the one group the Firm never fucks over: they never know where even the lowliest local stringer will land up.

The Yes Man tapped the folder in front of me. 'Unfortunately, there is mounting evidence that Dominik Condratowicz should be seen in an entirely different light.' He lifted the cover. 'This is what happened to one of our people last year.'

I opened the folder to see half a dozen colour eight-by-tens of a young Arab, maybe early twenties, sitting on wet concrete. He was held upright by a pair of over-inflated forearms. The right one had an ageing scar that looked like a badly laid railway track. I flicked through the pictures with no idea if the man was dead or alive. His body was a mess of cuts, bruises and burns. His face was so swollen his eyes were forced closed and his lips were like plastic surgery gone wrong.

'They were taken in Afghanistan. An illegal prison. Freelance bounty-hunters, normally torturing their victims for information about the Taliban and al-Qaeda.'

I shrugged. 'There's a lot of those guys about over there. It's the new Wild West. Bad things are going to happen.'

'Condratowicz was in Kabul at the time,

ostensibly filming a documentary. I have to ask myself whether there's more to that than meets the eye.'

One of the pictures was a wider shot of the room or cell. The door had a sheet of steel screwed over it and a gaoler's spyhole. The last one showed a tabletop with the legs removed, bolted to an oil drum. It looked like an oversized see-saw, but I knew this was no game. Two buckets of water stood next to it. A tap stuck out of the wall. A fat roll of clingfilm sat on a pile of empty hessian sandbags.

Waterboarding is guaranteed to get its victim telling everything he knows, and even some things he doesn't – anything to keep breathing. The physical experience is like being trapped under a wave. But that's fuck-all compared to the psychological horror. Your brain screams at you that you're drowning. And the reason I knew all this was because the Americans and the Brits had invented this shit.

'Then we have a major drugs haul unearthed in Basra, and yet again it happens that Dominik Condratowicz is in town. There is more. Believe me, I could go on. Stack up enough of them, Nick, and you have to start asking yourself whether they're not coincidences, but positive correlations.

'I know that he was with the FCO in Basra the day before a raid that resulted in the confiscation of a huge haul of heroin. What are we to make of that? Was Condratowicz colluding with others to misbrief the military for certain ends – for example, to disrupt or stamp out any competition to their trade? I just don't know. I don't know any of what he's been up to for sure, but I've started to wonder, for example, how a television reporter can afford a seven-million-euro house in the best street in Dublin . . .'

The Yes Man fixed his gaze on the garish neon across the road. The pause wasn't to give me a chance to ask a question. It was to give his words time to sink in.

He cleared his throat. Even in profile, he looked appalled. 'So, has he been abusing his position as an asset to help others ship heroin out of Afghanistan? I don't know. Might he have been doing it for the last two years? I can't be sure. Has he profited to the tune of millions? Nick, you look at pictures of that house and can't help asking yourself the question . . .'

He settled his gaze on me. 'I suspect this is a large and far-reaching network. People in the FCO could be involved. Maybe people in this very building.'

'Do you think the cameraman was implicated? The story is that he got shot by insurgents.'

He shook his head. 'Like everything else in this mess, I can't say for sure, but I very much doubt it.' He placed his cup carefully back on its saucer.

'Perhaps he saw something he shouldn't . . . Who knows? But get Condratowicz back to me and it's one of the things I stand a chance of finding out. You're independent of us, Nick, and that suits us very well. There's much less risk of anyone getting tipped off. You—'

I raised an eyebrow. 'Dom was against the heroin trade. Vehemently against. He wanted to expose it, not encourage it.'

The Yes Man leant across the veneer. 'Afghanistan now produces over ninety per cent of the world's heroin. One of the trafficking routes is into Iran and thence Iraq, alongside Iranian weapons and ordnance. The network knows this. They know those weapons kill British soldiers, they know the drug money finances terrorism, but it hasn't stopped them. So what would prevent them killing a cameraman who got in their way?'

He sat back. 'I know we haven't always seen eye to eye, and I know you probably feel you don't owe me too many favours, but this isn't about you and me, Nick. Think about the soldiers. Think about their families. This has got to stop. Bring me Condratowicz and I promise you it will.'

'Is there any kind of trail?' There was no harm in asking.

'The FCO made some enquiries. They say he left Basra with a fixer, and crossed the border into

Iran soon after. But in the light of what I've told you, can we trust what they say? I've had to soft-pedal. I don't want anybody to find out who's looking for him – the whole network could go to ground. But your name came into the equation, Nick, and it started me thinking. You know the man. You know his habits, the way he thinks. You, I believe, are the best chance I have of reeling him in.'

31

Dublin Airport
Tuesday, 6 March
1415 hrs

Rain dripped off the canopy outside Arrivals as I stood in line for a cab. The bus would have been just as quick, but I wouldn't have learnt as much. It was a long time since I'd been there, and a chat with a cabbie's the best way of getting up to speed.

That was the excuse I gave myself. In truth, I wanted to squeeze myself a bit more thinking time. I needed to be in control of the situation and keep on my toes. Bullshit baffles brains, but the Yes Man was spinning too much of it my way. He must take me for a complete dickhead if he thought a few rubber stamps on a folder were going to make me think it now had a yellow card.

The only known points of contact for Dom that remained were the station, his wife and his step-son. I'd told the Yes Man to have surveillance put on Dom's mobile and his wife's, all landlines and the house computer. No flies on him. He already had that in hand with his Irish counterparts.

OK, so there was no signature page on the inside flap and never would be. That didn't matter. I was going to use the Yes Man and all his resources to help me find Dom. But after that it would be me who found out what he knew – and dealt with it, if necessary.

Siobhan had been Dom's last point of contact. He had called her from the COB before he'd per-manently closed down. I should have gone straight there, but his file hadn't revealed that much about him, let alone her. It wasn't known if she worked, spent her days in the gym or just shopping. What was the point of getting there early and hanging around for hours on the street corner? It made more sense to go where I was going.

The driver of the cab that rolled towards me had to have been seventy if he was a day. There were creases in his face that even a steam press wouldn't get out.

'O'Connell Street, mate.' I jumped into the back with all my worldly goods still in my Bergen. The Yes Man had sorted me with a UK bank account, and I now had ten thousand euros in cash in my pocket. I'd drawn it all out because that gave me control of it. He wouldn't be able to track my movements whenever I made a withdrawal. I hadn't got changed. My clothes could have done with a bit of attention from that steam press as well.

'Been to Dublin before, have you, sir?'

We nosed out into a queue.

'Many times, but not for maybe twenty years. Stag parties, rugby matches ... You know the sort of thing.'

'A bit of that still goes on. But you'll see a lot of changes. A rags-to-riches story, Dublin is. I wish I was young enough to enjoy it.'

I'd had enough fun mixing with the stag and hen parties and rugby supporters, but that had had nothing to do with getting drunk enough to vomit over a policeman. We used the weekends to our advantage when I was in the Regiment. We used to come down here from the north on a Friday night to lift people Special Branch wanted to have a private one-to-one with.

The last time, it had been just like this: grey, wet and miserable. But instead of driving the couple of hours down we'd flown to London and out again on a Friday night Five Nations special. The pubs heaved with Brits in rugby shirts, so we'd blended in nicely in the ones we'd bought duty-free at Heathrow. Our target was a Provisional IRA war-council member, who'd thought he was safe conducting PIRA's drug-trafficking activities in the South.

Connor McNaughten spent most of his time in Dublin, only venturing up to Belfast or Londonderry to kneecap someone or collect another suitcase full of profits from the Provos' drug rackets. Towards the end of the war, once most of the PIRA ASUs (active service units) had been wiped out, it had felt as if most of our operations were against drug barons rather than terrorists.

We lifted him in the early hours of Saturday morning when he was out on the piss. We dragged him into the boot of a car that had been driven down by one of the other lads, and took him north, straight to Castlereagh police station. The big stone fortress was the Abu Ghraib of Northern Ireland. No fucker, no matter how hard they were, wanted to be interrogated there by Special Branch. Go into Castlereagh and you'd come out minus a couple of fingers and with a few bones bent out of shape. And it wasn't a myth. Twenty-four hours, maximum, that was the longest anybody ever lasted before they spilled whatever beans they had to spill.

Connor was a little fat boy, but hard as fuck. He lasted more than twenty hours, and after that SB had a grudging respect for him.

Later, he was bundled back into a car boot and returned across the border before the weekend of

Dublin jollity was over. Once back in the city, with his right hand short of a pinkie, I'd told him in no uncertain terms that if he breathed a word to anyone about what had gone on Special Branch would spread the whisper that he'd come up with the information willingly.

All that was required of him was that he went back to his seedy little existence, and when called upon for information, he would give it. Otherwise he'd be lifted for another night or two at the castle, or bubbled to the Provos. Some choice: lose a couple more fingers or have a paving slab dropped on your head. No wonder we ended up with more supergrasses than Kew Gardens.

All that has stopped since Gerry Adams and Ian Paisley started their power-sharing love fest. I wondered what Sundance and Trainers made of it. After all those years fighting with the UDA, and the Prod 'never surrender' business, that was exactly what the Loyalists – and Nationalists – had done. They probably saw it as a total waste of a war. I doubted I'd ever ask them. I liked having teeth and unbroken bones.

As for Connor, he'd kept well quiet about his little visit to the castle and done as he was told. But even better than that, he'd become a Dublin Sinn Fein councillor a year later. It meant the Brits had a source there, too.

I looked out of the window as we nudged

through the outskirts. The driver was right. Dublin had gone from rags to riches since Ireland had joined the EU, and it obviously wasn't just the Irish themselves who were fuelling the economic miracle. We passed a billboard advertising a newspaper. All the text was in a foreign language, but I recognized 'Polski'. 'You got many Poles here?'

'They even have their own TV show. Good people, I like them. We have all sorts. We got those Lithuanians, Africans, Spanish, and loads of those little Chinese fellas. We've even got a mosque.'

'That it?' I was looking at a silver pole pointing skywards over the city centre.

He chuckled as he wove in and out of the traffic. 'Bertie Ahern wanted to build some sort of sports stadium, but in the end they decided on a spire instead. We call it Bertie's Pole . . . or the Stiffy on the Liffey.' His face creased into another thousand lines. He enjoyed that gag so much he jumped the lights. Not because he was impatient, he just hadn't seen them.

We drove down a street I sort of recognized. I remembered it in a shit state, women selling fruit and veg and bits of fish from babies' prams. Now there were African hairdressers, Arab delis, Chinese restaurants and loads of Internet shops. Places selling coconuts and all sorts. It reminded me of parts of New York, the city where you think everybody smokes because the new laws have driven the lot of them outside.

And judging by the size of the huddle puffing away on the pavement, TVZ 24's entire staff had been recruited on the other side of the Atlantic.

32

Glass doors hissed open. Ahead, a torrent of water coursed down a huge angled sheet of steel. Beautiful people glided over white tiles doing important things with a mobile in one hand and a paper cup of cappuccino in the other.

I went up to the reception desk. An entire wall of flat screens showed footage of Pete fucking about with his cameras, getting ready to film. A tickertape caption announced the sad death of one of the station's finest cameramen.

'Hello, my name's Nick Stone. I'm here for Moira Foley.'

The girl had a little Bluetooth thing in her ear. She gave me a big smile and tapped her keyboard.

'She is expecting me. We spoke this morning.'

I'd called on the pretext of seeing Moira about my invoice. I needn't have worried about getting a meeting. She was the one who asked me.

My name obviously turned up on her monitor. Now the receptionist was tapping phone keys. 'Could you sign in here, please?'

By the time I'd done so and she'd finished her call, a machine had spat out a nice little plastic credit card with my name printed on it to hang round my neck on a nylon tape.

'Would you like to take a seat over there? Someone will be down.'

It was just like the office at Vauxhall Cross, only with a hint of politeness. They even had black, steel-framed leather settees. Above them, glass cabinets were crammed with silver and glass trophies. They'd obviously won a lot of awards and didn't mind everyone knowing.

I pulled my invoice from my bomber. Three hundred euros a day for ten days, printed out at an Internet café near Paddington station on the way to the airport.

Another battery of flat screens showed Dom waffling with an attractive, petite Arab woman in her thirties. Her head was covered with a white scarf. The rest of her garb was long and black. As they talked, they walked across a dustbowl strewn with rubble. It just had to be Afghanistan. The mountains in the background gave it away – and if they hadn't, the figures in blue burqas did. They scuttled about like big blue pepper-pots. The camera focused on her head. She waffled away silently above the caption: 'Afghan women's aid worker'. She seemed too un-weathered and beautiful to be working in the dust.

A new caption told me this was an excerpt from *Veiled Threats*, the documentary that had made Pete and Dom famous. It had won two Emmys and a host of other stuff. The station was very proud of them.

The tribute was working. It made me think of Pete fucking about with his tin hat on.

'Mr Stone?'

I dragged myself back from the last time I'd seen him. I didn't know why the Polish accent surprised me. It was a Polish station, after all, and I knew the voice. I looked up to see a girl in jeans and a polo-neck jumper.

'I'm Katarzyna. Everyone calls me Kate.'

I stood up and shook hands with a very smiley young woman. She looked just as her voice had told me she would. She pointed at my arm, a little unsure what to say. She managed, 'Ouch,' and a sympathetic smile.

'It's OK. What do I do with this?' I held up my invoice.

She took the sheet of A4. 'I will try and get a cheque for you today.'

I followed her to the lift. She was embarrassed. She was seventeen or eighteen, just starting out in life. She was getting the hang of it and wasn't quite sure how to act, and I was fed up with it. We didn't say any more to each other. I was fine about it and so was she.

The lift doors opened and three of the smokers rushed in to join us. The reek of nicotine breath filled the metal box.

The doors opened again into a large, open-plan office. Again, it could have been Vauxhall Cross if it hadn't been for the trendy water-bottle dispensers and coffee machines. People were on the phone or hunched over their PCs. Worktops were littered with piles of magazines and newspapers. At the far end the newsreaders' desks were in plain view so we could see how hard-working they were. That particular section, however, was cut off by soundproof glass so the newsreaders could shout at each other and call each other dickheads without it going on air.

Glass-walled offices lined the left side of the big open space. My very quiet new mate led me to a fanatically tidy desk. A woman I assumed was Moira sat behind it.

She wasn't what I'd been expecting. For starters, I wouldn't have predicted the inch-thick layer of makeup. She was maybe mid-fifties, and didn't show a wedding ring. Maybe she was trying hard to compete with the likes of Kate. A far-too-thin blouse revealed her bra, and the look continued with a mini-skirt and knee-high boots. Her hair was jet black. Her eyelashes were so long they looked like spiders' legs. Either everyone was too scared to tell her, or they disliked her so much they couldn't be bothered.

'Come in, Nick.'

Her accent was as Irish as Bertie's Pole, and her arrogance levels twice as high. She glanced at my friend. 'Coffee.'

I turned to Kate. 'No, I'm fine.' I'd always hated the girl-go-get-coffee thing. I'd had enough of it myself when I was a young squaddy, getting pushed around from pillar to post. I didn't wish it on others, especially if the order came from someone like Moira.

I sat down where she pointed. 'I'm sorry to have to let you go.' She settled back behind her desk. 'If it was up to me, I'd have kept you on. But the MD took the view he'd paid for close protection and not got it. Did you bring the invoice?'

'Got nothing else to do, have I?'

She leant forward, hoping her expression of deeply sincere concern would help us move on from the sacking. 'How's the arm, Nick?'

'Fine. I had it cleaned up this morning in Harley Street.'

She took a breath but I beat her to it. 'Don't worry, I'm not billing. Look, I've been calling Dom but still can't get an answer. You heard anything?'

Her face fell. 'I was hoping you might have. That wife of his – you've met her?'

'No.'

There seemed to be no love lost there.

'Well, *she* says he's taken a break. You know, clearing his fucking head or something. *She* won't say where he is, when he's coming back.' She raised her hands in frustration. 'I'm trying to run a news organization here.'

'Has he done this before?'

They dropped back on to the table. 'No – but, then, he hasn't had a cameraman killed before either. That bloody wife of his, she knows where he is.'

'Did he say anything about filming in the city before we left?'

'He's my war correspondent. He doesn't do new one-way systems. That was just the fucking cameraman trying to get some expenses out of me. Old habits die hard.'

She sat back, her hands stretched out on the desk. The spiders' legs flashed up and down. 'Perhaps we could arrange some extra work? Here in the studio? We've got a great story, all this great footage, but no one to follow it up. We could get massive exposure on this. All the outlets have been clamouring.'

She looked at my arm. 'You're a film star now, Nick. What about you giving an interview, just talking to camera, nothing hard, telling us what happened? You could talk us through it. They're hungry out there, Nick. People want to know the pain you've gone through. It would be a lasting tribute to Dom's cameraman.'

Moira couldn't have pulled off concerned if there'd been a gun to her head.

I stood up and so did she. She was waspish. 'You're wasting an opportunity to tell the world what happened. If you don't do it, there are others who will.'

I had to put her right there and then, before she barged her way into their lives and fucked them up even more. 'Do not go near Pete's family. They've had enough shit already. If you do I'll go to the BBC – in fact, any fucker – and do the inter-view with them.'

Her face went red with anger, which was quite an achievement, given the thickness of her makeup. 'Then your invoice will take a fucking long time coming through, that's all I can say.'

I walked out.

Kate had been hovering outside. She followed me to the lift. As the doors closed, she jumped in.

'Mr Stone, I knew she wouldn't pay you if you said no, so here . . . I prepared.' Out of her bag came a wad of euros and a receipt for me to sign.

'You'll burn in hell for this, Kate. Thank you.'

She smiled, then got embarrassed and looked down. 'She's already asked Peter's family.'

'What did they say?'

'They said no. I think that is good thing.'

'So do I, Kate. So do I.'

We shook hands by the steel waterfall and I headed for the door.

'There is one more thing, Mr Stone.'

I turned.

'She really didn't believe Peter's invoice. But he had been filming in St Stephen's Green. You wouldn't believe how tight she is. She wouldn't reimburse Dom for his donation to the refuge either.'

'The one in their documentary?'

She nodded. 'It's very close to his heart.'

33

'Herbert Park in Ballsbridge.'

The cab edged out into traffic.

'One of the embassies, sir?'

'Nah, just an old mate who's moved there. Smart area, is it?'

He chuckled. 'On the Dublin Monopoly board, the roads in Ballsbridge are the fockin' big bucks squares.' He threw a newspaper to me. 'Here, have a read of that. We're going to be stuck in the rush-hour for a while.'

He wasn't wrong. We were surrounded by commuters with their heads down and telephones to their ears as they made their way home.

The street-lights glowed on the paper through the rain-stained windows. I opened it up on a big spread about extraordinary rendition. A cleaning woman had boarded a supposedly empty

American plane to find a prisoner handcuffed, hooded and wearing an adult nappy. The Irish government were hugely embarrassed: they'd given public assurances that war-on-terror 'rendered' prisoners didn't come anywhere near the place on their way to Guantánamo Bay or the CIA's secret prisons in Afghanistan, Pakistan or wherever their interrogators had been able to set up shop.

The piece said:

> The practice has grown sharply since the 9/11 terrorist attacks, and now includes a form in which suspects are illegally arrested, sometimes straight off the street, and delivered to a third-party state. There, the suspects are tortured by many means, including 'waterboarding' . . .

We used to do it out of this very city, only it wasn't called rendition in those days. They were just lifted. It got me wondering if Special Branch had ever used waterboarding. We never hung around at the castle long enough to see what went on. Better not to know, and have a clean pair of hands.

I checked the property pages but there was nothing for sale in the whole suburb of Ballsbridge, let alone Herbert Park.

'What do the houses go for round here?'

'Put it this way, last time you were here you could have picked up one of these little beauties for fifty thousand punts. Last one I saw advertised went for well over seven million euros. We're nearly there. Which end?'

I folded the newspaper. 'Drop us off here, mate. I'm going to walk down and surprise them.'

I paid him thirty euros and walked along Herbert Park in the rain, looking for number eighty-eight. Actually, it wasn't really rain, not even drizzle, more a mist that soaked everything through. I pulled up the collar of my bomber, hooked my bag over my shoulder and started walking.

If Pete had done good, Dom had hit the jackpot. These were substantial four-storey red-brick houses set back from the road, with large rectangular windows, designed for the grand and merchant classes during old Dublin's previous heyday. Raised stone staircases led one floor up to very solid and highly glossed front doors. The ground floor was reserved for the servants. Either Dom had married into money or the Polish celeb mags paid much more than I'd imagined for their double-page spreads. Or the Yes Man hadn't been talking bollocks.

Lights were on in several of the houses, and curtains were open to display the gilded furniture and big chandeliers to best effect.

I was still trying to work out what to say to Siobhan. Did she know Dom was an asset? I wasn't sure how that worked with spouses. I'd never been put to the test.

I walked past 6 Series BMWs and shiny 4x4s.

For all I knew, Dom could be sitting at home with his feet up watching telly, and Siobhan was putting the kettle on to make him a brew.

I neared number eighty-eight. The hall light shone through a glass panel over a wide, shiny wooden door. I couldn't see any movement through the front windows or upstairs. There were no milk bottles on the front step, empty or full, but that meant nothing nowadays. There was no condensation on the windows, but I wouldn't expect it. This was no minging old council house with poor heating and no ventilation.

I carried on past. Keeping a mental count of the houses, I reached the end of the street. The last time I'd walked past so many brand-new cars I'd been in a Kuwaiti showroom. This place was awash with money. I picked up a flyer from the pavement advertising a luxurious spa with a helipad on the roof in case you needed some emergency work on your cuticles.

I turned left at the end of the terrace and worked my way round to the back of the houses. There was a small service road about four metres wide that the gardens on each side backed on to.

I walked past all the wheelie-bins and counted up to sixteen. Each property had a six-foot brick wall and either an old wooden gate or a fancy wrought-iron one. Mature trees towered over the gardens.

The lights were on at the back of eighty-eight on the first floor.

There was movement in what looked like the kitchen, but the blinds were half down. I couldn't ID the shadow, but it seemed too small to be Dom.

I turned back and it wasn't long before I was knocking with the heavy iron lion's head on the front door.

'Who is it?'

The voice was female and Irish.

'My name's Nick. I'm a friend of Dom's. I was with him last week in Basra.'

34

Siobhan was dressed in jeans, trainers and a black sweatshirt. Her big brown eyes were red-rimmed, and her short, straight hair needed a brush. She looked like she hadn't slept in days, but she was still beautiful. She must have been at least ten years younger than her husband.

'I know who you are.' She smiled weakly. 'You'll have to forgive me. I've been in bed for two days. It's a flu thing.'

I smiled back. 'Is Dom home?'

'I wish.' She touched my arm gently. 'How are you?'

'A few stitches, no bones broken.'

'He called me, and then I saw it on the news.' She bit her lip. 'I feel so bad about Pete. When is the funeral, do you know?'

I shook my head.

'His poor family . . .' Her voice was educated and soft, full of compassion.

I nodded slowly. 'I've been calling him for days and just get his voicemail. It's not like him. I'm worried maybe he's not picking up because he blames me. I feel responsible. I was supposed to be the one protecting them. I want to find him, clear the air.'

She started to look about her.

'Sorry for just turning up on the doorstep – your number's ex-directory but he gave me the address back in Basra. So . . .'

'Did you go to the studio? Did they tell you to come here?'

'No. Listen, Siobhan . . .' I hesitated. 'OK – I'll level with you. There's something about Pete's death that doesn't add up. I really need to talk to—'

She stepped aside. 'Please come in.'

I crossed the threshold and wondered if I should be taking my shoes off altogether instead of just wiping them like a madman to scrape off the wet grime. The highly polished black-and-white chequered tiles were clean enough to do surgery on.

I put down my Bergen. A crystal chandelier hung from the high ceiling. Landscape paintings gazed down at us from every direction. I caught a faint whiff of cigarette smoke.

'Nice place.'

'Thanks.' She was already walking down the hall. 'What can I offer you? Coffee, tea?'

We passed two antique half-tables. Glass trays held keys and change.

'Coffee would be great.'

We passed the open door to a front room or reception room, or whatever they called it in a house this size. I saw no framed prints on the walls of Dom being heroic with a microphone, just lots more landscapes. The mountains were too big to be Irish. Maybe they were Polish, or Transylvanian.

We finally arrived in the kitchen.

'After Pete got killed Dom just left me a message and did a runner. He OK? I was worried about him.'

It was a large knock-through that took up the whole of the rear of the building. In the far left corner, the steel banister of a spiral staircase disappeared into a round hole in the floor.

'Yes, he's fine, still out there. Moira got all excited about another story and Dom said he'd stay on and research it. He needed something to throw himself into, get his mind off things – you know Dom . . .'

There couldn't have been a bigger contrast with the antique stuff in the hall. We were in a world of stainless steel and glass, limed oak and spotlights. Four gas rings seemed to float in a polished granite island in the middle of the room. Nearby were a BlackBerry and a pack of Marlboro Lights, a lighter and the day's unopened mail. A dead, half-smoked cigarette balanced precariously on a mountain of ash and butts in a nearby ashtray. And, by the look of it, nicotine wasn't the only medicine Siobhan was taking for her flu. A bottle of white wine stood next to a glass. Both were half empty.

She followed my gaze. 'I'm sorry, would you prefer something stronger?'

'Thanks, but no.' I tapped my arm. 'Antibiotics . . .'

She selected a coloured capsule from a tin and dropped it into a sleek, cube-shaped coffee machine and closed a lever. They really did live in a Sunday supplement. One where the necks of two empty wine bottles stuck out of the recycle bin.

I didn't buy into the flu thing.

She'd been crying.

Mourning Pete? Possibly. But had they ever met? Pete said he'd never been to the house.

'Do you know how I can get hold of him? Has he got another number? I'd really like to talk to him.'

The machine spat a thin stream of coffee into a small cup.

'Me too.'

They were the first words she'd said that I really believed.

Her eyes stayed on the coffee machine. 'It's nothing unusual for him to be out of reach for weeks sometimes, while he's up in the mountains or wherever. It hasn't been a week yet. Work, it's just his way of dealing with things.' She fiddled about in a tin for another capsule. 'I think I'll join you.'

'So he's in the mountains? Still in Iraq?'

She shoved another capsule into the machine. 'I think he left some time yesterday. Sorry, my head's all over the place. Sugar?'

I shook my head. She placed stuff on a tray and got ready to move. 'Let's go in the front room.'

I followed her through double doors that had been punched through the dividing wall. She offered me a blue velvet two-seater on one side of the low coffee-table and sat down opposite.

The fireplace to my left was tiled. The black grate was far too shiny ever to have been used. The mantelpiece was covered with all the usual pictures of two people's lives together, but instead of picnics on the beach or family gatherings, they featured sailing boats or horses. There were also several of the same boy, from about ten to his teens.

'That Finbar? He's twenty now, isn't he?' There hadn't been much in the file about the boy either, only his name and DOB.

She stared at the row of grinning faces. 'Twenty-one this August.'

'He's the spitting image of you.' I kept my eyes on the frames. 'He still living here, or has he legged it?'

She turned back to her coffee. 'He's gone now.'

'This is the time you get to see more of Dom, eh?'

She gave another weak smile, but concentrated on her cup. The silence quickly became uncomfortable.

'He at uni?'

'He works. He's in the financial sector.' There was no gush of pride from a beaming mother.

'Here in Dublin?'

She put down her cup and gave a couple of short sharp nods instead of an answer. 'Excuse me – my cigarettes.' She waved in the general direction of the kitchen. 'It's a filthy habit, do you mind?'

I stood up with her, all smiles. 'Course not. I won't send you to smoke on the street.'

I sat down again and sipped the brew. She returned in a cloud of smoke. Her hand shook slightly as she sucked at her cigarette. She hadn't brought the packet and the lighter with her. She wanted me out.

I raised my cup. 'Thanks for the coffee, Siobhan. Sorry again to barge in on you. Can I leave my mobile number in case you need to get in touch?'

She went over to a small table covered with

style magazines. She pulled open a drawer stuffed with pens, pencils, electricity bills, all the normal shit. Nestling among it all was a grey mobile phone.

I stood up. 'Can I use your loo before I head off?'

She did her general wave once more. 'Through the kitchen, down the stairs. First on the right.'

I left as she pulled out a pen and something to write on.

35

Once in the toilet the first thing I checked was the window. It was a wooden sash, as I'd have expected in one of these houses, but this one was new. The frosted glass was double-glazed, with a decorative brass latch in the centre of the frame. A hole each side indicated an internal deadlock operated by a star key. It didn't worry me. Keys tend to be left in toilets so no one gets embarrassed after a big hot curry. I dug about in the unit under the sink cabinet and found what I was looking for, right next to the Toilet Duck.

I pressed the flush, and unwound both deadlocks while it was noisy. I left the latch closed, so everything looked normal.

I replaced the key in the cabinet, and washed my hands with plenty of scented liquid soap. I wanted her to know I'd gone where I'd said I would.

As I came out again, a motion detector in the hallway gave me a flicker of blue LED. So did another at the top of the stairs.

The door opposite opened easily. It was a teenager's room. There were posters on the wall but no bedding, just a folded duvet on the mattress.

I took a step inside. Even if Finbar had moved out, there might be something that would give me a clue as to where he was now. I didn't care what the Yes Man had said about the boy not being important. If I found him, I might find Dom. That was why the Yes Man hadn't got a river view.

Nothing stood out at first glance. The laptop looked steam-driven, and the GameBoy wasn't even from this century.

Then something caught my eye. A Vodafone USB modem. They'd only come out a few months ago, but you couldn't move for the adverts.

By the time I rejoined Siobhan, there was a blank index card and a pen waiting for me on the coffee-table. I sat down with a big smile. I could smell the soap on my hands as I wrote out my number.

I got to my feet and handed her the card.

She looked at it as we headed towards the front door. I kept my eyes busy. The alarm-system keypad was midway up the wall. Another little blue light flickered below the picture rail.

I hooked my holdall over my shoulder.

She glanced past me at the dark wet street. 'Don't you want me to call you a cab?'

'It's OK. I'm going to walk for a while.'

We shared a nod. 'Thanks again for the coffee.'

I headed down the steps, and when I hit the street, I turned right. My mobile was out the moment I heard the door shut.

I hit the new number I'd burnt into my brain. It was fine to talk in clear. These mobiles were secure. Calls were masked by white noise, courtesy of the Firm's version of the Brahms secure speech system, developed by GCHQ. Not even the NSA could eavesdrop.

It gave four rings.

I pulled up my collar against the damp. 'You're sure the house only has their two registered mobiles and the landline?'

I heard the rustle of paper at the other end. 'Only three numbers registered. Why?'

'And just a PC desktop on broadband, yeah?'

'Correct.'

'I need to check something out tonight. I'll call you.'

There was no reply. The telephone went dead. Not much of a one for small-talk, the Yes Man.

I didn't give a fuck. I was in control, and I planned to keep it that way.

36

I must have looked a complete dickhead as I checked into the Conrad with my holdall and the world's supply of cheap shopping bags. The other guests' bags said Gucci and Hugo Boss, but mine were from Spar, a corner chemist's, an electronics shack and a charity shop. The receptionist had raised an eyebrow at the half-drunk two-litre bottle of own-brand cola sticking out of one of the carriers.

It was just as well she hadn't seen the rest of the stuff now spread out on the bed in my very swanky room. There were a couple of shower caps, floral-patterned with some frilly stuff round the sides, a notebook and pencil, a box of forty pairs of surgical gloves, a pair of scissors, a little keyring torch, and a SIM-card reader that I'd have to work out how to use before I left.

I also had some fishing-line. I hadn't been able

to find an angling shop, so I'd bought a reel of four-pound breaking-strain stuff off one of the guys on the banks of the Liffey. Twenty-pound would have been ideal, but this would have to do.

There'd been an amazing number of druggies down by the river. Even at this time of night, young guys looking like ghosts shivered under blankets beneath a bridge not a stone's throw from Bertie's Pole. I tried to talk to one to ask where the fishermen hung out, but he just stared back, too out of it to string an answer together. This city really did have a problem. But then again, show me one that didn't.

I had also bought new boxers and socks and a couple of long-sleeved T-shirts. I might be spending the Firm's money on this posh room but even I wouldn't squander it on hotel laundry when it was cheaper to buy new.

Especially for tonight, I'd bought some grey trousers in a charity shop and yet another shitty brown fleece. I'd also picked up a black balaclava I'd found on a shelf of odd gloves and woolly hats. In the old days, the housing-trust shop would have made a few bob selling them in this part of the world. I'd given the old dear at the till a big grin when I'd handed it over. 'Let the good times roll.'

None of the stuff needed much doing to it, apart from a bit of remodelling to the cola bottle.

I poured myself another glass before tipping the rest away and giving it a rinse. Then I took off the wrapper, and cut off the top and bottom to leave an open cylinder. It was *Blue Peter* time. I cut up the side of the cylinder and flattened out the rectangle I'd created on the floor, then cut the biggest circle I could from its centre. It curled into a tight brandy snap as soon as I let it go and that was it, I was almost done.

All I had to do now was shove everything in the cupboard, jump on the bed, get my boots off and check out the room-service menu while I read the instructions for the SIM-card reader. I wouldn't be leaving until dark o'clock.

I finished off the glass of flat cola. It was just like old times. I remembered being pissed off as a nine-year-old when my mum wouldn't buy real Coke because it was too expensive. I wondered if it had been the same for Pete over Brockwell Park way. I shoved a couple of antibiotics down my neck and ordered up a steak sandwich and chips.

Siobhan's compassion for Pete had been convincing, I supposed. And she clearly missed Dom terribly. But she'd avoided eye contact on every other subject. She had to be the only mother on earth who wouldn't open up about her little boy when given half a chance. Well, tonight we'd be finding out what she was hiding.

After my sandwich, it was downstairs to the

business suite to get online and see if I could find Finbar on the electoral register. I'd trawl Facebook and MySpace too. I had a few hours to kill.

37

**Wednesday, 7 March
0326 hrs**

I heard someone come out of a back gate and the sound of a garbage bag landing in a wheelie-bin. A dog got a bollocking for something or other.

I was standing outside the toilet window. I'd been playing Peeping Tom since about midnight. I'd had to wait more than two hours for Siobhan to go to bed, and then another hour or so to give her time to nod off. It was really unusual for someone to be up as late as two during the week. My brain worked overtime. Could she have been waiting for a call from Dom on that second mobile of hers? I'd find out soon enough.

I had one last feel about in my grey trousers and shitty brown fleece pockets to make sure I hadn't overlooked any coins or anything that was going to rattle or fall out. ID-wise I was sterile – no wallet, no credit cards. It wasn't about what would happen if the police caught me. With luck, that was when the Yes Man would come into his own. It was to do with leaving nothing behind. Why take stuff on target you don't need? All I had was forty euros shoved down my socks in case there was a flap and I had to run for a taxi.

I checked that the fishing-line I'd looped round my wrist hadn't unravelled.

I could feel my mobile in the inside pocket of my fleece and checked again that it was turned off before rezipping. You can never tell when the bad fairy might pay you a visit and sprinkle the fuck-you-up dust.

Finally, I checked that all the other bits and pieces for the close target recce were good and secure in their pockets. Everything I was taking in was tied to my clothes with fishing-line.

As a car rumbled along the street I pulled the curled-up cola-bottle disc from the front of my fleece. I shoved it up through the narrow gap between the two sash window frames and watched it curl round the other side.

'Lottie, you bollix!' Wheelie-bin man was getting pissed off with his little furry friend. 'Come here!'

I wiggled the plastic circle until it rested against the brass latch, then turned and pulled it along the frame. The latch started to swivel open under the pressure of the coiled plastic.

The device was also magic for opening Yale locks on doors. Credit cards don't work like they do in Hollywood because there are two right-angles to negotiate before getting to the deadlock. As long as you keep on turning and pushing, the curly stuff will get round them and push the bolt open. But it wasn't so easy, these days, to find nice thick plastic bottles. This going-green business was fucking up the method-of-entry trade for sure, but luckily the cheap stores' own brands were still up to spec.

Within seconds the window was unlocked. I pulled the plastic back through and put it down at my feet.

The bottom of the frame was stuck, but it didn't take much effort to budge it. I pushed up, just a couple of centimetres at a time. When it was open as far as it would go, I heaved myself up on my stomach. Once inside, I made sure I kept on my knees instead of my feet.

I was sitting on the varnished wooden floor-boards. I cocked my head and listened, tuning in to my new environment. I'd just been making a lot of movement and wanted to be sure nobody had heard it and was reacting. I'd also opened a window. Even when people are asleep, their eardrums can be sensitive to minute changes in air pressure. It was probably caveman survival stuff – you needed a little advance warning if a brontosaurus was coming into the cave to eat you.

I waited a little longer. There was no rush. The hard part was done. This toilet area was the buffer zone between the outside and the in.

There was still no movement, no late-night snackers raiding the fridge in the kitchen above me. No sound from a radio or TV.

I pulled the two plastic shower caps from my jeans and put them over my boots, tucking them in at the sides for extra grip. I didn't want to mark the tiles or drag in any of the wet, grimy shit from the street. Siobhan was probably not out there with the Hoover every day, but people notice these things. And while she didn't look like the kind of girl who pulled on the Marigolds, staff have eyes too.

The next problem was going to be the motion detectors. Was the house zoned? Did she put the alarm on when she went to bed? Chances were she didn't, but I had no way of telling. All I knew was that when she had finally thrown her hand in, there wasn't a long delay between her coming out of the kitchen and the hallway light turning off. She'd not had time to stop and tap in a code, just turned off the light and walked straight up the stairs. I didn't think she'd gone to the pad I'd spotted in the hallway. But for all I knew there might be another upstairs.

I took the black balaclava from the front of the

fleece and pulled it over my head. I had cut out two holes for my ears. In the dark they're more important than eyes so there was no sense in keeping them covered.

Easing down the handle a fraction at a time, I opened the door a couple of inches. The hinges didn't squeak. I opened it some more and slipped out of the buffer zone.

The first thing I looked at was the blue light on the motion detector. It flickered as it sensed me. I held my breath, waiting for the initial warning tone that normally kicks in after about twenty seconds.

Nothing happened.

I rocked backwards and forwards. The motion detector kicked off again and the blue light flickered – but again, no response.

I went back into the toilet, pulled the window closed and eased the latch back into place. Everything had to look normal while I was inside the building. It wasn't very likely she was going to come all the way downstairs to use the plumbing, but if she did, that was the job fucked.

Back in the hallway, I stopped, looked and listened. The wool of the balaclava was warm and wet around my mouth. I let my jaw drop open so that all the internal noises like breathing and swallowing didn't intrude. The house was almost completely silent: no ticking clocks, not even the common night creaks as bits of the building settled after the day.

First stop was the boy's bedroom. I eased myself in and pulled the keyring torch from my pocket. The fishing-line attaching it to my jeans belt loop had to unravel before I was able to get the beam shining where I wanted it.

The laptop and modem were still in place. I'd deal with them later if I could. The mobile was the priority. The laptop would take some fiddling. If I was compromised I'd deck whoever it was, then leg it with the laptop and maybe her handbag or something so it looked like a burglary.

I closed the door and took a few careful paces to the spiral staircase. I put my foot on the first step, right against the wall. It took my weight without protest.

I headed up, taking each step gingerly.

Slowly, slowly, my head came level with the kitchen floor. No lights were on. A little ambient glow from the end of the street washed through the rear window, and a little more from the adjoining door from the front room. The only other source was the standby lights on the microwave, cooker and all the other gadgets.

The smell of cigarettes and pizza got stronger as I moved up the stairs.

The empty delivery box sat with its lid open on the wooden island, alongside an empty bottle and a glass with only a drop left in it. The mail had been opened and lay next to the now over-flowing ashtray.

Slowly and deliberately I made my way through the double doors and into the front room. The neck of yet another bottle stuck out of the bin.

The drawer had been pushed right in. I made a mental note. That was exactly how I had to leave it. She would know every detail of this house and its contents, whether she realized it or not. Maybe the drawer was really hard to close, and had to be given a bit of extra force that took it less than flush with the front of the desk. If I didn't do exactly the same, her alarm bells might ring.

I eased my left hand under the drawer, lifted the handle with my right and pulled, slowly but firmly.

The drawer opened six inches, enough to expose the grey plastic mobile sitting in the bottom-right corner. I studied its exact position in relation to the biros and bits of paper, then lifted it out.

I took off the back. No way was I going to switch it on and let it blurt some happy tune. A quick sniff of the SIM card was all I needed.

The stairs creaked.

And then the hall lights came on.

38

I pushed the drawer shut and dropped behind the blue velvet two-seater. The mobile phone was still in my hand.

The slap of flip-flops approached along the tiled hall floor. They came at normal walking pace, not agitated, not tentative, and padded into the kitchen.

The spotlights went on.

The movement in the kitchen would cover my noise. I half turned, reached up, opened the drawer and pushed the phone as far back as I could. Siobhan or whoever it was might come for it. Perhaps I'd find out where Dom was just by listening. If not, I'd wait, as planned, until I could copy the SIM card.

The feet slapped their way down the kitchen stairs. There was nothing to tell me whether they were Dom's, Siobhan's, Finbar's, or someone else's altogether.

I was waiting to hear the toilet door close but it didn't. Soon the feet were heading back up the stairs.

There were a few noises I couldn't make out, and then the unmistakable pop of a cork. Seconds later came the glug of pouring, then the click of a cigarette lighter. I could smell smoke.

Fingers began clicking at a keyboard. I heard a couple of sighs and sniffs.

I was pretty sure it was her now. She carried on typing.

I inched my way to the corner of the settee. It was in shadow, but I wanted to make sure I wasn't in her line of sight.

I moved my head until I could just see her with one eye, keeping my mouth open to control my breathing.

She was sitting on a stool at the island, sideways on to the open door. She was wearing mule-type slippers and a towelling dressing-gown. Her hair fell forward as she looked down at the screen. She wasn't reading. She was waiting.

She reached for the wine bottle, poured herself a second glass, and wiped her nose on her dressing-gown. Halfway through the second mouthful, she slammed the glass on to the worktop. She needed both hands to work the keys.

Whatever she was reading wasn't good news. Her face contorted and a gasp turned into a sob. Tears ran down her cheeks. She refilled the glass with trembling hands and tried to compose herself, drink and smoke at the same time.

She sniffed some more as she placed her cigarette on a corner of the ashtray, the only vacant spot left for it. Then she got up, walked away from me and disappeared down the stairs.

I was out from behind the sofa and heading for the kitchen.

I heard the toilet door close.

Cigarette smoke worked its way through the wool and into my nostrils as I looked at the screen. The Sony laptop was a few years old, but had USB ports. The white Vodafone modem dangling from one was about half the size of a pack of playing cards. It would contain a SIM card, but there was no time to extract it.

I read the screen. She was replying to a Hotmail. The sender had had plenty to say but I didn't have time to read it. The important stuff was in the header. The message was timed at 8.37 a.m. GMT today. The laptop told me it was now 04:10, so the email had come from the east.

The toilet flushed.

I pulled the notebook and pencil from my pocket and scribbled the IMEI and SN numbers from the back. They'd mean something to somebody who knew about that shit. I wrote down both Hotmail addresses.

I moved quickly and was back behind the settee before she settled down at the island again. A few seconds later, she was pounding the keys.

She kept it up for another twenty minutes before I heard another glug followed by a click. The stool grated on the floor and her mules clacked back down the stairs accompanied by a few more sniffs and sobs. Seconds later they came back up, and towards the front room. She carried on past and up the stairs. I looked out. Her glass had gone but not the cigarettes.

I moved down the hall to the kitchen.

She'd left the mail. Only a couple of letters were open. One had a green motif and was headed Dublin Drug Outreach. It was addressed to Finbar in St Stephen's Green. Maybe he did live here and his mail was forwarded. Maybe she was picking it up for him. I read the letter quickly. He hadn't attended any sessions for the last four weeks and had made no contact with his mentor. They were worried about him.

The letter underneath was from an estate agent. He was jumping for joy that she'd accepted an offer for €6.5 million for 88 Herbert Park.

There was a noise upstairs. Probably her going to the bathroom again, but maybe not. I wasn't going to risk going back for the mobile in the drawer. Fuck it, it was time to go.

Back in the toilet, I unwound the fishing-line from my left wrist. I'd already prepared the loose end into a three- or four-strand loop. Four-pounds breaking strain was a little weak. I put the loop over the end of the latch, fed the free end through the gap between the frames and opened the bottom window. Then I grabbed the free end of the line and pulled it through.

I lowered myself into the garden. A couple of dogs a few houses away were too interested in growling at each other to worry about me.

Gripping the line to keep it taut, I pulled the window closed. It took just one smooth pull for the latch to flick across, and the loop jumped free. The internal frame locks weren't a worry; nobody ever checks them.

I made my way to the back wall, pulled myself up and rolled over the top, the way I'd got in. There was a gate, but I couldn't use it. I wouldn't be able to bolt it again once I was streetside.

I turned left and headed up the service road. I got out my mobile and dialled as I walked.

It rang just once.

'I couldn't get the mobile but I think they're in contact via Hotmail. She's using a modem.' I read him the IMEI and SN numbers. 'But listen, there's more. There's a letter from an estate agency – Fitzgerald Drum Maguire & Walshe. It was addressed to just Mrs, not Mr and Mrs. She's selling the house.'

This time I closed down before he did. He would have to wait for me now.

The time difference on the email was four and a half hours. She had taken a couple of minutes to read the thing before going into water-fountain mode. There was only one time zone that was four and half hours ahead of GMT, and I was prepared to bet good money on finding a man called Baz there.

I was feeling quite pleased with myself, until I walked out on to the main road and looked down to see my boots still covered with the two flowery shower caps.

39

St Stephen's Green
0908 hrs

At least it had stopped raining.

You could smell the money round St Stephen's Green. Not as strongly as down Ballsbridge way, but it was getting there. The park was beautifully kept and dotted with memorials to the great and good. There wasn't a statue to celebrate EU subsidies yet, but it was only a matter of time.

I came out at the northern edge of the square and counted down the numbers to the one on the letter. It was an elegant Georgian townhouse. The big black door looked just like the one at 10 Downing Street, even down to the large fanlight and thickly glossed white columns. Black railings lined the stone steps.

I carried on past with my takeaway latte in one hand and a big map in the other, then parked my arse on a doorstep a couple down and played the dickhead tourist. Leaning against my Bergen, I spread the map on my lap and got very interested in orienting it with the street.

A guy in painter's overalls came out of the black door and fetched some brushes and rollers from a Transit. He went back in.

The Yes Man mightn't have thought it worth checking this place out, but I did, for two reasons: Pete had filmed there and Finbar lived there. And it looked like I'd been vindicated. I'd been expecting a junkie's squat, but it was smart enough to be the Saudi embassy.

The two windows on the top floor, the third storey, were open. The guy in overalls eventually appeared behind the one to the right.

None of the windows at the front had curtains or blinds. The ceilings had no lights hanging. Just like the flat being decorated, no one was living there. Was the whole place being made ready to go on the market?

There were four buttons on the polished brass entryphone. I pressed number four.

'Hello there?' He sounded much older than the guy in overalls, and a forty-a-day man.

'I'm a friend of Finbar's, number four – can you let me in?'

He didn't answer but the door buzzed. I

pushed it open. There was a strong smell of fresh paint.

'Up to the top.' A head came over the banister. 'Hope you got oxygen.' He chuckled to himself and disappeared.

The four pigeonholes held nothing but flyers for pizzas and taxis.

I headed up. The building had been gutted and rebuilt. New deep-pile carpet was laid on York stone. I reached the top floor, where the smell and gleam of fresh white gloss nearly over-powered me.

The head turned out to belong to the older of two guys. His overalls looked like a Jackson Pollock painting. Not much of an ad for his decorating skills. I followed him through the open door. Dustsheets covered the floor. A third guy clutched the top of a very tall ladder and worked his brush over an elaborate ceiling rose.

'This Finbar lad is very popular. You're the second one to come looking for him in as many days.'

'Who was the first?'

'His mum. Well, she said she was. She took his post.'

'We were supposed to meet up today.'

He winked. 'Who? You and his mum?'

'Finbar. Young lad – twentyish?'

'Never seen him.'

'Who gave you the job – his mum?'

'No. All the places we do belong to one of these fancy London property companies. We finished this building a few months ago. Got the call to come and redo this flat before the whole thing's sold.'

'Oh . . . I thought he owned it.'

He shook his head. 'Like I said, it's a developer.'

'So you never saw Finbar . . . You don't know where he's gone?'

'Not a clue. I didn't even know anyone was living here until his mum came round.'

'Thanks anyway. If he turns up, can you tell him Chris called?'

My mobile rang as I headed down the stairs. I knew the Yes Man had been wrong not to go down this route. I tried not to crow. 'The house is going cheap and the stepson lived in a flat that—'

'Stop wasting time. We know this. Once you do your job we can do ours. We traced the email.'

'Afghanistan?'

For once, the Yes Man was silent.

'It's the only place I know that's four and a half ahead.'

'Quite so. The email was sent from Kabul.'

'Is it Dom?'

'Possibly. They claim to be from him, and there have been a number of exchanges. If so, they're using him to negotiate with his wife.'

'I want to see them.'

I hit the street and headed for the main. 'Any idea why he went to Afghanistan?'

'Heroin? Looking after his interests? He was probably lifted by the local Islamafia or one of the bounty-hunter groups – they know he has cash. I'm trying to discover which group may have him.'

'OK, I need you to make sure this mobile works over there. I need a visa, a cover story, and a laptop with Internet access. I want to be able to read any more emails coming through while I'm there. Also, as much mapping and photography as you can lay your hands on.'

I waved down a cab. 'I can't talk. I'll be coming into City airport. I'll call to confirm.'

I threw my Bergen on to the back seat and jumped in.

40

Arrivals buzzed with City boys and girls flying in from Europe with a few more zeroes on their annual bonuses. Most were being met by men in grey suits who held up name cards. It made the Yes Man easy to spot. He'd taken off his jacket and tie, and was in a checked business shirt with gold cufflinks, suit trousers and shiny black shoes.

I aimed for the coffee shop. 'I've been up all night. You want one?'

'No, thank you.'

I asked for the large latte-and-muffin deal, and was just about to organize a mortgage to pay for it when he got his money out.

We didn't exchange another word until we were through the automatic doors and walking past the lines of cabs and buses. The airport was slap in the middle of Docklands. Blocks of new million-pound apartments stood uncomfortably alongside estates built to house dockers after the Blitz.

'You get all the gear I asked for?'

The Yes Man clenched his jaw. Maybe he wasn't used to meeting in public. He certainly wasn't happy taking orders from his underlings. 'Yes, and I have the emails. You're right, by the by. He launders money via a property company here in the City. We knew that. We had it covered.' The Yes Man pulled an A4 sheet from his pocket. 'There have been three emails from Dominik, starting last Sunday. All originate from the same location in Kabul. The ransom is eight million US.'

I gave him a frown. 'If he's the big-time drugs baron, why the need to sell the house?'

He was getting annoyed now. 'He has the cash, believe me. He probably wants it to look as if they're giving up everything, just to keep the price down. Back to the matter in hand . . .'

I read the page. Dom's emails were basically messages of love and hope. Siobhan's were about progress in raising funds.

We've got a buyer at 6.5 [she wrote]. Please beg them to hold on, I will get the rest. It will take time.

She'd spoken to Patrick, she said. I presumed he was their money man. Patrick was trying his best to liquidate their portfolio.

I've told him we've gone broke. I will get the
money, Dommy, I will. Please tell them I need
time. I don't know how long. Explain to them it
might have to be in instalments. The house
money very soon, they can have that, then the
rest. Please show me again that it's you. Please
tell me what colour the sofas are in the living
room.

I was right: it hadn't been the flu making her
sniffy and red-eyed in the kitchen last night.
Maybe she didn't normally drink or smoke.
Whatever her state of mind, she was on the ball
enough to ask for proof of life each time. Last time,
she must have asked him about a suit, because
Dom's email started:

My Paul Smith is grey and it came back from the
cleaners with double creases in the trousers. I
was upset because I was going to wear it for dinner at the Mermaid the night before I left.

It ended:

I love you darling, but they need to know how
long.

One thing we knew for sure, then: up to the
point he wrote those words, he was alive. They
could only have come from Dom.

235

Proof-of-life statements are an important part of any hostage deal. A trained negotiator would also be looking for clues that Dom was either bull-shitting or under duress. Prone-to-capture troops and business people working in hostile zones have a ready-prepared under-duress sign, and maybe even a coded means of identifying locations. All Dom's had been sent at around eighty thirty, local. That was why she had been up, online and waiting.

We'd reached a bank of pay stations for the short-stay. I handed him back the sheet. 'Any idea yet who's lifted him?'

Criminals would demand a ransom and hold out for it. Only if it didn't eventually materialize would they offload him in a fire sale to another gang – or, in Afghanistan, the Taliban. That was when things usually turned nasty. Each gang would sell him on to the next like a girl passed between sex-traffickers; he'd spiral down a chain of extremist groups with life getting worse and worse until he ended up with one who didn't want anything except to hack off his head in front of a camera.

The Yes Man shook his head. 'It could be free-lancers, it could be another drug cartel. I don't know and don't care.' He put the sheet into his pocket and paid for his ticket. 'I just want him back and in a fit state to talk.'

We stalled as four guys walked past with

suit-carriers over their arms and overnight bags trundling on wheels behind them.

'Is he emailing anybody else?'

'No.'

The Yes Man had phenomenal electronic fire-power at his beck and call. Using the Echelon system, GCHQ could capture radio and satellite communications, telephone calls, faxes, emails and other data streams nearly anywhere in the world.

'This could all be bullshit to get the cash from the house and fuck his wife off.' He gave me a strange look and I wondered if he thought I'd lost my marbles. 'Why not?' I raised my palms. 'We don't know what the fuck is happening.'

He did it again. I suddenly realized it was the profanity and not the idea he didn't like.

'There's no other traffic from that or any other email address while the user is logged on. But his emails have all been sent from the same location.'

He'd stopped by the boot of a navy Audi A4 and produced a key fob from his trouser pocket. He pressed it and the boot unlocked. A laptop bag was sitting on top of picnic blankets and welling-ton boots.

'Everything you need is loaded in here. New ACA, the lot. The Read Me file will start you off. If you have information, you send it directly to me the moment it happens.'

He handed me the case. 'The password is your

old army number. You know how to work Schubert?'

I nodded. GCHQ had developed the secure hard drive and email system so not even the Americans could suck it up. There wasn't anything to know about it. It just, like, worked.

'Good. The mobile will still be secure there.'

He unzipped the front pocket of the bag to show me the airline tickets.

He took a step closer, as if airport car parks had ears. I could see inside his collar. He'd been squeezing that boil.

'I want to keep foremost in your mind the sensitivity of this operation. There are people in the FCO in Kabul, embassy officials, who may well be part of the problem. We need him back without anyone knowing.'

He held out a hand, but shaking wasn't what he had in mind. 'Why don't you let me have your own documents, for security? I'll hold them until you get back.'

I zipped up the laptop and put it over my shoulder. I smiled, shook my head and walked away.

PART THREE

41

Thursday, 8 March
1305 hrs

Well over an hour behind schedule, and six security checks and X-rays later – including one right at the door of the aircraft – the Indian Airlines Airbus 320 took off into the hot blue sky over Delhi and pointed north-west for the two-hour flight to Kabul.

Departures had been a nightmare. We'd even been segregated in our own little holding area. It reminded me of the Belfast to London flights during that war, except that here the whole terminal, including our Kabul leper colony, was plastered with flat screens showing non-stop Bollywood. No matter which film it was, they all seemed to star the same tall guy with a grey beard; he even popped up in the commercial breaks, advertising mobile phones and aftershave. Then one of the channels ran a documentary about his waxwork in Madame Tussaud's.

The aircraft could have carried 150 passengers but was only half full. Kabul was hardly competing with Amsterdam or Prague for the city-break crowd. The Gurkhas and Filipinos in economy, paid to guard compounds, were proud big-time of what they did, and didn't care who knew it. They toted US Army camouflage print or Brit DMP day sacks, and their T-shirts were emblazoned with eagles wrapped in the Stars and Stripes and messages about Operation Enduring Freedom.

Up in business class, Indian men in pressed, short-sleeved shirts scribbled furiously on notepads, arranging the shipment of another twenty tonnes of Fairy Liquid and marmalade into the war zone.

Some of the Westerners looked like seasoned contractors, the sort who supplied the armies with everyone from cooks to radar operators. They were the ones in black polo shirts with embroidered company logos. There were also a few of the bigger-buck contractors. They wore Gucci safari vests, and their hair was longer to show they weren't military. One had a Mohican. They didn't want a sergeant major shouting at them by mistake. Me, I was in my normal shit state, but at least I had brand-new boxers and socks on. When I pulled off my boots the stink wasn't half as bad as usual.

The seat-belt light pinged off and the attendants started serving our pre-ordered drinks. I'd gone for Pepsi to wash down the antibiotics. I gazed out of the window. I'd thought I'd never get shot again, and I had been. Afghanistan was one place I'd thought I'd never come back to, and here I was. Whatever happened, I didn't want to be running up and down those fucking hills again.

When the Russians invaded in 1979, it had been for much the same reasons as we did in 2001. They were 'liberating' the country. The West didn't see it that way. Soviet troops weren't welcome so close to the Gulf oilfields.

As a young Green Jacket squaddy running round Tidworth garrison in Wiltshire, the invasion had about as much impact on my life as coastal erosion in Northumberland. It didn't directly hit my pay packet or interrupt the supply of curry sauce to the local chippie, so why should I give a shit? In any case, I didn't even know where Afghanistan was.

To start with, the invasion was a breeze. The Russians thought they'd cracked it. Their problem was, none of them had a clue about mountain warfare or counter-insurgency, and their weaponry and military equipment – particularly their armoured vehicles and tanks – were crap. Their other problem was the mujahideen.

The Dad's Army in cowpat hats finally started to get their act together and kick ass – until the Russians brought in the Hind gunships. Basically an airborne artillery park, the Hind was the most formidable helicopter in existence. It turned the tide. By the mid-eighties, the Americans were flapping big-time. It was still the Cold War. The Kremlin needed to be taught a lesson.

Ronald Reagan was suddenly hailing the muj as freedom-fighters. A wealthy Saudi, Osama bin Laden, called on Muslim fighters round the world to come and do their bit. Weapons poured in from all over, and they didn't have a clue how to use them. Dickheads like me, by then a lance corporal in the SAS, were told to get cracking and give them a hand.

The only way the muj could win that war was by making the Russians pay such an unaccept-able manpower cost for the occupation that public opinion back home turned against them and the army rebelled. Simply put, that meant killing and wounding as many Soviets as possible, and fucking up their infrastructure any way we could. Just about anything was a legitimate target.

Before that could happen, the Hinds had to be eliminated.

The American Stinger ground-to-air heat-seeking missile was the best in the business at knocking things out of the sky. The trouble was, it was so good the Americans were reluctant to let go of them. The risk of them falling into the wrong hands was just too high.

Instead, the Brits were tasked with teaching the locals how to use Blowpipe, our equivalent to the Stinger. We'd round up about thirty at a time and get them out to Pakistan. Then we'd throw them on a C-130, and have a two-day trip to one of the little islands off the west coast of Scotland. We ran our own field-firing exercises, teaching the boys everything from how to use Blowpipe to how to drop electricity pylons. At the end of their couple of weeks of rain and cold, we'd put them back on the C-130 with a packed lunch and a can of Fanta, get them into Pakistan, then over the border to put theory into practice.

The trouble was, Blowpipe was a heap of shit. Not even the Brits used it any more: you had to be a PlayStation wizard to operate the thing, and that was before PlayStation even existed. It was soon clear it wasn't working. The sky was still full of Hinds. The Americans had to relent. They opened the toy cupboard and broke out the Stingers.

The muj had to be trained all over again. The west coast of Scotland reopened for mujahideen short-breaks and the C-130s resumed their shuttle.

The kit was filtering into Afghanistan via covert convoys, but the shifty fuckers weren't using it. Stingers were far too nice and shiny, and the muj were saving them for a rainy day.

It was then that we had to go over there ourselves and get our hands dirty. We were running all over the snow-peaked mountains and harsh rock valleys I was now seeing below us. We ambushed, attacked, blew up and killed anything that carried a hammer and sickle. Every time a Hind retaliated, one of us would loose off a Stinger and blow it out of the sky. All my Christmases had come at once.

Eventually the Russians had had enough. We'd helped make Afghanistan their Vietnam. One day they just got back into their tanks and few remaining Hinds and crept out of town.

We withdrew, only for the muj to start fighting among themselves all over again – as they do. If there's no enemy, they kick the shit out of each other. They're even worse than Jocks. Fifty thousand people were killed in Kabul alone during the civil war that followed.

The Taliban finally won in 1996, and they ran the shop until late 2001. That was when, after 9/11, the USA came calling with a few thousand tonnes of bombs so the Northern Alliance could enter the city and take over for the US forces that were 'liberating' the country. And so the show goes on.

Even today, the US are still shitting themselves at the prospect of Stingers being used against them, and rightly so. Pallet loads of the things are unaccounted for. They could be lying in some-body's shed, still waiting for that rainy day, or in Iran, being busily reverse-engineered.

42

'This your first time in Afghanistan, mate?'

The Australian in the aisle seat to my left was in his late fifties, with grey, well-groomed hair. He'd been dressed from head to toe by Brooks Brothers. The hand that took a gin and tonic from the permanently smiling attendant was manicured. He had 'diplomat' written all over him.

One look at my T-shirt and unbooted feet should have been enough to tell him how I fitted into the picture. There would be thousands of guys like me in-country, and our two lives wouldn't overlap. No invitations to the ambassador's party would be heading in my direction.

Nonetheless, he held up his glass. 'Cheers.'

I nodded. 'Yes, first time.'

He took another sip, then dipped into our bowl

of cashews. 'So what do you do? What brings you here?'

'Travel writer. I do guidebooks. We call them "Outside the Comfort Zone".'

He laughed, then threw a few more nuts down his neck. 'You really think people will want to come here?'

'Dunno. That's what I've come to find out.'

I sat back in my very comfortable seat, reclined it a bit more and picked up one of the Indian business magazines to fuck him off as nicely as possible.

The alias cover address and alias business cover linked me with Outside the Comfort Zone, a small independent publisher in the East End whose niche was extreme travel. The Firm had probably set it up donkey's years ago. The books it brought out featured all sorts of places the Firm was interested in. I was now one of their free-lance employees. My passport had had to go through all the normal channels. The visa appli-cation had been handled by a commercial company in London, and still had their sticker on the back.

The laptop told me I had a girlfriend, Kirsty. I could never remember her new number, which was why it was right there for me. If anyone called it, she would back me up as part of the ACA. No wonder I loved her.

I flicked through the mag. Uncle Sam wasn't

exactly flavour of the month. Nor was Uncle Tony, come to that.

I flicked through some more and saw a picture of Dom alongside a piece about 'Veiled Threats'. He was sitting with the woman I'd seen on screen in Dublin, on the bonnet of a 4x4. He was dressed in a safari vest and had an earnest expression. She was wearing the same gear as in the documentary, a white headscarf and long black dress. Her name was Basma Al-Sulaiman. Basma. Baz . . . A few blue pepper-pots stood around in the background to give the shot some depth. Well done, Pete.

The article was about the plight of Afghan women and the safe-house Basma ran in Kabul. She was talking about the promises made after the Taliban were kicked out. Their lives were supposed to get better once they were 'liberated'. Local women were supposed to be running multinationals by now, yet they were still third-rate citizens. Some of the girls in her refuge had been shot up with heroin at an early age to make them dependent, then used as mules by dealers to move drugs from around the country. It was perfect cover. Nobody paid any attention to them, and there was a lot of spare room under a burqa.

It sounded as if nothing much had changed since my last time there.

When the girl Farah died, I'd carried her body

a short way from the village that night and buried her. I found out from Ahmad a couple of weeks later that her husband had managed to get over his loss. He'd gone out the next day and bought himself a replacement.

43

'We've started our approach, sir.'

The attendant was giving me a gentle shake. I hadn't even realized I'd fallen asleep.

I looked down at the vast mountain plain, six thousand feet above sea level, which held the capital. I'd never set foot there. Last time round, it was full of guys with red stars on their hats goose-stepping about with vodka bottles in their hands. We'd stayed in the mountains that hemmed them in.

The Australian didn't waste a second. 'Kabul has swollen from less than a million to nearly three million since the Russians left, and now the Taliban are back in the mountains, refugees from there are pouring in.'

To dodge any more waffle, I studied the parched landscape ten thousand feet below. The city was a giant mosaic of low-level, grey-brown buildings, not more than a couple of storeys high.

He didn't get the hint. 'Do you know what the Australian government advice is about this place? Don't go. And if you're there, get out.' He smiled to himself as he leant forward to share the view.

'Welcome to sunny Kabul.' He laughed. 'Who in their right mind would want to come to this God-forsaken place?'

I kept looking out. 'Who knows? I file a first-person account exactly as I find it. It's more like a travelogue for their website, really.'

I sat back in my seat. He nodded, not believing a word. Private contractors wouldn't tell other private contractors what they were doing. Different bits of the military wouldn't tell each other either. In a place like this, everyone had op sec. Or bullshit.

We thumped the runway. Flashing past the window on our left were more fixed-wing aircraft than I'd ever seen parked in one place, military or civilian, then every size and shape of helicopter. HESCOed compound followed HESCOed compound, each flying a different national flag, but all part of the International Security Assistance Force. More than thirty countries supported ISAF, from Finland and Norway to Portugal and Hungary, but only four were doing the actual fighting: the Americans, Brits, Dutch and Canadians.

The Stars and Stripes fluttered over a collection

of stadium-sized tents. I bet some of them were bowling alleys and movie houses with milkshake bars.

The British compound would be the one with the Portakabin, a small TV, the boxed set of *Only Fools and Horses*, and a couple of teabags for the kettle. It was probably on the other side of the runway, where the husks of bombed-out buildings sat alongside the occasional intact concrete block, like a row of old man's teeth. Beyond, it looked like dustbowl all the way to the mountains.

Flags everywhere flew at half-mast. These days, they were probably like that permanently.

As we taxied past acres of armoured vehicles and steel containers, economy passengers were already surging forward to disembark. They chattered away on their cellphones as the aircraft still rolled.

The Australian had a suit-carrier handed to him. When the aircraft stopped and the seat-belt lights were switched off, he stood up and held out his hand. 'Well, nice to have met you. I hope it goes well.'

'And you.' I pulled my Bergen from the overhead locker. All it contained was the laptop and a bit of washing kit.

I detached myself from him in the crowd and walked down the steps into the blistering heat and blinding sunlight.

A pair of helicopters lifted off and cleared our

aircraft by no more than thirty feet. Two Humvees armed with .50 cals roared along the runway and pulled up at the bottom of the steps. I guessed they were just there to look mean and keep us from straying.

Razor-wired compounds flanked the terminal. It was a small, two-storey, regional-airport-type building, but with so much concrete involved it had to be a Russian legacy. Handpainted signs told me there was just about nothing I was allowed to do but stand in line and await instructions. To keep it that way, bearded men in thick grey serge uniforms and high-legged boots stood glowering at either side of the doors, AKs at the ready.

We filed inside. It was dark, and it took my eyes a while to adjust. The place was wrecked. I was just thinking it must have taken a major hammering at some stage when I spotted a poster. There was a major refurbishment under way, courtesy of the US and EU. Fluorescent lights dangled from the ceiling. Guys in overalls drilled away at the concrete floor. A guy in a blue suit and tie was having a go at a pillar with a hammer and chisel.

An Indian passenger at the front handed out immigration forms to the rest of the queue. They were poor-quality photocopies. Two forms had been reproduced on the same sheet of A4, then torn in half. I didn't have a pen.

Another bearded man in grey serge sat in a box

at Passport Control, surrounded by handpainted signs saying *No photography* and *No smoking*. He didn't even look at the form I hadn't filled in, just glanced at the visa in my passport, stamped it and waved me through.

I had to put my day sack through another X-ray machine. Once I was clear, I dug out my sunglasses, slipped the string round my neck, and exited the building.

This time I really did find a bombsite. We must have been on the fucked-up side of the runway. All I could see was rubble and dust, and the shells of buildings. There was a strike mark in every square inch of rendering.

Traders had set up shop in the back of old Russian trucks without wheels. They sold the two essentials: cigarettes and tea.

Beyond them, on a dustbowl the size of a football pitch, were scores of cars, trucks and 4x4s. A couple of boys in UK desert DPM, Osprey and sunglasses stood next to a filthy Toyota 4x4. Six or seven clean and shiny ones were parked nearby. Their drivers were also sunglassed-up and had all the party gear on, trying to out-cool the military.

44

I'd called the hotel from a phone box in Delhi to organize a car. I didn't know the score on taxis. Would there even be any? And, if so, would I be driven off to some quiet little corner of town and persuaded to hand everything over?

It had been a nightmare trying to get through. I'd had to dial the number so many times it was etched into my brain. Then it was even more of a nightmare trying to communicate what I wanted, because the notion was so alien to them. But in the end they laid one on especially for me, the mad Brit who didn't have his own vehicle and protection.

I squinted into the sun. They'd said a driver would pick me up in Car Park C. That was a joke. There wasn't any Car Park C, just a big dustbowl.

Three locals hit on me with baggage trolleys. They rattled over the rubble and the first guy to arrive tried to grab my Bergen. I shook my head. He tried again. 'Yes – it is law.' In conflict zones most speak at least a little English. It's the language of war.

No way was I letting it out of my hands. I gave him a dollar as *baksheesh* and carried on walking. You couldn't blame them for trying. There was fuck-all else going on for them.

Crowds of people milled round the area, being regularly checked by AK-toting men in grey serge. I carried on past the contract guys in wrap-around sunglasses and thigh holsters, and finally spotted 79 9654 000 in shaky letters on a sheet of A4. I'd asked for just the hotel number to be shown, and on a clear board.

Even in places far less dodgy than this I'd never have my name in full display. It's too easy for someone either to run it through their BlackBerry or recite down the phone for a mate to Google, looking for multinational heavy hitters and other good kidnap fodder. All they have to do then is fuck over the driver, take his place and drive you to a world of shit. It would have been madness to advertise myself on a Serena Hotel board, even with a cover name. I had no idea how many big-shot Stevenses there were on the planet, and I didn't want to be mistaken for one.

The young guy holding up my board was skin and bone. His shiny jet-black hair was parted on the left. Apart from a bum-fluff moustache, he was clean-shaven. His shirt was untucked over brown trousers and buttoned all the way up to a collar that was two sizes too big.

I gave him a smile and offered my hand. 'Hello, mate – you taking me to the Serena?' It never hurts. Let them have a nice day. Chances are they're treated like shit the rest of the time.

'Yes,' he said. 'Maybe.' He went to shake my hand but caught himself in time. He touched his chest in greeting first, then gave me a semi-toothless grin as we finally treated ourselves to a couple of shakes. 'Come, Mr Stevens. Come.'

I followed his dusty black plastic shoes through the maze of vehicles. Most were white and yellow taxis of all makes, sizes and stages of dilapidation. Among them were dusty 4x4s, a mixture of clapped-out Fords from the eighties and brand-new Mazda saloons.

He told me his name but I didn't quite catch it first time; his voice was like gravel and his English very accented.

'Magrid?'

'Magreb.' He beamed. '*Magreb*.'

I nodded. 'Nice to meet you, Magreb.'

His ten-year-old Hiace people-carrier was coming to the end of its days. It looked like the blacked-out side windows were only held to the bodywork by layers of dust, so it was hard to hide my amazement when the door was slid open for me by a smartly uniformed escort. No grey serge for this boy: his black ball cap co-ordinated with his trousers, high-leg boots and heavy body armour. Only the brown wooden stock of his AK was off-message.

I climbed into the back, next to a torn and food-encrusted baby seat. The escort closed my door and sat up front with Magreb. The air-conditioning was going full blast.

We only got a few yards before we hit the end of a queue. A couple of old guys in suits, polo-neck jumpers and Afghan pancake hats manned a homemade checkpoint. The drop-bar was two branches roped together and painted red and white.

Magreb pulled a dollar bill from his pocket.

I leant forward. 'Police?'

Magreb gave an Italian-style shrug. 'No, no – police come here later, Mr Stevens. They come to collect the money, maybe.'

We drew level and he handed over his bribe. The old men lifted the barrier. We drove out past the empty shells of bombed-out buildings.

The wrecks of Russian vehicles rusted at the roadside. Only one bit of Eastern hardware had stayed the distance. A MiG jet fighter sat at a forty-five-degree angle in the middle of the exit roundabout, as if it was about to take off. Its freshly painted camouflage gleamed in the sunlight.

We hit an official checkpoint, manned by guys in khaki serge. They waved us through for free.

We turned south on to a dead straight road. The sun was on my right. 'How long to the city, mate?'

'Twenty minutes, Mr Stevens. Maybe.'

'Please call me Nick.'

'OK, Mr Nick.'

His breath stank from too many cigarettes.

Even from this distance, Kabul was clearly dominated by the mountain at its centre. It was like London with Ben Nevis instead of Hyde Park.

Magreb followed my line of sight. 'TV Hill, Mr Nick.'

It had two peaks of roughly the same height, with a saddle in between. Two colossal antennae farms capped the summits. It might be a hill to the locals, alongside the snow-capped mountains that surrounded us, but in the UK it would have been a national park.

I gave him a smile. 'Let's see if this works.'

I waved my mobile, sat back and powered it up.

The buildings either side of us looked like they'd been out in the sun too long. Even the advertising hoardings were like bleached skeletons.

The potholes were the size of bomb craters, but that didn't stop the local drivers going for it at motorway speeds. Instead of a central reservation, there were just one-foot-high concrete bollards.

We came to a run of shops and stalls, mixed with mud houses and stark concrete apartment blocks. One sold bananas, the next oranges. The one after that seemed to have cornered the market in second-hand plimsolls. Old boys sat in the shade beside them gobbing off into mobiles.

I had five bars of signal, and a text from my new mates at TDCA welcoming me to Afghanistan. I tapped the keypad as kids kicked a football on a dusty make-do pitch with rocks for goals. A family had set up home in the bombed-out remains of a one-storey building. The roof was a moth-eaten tarpaulin.

Everything and everyone was covered with dust. I could already feel a layer of grime on the back of my neck, and that was just from the air-conditioning.

There were four or five rings, and then I heard a familiar voice.

45

'I'm in the city, heading for the hotel. Any more emails?'

'Yes. We have a problem. They want the money in position by Saturday morning. If not, he dies.'

'Chances are he's history anyway, right?'

'Correct.'

'I'll read it when I get to the hotel.'

I closed down the cell and leant forward again. 'This your wagon, maybe?'

He smiled proudly and nodded like a madman.

'Nice.'

He nudged us past a dozen pushbikes taking up half the road. The traffic was bumper to bumper. I saw plenty of 4x4s and orange-and-white taxis, but everything else seemed to be a Corolla.

High walls, razor wire and floodlights

sectioned off the buildings in this neighbourhood. They probably housed NGOs, big companies and government bodies, and were guarded inside by the entire male populations of the Philippines and Nepal.

Outside almost every one of them was a plywood guardhouse. Local guys in serge sat on plastic chairs in the shade, their body armour so thin it was more like a stab vest. Each had an AK across his thighs, a brass teapot and a glass at his feet. Nothing much seemed to be going on. They just sat and stroked their beards.

I tapped the baby seat. 'How many children you got, mate?'

'Four! All boys, Mr Nick!'

'You've been busy.'

He turned and gave me the world's biggest grin. 'Maybe!'

The escort nodded along, too, as Magreb explained what we were waffling about.

We crawled past rack upon rack of bootleg DVDs, mostly Bollywood by the look of it. A poster in the shop window behind them showed a beautiful woman with perfect teeth dancing around in blindingly coloured clothes as the guy with the beard watched on admiringly. The fucker was stalking me.

We reached a roundabout. Traffic in all directions was at a standstill. Four guys in a different style of grey serge pointed at vehicles and shouted, then kicked the ones that didn't obey. They wore oversized Russian-style white peaked caps they'd had to place on the backs of their heads so they could see. They looked like drunken sailors. A couple wore face masks, as if they were directing traffic in Tokyo.

Magreb made a tutting noise. 'A bomb in a car. The man killed himself, Mr Nick, maybe.'

The escort thought he'd better demonstrate. His arms went up in the air. 'Boom!' He pointed along the exit immediately to our right.

I watched one of the peaked caps land a kick on the side panel of an orange-and-white. Magreb tutted again.

'You work at the hotel?'

'I work in kitchen, Mr Nick. I am chef. They need someone go to airport, and I speak English. My English OK for you, Mr Nick?'

I gripped his shoulder and gave it a bit of a manly shake. 'Maybe, Magreb. Maybe. Thanks for picking me up, mate.'

Cars tried to worm their way into any gap. Magreb somehow worked the people-carrier forward. The traffic cops' brand-new green-and-white Toyota 4x4 was parked in the middle of the roundabout. A sign on the back announced in English that it was a present from the people of Germany.

An old man selling SIM cards took advantage of the jam and walked between the vehicles, his merchandise hung from a board held high on a pole, like a glockenspiel.

I tapped the escort. 'Give him a shout.'

Magreb translated. The window creaked down and the guard called him over.

The old guy wore about three coats and a cowpat hat. His eyes brightened at the prospect of a sale. Every card that hung from the board in a cellophane wrapper showed a footballer that even I could recognize. I pushed my arm between Magreb and the escort.

'How much?'

Magreb translated. 'Ten dollars each, maybe.'

My hand dived into my jeans.

The old boy's head almost filled the open window.

I spread my fingers. 'Give me five.'

He grinned like I'd made his year and handed over a set of Thierry Henrys. Perhaps he'd celebrate with a fourth coat.

Transaction done, the Hiace was moving again. I rummaged in my Bergen and pulled out the mobile I'd bought at Heathrow. The Yes Man didn't have to know everything I needed to do. And I certainly didn't want him tracking me on the Firm's mobile once I'd got my hands on Dom. I'd give him just enough information to make him happy and keep him letting me use his resources. It wasn't op sec and it wasn't bullshit. It was self-preservation. I didn't know what he had planned for me once I'd handed Dom over. *If* I handed him over.

As I loaded one of the Thierrys, a two-ship Humvee convoy barged its way to the detonation site. Both wagons had .50 cals on top and the American drivers were taking no prisoners. Faces shrouded by dust masks and goggles, they shouted, gesticulated, leant on their horns. It had no effect. In the end the Humvees decided just to bump cars out of the way with their bull bars. The gunners up top in the turrets swung their .50 cals in wide arcs. How to make friends and influence people, Washington-style.

'Kate, it's Nick. Top of the morning to you.' Well, it was Dublin. I got a sort of laugh from her as she tried to pretend no one had ever said that before.

I asked if she could have a little rummage in Moira's office for me and see if she could find where Basma Al-Sulaiman had her safe-house.

'I'm so sorry, Nick. It's a women's refuge. Part of the deal was that Dominik wouldn't divulge any details.'

Shit.

'But I have a mobile number.'

'Kate, you're a star. What are the colours of your national flag?'

She hesitated. Either she didn't know the Polish flag or it was just a stupid question. 'Red and white.'

'That's the colour of the flowers I'll send you, then. Has my number come up?'

I got lots of giggles and a thank-you before she gave the answer I wanted. 'Yes.'

'Great – can you text me the number? I'll get those flowers to you as soon as I can. I won't tell Moira if you don't.'

I closed down as Magreb eased in behind the second Humvee. The .50 cal gunner didn't like that. He swung the barrel and waved at us to back off.

Magreb pulled a face that said, in any language, *Yeah, right.* I liked this boy more by the minute.

We made some progress and passed a huge mosque shrouded in scaffolding. An army of plasterers was filling in strike marks and shell holes.

Just round the corner a fortress was disguised as the Serena Hotel.

46

Whoever had designed the place had made it almost impregnable to ground attack by anything except a Challenger or a Warrior, and with not a HESCO or roll of razor wire in sight.

The two main gates must each have been about twelve feet square, and built of thick steel bars in close grids. Marble columns at either side supported a thick stone canopy; whatever else it was meant to do, it provided shade. The guards underneath were impressive, too. They wore the same kit as my escort, as you'd expect in a place with a $35 million price tag. He gave them a wave.

I'd read all the stuff about it online at Heathrow. It had gone up last year over the ruins of the old Kabul Hotel, which had been bombed and shot to shit for years. Going by the pictures and blurb on the website, it was the safest and most luxurious place in the whole of the city, probably in the whole of Afghanistan. Unless, of course, you were bunkered in with ISAF.

The gates opened inwards and we drove into a stone-slabbed courtyard. It was lined with a pair of white Toyota Landcruisers with UN markings and three American GMC suburbans with blacked-out windows and enough antennae to double as NASA mobile control centres. The drivers leant against their bonnets in the new grey spotty camouflage, thigh holsters and wrap-around shades and watched us rattle past.

Magreb stopped under a huge stone and marble portico. A doorman dressed in the local turban-type get-up rushed out and opened my door. His London equivalent would have been decked out as a Beefeater.

I shoved them both a twenty-dollar bill and the escort discovered a little English. 'Thank you.'

It was probably more than they earned all day, and it showed.

Two young bellhops ran out looking in vain for bags. I pointed at my Bergen and shrugged. They tried to take it from me, but I held on. I shook hands with the security guy and he wandered back to his mates at the main gate.

It was Magreb's turn for a handshake. 'Do you want to drive me while I'm here, mate? Maybe buy a new baby seat for son number four?'

The handshake got more rigorous. This was a

good day for him, and of course he liked me. I was nice to him. 'But I work, Mr Nick . . . I cook nice food for you, maybe.'

'No problem. When do you finish?'

He looked at his watch as if it was going to tell him. 'Seven . . . seven.'

'Good, write down your number and I'll call you at seven, OK?'

He jumped back into his seat and found a pen.

Job done, I headed for the metal detector immediately to one side of the entrance. My new mate with the turban ushered me straight towards the tall glass doors. We might have been in a war zone, but it felt a million miles from Basra. There were no mortar rounds or rockets raining down, no armoured track vehicles, no helmets, no body armour jutting under my mate Gunga Din's robes. The only reminder was a printed sign telling me no firearms were allowed inside.

The lobby could have belonged to a five-star hotel in Paris or New York. There were marble floors, glass walls and gold finishing to all the surfaces. Local carpets and dark wood added to the palatial impression. The only thing out of place was the reggae music coming over the speaker system. Either they'd got their lobby and party disks mixed up, or there'd been a cock-up in the mailroom at the hotel chain HQ and a Caribbean pool party in Jamaica was trying to dance right now to traditional Afghan folk songs.

Thirty-five million dollars for a hotel in Kabul made good business sense. The oil companies had their guys exploring the north of the country to see what could be sucked out of the ground up there. When their top brass jetted in for a visit, they could hardly be put up in a downtown flophouse. There always had to be wartime melting pots for the so-called great and good. There was a Serena lookalike in every war zone, maybe not as luxurious as this one but they existed all the same.

I started checking in. In this part of the world they don't trust plastic; it's folding money all the way – and preferably green, with presidents on.

I thanked reception profusely for organizing my lift and handed over fifteen hundred US for the first five nights I'd booked.

As I signed the register, seven or eight guys swaggered past, all in BDUs with razor-sharp creases and desert boots straight from the quartermaster. Each carried a laptop bag over his shoulder, and a small fancy box in his hand. The pink ribbon they were tied with looked bizarre next to the thigh pistols. I took it that the sign outside was for the bad guys only.

They headed for the reception desk flashing credit-card-sized IDs on their armbands, just in case we hadn't realized they were American officers.

47

I headed upstairs. The hotel was only three storeys, with rooms on the first and second floors. I'd asked for one on the first. In theory it would be harder to hit with an RPG from the outside because of the perimeter wall. With luck, anyone taking a pot shot would only zap the top floor.

My room was huge. Plush carpets, lots of dark wood, all the gear. There was even a little office area and a torch in case the emergency generator didn't kick in when they lost power. The air-con hummed above me as I looked through the sealed, double-glazed windows. Maybe I was wrong about RPGs. The perimeter wall was being heightened to give a little more protection from direct fire.

Down in the compound, the neatly pressed Yanks had just placed their pink-ribboned boxes into their three-ship GMC convoy. They lifted out M4s, a shorter-barrelled version of the M16 with a collapsible butt, and loaded them up before climbing into the wagons.

I left them to it. First things first. I powered up the laptop and connected to the room's ADSL.

I had no idea how the secure comms worked on one of the Firm's machines, but there was encryption and decryption at each end, and that was all I needed to know. Normal email addresses were used. I was on AOL, paid for by direct debit from my ACA bank account at the Royal Bank of Scotland. I'd be sending to a Hotmail account belonging to the Yes Man. Echelon wouldn't be able to intercept: it would be a load of old mush bouncing around in cyberspace until the Yes Man opened up his own computer and retrieved it.

The mailbox was full of emails about jobs I was planning and had already done for the publisher. Their emails would keep arriving all the time I was away. There was also a healthy amount of spam. In fact, it looked so normal I was amazed the Firm hadn't downloaded some porn on to it.

The hidden bit of the hard drive prompted me for my password. I keyed in my eight-digit army number and it took me straight online.

There was one email with an attachment waiting. It was from the Yes Man.

Dom's reply this morning to the email Siobhan

had sent from the kitchen wasn't good news. The language was controlled, but you could tell he was sweating.

> The sofas are blue – remember it took us a month of shopping to find just the right shade? Darling, they have told me that if the money isn't ready by Saturday, they will kill me. Please make sure all the funds from Patrick or whoever come in by electronic transfer – no checks – so the money is ready to move. I will give you details of how and where as soon as you tell me you're ready. I love you. Dx

Siobhan's email, in contrast, was all over the place. I imagined her sitting at the island sobbing into her alcohol.

> I WILL HAVE THE MONEY . . . patricks nearly got everything sorted . . . i will have the money darling . . . please tell them to hold on I have it, it will be ready for them anywhere anytime . . . please tell them not to harm you, i will have their money. When you reply, wherever you are, we'll have good news – 1 promise. I love you. Please tell me what happened to John's black BMW last winter. Please show me you are still alive. I love you . . .

I reread them both. There was something

wrong with Dom's. The proof-of-life statements showed he was alive around the time they were sent, but it didn't feel like Dom was sending them.

He was a clever lad with a degree in English literature. Under duress he might spell the odd word wrong, but he wouldn't have spelt 'cheque' like an American. In fact, I knew he didn't. I'd seen the proof in Pete's files. So had I got an American at the end of these emails? Could be; there were enough of them in-country.

The Yes Man told me they were being sent from AM Net Café. It was on the corner of Flower Street and Jadayi Sulh, two shops in from the junction opposite the Emergency Surgical Centre for War Victims.

There was no welcome pack in the room and no courtesy map, no bus trips on offer to see the sights or visits to the ballet. One day I guessed there'd be guided tours of bin Laden's caves and the glorious poppy fields in bloom, but not yet.

There was a PDF map of the city on the desktop. I'd try to correlate the main routes with satellite imagery. It was important to know exactly where I was, and exactly where I was going – there was absolutely no room for fuck-ups.

I could have used the Firm's satellite imagery to study the location, but Google Earth was just as good for the detail I needed.

The street map itself wasn't detailed enough to

give street names, but the sat imagery was good.

I found the café. It was only about a K and a half away, but I was going to need to burn the routes there and back firmly into my memory. I switched between the PDF and Google Earth and soon had my bearings.

I found a bottle of water among all the mock-tails in the minibar and went back to the laptop. This was a dry country. If you wanted alcohol, you had to smuggle in your own – or go to a place like the Gandamack Lodge.

It was next on my list. I'd have to check all Dom's known locations to find out where the fuck he was by Saturday morning. Even if the cash was handed over, he was still going to get a round in the back of the head. And if I discovered he'd killed Pete, I wanted it to be me who pulled the trigger.

The Gandamack Lodge had opened in the days following the overthrow of the Taliban in 2001, when a glut of news crews found them-selves with nowhere to stay. It very quickly became a Mecca for journalists. That, in turn, made it a Mecca for another breed of war veteran, the fixer.

I checked Google Earth again. It wasn't easy to work out where exactly it was on the map when all I had to work with was an address that read: 'Next to the UNHCR building and just up from DHL'.

This wasn't unusual. I'd worked in plenty of cities where the directions were just as vague. Phrases like 'round the corner from' or 'at the back of' keep cropping up. My favourite had been in Jalalabad. One address had been 'street number two, second alleyway, house fifteen, four doors left'.

I thought I'd worked out which building I was looking for. UNHCR (United Nations High Commission for Refugees) was marked on the PDF, but I still wanted a decent local map. I wasn't going out there on the streets without one. TV Hill stuck out like a sore thumb, but Kabul was a city of three million people. That was a fuck of a lot of streets and alleyways.

I closed down the laptop. The Firm's disk would close itself down automatically and go hide somewhere in the main drive. It would also be defended against interrogation by sniffer devices, which could read a hard disk from a few metres away. Targets of industrial espionage can have their hard drive downloaded while they're checking in at an airport without having a clue that it's happening. Even the new biometric passports aren't immune. IDs are routinely stolen this way, especially by people-traffickers.

I sparked up the personal mobile and a text was waiting. Kate had sent Basma's mobile number.

I highlighted and hit send. It rang four times. It

was answered, but whoever was at the other end didn't speak.

'Hello, Basma? My name is Nick.' I could hear rustling and distant traffic.

'Basma, I'm a friend of Dominik Condratowicz.'

'Where did you get this number?' The voice was female, and spoke perfect Home Counties English.

'I need to see you. It's about Dom. He's in trouble and I think you can help. I know he's there. I was with him when you phoned a couple of days back. Where are you?'

There was no hesitation this time. 'Do not call me again.'

The line went dead.

I stored her number, and closed down to save the battery.

The laptop and the Firm's mobile went into the room safe, and my two passports, cash, room card, RBS card and, of course, my Thierry Henrys went down between my socks and my Timberlands.

I'd bought a black nylon bum-bag at Heathrow at the same time as the phone. I went to the bathroom and padded it out with the flannel and half a roll of toilet paper, then fixed it round my waist so the pouch was on my right hip and protruded from under my T-shirt. The personal mobile went into the pocket of my jeans.

I switched on the TV. I looked back as I hung the Do Not Disturb sign outside, and the first face I saw on the screen was the grey-haired bloke with the beard.

48

'A map? You don't need a map, sir.'

They didn't have any at Reception either. No one who stayed at the Serena had ever asked for one. Maps implied walking or giving a driver directions. The manager said no Westerner should go round Kabul on foot or without a driver and escort.

He pointed me in the direction of the pastry shop and asked me to wait there while they tried to track one down. He was sorry I couldn't have Magreb again but he was needed in the kitchen. Was I sure I didn't want him to organize a convoy with one of the security companies? It would only take an hour or two.

'Thanks, but I'm quite sure.'

I headed for the pastry shop and ordered a coffee. An Afghani in a suit walked past with three women, two of them in the old-style

American desert camouflage, one in the new. The talk was about contracts. I half listened, but my attention was diverted by the black woman in the old-style stuff. Her stomach was so pronounced she had to be at least six months gone. It was bizarre to see someone pregnant in uniform.

I picked up the *Afghan Times* to stop me lifting the Tubigrip and picking at the scab. My arm still hurt, but not so much that I was constantly thinking about it.

A story about an Italian and his Afghan interpreter who'd been kidnapped off the street a week ago dominated the front page. The Taliban had got hold of them. Their demands weren't met, so they cut off their heads. The bodies had been found on wasteground to the south of the city. The newspaper urged Westerners not to travel anywhere without an armed guard.

The three American women returned, carrying the same little boxes with pink ribbon I'd seen before. The ribbons were soon undone and the boxes opened. They munched pastries. Maybe she wasn't pregnant after all; maybe it was just big-time wheat intolerance.

Eventually the manager arrived with a map. One of the bellhops had been sent out to a local bookshop to buy it.

I studied it as I finished my coffee. It showed all the embassies, hospitals and main mosques, and the ministry of this and the ministry of that.

It sort of correlated with what I remembered of the satellite imagery, but I didn't know which had been produced first. The map still showed this hotel as the Kabul, so it was at least a year old. It didn't really matter. It would still get me to AM Net and the Gandamack.

I slipped it into the empty Bergen, which I threw over my shoulder as I headed for the door.

Two businessmen in suits exited in front of me. Both carried briefcases and dripped with sweat as they waddled towards the 4x4 two-ship waiting in the courtyard. Their BG watched as they climbed aboard the rear vehicle. Then he took the front right of the lead wagon, and they were ready to go.

I walked towards the pedestrian door at the left of the main gates. I couldn't waste time waiting for Magreb to finish work and certainly didn't want a security company to send a convoy. I had to get on.

The guard from the Hiace sprang out of the guardhouse. He lifted his upturned hand. 'No Magreb? No car?'

I smiled and shook his hand. 'It's OK, I know where I'm going. It's just round the corner.'

I overrode him with my happy face, and machine-gun English that he didn't understand. I just hoped I'd done it without pissing him off. I might be running back in about five minutes and needing that AK of his to spread the good news.

49

I turned left. I knew that the road soon bent round to the right, towards a roundabout. The second right after that would have me heading north into the diplomatic quarter. The Internet café was close to the Iranian embassy.

I was facing south. The sun was on my right. It had maybe two and a half, three hours' burning time left.

The air was hot but not sticky. Without humidity to damp it down, dust was king. Every vehicle carried a thick layer. A little kid of five or six scrawled a message on a door panel with his finger.

Traffic was heavy and slow-moving in both directions. The pavements were clogged and pedestrians spilled on to the road. People dressed in grey, white and brown wove in and out between the cars.

I passed the big mosque I'd seen from the cab. Its twin towers were sheathed in scaffolding. There was a big regeneration programme under way. The signs stuck to the railings explained that some nice Italians had signed the cheque.

The two-ship passed me, and the businessmen swivelled and stared. I gave them a glare back that said, 'Yeah, that's right, I'm walking.' What else could I do? Like Basra, Kabul wasn't exactly a hail-a-cab sort of place for foreigners. At least I kept control of where I was going – and by the look of things I'd be quicker on foot anyway. I needed to recce the café in daylight.

I kept my head up and strode along as if I belonged there, trying not to make myself look like a target. The traffic on the road skirting the mosque was at a standstill. I guessed it was a tail-back from the drunken-sailor roundabout, but then I heard shouts and screams, amplified over the speaker system. Fuck, here we go – a mad mullah sparking everyone up on a demo, hatred for the West, that sort of shit. Why couldn't he have waited an hour?

I was against the clock here. I'd have to keep going. AM Net was one of only three known locations for Dom – I needed to find out how it would look when I came back in the morning and waited for whoever was sending the emails; I didn't need to know how it looked at dark o'clock when everyone had gone home. I also didn't want to be on the streets at night, sticking out even more like a sore thumb than I already was. If I turned the corner to find a mob, I'd just have to leg it.

Books were stacked by the hundred against walls and railings. Guys in suits and local get-up, and women, some in burqas, flicked through the pages. Nobody seemed perturbed by the noise of the demo. Stalls sold newspapers with headlines and pictures of their war in both English and Pashtun. Kabul used to be the capital of the Mughal Empire. These boys had been playing war for five hundred years.

I reached the roundabout. A bunch of drunken-sailor policemen stood in the middle of the mound. One of them yelled into a micro-phone and gesticulated at vehicles like a TV evangelist on speed. Behind him, a huge PA system was mounted on the roof of their green Toyota.

A guy selling olives tried to grab me. He dipped a glass into a big drum and dragged some out for me, but I brushed him off without breaking my stride.

I didn't know if it was kicking-out time in offices or some kind of public holiday, but there were thousands on the streets. The traffic was chaos, and the drunken sailors just added to it. It would have been suicide to cross now to take the right I wanted.

There was a metal pedestrian bridge just short of the junction. A poster stretched along almost the whole of its span. A smiling granddad type with a shiny bald head and perfect white teeth offered a free mountain bike in two languages to anyone who just said no to drugs.

The bottom of the steps was seething with newspaper, fruit and tea stalls. I pushed past and took the steel stairs two at a time, bobbing left and right to avoid people in the tunnel created by the roof and the hoardings that lined the sides.

I reached the far end and was about to come down. A woman laden with shopping bags laboured up the last couple of steps. I did my bit and waited for her to pass. While I waited, I looked down at the pavement.

Three guys in Gunga Din gear were staring up at me, checking me out. Their faces were gaunt and creased, a lot harder than anyone else's round here. Each had a little flower in his waistcoat, and that was the big giveaway. They were Taliban, down from the hills for a few days' R&R after shooting at ISAF or cutting off some Italian heads.

They watched me with total hatred in their eyes. Those boys wanted to rip me apart.

I was committed. There was nothing I could do but keep going down. If I turned and ran they'd come after me. I had to front this out.

Both hands shot to my hip. I unzipped the

bum-bag with my left and jammed the right inside. My fingers closed round the padding as if it was a pistol grip.

They muttered to each other and exchanged a quick glance under their cowpats.

Two of the traffic cops stepped into the frame as I was about halfway down. They seemed interested in finding out what the three were getting sparked up about.

The cops looked at me, then at each other. At that point they also spotted the small flowers and turned on their heels.

Fuck it. I got about three-quarters of the way towards the cowpats and flicked my left hand to wave them back. 'Fuck off! Fuck off!'

People who'd been making their way up the stairs melted to either side. The ones right at the bottom decided they'd gone off the idea altogether.

'Fuck off! Fuck off!'

Three sets of eyes locked on to mine, but I kept coming. They looked at each other again, suddenly unsure what to do. This was the OK Corral, Kabul-style.

They edged back a step or two.

I had to keep the initiative. 'Fuck off! Out of my fucking way!'

They were close enough to spit at me, and they did. They growled what I guessed were obscenities.

I pointed at each one in turn. 'Fuck – off – *now*!'

I moved past them and on to the pavement. The two policemen were standing under the bridge, eyes fixed on the very interesting summits of TV Hill.

I leapt the barrier and ran like a man possessed against the flow of traffic.

Horns honked. Angry fists waved. My sunglasses bounced up and down on my chest as I pumped my arms.

I dodged, wove and jinked round vehicles. Drivers went ballistic. A chorus of shouts went up behind me.

Fuck 'em. I was making distance. That was all that mattered.

50

Up ahead, the street broadened into a wide avenue bordered by imposing buildings hidden behind high walls. Their tops bristled with security lights and concertinas of razor wire. Plywood huts jutted on to the pavement. Guards sat outside on plastic chairs.

A three-ship Humvee patrol was speeding down the road towards me. I jumped back on to the pavement. The pedestrian traffic had thinned and the Taliban hadn't followed. They wouldn't come up this far into the embassy area. There was too much security.

The centre Hummer towed a trailerload of suitcases and camouflage-pattern day sacks. The gunner on its .50 cal jerked his thumb at the rear of his vehicle, shouted and screamed at the traffic behind. As they passed, I could see a big red sign dangling beneath him. Judging by the way he waved his arms, it said something like *Fuck off, suicide-bombers*. The Corollas and orange-and-whites didn't take the slightest bit of notice.

I slowed to walking pace to get my breath back. My arm throbbed. I began to see one or two more white faces, but they were all in vehicles.

On my right, a big set of gates swung open and two black Cadillac Escalade SUVs surged on to the pavement. Both had a big antenna on the roof. I couldn't tell what nationality they were. There weren't any flags flying on any of the buildings, no ID to show which embassy was which.

The two guys in the front wagon glanced through their wraparounds at the dickhead in the T-shirt and Timberlands, then studied the heavy traffic carefully before driving straight across all the lanes. The Highway Code didn't seem to apply to them.

It was only when I got level with the closing gates that I saw a small plaque. It was the Chinese embassy. The plywood huts outside were painted grey and red. I half expected to see Red Guards with flags sitting on the chairs instead of the local lot.

I approached the first shed. The four guards glared at me from under their hats. Two got to their feet. They didn't look happy, but they were paid to look that way. This was Kabul.

I smiled and gave them a wave as I got nearer,

as if I was on a morale-boosting visit. 'Hello, mate, how are you?' I held out a hand, shook, and kept walking. I got a smile back from the smaller of the two. He touched his chest and gave me a nod. The next guy offered a hand. I did it on the move, not missing a step.

There were still remnants of the Russian occupation here. In an open space between two walls lay the rusting hulk of an armoured personnel carrier, its tracks splayed out from the wheels and the mother of all big fuck-off holes ripped into its side by a HESH (high-explosive squash head) round.

I pulled out the mobile and sparked it up. I went into Tools and made sure Number ID was off, then called Basma.

Two armoured vehicles came down the street towards me and stopped. I couldn't tell whose army they belonged to. All I knew was they were green and had six wheels. Matching green uniforms sprang out, helmeted, body-armoured, all tooled up.

Her mobile rang and rang. She probably ignored calls from numbers she didn't recognize just as much as the ones she did. But at least her mobile was still on, and if it stayed that way I'd locate her – once I'd found myself a fixer.

I was nearly on top of the armour by the time I closed down. The arm flashes told me they were Turks. One wagonload ran across the street to cover from that side. Maybe one of the walls belonged to their embassy. Whatever, it looked routine. It wasn't me they were interested in.

I turned the corner and immediately hit another set of guardhouses. I smiled, shook a hand or two. A sign said the steel double gates belonged to the Embassy of the Islamic Republic of Iran.

Jadayi Sulh was signed on the junction opposite. Flower Street had to be close by.

I turned back to the guards and gave them a smile. 'The hospital?' I pointed down the road. 'The war-victims hospital?'

I gave them a peek under the Tubigrip.

They had a quick discussion and a laugh, then showed me.

I ran across the road in the direction they'd pointed.

51

The stone wall directly opposite me was ten feet high, and the sign that ran the whole length of it confirmed in red that I was at the Emergency Surgical Centre for War Victims.

A corrugated-iron canopy shaded two long benches at either side of the entrance. It was guarded by a huddle of grey serge and AKs. Old guys occupied the benches, smoking, waffling, reading the paper. I couldn't tell if they were patients, visitors or just waiting for a bus.

On my side of the junction, a couple of guys sold glasses of tea as black as boot polish. Above their heads, a small blue handpainted sign with an arrow said AM Net was round the corner.

This was the sort of thing I needed to know about – what was happening during working hours when I'd be hanging about and waiting for someone who spelt in American English.

Flower Street was narrow and the sun had stopped shining on it for the day. Every shop sold either flowers or cakes. There were pavements both sides. It was potholed, but there were still traces of tarmac. Large open concrete drains lined one side.

AM Net was exactly where the Yes Man had said, two shops in from the junction. I walked under the rusty corrugated-iron awning and glanced through the grimy window. The room was small and dark. No one was using too much electricity here. I saw two rows of four grey monitors, maybe three or four people hunched over them. An old guy waited at the desk by the window to take their cash.

I kept going without looking back. If I'd missed something, tough shit, I should have done a better job. Enough people were looking at the white face as it was and quite a few didn't like what they saw. I lengthened my stride.

The smell of grilled meat reminded me I hadn't eaten since getting off the plane. I came to a steel trough, maybe three metres long. Lines of kebabs sizzled away over glowing embers in the half nearest me. Two kids up on boxes fanned the charcoal at the other end, keeping it sparked up. At least they gave me a cheery wave.

I kept walking, past yet more flower and cake shops.

My time with the muj had taught me they loved

flowers – and not just poppies. Maybe it was something to do with the barren mountains they had to
live among. The Taliban were the same, and a lot of
the guys we trained and fought alongside were
now with them. They liked to put them down the
barrels of their AKs as well as in their waistcoats
when they had the chance. But the idea of going to
San Francisco never crossed their minds – unless it
was to bomb the fuck out of the place.

The deep ditch on the right was obviously a
great place to park your bike. All I could see were
seats and handlebars. The people milling round
were doing exactly what anyone else on the
planet would be doing right now, just getting on
with their lives – picking up a birthday cake or
some treats for the family on the way home. It
always amazed me how people so fucked-up by
war still managed to carry on. Maybe they had
no choice.

Word had definitely spread that there was a
white guy in town. Kids materialized from doorways and held stuff up. 'Mister! You buy this!'

No, thanks. I didn't need twelve boxes of
matches wrapped in cellophane.

'Boots dirty, Mister – I shine!' A ragged little
boy thrust his shoe-cleaning kit and black
brushes insistently at me. I pointed at my scuffed
brown Timberlands and shrugged.

I pushed on and most of them faded away
within ten or fifteen paces. A group of pepper-pots

headed my way and stepped out on to the road. I was careful to wait until they'd got back on the pavement and walked past.

Flowers and cakes gave way to furs and leather. Skins of all shapes and colours hung from awnings or were stretched on frames. Large hides were being prepared as rugs. A couple of white spotted cats looked mildly surprised, thanks to their new glass eyes. When the Taliban weren't shooting ISAF, they killed anything else that moved on the mountains to make a few bob. Maybe my three new mates were in town to drop off pelts.

I could see the crossroads maybe fifty ahead. Turning left would take me to a main drag. Then if I turned left again I'd get to the junction near the Gandamack.

But that wasn't going to happen. There were too many cowpats with pissed-off faces gathering at the junction. Young men smoking, staring, waiting. I didn't know if it was the prospect of money, wanting to know what the fuck I was doing there, or just because I was white. I wasn't going to hang around long enough to find out.

I crossed the road as casually as I could, heading towards the nearest alleyway. As soon as I was out of sight, I broke into a run. I took the first left, then a right down a rubbish-filled gap between two buildings. I wanted to put as many angles between them and me as I could. I jumped a low wall and landed in a small square. I was losing my bearings as I ran into another street, but at least it was quiet, just closed doors and growling dogs.

Shouts bounced off the houses behind me.

I charged down another alleyway, not looking back, just trying to make distance. The shouts seemed to follow me. My sun-gigs bounced even higher as I took a right between two mud buildings. I spotted a mountain of firewood and burrowed in behind it.

My throat rasped as I lay there gulping air.

Woodsmoke and the sound of Bollywood wafted from the house above me.

I fought to control my breathing as I heard more shouts and the slap of sandals and boots on what was left of the tarmac.

I moved my head very slowly and peered round my cover. Three or four were running, searching, sounding more and more pissed off at not gripping me.

It was getting close to last light. I would have to sit it out and wait. This wasn't the time to get out my map and play tourist.

52

I wondered if it was the Indian guy with the beard who'd been singing and dancing on their television for the last thirty minutes.

It was fully dark, and the crowd had dispersed. I pulled the mobile carefully from my jeans and powered it up, shielding the glow of the display with my hand.

'Magreb, mate. It's Nick. The Gandamack – do you know where the Gandamack Lodge is? The hotel?'

Pots and pans clanged in the background as the Serena's answer to Gordon Ramsay yelled orders at his sidekicks.

'Yes, yes. You want me drive you there, maybe?'

'No, I want you to meet me there after work. But right now I need you to tell me how to get there on foot.'

His voice took on a strangulated tone. 'Not walk, Mr Nick. Very bad men there. Wait until I finish work, maybe—'

'Too late, mate. Listen, if I describe where I am could you get me on the right road? I know I'm not that far away from it.'

He didn't sound too happy. I wasn't sure if he was concerned for my safety or for lost income if I got lifted.

I extricated myself from the woodpile. 'I'm looking at a big road just ahead. By the junction I see a sports shop – Gym Tonic. The windows are full of running machines, mate. You understand, multigyms? Punch bags?'

It seemed so out of place. I'd have thought the last thing the locals would be worried about was toning up for the beach.

'OK, OK.' He was thinking. 'Mr Nick, walk past sport shop and go right, then—'

'I'll stop you there, mate. I need to keep on the side-roads. The bad men have already found me. I'm hiding from them. I don't want to be under those shops' lights, do I?'

It took a few seconds to sink in. Either that or he couldn't hear me above the din of Gordon's latest wobbler.

'OK. You walk away from sport shop, maybe, the other way, and tell me what you see.'

I did what he said. I walked for the next ten minutes without hitting a landmark. At last I found a handpainted street name and spelt it out for him.

We worked our way down streets where occasional slivers of light forced their way between shuttered windows. Traffic groaned incessantly on parallel roads. I imagined the pavements full of angry young men in cowpats.

'What can you see now, Mr Nick?'

I stood between two trucks. 'There's a crossroads. On the far side there's a high wall with razor wire, maybe an embassy. I might be at the start of the diplomatic area.'

'Yes, Mr Nick. What is in the middle of road? Concrete, maybe?'

The road had a central reservation of scabby bushes. 'Bushes, mate. Not concrete. To the right I can see the lights on TV Hill.'

'Go left, Mr Nick. Left and you will come to the Gandamack.'

I jumped the junction and headed left, hugging the wall. Headlights caught me in their glare but there was fuck-all I could do about it.

'Go up the road, Mr Nick. Walk more. You see computer shop, maybe?'

'Yes.'

The little fucker was spot-on.

'The Gandamack is on this road, on same side as computer shop.'

There were shouts from behind me. I spun

round to see cowpats, maybe five or six of the fuckers, running my way.

'I'll call you later.'

I closed down as I legged it, and within a few strides I could make out the shapes of guard huts sticking out from the line of buildings.

The cowpats were gaining on me but I was getting closer to the huts.

Bodies spilled out to investigate the commotion. They couldn't have been sure what the fuck was coming at them out of the dark.

A couple had their weapons up. Another two were already checking their safety catches.

I held up my hands as I ran. 'It's OK, it's OK! Gandamack!

My hands stayed up. I got to within about fifteen metres of them. 'The Gandamack! Where's the Gandamack?'

One pointed down a dark gap that loomed on my left. I couldn't tell if the building behind had been bombed or was being repaired, but these guys had to be guarding something.

Their weapons lowered. I checked behind. The cowpats weren't that brave.

My hands dropped to my knees as I fought for breath. 'No need to shoot me. I won't complain about the food, honest.' I held out my hand and they shook.

I picked my way over rubble and bricks.

Plastic buckets full of the stuff sat waiting to be moved.

There was a pedestrian door to the right of the gates. Set into it was a sliding peephole.

I gave the gate a couple of punches. The steel rattled. The slide was pulled back and a set of dark brown Afghan eyes wanted to know what the fuck I wanted.

53

I gave him a big smile as the door swung open and I got a big row of brown teeth back. He was dressed for winter warfare in a thick black polo-neck jumper beneath an even thicker stripy tank top. Me, I was wiping sweat off my face. On the floor of his plywood gatehouse were a bedroll, bottled-gas burner, kettle, teapot and glasses. He was set for the night.

A dozen or so dusty 4x4s were jammed against each other in the courtyard. The house was large, with additions all over the place. I followed the gravel path across a patch of garden to a set of concrete steps that led up to the glass-fronted entrance.

The first thing I saw in the hallway as I stepped inside was a long rack of old Martini-Henry rifles, probably relics from the last time we tried to control the area and got fucked off big-time.

The Khyber Pass to Pakistan wasn't that far away.

The reception desk wasn't manned. A card told me the name Gandamack had come from the fictional home of Harry Flashman, the nineteenth-century answer to James Bond. It was also the name of the village that had seen the slaughter of about sixteen thousand British troops by the Afghans in 1842. I wondered if some of the gear in the racks had seen action there.

I wandered into the eating area. The tables were laid for dinner later tonight, with starched white cloths and china. All the breakfast stuff – jars of marmalade, jam, honey and Marmite – were stacked ready on a side-table, just like in a B and B. The walls were decorated with hunting and fishing prints. Stuffed parrots flew around in a glass-fronted cabinet. The only thing to remind you that you weren't in an old Surrey inn was the neatly stencilled sign on the door: *Only side-arms allowed in the restaurant.*

I looked through the open windows and on to the grass. Two big, muscular guys had squeezed into a couple of wicker chairs under the external lighting. They sat with their tree-trunk legs splayed apart. With their dark skin and black leather jackets they could only have been from the Balkans. My money was on them being Serbs.

They had been taking afternoon tea. A wicker

table was set with china. Ducks waddled round their legs scavenging scraps of sandwiches.

Neither looked the afternoon-tea type. One's head was shaved bald, and reflected the light like he'd been having a go with the Mr Sheen. The other had greasy brown hair down to his shoulders and a top lip like John Major's. He was talking into a mobile.

I moved closer to the window. He wanted to know why they hadn't got the equipment they'd asked for. If it didn't come soon, someone was going to pay. That would have had the person at the other end sitting up and taking notice. To a Serb, payment didn't necessarily mean cash.

A young lad in a white shirt appeared behind me. He was all smiles.

'Hello, mate – where's the pub?'

'The Hare and Hound? Downstairs, sir. I'll show you.'

He led me out of the restaurant, past the weapon racks and back outside towards a flight of steps down to the basement.

'Is my mate staying here? Tall Polish guy, irritatingly good-looking? His name's Dom, Dominik Condratowicz. Might have left a couple of days ago, I'm not sure.'

He thought for a while. It couldn't be that hard. The card had said there were only fifteen rooms. 'I do not think so, sir.'

'Could you find out, mate? Maybe at the desk?'

He nodded and gave a smile as five dollars found their way into his hand.

I carried on down a couple of stone steps to a large wooden door. I took off my Bergen as I went through. It was like walking into an olde-worlde pub, right down to the low-beamed ceiling. The only giveaway that we were still in Kabul was the two hundred years of rifle and machine-gun history stuck on the wall.

It wasn't busy. There were a couple of guys at one of the tables in a corner, and a couple of women at another. An overly Western-dressed local nursed a Coke at the bar. Bob Marley was on the speakers. Was it the anniversary of his death or something?

The young barman wore jeans, a tight T-shirt and had long, centre-parted hair. I asked for a Coke. All the drink was in bottles or cans. Löwenbräu was the only stuff on tap.

I took my cold can and glass and headed past the dartboard to one of the vacant tables.

The two huddled in the corner were big lads, maybe in their late twenties. They'd obviously been hitting the weights before slapping on the hair gel and heading out for the night. They hadn't been working on their lower bodies, though. They'd just been hitting the chest and arms so they looked good in their spray-on T-shirts.

Sundance and Trainers wouldn't have approved.

54

They had holsters and mag-carriers on their belts but nothing inside them. Maybe it was different rules downstairs: not even side-arms allowed in case things got out of hand after a few Löwenbräus.

They cracked into their cans of Guinness and cast an eye over the other table. The girls sounded as though they were from London. Both were wearing red and white Arab *shemags*, slung fashionably round their shoulders. Not only wrong country but wrong ethnic group. They checked their Thuriya sat phones for messages. I doubted they'd have many: Thuriyas are the dog's bollocks of the mobile world, but even they aren't too clever in basements.

It was the local guy at the bar I was interested in. Maybe mid-thirties and clean-shaven, he was trying too hard to do the Western thing. His shirt had the little polo-player motif; his jeans had a sharp crease down the middle. His navy ball cap had KBR embossed across the front. Kellogg, Brown and Root were a military contractor and Halliburton subsidiary. He wanted everyone to know he was in with the in-crowd. He just had to be a fixer.

He finished his Coke and started to say his goodbyes to the barman. I powered up the mobile, left some cash from my sock on the table, and followed, dragging my Bergen by one of its straps.

He'd got to the top of the stairs.

'Hello, mate – I was told you're the fixer. You working for anyone this week?'

He adjusted his baseball cap so it covered his eyes. 'I have work, but maybe if you need someone I could . . .'

His English was good.

I held up a hand as I climbed the stairs. 'It's you I need. I want you to track a mobile phone for me. It's in the city somewhere.'

'I'm sorry, I wouldn't know how to do that.' He headed on up, but I held his arm. 'Look, mate. You're a fixer. The only reason you can do the job is you know the Taliban – you might even have been one. Otherwise you'd get fuck-all fixed, wouldn't you?'

'I have to go—'

I held up the cash so it was level with his eyes

and close enough to smell. 'I got two hundred for you now and two hundred more when you tell me where the number is. Get one of your Tali mates to do the same for me as they do for the guys in the mountains.'

He didn't think too much about it before the wad disappeared into his jeans.

'Do you want the name?'

'No. I know his fucking name. He owes me money and I want it back. How long will it take?'

I kept a grip on the fixer's arm to make sure he came with me. I guided him up the gravel and towards the glass entrance.

'Maybe half an hour.'

As we started up the steps the guy with the brown teeth swung the gates open and a wagon rolled into the compound.

Next to the Martini-Henrys was a table with newspapers, postcards and pens. I copied Basma's number from the mobile on to a hotel business card.

'Talk to your mates. If they get a location, you'll get another two hundred.'

He took the card and disappeared into the dining area. His mobile was already to his ear.

I went to the desk at the other end of the hallway. My white-shirted mate was there, studying the computer. 'I'm sorry, sir. No Polish man. He hasn't been here for over one year.'

He got another ten dollars. 'Thanks anyway.'

A side-door took me out into the garden. The two big Serbs were still sitting and enjoying their cigarettes. Small bats darted about over a tiled veranda overhanging a set of rooms along the side of the lodge. The ducks rooted in the long shadows cast by the lights.

Serbs are to war as Jocks are to kilts and whisky. They'd finished their own in the 1990s, but had had a finger in everyone else's ever since. They weren't the type to lay down their arms and take up bookkeeping positions in a Belgrade bank.

As I walked across the grass towards them I gave a nod and a smile. 'Evening.'

They stared, waiting to find out what the fuck I wanted while they sucked away at their cigarettes and admired the red glows in front of their faces. They were ready for a night out by the smell of them. It was heavy cologne all the way.

'I need a weapon. I'm heading south. Do you know where I can get one, and quick? I'll pay.'

Top Lip couldn't have been less interested. Mr Sheen looked me up and down as if I shouldn't even be near them, let alone talking. 'Cowboy or newsman?'

'Cowboy.'

I hated that shit. They'd been watching far too many films. They waffled between themselves. It wasn't intense; it wasn't as if there was a law against having guns here. Top Lip was just telling

Mr Sheen to fuck me off. But there seemed to be a good enough reason for helping me. Top Lip finally shrugged and Mr Sheen pulled out a pen. He beckoned for my hand. He gripped it with his rough and massive one and wrote straight on to the skin. If he'd pressed any harder it would have turned into a tattoo. 'Don't go until early hours. No one will let you in. Tell him I sent you.'

'What's your name?'

He blanked me. 'Just tell him. If you can't find it, you shouldn't be allowed to ride.'

I nodded my thanks and left. I could see the fixer in the dining area as I headed for the bar. He'd just finished his call.

55

Back in the pub a waiter walked past me with two heaped plates of steak, chips and peas, and a bottle of ketchup. An early dinner for the big lads, who were now flexing away at the girls' table.

More drinkers had arrived. All three of the thirty-something males propping up the bar looked like they'd gone native. Their faces had maybe three months' growth, and they wore all the local gear – baggy trousers, waistcoats, cowpats and shirts down to their knees. They weren't taking the whole thing to extremes, though: one was in the process of ordering them Guinnesses and shots of Famous Grouse. Until I heard them shooting the shit, I couldn't make up my mind whether they were serious players or members of a ZZ Top tribute band.

Cigarettes came out as they perched on stools and waffled on about being down south, and how they were coming up against the Taliban and getting some awesome film. Everything was fucking awesome, man – and I mean awesome.

They lifted their shot glasses and toasted each other, then tilted back their heads and wiped their beards with the back of a hand in true Afghan fashion. With their suntanned faces, they certainly looked the part. They would have passed as Taliban at a glance, and that was probably all they needed.

I wandered over. 'How long you guys been back from Helmand?'

'Five days, man.'

The one who'd ordered the drinks had the longest and bushiest beard of the three. Cigarette ash distributed itself generously across it as he bounced a Marlboro up and down on his lips. 'We go back in another two.'

'You seen a Polish journo about? Dominik Condratowicz?'

'Shit, man, I know who he is – he's like a fucking superhero. He here now?'

'You seen him?'

'No, but you know what? Two fucking guys came here last week, maybe Saturday, who knows? Anyways, they were high, man, up on H, and they were shouting for him. Pushing every fucker around saying they know he's in the city, wanting to kill the guy or something fucked-up like that.'

'American?'

'Yeah, well, one of them, anyways . . .'

He pointed over at the two guys flexing, eating and chatting up the two women, all at the same time. 'Some of those contract guys? They had to run to their wagons and draw down to get them outta here.'

'You know who they were? You seen them before?'

'No, man, no one knew them. The American, big guy – and a Brit. They were like just fucked-up and crazy.' His eyes lit up and he pointed his cigarette at me. 'You know what? He talked like you.'

'What did he look like, the American? You said he was tall.'

'Yeah, like six six, fucking huge ginger guy, fucked-up skin. But, hey, they'd really gone local, know what I'm saying?'

'What about the Brit? He's smaller, right?'

'Yeah, your size. His hair and face, man, it was like matted and fucked-up.' He turned to his mates and grinned. 'We're like fucking dinner-party guests compared to those guys.'

All three got into their cans and drank to that. I said my goodbyes, good luck down south and all that shit, and headed back upstairs. The only sound was the crunch of my boots on the gravel.

American spelling . . . American looking for Dom . . .

The fixer was waiting by the rifle rack. 'The phone is in Khushal Mena. Well, it was when it was located. It might have been in parked car, or maybe the owner was in friend's house.'

'Where's this Khushal?' I dumped my Bergen and took out the map. I grabbed another pen and let him show me.

'On Ghazni Street, where it meets Sarak Street.' He circled the map. 'There.'

It was on the west side of the city, near the polytechnic. If it was still standing.

He got his other two hundred and left without a thank-you. Fair enough. He hadn't got one either.

It was just before seven as I sat on the steps and watched him climb into his Honda 4x4 and head out of the gates.

I put a new Thierry Henry into my mobile. Just like a soldier's weapon and Pete's camera battery, it also needed to be fully loaded.

Magreb's phone was soon ringing in my ear. He answered quickly.

'Hello, mate, it's Nick.'

He was a very happy bunny. Maybe there would be some work. 'You found the Gandamack OK, Mr Nick?'

'No drama, thanks to you. Can you pick me up? You'll be finished by about three in the morning. That OK?'

'Of course, Mr Nick. I sleep in kitchen.'

'Listen, I need you to bring some stuff. I want a set of local clothes. You know, hat, waistcoat, *shemag*, like the SIM-card seller but without the overcoats, yeah? I want to look like him.'

'Not be clean, maybe.'

'No problem, mate. I'll pay you for them. I'll wait for you inside.'

'Good idea, Mr Nick.'

I closed down and went into the deserted dining room. I took my Nick Stone passport from my boot and slipped ten hundred-dollar bills inside. When I left again a few seconds later, the side-table was minus one of its jars of Marmite.

Then I became the world's greatest admirer of Martini-Henry rifles. I went over to the rack and almost caressed them. Each one had been lovingly restored; there wasn't a speck of rust to be seen.

I checked the corridor for bodies and CCTV before realizing my bootlaces needed retying. I bent down, and quickly shoved the slim bundle behind the rifle rack, right at the bottom where it met the floor. I wedged it in deep, but all it would take to retrieve it was a bent coat-hanger.

Sitting on the steps again, I watched as wagons rolled into the compound, their occupants looking forward to a good night out.

56

Magreb took just one glance at the map and we were off. He knew exactly where he was going, even if he didn't know what was there. I left him to it and sifted through the bundle of Gunga Din gear he'd left on the back seat. It was perfect. I wondered if a certain SIM-card salesman had gone home tonight a few dollars richer but bollock naked under his three overcoats.

We passed Flower Street. It was all lit up and packed with people.

'Thanks for these, mate. I think I'll go local from now on.'

He turned his head and gave me a big, long smile. The Hiace swerved. I'd have preferred him to keep his eyes on the road.

There was no street-lighting as we drove through the embassy area. Vehicle headlights and the security lights on the walls and inside the compounds were doing that job.

'How much do you get paid a day?'

'Eleven dollars, maybe.'

We passed another compound. This one was protected by a sangar, and probably stuffed with Filipinos and CCTV. It didn't look military or diplomatic. Maybe it was one of the private security companies. The big lads might be back hitting the weights in there later if they didn't score.

'OK, here's the deal, Magreb. One hundred a day.'

We swerved again. His face lit up and he took a breath to say something but I raised a hand. 'But only if you concentrate on the fucking road, OK?'

He grinned, but his brow creased as he turned back to the road. 'But what about my work?'

'I'm only going to need you from time to time, and for a couple of days. We'll do it at night. I'll pay for each night whether I use you or not, OK?'

An emphatic nod said fucking right it's OK. And not just maybe.

'Make sure you have your phone with you all the time, so if I'm desperate I can call you.'

He nodded again.

A couple of police 4x4s screamed past, the kind of Toyota flatbeds the muj and later the Taliban had liked to cruise round in. These ones were straight from the showroom. They'd had seats installed on the back so four or five police could sit with their weapons pointing out.

Magreb gestured to his left. 'British embassy, maybe.'

As if I couldn't have guessed. High walls and razor wire weren't enough for the FCO. The set-up looked more like the Old State Building in Basra. HESCOs surrounded it, and a big sangar stuck out on both corners. The barrels of SA80s moved about above the sandbags. Fuck knows how bunkered down the US embassy must have looked.

Magreb wove in and out of the traffic as if he'd receive a bonus if he got there quicker. Maybe he would. Fuck it, it wasn't my money.

I looked behind us at the car seat. 'How old are your kids?'

'Five years, four, three, and two, maybe.'

I slapped him on the shoulder. 'I think you need to spend more time out of the house, mate.'

He didn't really understand but grinned anyway.

We hit a busy junction. Neon glowed. Strings of lightbulbs festooned the fronts of shops selling food, TVs and clothes. Hundreds of locals were out strolling, listening to the music blaring from bootleg music shops, or just sitting drinking tea.

'Where do you live, Magreb? Near the hotel?'

'No, no.' He tapped his window. 'Up there, maybe.'

I looked past him to see headlights climbing steeply in the distance. The two peaks were floodlit, and a couple of mini-lighthouses flashed a warning for short-sighted pilots.

A couple of minutes later, we were almost where we needed to be, maybe. That was what Magreb said, anyway.

We'd driven into an area of dark, narrow residential streets formed from rocks compressed into the mud. Every house hid behind a concrete-block wall. The Hiace lurched in a pothole and we bounced in our seats. There was no street-lighting, and no one about. The only noise as our engine closed down came from a dog going apeshit and the drone of traffic on the main, two or three blocks away.

I sparked up the phone and once more made sure my number would show. 'I'm going to jump out for a while, mate. It could be five minutes, it could be an hour – I'm not sure. You OK to wait here?'

He looked at me wide-eyed. 'For hundred dollar? Maybe!'

I closed the door behind me and stood against a wall. He might be my new mate, but he didn't need to know what was happening, for both our sakes.

The phone rang. I hoped she'd answer. I didn't want to start jumping over walls to find her refuge.

Within five or six rings her voice was in my ear. 'I told you not to call again.'

There was no time to beat about the bush. 'Basma, listen to me – Dominik's in the shit and I need your help. I was with him in Iraq. I was there to get him out of the shit, and that's why I'm here now. You're the only one who can help me do that. I'm outside your house right now. Come out and meet me. I don't want to have to come in.'

There was hesitation. 'Where did you say you are?'

'Right outside. On Ghazni where it meets Sarak.'

More hesitation. 'OK, wait.'

I listened for the rattle of a steel door or to see some light or movement. It took a few minutes, but at last I heard bolts being thrown. The sound came from further down on Ghazni. I ran the fifteen or so metres just to be there the moment she appeared. It was a set of wooden gates, wide enough for vehicles. They were blue, and the paint was peeling.

The right one opened just a few inches. It was on a chain. I moved my face close to the gap. 'Basma, I'm Nick.'

The door closed, the chain rattled, then it opened properly. She came out on to the street and closed it hurriedly behind her, as if that was going to stop me. It wasn't locked.

We stood there awkwardly, like a couple of teenagers on the doorstep after our first date. She came to about chest height, and was even better-looking in the flesh than she had been onscreen.

'Who are you, Nick?'

'I told you, a friend. I was in Basra with him.' Dom seemed to know all the beautiful women. She wasn't local but Arab. 'Dom's missing. He's probably here in the city. Has he made contact with you? Did he come and see you a few days ago? Don't fuck me about, I'm trying to save his life.'

She put her hands to her mouth, but not very convincingly. What I was telling her wasn't news.

She lowered them slowly. 'Do you know what's happened to him?'

'He's been kidnapped. Did he come and see you?' I studied her face. 'He did, didn't he?'

She nodded and sank back against the door.

Now the chink in the armour was exposed, it was time to scream in. 'He came straight here from Basra. You know why? He tell you?'

She tried to look blank. She wasn't very good at this stuff.

I stabbed a finger towards her, stopping just short of her shoulder. 'I've got no fucking time to piss about. I'm here to get him out of the shit. Do you want to help me or not? Did he come and see you?'

She nodded. 'Yes, he was staying here. He wanted somewhere he wouldn't be spotted.'

'Glad we cleared that up. Now, why was he here?'

No more evasion. She gave me eye to eye. 'He's investigating heroin-trafficking. He was trying to fix a meeting with someone from the Taliban. He said they're supplying heroin to the British.'

My finger came up for another stab but she beat me to it. 'No, he didn't say who it was. He didn't want to tell me because he wanted to protect me. All I know is that it's to do with the British. People high up in the embassy, right here in the city. I told him it was madness trying to expose such things, but Dominik said he had a film as security.'

'What did he say about the film? Did he mention Dublin?'

She shook her head. 'I'm sorry, that was all he told me.'

'Tell me about his movements. When did you last see him?'

'He was in and out a lot, mainly at night. He didn't want to be recognized. He said he was seeing fixers, trying to find somebody who could get him a meeting with the main Taliban dealer. I don't think he did – he was getting quite frustrated. Then he went out on Monday night and never returned. I've been worried sick. I

didn't know whether to report him missing ...
I didn't want to go to the embassy because of the
connection ...'

Her voice trailed off and her hand came up to
her mouth once more. This time the shock was
genuine. 'Oh, Nick, do you think the British have
him in one of their secret prisons? We hear about
them ... People never come out of those places.'

'Stop there – no, they definitely don't have
him. He's been kidnapped. I'm here to get him
out.'

A heli rattled high over the city, its navigation
lights flashing like strobes. I waited for its noise
to fade.

'Basma, there's an American and a Brit been
looking for him. They've gone totally local –
beards, Afghan dress. The American's very tall,
and has ginger hair. You know anything about
them?'

Her eyes widened. 'James. Noah James. An
animal.' She looked away. She was no longer
scared or sad, she was angry. 'They're the scum
that sprang up after the Taliban. They use the city
like some big anarchy theme park.'

'Why would they be looking for Dom? Are
they dealers?'

'Of a kind.' She put both hands together and
rested them on her chest. 'The documentary he did
about the refuge ... he exposed them for what they
are. Dominik found some of the girls they'd been

keeping high on heroin and brought them here to safety. They hate him, they hate me. We've had to move the safe-house twice because they tracked us down.'

'Where do they hang out?'

'I don't know. They closed down after the film came out, but they'd have started up again some-where else. Bringing young girls off the hills, turning them into addicts, making them prostitute themselves or carry drugs round the city . . .'

'How many of them?'

'Sorry, I don't know. They find each other. They gravitate together like pack animals.'

I risked a hand on her shoulder. 'Listen, Basma, it's going to be OK. Nobody knows I'm in the city. Nobody knows I've come to see you. Don't tell anyone. I'll contact you soon. I will get him back.'

I ran back to the Hiace, climbed in next to Magreb and closed the door gently. 'Back to the hotel, mate. We've got a while before we go out again.'

He turned his head. 'The lady – she is . . . special friend, maybe?'

I laughed. 'No, mate, maybe not. I'm just try-ing to arrange a reunion, that's all.'

57

It was only nine, still too early to go and visit J's Bar. At least, that was what I thought the Serb had scribbled on my hand. I'd have to wait at least another couple of hours to find out for sure. After dropping me back at the hotel, Magreb had gone to see his family. He was picking me up again at 0215. Maybe.

The plan was to get a weapon, then stake out AM Net until whoever was sending the emails showed up.

I sparked up the laptop and searched for J's Bar on my map, Google and Google Earth. There was no reference to it anywhere – no blogs from journalists talking about the city, no mention of it in news articles, no nothing. I wasn't surprised. It was probably illegal, and that would have nothing to do with being able to obtain a weapon from the place. It would have to do with it selling alcohol.

The address was in the Kartayi Seh district, a couple of Ks south of TV Hill, and a block or two the other side of the Kabul river. According to my map, the Russian embassy was down there too. I wondered why Putin's boys were so far away from the rest of them. Maybe there just wasn't much call for their services, these days. After all their years of liberating the country, they would hardly be flavour of the month. Only a matter of time before the Brits and Americans moved in next door, then.

I'd done as much checking as I could. Finally I could eat, and room service was just snacks.

The only restaurant open downstairs was the Silk Route. It served South East Asian food. I could see from the doorway that almost every table was packed with the élite. Afghan businessmen and diplomats were easy spots. And even in suits and ties instead of uniform, the senior military looked like senior military. This was where the country was being reinvented. This was where the aid, arms and oil clans gathered and had a chat over a couple of hundred dollars' worth of noodles and stir-fry to make sure the reinvention suited the West. I wondered how many multi-million-dollar contracts were changing hands, and how much of the proceeds was getting kicked back under the table.

I was shown to a table for two. The spare white

napkin and cutlery were whisked away, and they asked if I wanted the little flower to stay. I didn't, so they took that too. My Pepsi arrived very quickly with some bread.

Three middle-aged women were at the next table, talking to an Afghan man with a Donald Trump-style comb-over. He was dressed like he belonged to the MCC, in a blazer, striped tie and white shirt, and maybe he did. He spoke slowly and carefully in that I'm-foreign-but-I've-been-to-Oxford sort of accent.

The three women wore neatly tailored trouser suits, and tackled their clear chestnut soup like woodpeckers. I knew that was what it was because they'd spent so long discussing it that my green curry had turned up before they'd even made their decision. I also couldn't help overhearing that they had another friend coming, who'd told them to carry on and order. He'd be there when he could.

I concentrated on the table so I didn't have accidental eye-to-eye. In environments like this, everybody thinks they're all part of the same club and wants to draw you into their conversation – even if you're wearing a long-sleeved blue T-shirt and jeans. It can lead very soon to 'Who are you?' and 'What do you do?' and you can find you're digging yourself into a hole.

Two of the women were American, the other a Brit. The Yank at one end of the table had a shock of white hair, more through stress than age by the sound of it. 'I still find the mere sight of a gun so . . . painful and so . . . upsetting.' She looked like she was going to burst into tears. Fucking hell, if she'd been here more than a week no wonder she'd ended up with Albert Einstein's barnet.

I got among the curry as the waffle next door went off the pain-in-the-arse scale. They went on about the 'big building project', the 'big factory project' and then the 'big road project'. Mrs Einstein nodded earnestly. 'The sooner they learn our way of doing things, the sooner we can go home.'

Donald sat there nodding and agreeing, but deep down all five of us knew no one was going anywhere in a hurry.

The chat switched to ISAF and its success or failure in the war being waged just a couple of hours away in the mountains. I loved armchair generals. I could listen to them all day. The Brit one even threw in a mention of the Great Game. So many people loved to trot out that old line to illustrate the region's geographical significance and their suddenly acquired detailed knowledge of it. Whatever, there was no disputing Kabul had become one of war's latest boomtowns. Apart from the rebuilding contracts, the whole world knew they were already prospecting for oil up in the north.

I managed to finish not only the curry but also

apple strudel and a coffee quicker than they did their starter, and they'd been there when I arrived. I'd often wondered if I had a bit of Arab in me. When it came to food, I just wanted to eat, belch and fuck off.

I also had to prepare and pack my Bergen for tomorrow. Once Magreb picked me up, I wouldn't be back until Saturday. By the morning, I'd either have got Dom back or he'd be dead.

'Hello, Nick, this is a strange place to write about being' – the Australian who'd sat next to me on the plane put his fingers in the air to make the quote sign as he sat and joined them – 'Outside the Comfort Zone . . .' He gave me one of those knowing nods that diplomats do in films.

I left him with his friends. I felt more at home with Magreb.

58

Kartayi Seh District
Friday, 0243 hrs

Magreb had parked the Hiace between two truck containers while I checked my map. We were looking out over a sort of village square a couple of hundred metres wide. In the middle stood a small 1950s Russian anti-tank gun with a steel plate at either side of the barrel. The rubber tyres were decaying; it seemed to be there as decoration. Maybe the people of Russia couldn't afford to donate a shiny new Toyota.

The road we'd taken off the main drag south was tarmac and pothole-free. The two-storey, flat-roofed concrete houses either side of it seemed a lot more upscale than round Basma's way. All of them sheltered behind walls, security lights and rolls of razor wire. Many had plywood guard huts. A couple looked like they'd been on the wrong end of a B52's payload, but even so, the rubble had been neatly swept up and piled inside their remains.

Headlights came up the road behind us and carved through the square. The beam bounced along the different-coloured walls before eventually reaching the gates of the corner house. They swung open.

'That has to be J's, mate.' I showed him my hand. 'House fifty, blue gates, in the corner.'

The area might be high-rent by Kabul standards but Magreb didn't like being there. 'Mr Nick, I hear about this place. Is dangerous, maybe. Bad people come here. Very bad. I wait, maybe, take you back to hotel, be safe.'

Two silhouettes moved round the vehicle to check it before it drove inside.

'Don't worry about it, mate. Just drop me off and I'll give you a call later, yeah?'

The headlights splashed across more vehicles inside the compound, and I saw house lights still further on. The gates closed as I pulled out three hundred-dollar bills and tried to hand them over. 'This is for tonight and the next two. Remember, I said I'd pay you anyway.'

He took them, but gave two back. 'You pay me when I work, Mr Nick.' He pocketed the equivalent of nine days' pay and the rest went back into my jeans.

I climbed out and lifted my Bergen from the footwell. 'OK, mate. But in my book, if you're on standby for a call, that's working.'

He held out a hand to stop me closing the door just yet. 'You really not want me wait and take you back to hotel? Your friend look too nice be with man who go to this place.'

More headlights bounced towards us from the main.

'I'll call you tomorrow. Go on, mate. Go and get your head down.'

I closed the door gently and took the Hiace's place between the containers as Magreb drove off.

An Italian armoured-vehicle two-ship trundled into the square, probably a neighbour-hood-watch thing to make the residents feel safe. Two guys on .50 cals stuck out of the tops. They did a lap before heading off to look good elsewhere.

I had a quick scratch of the sutures, swung the Bergen over my shoulder, then moved out of the gap and made my way across the packed-mud square. At the gate of number fifty, I could hear the steady thump of music. I gave it a couple of bangs.

A small peephole slid open. It was too dark to see eyes.

'No car? You no car?'

'I live just round the corner, mate. No need. You letting me in or what?'

The gate opened just enough for me to slip through. A Tilley lamp hissed away inside yet another plywood guardhouse. Blankets were heaped on the floor. A kettle steamed above a portable gas burner.

The music got louder and light spilt from a door fifty or so metres away. Vehicles looked more abandoned than parked, like the place was so hot the punters couldn't wait to get in.

59

The two guards were bearded lads in their fifties. They toted AKs and had Osprey, but without the collars and bat-wings.

They shone their torches to draw my attention to a couple of printed signs, covered with dirty plastic and pinned to the plywood of their hut.

One said:

Two more killed last week. No more weapons allowed in the house. Leave them in your vehicles. We will search you.

And the other:

If you have a gun or no folding money, you get no drink or fun with the honey.

They pointed at my Bergen. 'In here, leave here.'

I smiled as I dropped it from my shoulder. 'No, no, mate, I'm going to keep it with me. You can search it here, yeah?' I stepped inside and unzipped the top. 'See? No guns.'

One knelt and had a rummage while I held up my hands for the other to frisk me. It wasn't a very good search: Afghans don't like touching strangers that intimately. They hold hands with each other as they walk down the road, but they aren't too keen to feel someone's bollocks to see if there's a little revolver nestling between his legs.

My Gunga Din gear came out and was piled on the floor, along with my map, my bum-bag, now stuffed with money instead of toilet paper, and the Yes Man's phone wrapped up in a black-and-white *shemag*, the sort the two girls in the Gandamack should have had. None of it raised an eyebrow. All they were interested in was weapons.

Next out was my jar of Marmite. The guy held it up like he thought it was high explosive.

I smiled and squatted down next to him. I undid the lid and mimed digging in with an imaginary spoon. 'Mmm, yum-yum.' I dipped in a finger and gave it a suck. I offered him some. He took a sniff and recoiled. The other lad had a taste, and looked like he was going to throw up.

'You either love it, mate, or hate it.' I packed it away as if I'd been given permission to go.

I shook them both by the hand before I turned and left.

The music got even louder as I picked my way round the vehicles and towards the large two-storey house.

Two more beards sat cradling AKs on the doorstep. They had no body armour, and looked bored. They waved me through.

I pushed open the heavy wooden door and felt like I was about to step into a Wild West saloon. A thick fug of cigarette smoke hung in the air, but this being Kabul, it was sickly sweet. Instead of a pianist on a honky-tonk, Justin Timberlake yelled from invisible speakers. Or maybe Justin was actually there – it was impossible to see much beyond the end of your nose.

The whole of the ground floor seemed to con-sist of one huge room. Old sofas and armchairs were dotted around on bare, beer-soaked floor-boards. Dining- and coffee-tables had been stained and bleached by years of spillages and cigarette burns.

There was a sea of faces, and every guy was white. The girls looked Pakistani. Some were dressed in green Russian uniforms with drunken-sailor type hats. Some were in saris. The rest catered for other tastes as they tottered round serving drinks in high heels, ripped fishnets and tight mini-skirts.

There were lots of wide eyes, sunk behind gaunt cheeks, just like in any other opium den on the planet.

60

I ventured further in and found it wasn't just whores and punters having fun. Small monkeys, about a foot from head to tail, jumped about the place dressed in little camouflage uniforms. Miniature plastic AKs were strapped to their backs. They jumped on tables and grabbed drinks or cigarettes. One was smoking a joint. Another soaked its face fur with beer as it tried to drink from a can.

I headed towards the one boy who looked as though he still paid fleeting visits to my planet. He had a straggly beard that came down to his chest and made him look like he should be taking over Middle Earth from the Good Wizard. His hair was tied back in a ponytail. He stood behind a makeshift bar in the corner.

Bottles were stacked on shelves. Pictures, flags, college pennants, all sorts were plastered across the wall: Union flags, Stars and Stripes, soccer teams, American-football sides. A poster showed Mel Gibson doing his *Braveheart* thing. His face was peppered with 9mm holes. The ceiling was the same. There were so many strike marks it looked like a dartboard. This room had seen a few party-size bursts, that was for sure. Either the president was too shit scared to shut the place down or he was a regular.

I could hear Brits, Americans, French, Italians. There were other languages I couldn't make out over the music, but then I heard one I did recognize, even with Justin going full blast.

The Serbs sat on a sofa; each had a whore on his lap. Mr Sheen's fifteen-year-old wore a sari that was up round her waist. Top Lip's was in Red Star gear. She kept stroking his long greasy hair away from his sweating face. Mr Sheen pushed his girl out the way so he could gob off to his mate. Then he leant back and shouted at a group of three guys I took to be Americans. He jabbed a finger at them and repeated himself, but they ignored him and carried on laughing and drinking.

The whole lot were probably freelancers, bounty-hunters drawn here from all over the world like gold prospectors to the Klondike. Only here the prize was Osama, al-Qaeda and any of the Taliban leadership. There was still a price of something like fifty million dollars on bin Laden's head, but most of these guys wouldn't have a clue where to start.

I'd played with the idea of coming here myself for a while, until I did a little digging. It soon became clear I'd be hanging around like this lot. Some had resorted to séances in one of Osama's old houses in the city, the one he'd used to accommodate wives number one and two. They'd legged it when the Americans started bombing, leaving behind just an old bra and a kettle.

Their landlord, the next-door neighbour, wasn't happy. Bin Laden owed him five hundred dollars in rent so he had to make up the cash somehow. He came up with the ingenious idea of installing a few local Mystic Megs, lighting a couple of candles and charging bounty-hunters through the nose to come and get guidance from the other side.

Nobody challenged me. In a place like this nobody asks you your business, and nobody gives you eye-to-eye. Not that most of the guys there tonight could have focused that well anyway.

A couple of monkeys sat and licked at puddles of beer. Maybe they'd had their cans confiscated.

Pictures ripped from magazines were stuck to the wall. The Tora Bora caves getting the good news from a squadron of B52s. Members of the Northern Alliance grinning as they propped up dead Taliban. A double-page spread from a porn mag of two guys and a girl, with Bush's and Musharraf's heads stuck over the men's at either end, and Blair as the meat in the sandwich.

The bar was built entirely from old steel mortar-round containers. They were a bit rusty, but the Cyrillic writing was still visible. The top was a couple of beer-soaked planks.

A couple of girls in laddered fishnets took drinks away on trays. My eyes stung from the smoke. The wizard behind the bar took a long look at my Bergen. 'You planning to stay the weekend, man?' The shelf behind him was packed with whisky bottles. A monkey, either drugged or drunk, lay flat out on his back, an arm and a leg dangling into space. The bottles had been relabelled with pictures from magazines. Hitler stood in the Bavarian mountains. Mussolini looked dead hard with his helmet on. Bin Laden, in his robes and combat jacket, nursed his AK beneath the CNN logo.

'No, mate.' I had to lean across the bar and meet him half-way to make sure I could be heard. 'I was told I could buy protection here. I'm heading south and I need at least a short.'

He certainly had enough protection at his feet. Parked on the lowest shelf was an HK53, a sort of 5.56 version of the MP5. It was loaded with a thirty-round mag and two more, taped together, head-to-toe, sat within easy reach.

61

'You on Osama watch?'

'Nah, just fishing about for work.'

The look on his face said he'd heard that one too many times before. 'You're going the wrong way, man. He's up north.'

I smiled and waited for a yes or no. If he didn't have a weapon, I'd try my luck in the car park. But it would be risky with the guards out there, and I had no time to fuck about.

He pointed through an open doorway that led to the back of the house. The door had been removed – or pulled off its hinges. 'Up the stairs, look for Stu.'

Justin finally shut up and some Indian music came on. A couple of girls in saris got up and began gyrating. The wizard gripped my arm. 'I'm telling you, he's with those Pakistani bitches way up north, getting high and laughing at us all, man.'

The flat-out monkey awoke with a jolt, maybe startled by the change of music. He rolled right off the shelf and landed in a puddle of beer on the floor. He got to his feet and staggered away to war, leaving his hat behind. But, like a good soldier, he kept his weapon with him.

The corridor took me to a set of stairs. A naked bulb burnt on the landing. The noise filtering down was a mix of drunken shouts and girly squeals.

Somebody had propped a mannequin against the wall at the top of the stairs. They'd given him a rubber bin Laden mask. An unlit cigarette dangled from the mouth, and he was plastered with lipstick and eye-shadow. The finishing touch was a pair of fake women's breasts, the sort the local dickhead would wear while cooking a barbecue.

A rough Jock voice came from a room at the far end. I followed it. That door was missing too. The ones either side of it were intact and closed. From behind them came the rhythmic pounding of mattress springs and a chorus of moans and groans.

The open room was piled high with six packs of plastic two-litre water-bottles. The bare floor-boards were riddled with holes. The wood was splintered inwards. No wonder weapons weren't allowed downstairs. Punters who'd come up for a shag would have ended up with their bollocks shot off. Not much repeat business in that.

The walls were plastered with more pictures and magazine cuttings. The connecting door to my right seemed to be a shrine to Jonathan 'Jack' Idema. I remembered him. He'd become world news when he'd got caught running his own private interrogation centre a few years ago. During his trial, he said he'd been given a passport and visa by an unnamed American agency. He claimed he'd been fitted up – the FBI was out to get him because he refused to name the sources who had tipped him off about a nuclear smuggling operation in Lithuania.

Idema might have been away with the fairies, but his victims weren't. The pictures on the door showed what the police had found inside his homemade torture chamber. Three Afghans hung upside down from the ceiling, naked and totally covered with blisters and burns from boiling water. Another eighteen or nineteen were found dead in a trunk. They'd crammed the poor fuckers in there and locked the lid. Three more were in a cupboard, their flesh whipped raw.

The pictures could have come straight from the Yes Man's folder.

62

The shrine shifted suddenly as the connecting door opened. One of the girls came out carrying a red plastic bowl, some liquid soap and an old grey towel that had probably once been white.

The picture on the door was now at an angle but I could still see our mate Jack in court, pointing and ranting from the dock. He had a beard, and wore sunglasses and combat fatigues with US flags stitched all over them. I remembered him claiming he'd been working for the US government and had received orders from Donald Rumsfeld. Nothing to do with multi-million-dollar bounties, of course. Fuck it, I might still have a go myself when this was over.

I passed the door to see a stained stripy mattress. Sprawled across it, an overweight and hairy white man scratched his bollocks with one hand and smoked with the other. Next to his pile of clothes on the floor, a used condom leaked its contents.

'Stu?'

His well-fed head lifted from the mattress long enough for him to suck in another lungful of nicotine. 'Fuck off.' His French accent certainly didn't belong to a Stu.

I carried on to the end of the corridor.

'Stu?'

The guy in the open room was playing chess with a young local lad, maybe fifteen at a push. Their board lay across a couple of cases of Miller Lite.

His head jerked up. 'Aye?'

It was a challenge, not an answer, and it came straight from the Gorbals. He had a wiry grey barnet and a beard that needed a good trim. So did his nostril hair, which grew straight into his moustache. He was early sixties, with pale skin and a nose that had been broken so many times it was almost flat. I nodded appreciatively at his blue Hawaiian shirt. 'Nice. The guy from downstairs sent me. I'm looking for a short. I was in the Gandamack and—'

'I know.' His eyes were back on the chessboard but he put up a hand. 'They called. The two of them want to shoot up for free if I sell you something. What am I? A fucking charity?' His head came up slowly. 'You people, you never give up, do you? Why have you come all this fucking way? English, I suppose?'

His attention went back to the chessboard. The white pieces were carved soldiers, Western-style, with helmets and body armour.

He stood up and waffled in local to the boy. Whatever he was saying, it sounded along the lines of 'Move any of these and you're history.'

I looked at the black pieces. They had turbans, beards and Gunga Din kit.

He looked me up and down as he came towards me. 'You've come to play big boys' games and you don't even have the brains to sort yourself out with a fucking weapon. What are you, son? A fucking bank clerk, thinking all this shite is some sort of great adventure?'

He needed a dental plan even more than Magreb. The few teeth that weren't black had an inch of nicotine on them. And he stank.

I nodded and smiled. He had what I wanted. 'I just need a weapon.'

'You got money?'

I stepped back from his BO. 'Enough.'

'What are we waiting for, then?' He turned back to the light-skinned boy and gave him another warning. He left the room and I followed. I grabbed a bottle of water from a pack that was already ripped open.

We passed the sound of more humping and grunting and headed downstairs. We went through the bar just as the dancing girls, now semi-naked, were having some fun with empty beer bottles. I followed the Jock through a door, into what would once have been the kitchen.

Two girls stood next to the sink, chatting away together and soaping themselves with flannels as if we weren't there.

The Jock led me across to two rusty and disconnected chest freezers with hasps and padlocks drilled into them. He unlocked one and lifted the lid to expose longs and shorts of all makes and sizes.

This place didn't do pub grub.

63

I dug around in what amounted to a big collection of rust.

'The semi-auto pistols are two hundred. Revolvers one fifty. AKs two fifty. Anything else, I'll tell you.'

'You heard of a Polish guy, Dominik Condratowicz?'

He leant against the other freezer, eyeing the two girls. They were now up on chairs and squatting over the sink to give themselves a final rinse with running water.

'No. That who you gonna kill with one of these fucking things?'

I picked out an old MP5 and fished about for some mags. There were two. 'You got any nine-millimetre for this?'

He slapped the freezer beneath him but kept his eyes on the girls. One was towelling herself and the one I'd seen upstairs was giving her makeup a bit of a retouch, ready for the next round. 'I've got to keep the fucking lot locked up. Fucking thieving bastards.'

The MP5 was knackered and rusty. I needed to look inside to check it had the basics – like a firing pin. These Heckler & Kochs were very quick to disassemble. I pushed back on the two pins at the rear, which opened up the backplate and one end of the pistol grip.

He was taking an interest in me now that he saw I knew what I was doing.

I pulled out the working parts. There was nothing but rust around the chamber, and so much corrosion in the barrel I could only just about see light through it.

'What about Noah James?'

The Jock's eyes jerked away from the girls. He went ballistic. 'Fucking animal! You anything to do with him?'

'No, just heard he was about. You know where?'

I started to reassemble the weapon.

His finger came up to my face. As long as his breath stayed away that was fine. 'I don't fucking know and don't care. If they come here again I'll do Kabul a favour and kill the shites myself.'

'He come in with the Brit?'

'Joey fucking Wallings. Arsehole used to work here. He was a good lad until the gear got him.'

The Jock mimed injecting his arm. 'Fucked him up and he started running with James. They tried to sell me Afghan whores. So smacked up, some of them, they could hardly stand.' He pointed at the legs and heads of the girls at the sink. 'Fucking burns all over them, whip-marks, cuts . . . They stole them from villages, sick fucks.'

He sat on the freezer and lit a Chesterfield with a Zippo. He sucked deeply to calm himself. His eyes flicked down towards the MP5. 'You not interested?'

I shook my head and put the weapon back in the freezer.

'Well, maybe you're not some bank clerk.' He nodded at the weapons. 'They're all shite.'

I spotted a mini Uzi, like the regular Uzi only a lot shorter. It was stuck under a pile of rusty old .303 Lee Enfields, probably left over from the Second World War.

I pulled it out to discover it was a Mini-Ero, a shameless copy. This one was the older version, with pistol grip safety and mag housing, and big chunky working parts that operated on the blow-back system. The only difference I could see was that the safety-catch markings were in Serbo-Croat.

The girls left and Stu helped himself to a hand-ful of arse from both on their way out.

The Mini-Ero wasn't in bad nick. A bit rusty, but at least it had a firing pin.

I'd always thought the Uzi overrated. After the Six Day War it got rave reviews it didn't deserve. Both the Uzi and the mini Uzi were heavy for their size. Almost every comparable weapon did the same job more efficiently. It was just marketing that made the weapon so popular in the eyes of people who didn't use them. Bank clerks and south London drug-dealers would be the only people ignorant enough to part with good money for one.

There were three mags taped round the barrel. 'I'll take this and two hundred nine-millimetre. How much is that going to set me back?'

Whatever the figure should have been, he probably doubled it. 'Three hundred.'

No point haggling. 'Done.'

He unlocked the freezer as I put the weapon back together. I took off my Bergen, bunged in the bottle of water, and waited to add the weapon, mags and rounds.

'You going south for long?' He handed me four cardboard boxes of fifty 9mm and I ripped one open. I'd always found it easy to speed-load, even as a boy soldier. Many guys try to position the rounds in their hands so that the percussion cap is going to be fed in first, but the easiest thing is to pick the things up and turn them between your thumb and forefinger as you press them into the magazine.

'Don't know.'

'Well, son' – he locked up the ammo freezer– 'you come back with that thing and I'll buy it back. But I don't give money, we just trade with honey.'

He locked up the first freezer and came over to do the same to the second. I moved the magazines and kit. 'That's how half of these shites pay. Some, they come in, they've got fuck-all left but their weapons.'

I shrugged. 'Maybe I'll bring it back.'

'I'm not sticking my nose in your business, son, but that James shite and his like – stay away from them. They're fucking acid.'

I finished the first mag.

'You liked my chessboard, didn't you?'

'Yeah, nice.'

'My boy.' He was grinning. 'He carved them. He's good at that sort of thing. It's a special edition, black Taliban, white ISAF. I'm going to try and get it marketed.'

He took a last drag and flicked the butt on to the floor. 'You see, son, you got the Taliban pawns in turbans, but the ISAF pawns, none of them match. That's because we spend so much time out here wondering if they're on the same fucking side.'

I was treated to another flash of his black stumps. 'If it was going to be true to life, obviously the Taliban king would be missing –

there'd just be a video of him in a cave. And no Taliban knights, no Taliban castles. They'd all be bishops, see – mad mullahs.

'And once the ISAF pieces were set up, most of them would refuse to move from their own squares. The bishops, well, they'd have to be paid regularly or they'd move over to the Taliban side. Are you getting this, son?'

I sort of was and sort of wasn't, but I nodded anyway to make him feel a bit better. I finished loading the last mag and counted out three hundred-dollar bills.

'Sorry for being a bit of a shite with you in the beginning, son. But when they called they said you were one of those cowboys. People like that, they come here and fuck it up for everybody else who's trying to make a living.'

'No worries, mate.'

The money went into his jeans pocket.

I shoved the mags and spare ammunition into my Bergen and he fired up another Chesterfield.

The other side of the door, somebody loosed off a double-tap in the bar. The music kept playing, but the background noise changed. Girls screamed. Men shouted, more pissed off than afraid.

I threw everything except the weapon and a mag on top of the Gunga Din outfit and hoisted the Bergen on to my back.

Somebody out there yelled for calm, but the

monkeys weren't having any of it. They screeched their heads off.

There was another shot, then a burst of .53 on automatic drowned them out.

64

The cocking handle was sited on the top of the weapon. I shoved a mag into the housing in the pistol grip and listened for it to click home, then pulled back.

The Jock was off the Richter scale. 'I'm trying to run a fucking business here!'

He stormed out and I went straight to the back door. I'd got what I'd come for. Time to fuck off. But everything round the back was more than just locked: nails had been punched through the door into the frame. I decided to wait for things to calm down in the bar. It wasn't my fight.

I went to the part-open door. Stu was trying to make himself heard over the music. The two Serbs were up on their feet and carrying. Mr Sheen had rammed his pistol into the fifteen-year-old's mouth. She was on the sofa, her head pushed hard against the backrest. Her chest heaved with fright and tears streamed down her face.

One of the Americans he'd been yelling at before lay motionless on the floor behind her. He had a hole in the side of his head that leaked on to the wood.

The old wizard lay in a pool of blood this side of the bar. His .53 lay next to him, the empty cases scattered about.

Everybody else had faded to the edges, but Stu was as close to the Serb as he could get. 'Fuck off, and don't come back. I don't want no more of your shite. Go!'

They weren't impressed. Top Lip pointed his weapon at Stu's head. Like Mr Sheen's, it looked to be a PPK, a small weapon, easy to hide down by your bollocks. 'No. We're staying.'

Mr Sheen nodded back to the body and his three mates hovering round it. 'That fuck started this. They should be kicked out. Kick them out now, or we will kill your whore.'

Stu was coming to the boil. 'I don't think you heard me right, son. I'm not having no more of your shite—'

Mr Sheen pulled the trigger.

Settee stuffing exploded behind her head, then got soaked with blood and brain. The monkeys' screeches filled the air once more.

Fuck this. Stu was about to get it and I might be stuck here all night.

Gripping the Mini-Ero like it was a pistol, arm straight out, right hand on the pistol grip, left hand over right and pushing back with a bent arm to make a stable platform for the weapon, I kicked the door wide open and charged into the room.

The two of them were straight ahead of me, maybe eight or nine metres away.

I stood ready to fire, the web of my hand hard against the pistol grip to release the safety, both eyes open, legs shoulder-width apart, left foot forward, left toe pointing where I was intending to shoot. Almost the classic shooting-range stance, so there could be no doubt that I knew what I was doing.

They swung to face me. There was fuck-all to say. They knew what was required. But Stu didn't want them to be in any doubt. 'I told you – fuck off, don't come back. Fucking animals.'

He was just noise to them. It was me they stared at.

Would I? Would I open up?

My eyes broadcast I would. They were clear – and the weapon stayed rock steady.

They exchanged a glance. Very slowly, their PPKs came down. Without saying a word, they walked to the door. Mr Sheen wiped the girl's blood off his hands on a seat cover on his way out.

Stu bellowed for his son. He came running

downstairs. Then, as the Serbs' wagon sparked up, he called for the guards. They stumbled in and he barked commands. They shouldered their AKs and started dragging the bodies away.

Stu looked from them to his boy, and then to me. He stretched out a hand. In it was my three hundred.

'I owe you, lad. Fucking animals, they should leave that sort of shit out on the street.'

The guards were getting very busy now the shooting had stopped. They grabbed hold of the wizard's feet and dragged him past. We both looked down.

Stu spat on his face. 'He was also a shite. He gave two of the girls gonorrhoea last month.'

The boy came over to his father and he slapped him affectionately round the back of his head. 'One of them's his mother.'

I followed the body outside and stepped back into the shadows as the Serbs' 4x4 screamed out of the compound.

I pulled out the mobile and dialled. 'I'm going to AM Net. I'll phone you when I get there. Be ready for the call.'

I threw the phone back into the Bergen and got out the Gunga Din gear. I wasn't going to use Magreb. I didn't want him hurt. He also needed to keep his job, and if things got noisy I didn't want to be worrying about him.

I had a long walk ahead.

65

Emergency Surgical Centre for War Victims
0758 hrs

The old guy who'd joined me on the left-hand bench under the corrugated-iron canopy pointed at the manic traffic and waved his arm with disgust. I agreed. Then he said something else and clearly expected an answer. I pointed at my ear and made a strangled sound. He nodded knowingly and looked to the other bench for someone to chat to just as the Yes Man's phone vibrated in my hand. I pushed my head down under my *shemag*. Now I was mad as well as deaf and dumb.

'No sign?' He sounded edgy. 'You still have eyes on?'

I cupped my hand over the phone to make

doubly sure this stayed local. 'Don't call unless he's online. I'm trying to do my fucking job. You just stand by and do yours.'

I cut the call. It wasn't the time to worry about him being a bit sensitive about profanity.

One of the young lads who'd been fanning the fire in the metal trough last night came out of the kebab shop carrying a tray. He went into AM Net.

I was facing the end of Flower Street, on the other side of Jadayi Sulh. Further down the main to my left, on the next junction, was the Iranian embassy. My new mates outside were probably having a hot brew as they sat and watched the traffic. I was almost becoming a local.

The only thing that mattered right now was finding whoever was sending Siobhan the emails and follow him – or her. The target might be on foot or might have a vehicle. A vehicle would be nice. I could just go back to the fixer and he'd find out the registered keeper. Even in places like Baghdad it was simple to trace a driver by his plate. US patrols were tasked to hunt specifically for unlicensed or unplated vehicles. It's one of the first things that had to be done to show some semblance of order. Every self-respecting terrorist or kidnapper operating in a city knows to keep his paperwork up to date. In the early days, too many got pulled over with a truckload of explosives or bodies wrapped in gaffer-tape in the boot.

An explosion rumbled up from the south, the direction of TV Hill. Nobody paid a blind bit of attention. Even the sparrows stayed chirping in the trees. The old guys on the bench had a bit of a tut to each other and waved their arms, but that was about it. They left me out of their gang this time.

It had been a long night's walk from the Jock's place. After changing into the Gunga Din gear, I'd used the bottle of water to mix scoops of Marmite into a lumpy cream that I worked into my face and hands. It stained me up a treat, but I smelt like a toasted sandwich.

I'd got here three hours ago. The shop had opened just before seven. Only four people had gone in – and one of those had been the old man who'd opened the shutters and now sat sipping his tea. The other three had been smartly dressed, Western-style, and in and out within ten minutes.

Soon afterwards the old men started filling up the benches. Nobody gave my Marmite tan a second glance. Some took a second or two to give me the once-over, same as they would with any stranger, but then they got on with their lives. They'd been there the best part of an hour. It couldn't be a bus stop. Maybe they were queuing up to ask where I got my aftershave.

The plan was simple. I sat there and kept the trigger on AM Net, while the Yes Man stagged on in London, waiting for the next email to be sent. There would be a fifteen-second delay between Siobhan receiving it and it popping up on his screen.

This wasn't an ideal spot to be keeping the trigger from because of the main in between. Vehicles cut my view and the target became unsighted for seconds at a time. But it was the best I could do. Anywhere else, I'd stand out like a bulldog's bollocks.

Flower Street was too narrow to hang about unobtrusively, and there were no options left or right close enough to the target where I could step back into the shadows. If the target came out of AM Net and headed my way, we'd have a head-on.

I couldn't just walk up and down the street, waiting. This was the city of kidnappers and suicide-bombers. Their kids were running around delivering tea and cooking kebabs. So there I sat with the main drag between me and the target.

Sirens warbled. The gates to my left swung open and two Merc ambulances screamed out, heading south. The traffic stopped briefly to let them through, then the trigger on the shop disappeared intermittently again as more vehicles drove between us.

There were a lot of old jeeps that had been rebuilt to carry sixteen people on the tail-bed.

They obviously kept these things on the road until they finally fell apart. There was plenty of old Russian gear still about as well: big trucks with bulbous noses that were made in the 1980s but might have been at the siege of Stalingrad. They laboured up and down blocking my view, overloaded with bricks and rubble.

My normal clothes, the map, the Mini-Ero and mags were stuffed into my Bergen, which I'd kept on my back. The straps were loosened so it fell back and rested on the top of the bench. My arm itched and I hadn't resisted much up to now.

The young lad came back out of the target with an empty tray. I could have done with a brew right now. I eyed the two old guys selling tea on the corner at the other side of the road, under the sign pointing to AM Net. They'd sparked it up about an hour ago and were doing a brisk trade. If only . . .

Another guy went into AM Net – maybe young, I couldn't tell under the beard and cow-pat.

I gripped the phone.

A knackered truck pulled up at the kerb and a gang of workers with shovels clambered out. They moved further along and started having a go at the ditches. A few had black and white *shemags* like mine, but all wore orange fluorescent jackets over their other gear. Health and Safety had even weaselled their way into

Kabul. They should have had a look round the back of the Jock's place.

He came back out of AM Net. The Yes Man hadn't rung.

I used the phone to give the sutures another rub instead. The traffic was binding, sometimes stopping altogether and blocking my view.

It was just after half eight when I felt more vibrations in my hand.

I got my head down again but strained to keep my eyes on target. 'They online?'

'Yes . . .' He hesitated, perhaps checking monitors. 'Is it him? Do you have Dominik?'

'No.' I kept my eyes on AM Net, waiting for the sender to sign off and come out.

'The email has confirmed proof of life. The tree fell on John's BMW in the storm last winter.'

The traffic snarled in front of me again. I kept my head pressed firmly to the phone.

The Yes Man read out the reply word for word as it came up on his screen. ' "They – are – getting – impatient – please – hurry . . ." ' Shit. Two trucks blocked my line of sight. I'd lost the trigger again. I cut him short. 'I don't give a fuck what's being said. Call me when the link closes down.'

'Just has.'

I closed down, too, and slipped the phone back into my pocket. I got up, resisting the temptation to run like a lunatic. I smiled goodbye to my friends and stepped off the pavement.

I squeezed between the two trucks and reached the other side by the tea stall. I checked right, then left, then back up towards the embassy, as if I was meeting a friend. There was no one but pepper-pots and kids within the time and distance anyone could have walked from AM Net.

I played phone call to the mate and glanced through the target window as I crossed Flower towards it.

I could see the old man near the window, but no one else.

I'd fucked up big-time.

66

The young lad brushed past me with another tray of tea glasses. He disappeared into a baker's as I started checking down Flower. There was fuck all else I could do.

I walked quickly down the street, head up. I was going to have to risk appearing suspicious. If I didn't find anyone who looked like a possible target I was fucked anyway.

A group of surly young guys who were probably best mates with the ones chasing me last night moved towards me, but carried on past.

It was no more than a hundred to the junction where my reception committee had been waiting. It was much busier than this stretch.

My arms were pumping now. The main was a blur of orange-and-whites.

Bodies milled on both corners, talking and

smoking. Women with shopping bags wove their way through.

I stopped and looked around. One cowpat, moving across Flower in the distance, was taller, much taller than the others.

I ran.

A taxi pulled up, an old Mazda estate, and I saw him slide into the back seat. As it pulled away, I couldn't believe what I was about to do. I waved frantically at the nearest orange-and-white and did the same.

67

I jumped into the back. The driver had a white beard and black teeth, and looked about eighty. He waffled some kind of greeting. I shoved my hand into my bum-bag and dragged out a bundle of bills. 'Let's go! That taxi! Follow, follow!'

I waved my hand urgently but he seemed more interested in the stink of Marmite. I shoved a couple of tens into his gnarled brown hand. 'Let's go! Chop-chop!'

He finally pulled away. He studied me in his rear-view, which had enough beads hanging off it to decorate a mosque.

The Yes Man's mobile vibrated in my baggy pockets. Fuck him, he could wait.

I leant forward between the two front seats, eyes skinned for the Mazda. I tried to stay all smiles as I gave his bony old shoulder a friendly squeeze. 'That's it, matey, let's go get that wagon!'

I shoved another note at him.

It was just after nine. The sun was behind us. TV Hill was on the left. We were heading west.

The road narrowed. The shops petered out. Concrete, flat-roofed two-storey houses took their place. I peered through the dusty, cracked windscreen but there was no sign of the orange-and-white estate.

A vehicle pulled out of our lane up ahead and cut left across the oncoming traffic.

'There! That taxi! Follow that taxi!'

I waved my hands and tried to get him to see what I wanted. He didn't understand until I produced another ten.

The orange-and-white disappeared down a compacted-rock road. It was definitely two up. A large body sat rear right. It didn't move, didn't check behind.

I rolled down the window. The noise and heat of the outside world rushed in. 'That's it. Left, yeah? That taxi, yeah?'

He grinned knowingly as he spun the wheel to get in among the oncoming traffic. He'd probably seen that bloke with a beard pull the same stunt in a hundred Bollywood films as he fought big-time crime in downtown Delhi.

He got halfway across the road and slammed on the brakes. I pitched forward. Two gleaming white GMC suburbans, all blacked-out glass, sped towards us. Red and blue lights flashed behind radiator grilles to tell us to keep the fuck out of the way. These boys were stopping for no one.

We turned in their wake. TV Hill was now ahead. We were heading south.

I kept eyes on target. The plume of dust that billowed behind it was maybe a hundred and fifty further ahead. A gang of kids cleaning cars had to jump out of the way as we slewed across the gravel.

The orange-and-white hung another left.

'That's it, matey!'

Our car slowed. He still faced forward, but gave me a sideways glance.

'Dodgy bastard!' I jammed another ten his way and he chuckled as we picked up speed.

We followed the Mazda through the residential area, sometimes fifty behind, sometimes more. A main drag was coming up in the distance, but I could see a tailback stretching almost all the way to us. I ripped off my Bergen and grabbed the map.

TV Hill was now about a K ahead. I could clearly see the antennae farms on the two peaks. The main had to be Salang Wat. A left would take us back to the city centre. A right would take us north-west – out of the city and off the edge of the world.

We crept towards the main. The target was now about four vehicles in front.

The driver was chatting away now as if I was

his long-lost brother. He smiled and sniffed the air. I could tell he was dying to ask the aftershave question.

Fuck it. I dug in the Bergen, eyes never off the target, got hold of the Marmite jar and opened it. I held it out so he could have a smell. He winced. It was official: Afghans definitely didn't like the stuff.

We rolled forward a couple of vehicle lengths. My face was covered with sweat, and that made the smell even worse. I could finally see the smouldering remains of a car bomb and the carnage it had created in the open-air market.

Italian armoured vehicles formed a partial roadblock, their .50 cals pointing every which way. Soldiers took cover in doorways while traffic cops in drunken-sailor hats shouted and pointed at the approaching traffic.

Body parts were scattered among the shattered metal and glass that surrounded the crater. Fire engines sprayed white foam as the larger pieces of the dead were retrieved and the injured were helped towards any available vehicle. The two Merc ambulances couldn't cope.

The market seemed to stretch all the way to the bottom of TV Hill. There it morphed into a shanty that reached most of the way to the summit. Somewhere in the sea of mud and corrugated iron lived Magreb, Mrs Magreb, and their four little boys.

68

The troops were diverting traffic to the right, out of town. The tailback had formed because everybody wanted to go left.

The area had been cordoned off big-time. Hundreds of shoppers and stall-holders were being herded away from the city side of the market.

The Yes Man's mobile kicked off again just as I saw our target raise his to his ear. I let it vibrate.

The street was wide and long, with a concrete central divide. Both sides were lined with what might one day be two-storey shops. Steel reinforcing rods stuck out of the first storey, like there was some Greek-style building tax dodge going on. Dead animals hung outside one, waiting to be skinned. Sparkling alloy wheels were piled outside another. The next down sold chip rolls.

Two helicopters circled our side of TV Hill. Police and military with white lollipops swarmed everywhere, marshalling the traffic like airport ground controllers.

The Mazda was only three ahead, but with so many orange-and-whites in the queue we blended in fine.

I checked the map again. Once we'd passed the hill, the diversion had to start heading south soon or we'd be up in the mountains.

We came to a spot where armoured vehicles had shifted the concrete blocks that divided the lanes. A cop in a drunken-sailor hat fed himself a chip roll with one hand and directed the traffic with the other. Sure enough, we headed south. We'd soon be in Khushal Mena, Basma's part of town.

It cost me another ten dollars. I tried five, but it seemed to make something go wrong with the throttle cable. At least he'd learnt one word of English. As I gave him the money he beamed. 'Matey! Matey!'

More armoured vehicles and Italians loomed. Their .50 cals kept the slow-moving wagon train channelled on the southbound road. A hand-painted sign pointed to the former king's palace.

The mobile kicked off once more and this time I opened it up.

'Never cut me off again! What's happening?'

'I'm following a possible.' I didn't need to

tell him where I was. He had the phone tagged.

'Who is he? What is he?'

'Don't know, but looking local.'

I could see farmland through the gaps between the bombed-out buildings. The rusting wreck of a Russian armoured personnel carrier lay stranded in a field. Wizened old men shepherded brown woolly sheep against the distant backdrop of snow-capped mountains.

'Where is he going?'

'Don't know. That's why I'm following him. Soon as I do, you will too.'

The traffic was picking up speed. On cue, Matey developed accelerator problems. I threw him another ten. Only fight the battles you can win.

It wasn't long before I was seeing what was left of the palace on the southern extreme of the city. It looked like Dresden after Bomber Harris had done his stuff. There was no way of telling which lot of liberators could take the credit: the Russians, the Taliban or the B52s.

Further down the road we had the makings of a military convention. Troops sat tightly inside their armoured vehicles and Humvees, body-armoured up, all the party gear pointing out at the traffic.

I could see why. About a K away on the plain to my right lay what had to be ISAFville: row upon row of 200-metre-long tented accommodation, vehicle compounds, HESCOs, razor wire, satellite dishes, the full Monty. They probably battened down their area like this every time a bomb went off.

The target was now just two ahead but the traffic had spread out as we finally headed back towards town. I knew where we were the moment we passed the Russian embassy. I wondered if I'd see the Jock carrying bodies out to the bins, still clearing up after last night.

We were soon at the river and the diversion lifted. It took a twenty this time to keep him moving. He must have sensed the end was in sight.

We stayed behind the Mazda as it approached the market, finishing up only about five hundred metres from where we'd started. The crowd was still being held back and had turned hostile. The Italians eyed them warily from behind their sunglasses.

The Mazda stopped. I squeezed the bony shoulder. 'Stop here, matey.'

Eyes on the Mazda, I grabbed my Bergen and shoved him one last ten. He could probably afford to drive straight home and begin his retirement.

I watched the target get out and skirt the crowd. It wasn't difficult: his cowpat was still a mile above the rest. He wasn't fucking around. He knew where he was going.

I followed, head down, eyes up, locking on to the back of his hat.

We reached a large car park among the cluster of flat-roofed, baked-mud dwellings that spread on up the hill.

He put his hands into his waistcoat pockets. He was searching for something. Keys . . .

Fuck.

He opened the driver's door of a battered black flatbed.

I spun round and broke into a run. Matey was still trying to turn round. I jumped in front of his bonnet, brandishing a twenty. His grin was bigger than ever.

69

As I jumped in, the black pickup had reached the last stretch of tarmac before the hill. Both of us soon hit the dirt road and started snaking through the shanty town.

We climbed steeply, past small, square, flat-roofed shacks. The cab lurched across ruts and potholes. The other wagon kicked up a dust-cloud a couple of hundred metres ahead. The city was soon below us.

As we got higher, a few brick and concrete houses jutted out of the hillside. Boys played football with bare feet. Women sat in groups on terraces carved out of the slope. Every hundred metres or so, we hit a hairpin. The cab was just inches from a sheer drop down into the valley. The road must have been built as access to the antennae farms, and these families had piggy-backed off it. There was no planning permission needed. It looked like they'd just scraped out a terrace with picks and shovels and used the spoil to build with.

I'd seen rougher and dirtier shanties than this in India and South America. At least some of the kids here were running round in school uniform, the boys in blue shirts, the girls in white head-scarves. And the packed mud was swept scrupulously clean. It seemed there was a whole lot more civic pride up here than I'd ever seen down in the valley.

A rusting Soviet hulk, ripped apart by the muj, overshadowed the next bend. It might have been picked clean by the buzzards. We lost sight of the black pickup for a moment, then found it again as we completed a sharp left-hander.

It was parked up alongside a two-storey rectangular house that was set back from the track by about ten metres on higher ground. It had three windows on the upper floor at the front, and one each side of the front door below. All were boarded up. No smoke curled from the chimney. No electricity cables ran in from the road and there was nobody in sight.

The next three hundred metres cost me another ten dollars, but there were no turns, just more dead Russian armour. We crested the hill on the saddle, alongside a group of old guys sitting cross-legged in a huddle round a cooking-pot. They gave us a look and got straight back to the business of cooking up dinner.

The track forked left up to one of the antennae farms, and right to the other. The driver stopped, turned in his seat, and gave me a triumphant but toothless smile. I gave him a final ten. 'I'll get out here, matey.'

As he embarked on a many-point turn behind me, I walked towards the barbed-wire fence round the installation immediately above the target, but not so purposefully that it might rattle the AK-toting guards hanging out by its gate. Both antennae farms were key locations; they needed to be protected. The big green circular ISAF signs told everyone that.

Kabul was so far below me it looked like a map. I walked along the saddle. The Serena and most of the embassies were to the north, down to my right. To my left were the Jock's bar, the Russian embassy and, out on a limb at the southern edge of town, ISAF.

I stopped and admired the view until the taxi was out of sight. Then I went and sat by the wreck of a Russian communications truck, surrounded by artillery-shell casings and ammo boxes like big sardine cans with the tops peeled back.

I pulled out the Yes Man's mobile and looked south, towards the Kabul river. I wasn't going to have any problems with a signal up here. I couldn't move for satellite dishes.

The phone rang twice. The Yes Man came straight on. 'Have you found Condratowicz? Have you got him?'

'I've just housed a possible, that's all.'

'Where is he?'

One of the old guys left the crowd with a can in his hand and went through the motions of washing himself ready for prayer.

'Ali Abad mountain. They call it TV Hill.'

'Where on the hill? Any idea yet if our man's inside?'

'No. Have you got access to anything in the air? I need you to keep a trigger on it and see what happens down there.'

'Nick, I cannot involve any other agency.' His response came with several degrees of frost.

I didn't give a shit. 'Do you want him or not? I need help, and you've got it on tap. I don't know yet if the fucker's in there so find me an airborne Predator. The Americans are bound to have one or two up there. Don't worry about compromise. They do this shit all the time. Just say it's an anti-terrorist op, for fuck's sake. You're the boss, aren't you? Think of something.'

One of the guards sauntered out on to the road. He had his weapon over his shoulder but wanted to take a closer look at the local gobbing off on his mobile.

The Yes Man said nothing.

'Just tap into whatever they have up there that

covers the north side of the hill. Then get the operator to stand by. When I do a walk-past I can ID the exact building for them. If Dom's in there, this isn't going to be some fucking shoot-'em-up. I want to get in there, try and find him, then get us both out alive – and not get shot by ISAF in the process. And some of their boys are a stone's throw away from me at the top of this poxy hill. So fucking think of something.'

'OK, wait out.'

He cut off and, for the first time in a while, I did what he said. The old guy had finished splashing his face, neck and arms and was now getting down to a serious chat with Allah. I watched him touch his forehead to the ground, then stand and pray over the city.

Another guard joined the first, and they both headed down the road towards me.

They were Turks. Their national flag filled the top half of the arms that were busy waving me away.

70

I moved back towards the saddle, past yet another pile of old artillery casings. Those two hills had been Russian strongholds. If you dominated the high ground there, you dominated Kabul. And that was exactly why a guy in blue body armour was climbing the south side of the hill, probing the ground with what looked like a row of kitchen knives. If you were in the mood to build there, I guessed you decided which bit of slope you wanted to carve out, then got a guy in body armour from the council to come and dig up the mines for you.

The old guys were just dragging whatever they'd been cooking out of the pot. I couldn't see the target. It was down to my left somewhere, but the angle was too steep. What I did see were the scorched remains of a blue burqa. So much for liberation.

The mobile vibrated in my hand.

'You got something up there for me?'

'Yes, we have one tasked. It's overhead.'

I looked up, even though I knew I was wasting my time. The Predator's video cameras and forward-looking infrared (FLIR) thermal imaging would be doing their stuff from fifty thousand feet. The ground crew would be able to see me, big-time. Even through cloud they could read a newspaper at a bus stop. To a Predator, it was always a bright sunny day.

Once they had imagery, it could be bounced anywhere, including to my laptop in the Serena. Down in Helmand and the south, they circled 24/7. They watched and waited for the Taliban to come out of their caves, jump on their flatbeds and scream across the plains. The operator, hundreds of miles north in the ISAF camp, just marked the target with a laser beam and kicked off a couple of the Hellfires strapped to its wings.

'You got coverage?'

'I'm looking at pictures now.'

'Tell the operator to focus on the saddle between the two antennae farms. I'm on my own, facing north.'

I stood there like a dickhead while the Yes Man steered the operator on target.

'They want to confirm it's you.'

'I'll walk down the road on their go. Tell them I'm in local dress and I have a rucksack on my back. Apart from their boys with the guns, I'm the only fucker up here who's standing. The rest of them are sitting and eating.'

'He's ready.'

'I'm walking.' I headed down the track. A couple of the old guys waved at me as I passed. I kept my head down, mobile to my ear. 'That's a hundred and fifty short of the target. White rectangular, two storeys, flat roof.'

'We have you, Nick.'

'Fifty short. On my left, building about ten metres back from the road. There's a black four-by-four parked to the left of the target.'

'I can see a white building ahead of you now, Nick.'

'That's it. I'm about twenty short.'

'There's movement!' His voice shot up an octave. 'Movement from the back. Someone's heading towards the four-by-four.'

I swivelled my eyes under the *shemag*. A massive body appeared from the back of the house and opened the wagon's hatch.

He was no more than five metres away. I heard him mutter to himself as he sniffed and chugged up the contents of his lungs.

He bent forward slightly from the waist, as if his massive frame was weighing him down. His head was down, maybe to hide his scabbed-up face, but he looked aware. Both hands were stuck inside his clothing. One would be gripping a weapon.

His gingery beard was almost as big as the wizard's last night. He could be local. There were plenty of big Afghans running around here, even ginger ones with blue eyes.

He lifted out a case of bottled water and dropped it on to his sandalled feet. 'Fucking goddamn fucking shit!'

So, not a local, then.

A few more paces and he was unsighted. I heard the rear hatch slam shut behind me.

'He's going back to the rear of the house, Nick. He's opening the back door. He's now inside.'

'It's no longer a possible,' I said. 'That's the target.'

71

Serena Hotel
1834 hrs

I came out of the shower still honking of Marmite but wearing a nice bathrobe. My arm was red and sore. My fault, I'd kept scratching.

The TV was tuned to an Iranian station. No need to buy any of those street-market DVDs of Americans getting blown to shit by IEDs. You could watch it all on state-sponsored news. I picked up the remote and flicked. It was all the normal shit. CNN, fuzzy HBO, some Russian channels, hundreds of Indian ones. I settled on some girls in bikinis playing beach cricket in Australia. I wondered what the boys up in the hills would make of it.

The Yes Man's mobile bounced across the desk

where it was busy recharging next to my personal one.

'The latest imagery is with you. If he's in there, get him down into the city and away from ISAF before contacting me. I will arrange pickup and fly you both out within the hour.'

I fired up the laptop with my left hand. 'You need to make sure the unmanned aerial vehicle is retasked and not covering the hill. Neither of us would want anything recorded.'

'Agreed.'

The mobile cut and I powered it down. I picked up the personal one and tried Magreb. It just rang and rang. Maybe he was at a crucial stage with the stir-fry.

The downloads finished. I was looking at a series of black-and-white thermal images. The hotter the source, the whiter it showed. A live human, even fully clothed, would show as a precise silhouette.

The 4x4 glowed with varying intensities of white. The bonnet was bright. The exposed bit of exhaust pipe was incandescent.

Scaled against the 4x4, the target looked about twenty metres by ten. There were no power lines going in, not even at the back, and the steeply sloping ground at the rear wasn't enclosed.

I scrolled down. Two pathways led from the rear door. One went left, towards where the wagon was parked. The other branched off right, meandering round the contours of the high ground to the other houses, thirty to thirty-five away.

There were no windows or doors in the side walls, and no heat signature leaked from the windows at the rear. Either they were boarded up as securely as the front ones, or nothing was being generated.

The last picture showed a body – too small to be Noah – taking a piss near the back door. The bright liquid ran back towards the house.

The UAV hadn't done much to help, except to tell me there were at least two people in the house. I was going to have to recce the target close up. I needed to find a way to make covert entry, and if Dom was there, get him out without compromise. Like I'd told the Yes Man, this wasn't a shoot-'em-up and drag-him-out job. That one, I might just lose – especially when those Turks came legging it down the road to investigate.

The Mini-Ero lay on the bed next to the mags. I'd emptied them to give the springs a rest so they'd have a better chance of pushing the rounds up. If things did go noisy, Plan B called for lots of speed, aggression and surprise. I'd have to get in there, grip him and get us out – whatever state he was in.

I sat down as the girls changed ends or whatever they did in beach cricket, and started to load. I was going to use thirty rounds a mag instead of thirty-two. It was all about giving the springs a bit of leeway. I wished my forearm would give me some. It throbbed as I gripped the mag and fed in the nine-millimetre.

As I was loading the last mag, the room phone rang.

'Hello, Mr Nick. I see you call me, but the noise, I no hear it ring. I sorry. I worry about you in that place. I no want call you because you with your friend, maybe.'

I kept loading with the phone jammed between my ear and shoulder. 'Don't worry about that, mate. Last night was fine. There was no drama and I even got a lift back with the man I was trying to make the reunion with.'

'Very nice, Mr Nick. I go home very happy and wait for your call, maybe.'

'Why don't you come up to the room right now and I'll pay you for tonight's standby? I was going to call you in an hour or so anyway to say don't wait up – just have your mobile next to your bed.'

'OK, Mr Nick.'

I finished the mag and packed the Bergen. The personal phone was clear of Magreb's, Basma's and Kate's numbers. It had to be sterile. I had been running Magreb's number in my head all evening. It was pointless remembering Basma's as well. I'd only fuck the numbers up and wouldn't be able to contact anyone. I knew where she lived. That was enough for now.

I zipped it into the top flap, along with the hotel torch. My jeans and T-shirt went in too, along with the Mini-Ero. The Yes Man's mobile would be staying in the safe with the laptop. If I did find Dom, I was going to keep him to myself until I found out what the fuck was going on.

It wasn't long before there was a knock on the door. I ushered Magreb in, but he clearly felt uncomfortable invading an employer's personal space.

'Here you are, mate.'

He took just one of the two hundred-dollar bills. 'No, thank you, Mr Nick. Tomorrow money tomorrow, maybe.'

I almost had to force him to sit on one of the luxurious armchairs and drink some water. 'Whereabouts on the hill do you live, Magreb? You on that road that goes all the way up to the top?'

He took a sip. 'Not all way. Halfway, maybe. Near United Nation school.' He beamed with pride. 'My children will go school there and be doctor.'

I stood up to let him out and we shook hands. 'Have a great evening with your family, mate, and remember – keep that mobile with you.'

He headed for the door and I jumped ahead to open it for him. He gave me a smile, and I couldn't help noticing that the school-fees savings fund obviously took precedence over a dental plan.

He paused on the threshold. 'Mr Nick, you go where bad people are. But I know you not bad, you kind. I listening for your call, maybe.'

It would have made my night a whole lot easier if I'd got him to drive me up the hill and back down again with Dom. But he was a real person, the sort who had a real job and a real family who loved him. I didn't want to be responsible for fucking that up.

I'd walk from here to the target in local gear, then get changed.

72

TV Hill
Saturday, 10 March
0146 hrs

The lights of the city twinkled below me. Above, the sky was clear and full of stars.

The wind was starting to pick up. It chilled the sweat on my back. I was still in local gear, but hadn't bothered with the Marmite this time. The *shemag* covered my face and I walked with my head down. Kabul wasn't exactly swamped with street-lighting.

A whole swathe of the city around the Gandamack was suddenly plunged into darkness. Even the embassies were affected. Then, one by one, lights came back on as their emergency generators kicked in.

It was pitch black up here, excepting the odd

glimmer from an oil lamp spilling under a door or past the sacks most houses used as curtains. A couple of dogs barked at each other in the distance. Apart from that there was no sign of life as the road wound upwards.

I came across two knackered American school buses, painted white with UNHCR stencilling, parked on a tight hairpin. A stretch of hillside close by had been scooped out to make way for a big brick building. A blue board drilled into the concrete-block wall announced that I'd arrived at the UN school.

Magreb's Hiace was tucked in by the wall. Any of the five or six nearby houses could have been his.

I kept climbing, fingers crossed that his mobile was taped to his ear while he slept.

It was another fifteen minutes before I came parallel with the target house. Not even a pin-prick of light leaked from the boarded-up windows.

The 4x4 was still outside, and didn't seem to have moved.

I carried on past, until I was sure I was out of line of sight of both the house and the Turks on the summit. Either might be on stag and equipped with night-viewing aids.

I slipped behind one of the Russian wrecks and changed. When the Gunga Din kit was back in the Bergen, I prepared the weapon.

A magazine was already loaded into the pistol grip. I pulled back on the cocking handle and the working parts stayed to the rear as I slid it back to the forward position. There would now be a round poking up from the magazine, ready to be snatched when I squeezed the trigger and the bolt went forward. I hoped I wouldn't have to use it. The ejection system was so poorly designed that, with the working parts held to the rear, the ejector-opening became a fucking big hole just waiting to suck in all kinds of shit and give you a stoppage.

I shoved the hotel torch into the front pocket of my trousers and a spare mag into each of the back ones. I felt in my sock for the cash and the Stevens passport. Finally I shouldered the Bergen, pulling the waist strap tight, and held the weapon vertically at my side to hide its silhouette. After a couple of jumps to check for noise, I started back downhill.

My mind was zoned in. The only thing in my head now was getting inside the target. And after that, nothing would matter but getting Dom out.

73

The target house, still in darkness, loomed on my left. Down in the valley, most of the Gandamack district was still plunged into darkness. The only ambient light up here came from the stars.

I walked carefully up to the wagon, bent down and touched its exhaust. It was cooler than the rocks after a day in the sun. A couple more dogs got pissed off with each other further up the hill.

I picked my way along the pathway towards the rear, lifting and lowering my feet in a slow-motion moon walk. I didn't want this to go noisy. There could be half a platoon inside for all I knew.

The back door was dead centre, like the front, with a window each side of it and three across the floor above. I stopped at the first window. It was boarded on the inside by what looked like scaffold planks. Whoever was in here was very determined to keep the rest of the world outside.

A key turned in the door.

I dropped to my knees and brought the weapon up, pushed the safety to its first click and squeezed my hand hard against the pistol-grip safety.

The door creaked open. Torchlight flooded out into the yard.

A shout came from deep inside the house. 'Shut that fucking door – keep the heat in, will ya?' The voice was American, and not sober.

The door opened wider. 'Yeah, yeah, fucking yeah.' This one spoke a lot like me. Joey and I were about to be introduced.

I lowered the Mini-Ero and laid it on the ground, then closed my hand round a rock.

A figure emerged, silhouetted in his own torchlight. His left hand was still on the door handle and he had something clutched in the right.

I jumped to my feet and grabbed whatever I could of him as the door slammed shut. I brought the rock down as hard and fast as I could. It hit the top of Joey's head with a dull crack. He groaned and I pulled him towards me, trying to control his fall. I toppled backwards with him on top of me, my Bergen taking the brunt. A long, matted beard covered my face and his blood trickled into my ear.

Joey was fucked and drowsy but not

completely unconscious. A roll of toilet paper had dropped from his hand and flapped in the wind like a kite tail.

He groaned again as he started to come round. I smashed the rock against the back of his skull, rolled him over and brought it down a couple more times for good measure. The wind carried the sound of his death up the hill.

I patted him for keys, sat back and wiped his blood from my face and ear, then retrieved the Mini-Ero. I took out my torch, stepped back to the door.

Two deep breaths and I eased it open, weapon in my right hand, web pushing against the safety grip, finger on the trigger.

Immediately I smelt cannabis. I brought the torch up to the weapon and gripped it against the barrel so I'd be able to see what I was firing at.

The American kicked off the moment I moved inside. 'Turn that fucking light off, will ya?'

74

The room took up maybe two-thirds of the ground floor. There was a concrete staircase to the right.

I stayed behind the torch. Four sleeping-bags lay on roll mats. Three were occupied. A ginger head stuck out of one. I jerked the beam in his direction and he screwed up his eyes. Noah was not pleased. It really wasn't his night. 'Jesus, will you turn that fucking thing off?' A joint dangled from his lips as he spoke.

The other two bodies looked like maggots and were totally out of it. Scattered around them were syringes, spoons, all the rest of the paraphernalia, and a variety of weapons.

I could have just fired. But I needed to find out if Dom was there and get him out. I'd only deal with these guys if I had to. It would bring ISAF down like a ton of bricks – and, besides, I might lose.

I pushed the door closed with my foot. There was another near the staircase, leading to the remaining third of the ground floor. I headed towards it.

Noah's joint glowed in the darkness.

'Hey, Joey, man! Get me a Mars, will you?'

It was only a makeshift kitchen. No sink or oven, just some bottled water on a table next to a couple of butane gas rings, and a pile of dirty pots. Another table boasted a week's worth of half-eaten food, liberally punctured with dog ends, on a couple of haphazard piles of metal plates.

The torchbeam hit on a box of Mars bars.

'You picking the fucking cocoa beans, man?' Noah definitely had the munchies.

A reply of sorts came from upstairs. Moans and murmurs of pain. A stifled sob.

'Shut the fuck up, cunts, or it'll be beasty-beasty time again,' Noah yelled, then chuckled to himself.

I grabbed a Mars bar and stepped back into the room. I threw it to him, then swung the torch up the staircase.

The wrapper rustled. 'Yeah, go on, Joey. Strut your stuff, dude.'

As he chuckled some more, I followed the torchlight up. The smell was terrible, a mixture of sweat and shit and stale cannabis.

The beam illuminated a bare hallway with a

door left and right. Another at the far end was heavily padlocked.

A pool of water had seeped under the door to the left. I switched off the torch. There was no light from under any of them. I switched it back on.

Weapon up, I stood in the puddle as I closed my other hand round the plastic handle. The moment it was ajar, I was hit by the stench of human shit.

Two naked bodies hung by their feet from the ceiling. One was still alive, though every inch of her was cut and blistered. She was able to support some of her weight by pushing herself up on the back of a chair. She screwed up her eyes against the torchlight and whimpered softly. I didn't understand what she was saying, but I knew she was begging. As I took a step closer, she sounded like she was praying.

Noah heard it, too. His laugh echoed round the building. ''Bout time that bitch learnt a little respect . . .'

The other girl was way out of Basma's reach. She hung like a tongue-dangling carcass in a slaughterhouse. Her teenaged body was covered with black scorchmarks and red blisters. In places, her skin peeled.

75

A flick of the torch revealed butane bottles, gas rings, a kettle. The fuckers made them watch the water come to the boil knowing what was about to happen.

I gave the live girl a slap. I had to make it sound like I'd come up here to carry on spreading the good news. Noah heard the scream and approved.

I left the door open and headed to the one opposite. It opened, but there was nothing inside except a tea chest in the corner. That left the padlocked room.

The keys hung from a nail punched into the doorframe. The reek of shit coming from the other side made me gag. I knew this wasn't going to be a good day out.

The Yale turned and I pulled open the door. The torchlight swept across a huddle of maybe twenty girls, heads bowed, bodies naked, emaciated, bruised and cut. Some were so young they didn't even have pubic hair.

The heads of the two nearest me were swollen from beatings. I pushed them aside. There was no sign of Dom. I moved through the middle of them. All they could see was torchlight, and they were flapping big-time. This wasn't whore-conditioning, this was sadistic shit. These fucks were enjoying this. That was why they were here in-country. They could get away with it.

I left the room and locked them back up for now. It had looked like a scene from a Nazi death camp, or the Idema pictures on the door at the Jock's. The guys hanging, burnt and whipped, the guys in the cupboard, the guy in the . . .

The hanging girl was still whimpering as I ran past and into the empty room. I shone my light on the tea chest.

Noah's laugh rolled up the stairs.

I ripped the nail holding the hasp closed and lifted the lid. The body was big, and white, its skin bruised and battered. They must have jumped up and down on the poor fucker to get him into this thing.

I leant closer. He was breathing.

I put down the weapon and torch, grabbed a handful of matted, blood-soaked hair and pulled. There was a moan. I couldn't make out what he was saying, but it was definitely Dom.

He rasped at me through swollen lips and gaps torn in his once perfect teeth. 'Please, please . . .' His eyes were so swollen they couldn't open.

I tipped the chest gently on to its side and pulled him out. He was cramped into a ball and his joints had locked. He couldn't unfold. Blood and saliva poured from his mouth as his begging went into overdrive.

It was Noah's kind of music.

'Only a few more hours, dude – he's gonna make us fucking millionaires!'

76

I ran back, unpadlocked the other room and threw the door open. The girls cowered in the corner, each not wanting to be the one the torchlight picked out.

'Go! Go! Get the fuck out!' I pointed the Mini-Ero at them, trying to get them sparked up.

A couple of heads lifted and stared. I dragged them out by their hair. 'Go on! Get the fuck out!'

I left the rest to it. They looked too scared to move, but they'd get the idea.

I went back to Dom. He hadn't moved an inch. These fuckers hadn't any intention of releasing him, and he knew it.

The hanging girl managed a scream. I ran to her room and grabbed the chair. She started pleading, wondering what the fuck new kind of pain was coming her way. I climbed on the chair and told her to shut the fuck up.

'Yeah!' Noah liked to hear his mate Joey having fun.

Fighting to keep control of myself, I yanked on the rope knot that secured her to the ceiling hook and tried to break her fall as best I could.

She crawled across and ran her fingers over the dead girl's face. She wasn't going anywhere either.

I stopped in the hallway as the first two girls from the room scrambled towards me. They froze in the torchlight like petrified rabbits and I hurried them towards the stairs.

Dom hadn't moved. I leant down and put a hand on his shoulder. 'Come on, Fat Boy, come on. Dom, get up, we're moving.' I couldn't tell if he recognized the voice. It didn't matter either way. We could have a hug and a love-in later on, when he understood what was happening. I put my arm around him and took his weight.

More naked bodies hobbled past us as I staggered towards the stairs.

Noah had a sudden rush of blood. 'The bitches are getting away, man! Get the fucks, c'mon!'

There was more movement at the bottom of the stairs as the other maggots stirred. 'What the fuck, Joey?'

Dom's body began to unfold as naked, scared but now increasingly excited girls streamed past us to freedom.

Noah was outside, hitting the ones he caught,

shouting at others melting into the darkness. The other two were out of their bags and joining in. It wouldn't be long before they stumbled across the real Joey. It was going to get noisy.

Weapon up, safety grip pushed in by the web of my right hand, I took my time going down the stairs.

'What the fuck . . . ?'

They'd found him.

I waited halfway down, torch up in my left hand and parallel with the barrel, ready to light up the targets.

The first body stormed back in, shoving the girls aside to get to his maggot and weapon.

I waited some more. I wanted the full set.

The other two ran in. The moment they saw them, the girls still on the stairs below me were screaming. I thought my eardrums were about to explode.

I wanted the fourth body, but the other two already had weapons and soon they would have light.

I had to kick off now.

I hit the torch button and caught them both in a tunnel of light.

All I could do was stand my ground and fire, both eyes open, bringing the torch and weapon to bear on their centre mass.

Double-tap.

Double-tap.

It was almost like a range day, and had to be. Otherwise I would make mistakes and die.

Cordite filled my nostrils and the blast of the Mini-Ero filled my ears as I kept on firing into the killing area below me.

A thick cloud of cordite now hung in the torch-light and there was no movement from the bodies. The two bearded fuckers lay at the bottom of the stairs. The black-haired one had died with a sneer on his face; the brown-haired one with a look of utter shock.

I lowered the weapon. The remaining girls needed no second bidding to get the fuck out.

I cleared the doorway and moved outside, but Noah had gone. He'd left the others to it.

I had no time to lose. The Turks would be here soon and I wasn't going to waste time looking for the wagon keys only for them to follow me down the hill.

I ran back upstairs to Dom and gripped his arms. 'Get up! Help me, Dom. I can't do this alone!'

77

'My legs . . .'

He was trying, but not much of him was working yet.

I got him as far as the top of the stairs and had to move down three or four so I could get my shoulder under him and lift.

His feet bounced off each step as I went down. The torch lit the way, sweeping across two dead bodies and one very live one. Noah's massive frame filled the doorway.

'Fucking asshole!'

He ran at me.

I tried to avoid him, but with Dom's weight on me it wasn't going to happen.

He body-checked me. Dom slid off my shoulders as I stumbled over one of the dead and fell on to the concrete, syringe-strewn floor.

Noah threw himself on top of me. He wasn't

bothered about grabbing a weapon. He was going to tear me apart with his bare hands.

'Asshole – fucking gonna die.'

He sat up, his entire weight pressing on my chest. His hands covered my face, then moved to my neck. I kicked and bucked to try to dislodge him, but it was like being trapped under a car. The Bergen dug into my back.

His huge fingers gripped my windpipe. I bucked again as he squeezed. I started to choke. My hands flew up to his wrists but I knew he was going to win.

I jerked my head from side to side.

'Fucking die.' His saliva sprayed across my face.

My hands dropped. My Adam's apple was being pushed deep into my throat and I couldn't breathe.

I felt a stabbing pain in my neck and chest. I thrashed and bucked, but more weakly than before. My right hand felt for a syringe. My brain was telling me to breathe, but I couldn't. I saw showers of white stars and the pain subsided. Not good. I gripped the syringe as the world blurred and faded and my head began to explode.

I focused on his eyes, or where they should have been in the shadow above me.

I swung my hand up and stabbed and stabbed.

He screamed and his scream became a howl.

His hands loosened on my throat as Dom tried to pull him off me.

I kicked and pushed, looking for a weapon in the torchlight.

Coughing and retching, I scrambled to my feet.

Noah swept Dom aside and got to his knees. His agonized screams reverberated round the room.

I spotted the Mini-Ero's muzzle jutting out from beneath Dom's thigh. I grabbed his foot and pulled him away from Noah's flailing fists, then lunged for the weapon. I gripped the safety and squeezed off the rest of the mag.

Noah jerked like a puppet as he took the bursts, then toppled over on to his mates and lay still.

Everything went quiet for a second or two until real life elbowed its way through the door.

I could hear engines rumbling down the hill and hysterical girls begging for help.

I should have moved but all I could do for now was sit. My Adam's apple was still most of the way down my throat. I could hardly swallow.

Dom was moving, trying to curl up and protect himself. I heaved a blood-soaked sleeping-bag from under Noah.

'Help me, Dom. Come on.'

I pulled him up, got him on my shoulder. I threw the bag over him and headed through the door.

A cold wind blew and headlights bounced across the night sky. Searchlights swung left and right from the top of the Turks' vehicles.

I took the path to the right, the one that headed further uphill. I stepped over Joey's body. Light was flooding from the houses about thirty metres away. Contouring the ground with the heaviest weight I'd ever had on my shoulders, I staggered a few paces, stopped, made a fruitless attempt to get the sleeping-bag round him to protect him from the biting wind, and staggered some more.

My ankles twisted on the uneven footing. Dom felt like he was getting heavier and heavier. His legs bounced off the ground in front of me as I tried to shift his weight more evenly on my shoulders.

We made maybe two hundred more across the face of the mountain, still level with the house, and gradually lost ourselves in the darkness. I unloaded Dom on to the rocks. He didn't react. I got him tucked inside the maggot as best I could and zipped it up. I couldn't see if he had his eyes open. There was starlight, but my night vision hadn't kicked in yet.

I crouched down next to him. A horrible rasping noise came from the back of his throat. 'Oi, Drac – it's Nick. Nick Stone. It's over.'

The kidnap might be. But once I had him sorted out there were questions that needed answering.

He moved an arm inside the bag and tried to grab mine through the material. His grip was weak. His lips moved soundlessly. I thought he might be trying to thank me. I patted him through the bag. 'You owe me big-time.'

His breathing became shallow and rapid. A hand snaked out of the bag and tried to grip my shoulder. His chest heaved and tears streamed from his eyes.

The wind whipped the sweat from my face, then forced its way between my wet back and the Bergen. I was starting to freeze.

I looked up at the commotion round the target. The two wagons were static. The house was lit up like an historic monument. Girls were being wrapped in blankets and comforted. Soon they'd be drinking hot tea and getting medical attention.

I eased Dom's hand off my shoulder. 'Let's get you warm, eh? Not long now. We'll be out of here soon.'

I tried to zip him up some more but he was just too big. The top of the bag came up to his chest. I took off the Bergen and dug inside for the *shemag*. I wrapped it round his head, then packed away the Mini-Ero and mags. I'd need both hands to grip him now he was in the bag.

From down in the valley, a long line of flashing blue lights was making its way towards us. The cops would be over the moon. They could take the credit for busting yet another freelance torture chamber, and the dead men were all foreigners.

I pulled out the personal mobile and slipped it into the front pocket of my jeans before re-shouldering the Bergen. I gripped Dom in the nylon sleeping-bag and somehow got him back over my shoulder. 'Not far, mate. If they're not broken, your legs will be working by tonight, no drama.'

I started to pick my way downhill. The blue lights were nearly level with me now. Their headlights splashed across a couple of Turkish armoured trucks and their .50-cal gunners looked as though they'd shoot at anything that moved.

I pushed on for maybe another ten minutes, with the buildings and the road to my right, but I couldn't keep it up. Dom was just too fucking heavy.

I laid him on the ground again and sorted out the sleeping-bag. I held his head and leant in close again. 'Dom . . .' Fuck, I wasn't too sure who smelt worse. 'Dom, I'm going to check the road, OK? I'll be two minutes.'

I slid between two mud houses and made my way down towards Magreb's Hiace. It was locked. So were the two buses. The school was battened down. I needed to get into cover with Dom, and it wasn't just to keep him warm.

The blue lights were still heading this way. In another couple of hours it would be light. Fuck the Yes Man, I'd deliver Dom when I was good and ready.

I moved back to the mud houses and sat under a corrugated lean-to with a pile of plastic bowls and a couple of old sacks. Below me, the Gandamack district was lit up again.

No curtains twitched in either house. Their inhabitants were either asleep or just wanted to get on with their lives and send their kids to school.

I powered up the mobile. It rang a couple of times, but I didn't hear where.

'Hello, mate, it's Nick. I'm going to need your van.'

78

'Mr Nick, I come to hotel now?'

'No need. I'm outside. I'm by the school.'

I could hear movement his end as he jumped out of bed and Mrs M gave him a hard time.

'You in the shooting, maybe?'

''Fraid so, mate. I just want your keys, OK? Can you meet me by the wagon? Keep the lights off in your house, OK?'

'I come now, Mr Nick.'

I closed down and went to the van.

A door opened just ahead and a skinny body in a pullover, trousers and flip-flops joined me. We ducked into cover as the flashing blue lights surged past, strobing the mud walls of the houses as they snaked up the hill.

His eyes widened. 'Mr Nick, your face – much blood . . .'

'Don't worry, mate. It's not mine.' I peeled off

some notes. 'I just want your van. I'll pay you for it. I've got eight hundred dollars with me.' I grinned. 'You could buy three vans for that, maybe.'

He held up his hands. 'Please, Mr Nick, I no want your money. You already pay. I drive you hotel.'

I got down on one knee and fished in my sock. 'That's the problem, mate. I'm not going back. All that shooting up there . . . It was a prison. There were young girls being tortured and raped. My friend was a prisoner too. I came to get him out, and now I must find somewhere to hide him while he recovers. He's been badly hurt.'

I stood up and offered him the money.

'Let me pay for your van. My friend's behind the houses here. I don't want to involve you in this, mate.'

'No. I drive you. I drive you where you want. I you friend, Mr Nick.'

I punched his arm. I knew I was beaten. 'Give us a hand, then. His name's Dom.'

He followed me into the darkness behind the two houses. The flashing blues had almost reached the target. The Turks' searchlights kept sweeping the hillside.

'Mr Nick, I take you to my brother woodstore, maybe. Not far. In valley.' He looked down at the mess in the sleeping-bag. 'Oh . . .'

'Dom, this is my mate Magreb.'

He nodded weakly, then kept mumbling, 'Thank you,' over and over. I wished he'd shut the fuck up.

I turned back to Magreb. 'He'll be all right. Come on, let's get him to the van.'

I slid my hands under his armpits and Magreb took his legs. We staggered down the hill.

'You go to bar to find these bad people?'

'No. The people in the bar were all right.' I nodded in the direction of Noah's place. 'The bad ones were up there. So bad they weren't even allowed into the bar.'

'They dead now, Mr Nick?'

'Yes. Very.' I didn't want to beat about the bush. I needed him to know what he was getting himself into.

We lowered Dom on to the ground when we got back to the Hiace, and Magreb went to open the side-door. 'No, mate. We'd better get in the back and you cover us over.'

He didn't miss a trick. 'Checkpoint, maybe?' He opened the tailgate and we lifted Dom in. I followed and unzipped the bag to cover us both.

Magreb stood motionless at the back of the van.

I reached over and put a hand on his shoulder. 'You sure you want to do this?'

He leant towards me, his expression serious. 'I want my children live in peace, Mr Nick.' He pointed at the building beside us. 'I want them go school, be doctor, maybe. Those bad men, I no want here. I want leave us in peace. You make my home little safer now, Mr Nick. You my friend . . .'

I smiled and gave his shoulder a squeeze before we went into gratitude overload. 'If we're stopped, act normal. Tell them you're going to work, OK?'

He nodded and stepped back. The tailgate closed, immediately sheltering us from the chill wind.

We huddled together in the space between the seat and the back of the vehicle. I held Dom against my chest to give him as much extra warmth as I could muster. His head rested just below my chin. He moistened his swollen lips and tried to talk. 'Peter . . . I did not kill him, Nick. I did not kill him . . .'

The van lurched off downhill and we were catapulted forward against the seats. I adjusted the Bergen lower down my back. 'Who did?'

'You must believe me . . .' His breath was warm and rancid.

'I know about the drugs, the FCO connection, all that shit. But what's so important about the Dublin film?'

'I did not kill Peter.' The boy was on a loop.

'Listen, mate. You need to level with me here. I need to know what the fuck's happening.'

Magreb had spotted a problem. 'Please, quiet, Mr Nick. Police . . .'

I found Dom's lips with my thumb and forefinger and held them tight. I hugged him to me, and tried to shuffle us a few inches lower. I checked that the bag was covering us as the brakes squealed and the wagon came to a standstill.

I could hear radio traffic. It got louder as Magreb rolled his window down. A voice gobbed off in Pashtun and Magreb responded in kind. It sounded like they were having an argument. It's that kind of language. Vehicles stopped, engines idled. The only words I could make out from Magreb were 'Serena' and 'hotel'.

Dom's breath rasped. I pressed my hand over his face as I heard footsteps making their way round the vehicle. A hazy light washed across the rear window and the cheap nylon sleeping-bag. Dom whimpered. I pulled his head more firmly against my chest. It was pointless flapping. There were only two things that could happen. Either they would find us or they wouldn't. All I could do was shut Dom up and wait.

The light faded and the footsteps moved back to the driver's window. There was another short exchange, and the van jolted forwards. We drove maybe fifty metres further down the track and then on to the metalled road. We were soon cruising along the flat of the valley. 'We're nearly there, Mr Nick.'

I lifted Dom's head and took my hand away from his mouth. Dribble poured down his chin and soon worked its way through my T-shirt.

'Siobhan?'

'She's OK. I saw her a few days ago.'

'Does she know I'm OK? Can I talk to her?'

'Not yet. Let's just get to my mate's brother's place, get your head straight. Then you're going to tell me what the fuck's going on.'

'Nick . . .' His stinking breath was just inches from my face again. 'I did not kill Peter, I swear.'

Magreb was getting a bit worried about the waffle. I didn't think he could hear Dom but he could certainly hear me. 'Mr Nick, please, quiet and stay down, maybe. Just few minutes. Thank you.'

We turned off the metalled road and bounced along another track. The brakes squealed and the van came to a halt. Everything went quiet. 'We here, Mr Nick.'

I didn't know why he was whispering. It wasn't as if he had a Stealth Hiace.

The tailgate opened and I pushed back the sleeping-bag. All I could see were huge wood-stacks, maybe fifteen metres high, tree-trunks, branches, bundles of twigs for tinder. I clambered out. In front of the wagon was a collection of corrugated-iron shacks. TV Hill was to our right, maybe a K away. The target was still floodlit and flashing blue like a UFO landing site.

Either side of us were runs of half-finished buildings, exposed reinforcing rods jutting into the starlit sky. A car drove past on the main the other side of the woodpiles.

We carried Dom over the tyre-rutted mud into one of the shacks. The place stank of old woodsmoke. We put him down on a pile of furry nylon carpets that had been spread across a minging old mattress tucked into the corner. Magreb lit an oil lamp. 'My brother get wood. Three days, maybe.'

There was a fireplace of sorts, with a badly sooted cooking-pot sitting on old embers. Hundreds of books were piled in one corner.

Magreb held the lamp over Dom. I touched his arm. 'Listen, mate, I'll get a fire going, heat up some water. You find some good stuff to drink, OK?'

It got him sparked up. 'Of course, Mr Nick. I get food also. I not long.'

As the rickety old door closed behind him I slipped the Bergen off my shoulders, took the lamp to the fireplace and tucked a couple of blankets round Dom.

The door creaked open again. 'Mr Nick?'

'What's the matter, mate?' As I opened my mouth I knew there were just too many footsteps.

The next thing I heard was 'Stay where you are, son – or you'll get it right now.'

I didn't need to turn to do a headcount. Where you had Sundance, you had Trainers.

'Now face me.'

They were both in the room, carrying shorts. Trainers kicked Magreb off towards the left of the shack. He wasn't controlling his fear too well. Dom just kept quiet and still.

Sundance and Trainers weren't interested in him, or even Magreb. I seemed to be the star of the show.

'Don't move a muscle, you fuck.'

A vehicle rolled over the mud towards us and pulled up. The engine stopped and doors opened.

Two more bodies joined us. Mr Sheen and Top Lip stopped for a moment and glared at me, then picked up Dom and my Bergen. Dom tried to put up a struggle rewarded by Mr Sheen with a blow to his face.

Magreb cowered, forehead down, knees up, arms wrapped round his legs.

Trainers covered as Sundance took a few steps towards me, a hand in his jeans. 'What's the matter with you, son? Do you really think you're so fucking clever you can do what the fuck you want?'

He threw something at me. The Yes Man's mobile glanced off my arm and fell to the ground. 'You thought you'd do your own thing, did you, and fuck everyone else?'

There was no point talking to these two but I couldn't resist it. 'If this is the courtesy car, what time's the flight?'

'Shut up, smartarse,' he snarled. 'Don't fuck me about or we'll drop you here and now. Then we'll do that fucking Pole.'

I kept my hands up and started moving. I wanted to get out of the building as quickly as possible. They might forget about Magreb curled up in the corner.

Sundance retrieved the mobile and came up behind me while Trainers moved towards Magreb. 'What about this fucking arse?'

Sundance didn't even draw breath. 'Drop the cunt.'

I swung round. 'He's just a fixer. You saw on Predator, he's no part of this.'

Magreb's head came up, eyes pleading. Trainers jammed the short against his forehead.

It was the last I saw of him.

Sundance bustled me outside to where a white GMC Suburban gleamed in the starlight.

A single shot rang out behind us.

Moments later, Trainers closed the door tidily behind him. He swapped a glance with Sundance and they burst out laughing.

The double doors at the back of the GMC were open and the passenger lights were on.

Sundance gave me a prod. 'They got big plans

for you, son. No quick exit like Sunny Jim back there.'

I hesitated at the back doors. Dom was already inside the vehicle, curled up behind the rear seats.

'Get in.'

Mr Sheen was at the wheel. Top Lip rode shotgun. A thermal-imaging monitor from the Predator glowed in the footwell.

Both Serbs turned and stared at me in silence. It was the kind of silence that told me we were in a bottomless pit of shit.

I lay down next to Dom. Sundance pulled a taser from his coat, pushed it into my stomach and gave me a 100,000-volt helping of good news.

I shuddered for two or three seconds, then blacked out.

79

I lay half on Dom, my cheek against his stomach, and half on the floor of the wagon. A blur of light flashed through the window as we raced past a line of shops. My head spun. My insides still shuddered. Fuck knew what lay in store. But the first chance I got to escape, I'd grab it. Then I'd come back to kill these fuckers for what they'd done to Magreb. And not just maybe.

The GMC smelt as if it had been brought straight from the showroom. My face bounced off Dom and on to the carpet as Mr Sheen threw us into a series of sharp turns.

I moved my hand slowly towards Dom's. He gripped it tight. I hoped it felt as good for him as it did for me.

He tried pulling my head towards his, but he wasn't strong enough. He wanted to tell me something. I pushed down slowly on the carpet with my feet so I could get closer to him.

'I'm sorry, Nick,' he breathed. 'I thought you were with them – the Irish guys. They're the ones that killed Pete.'

'Sure?'

'They dragged us out of the camp . . .' He shook his head and I felt his tears sprinkle across my neck. 'They took us out . . . and they shot him . . . right in front of me . . .'

A voice yelled, 'Shut the fuck up,' and a fist appeared over the back seat and punched us apart.

Occasional bursts of street-light strobed across the vehicle. There seemed to be no other traffic. The automatic gearbox stayed in fourth. We were moving with speed and purpose, and the road was long and straight.

We slowed after fifteen minutes or so and the GMC hung a right and stopped. A gate creaked open. We rolled forward maybe a hundred across rough ground and stopped again. Mr Sheen's window powered down and there was a muted conversation with someone outside. A gate opened with a metallic creak. We rolled another few metres and stopped. Then Sundance and Trainers threw open the passenger doors and jumped out. A gust of freezing air took their place.

The heat had been a security blanket, even for that short space of time. Cold meant shit was about to happen.

Top Lip opened the back. It was pitch dark, but he pulled a pair of blacked-out ski goggles over my eyes for good measure. I felt my feet being gripped and then I was on the move. My hand slipped away from Dom's and I fell on to a pile of rubble.

Sundance said goodbye with his boot.

Two sets of hands grabbed me under the armpits, frogmarched me across a stretch of gravel, then bounced me up a couple of steps. There was no talking but plenty of grunts as they struggled to get through a doorway without letting me go.

I knew we were inside, because the screams and pleading echoed off the walls. I was being dragged along a corridor. I listened for Dom's voice, but he wasn't doing the begging. Unless someone already had his balls in a vice and he'd suddenly become fluent in Arabic.

I could smell cigarettes and kerosene. We halted, and a set of ear defenders was pulled over my head. That meant only one thing. Everything I'd heard so far, they'd wanted me to.

I could feel rough concrete under my boots now. They'd taken me into another part of the building. It was much colder here.

Hands pushed me to the ground, rolled me on to my back and tore off my boots and outer clothes. Something cold and hard bit into my shoulder muscles as a heel pressed against my chest and my boxers were pulled off.

I had no idea of the size of the room I was in, but I was naked and had no control, so the space around me suddenly felt large and I felt very small.

I was hauled back to my feet and swung round. My head slammed against a wall. But fighting back would get me nowhere. I'd only get filled in, and I needed to keep as fit as I could to get us the fuck out of here.

They repositioned me and kicked my legs apart. Then they made me lean forward until my outstretched hands touched the brick.

I breathed long and deeply to slow everything down. I tried to listen, but all I could hear was the sound of the blood pulsing through my head.

My hands went numb, then pins and needles kicked in.

I clung to the only positive thought that came within reach. At least there was a system. I wasn't being kicked to shit – not yet, anyway. I must be in a holding area. I'd probably stay there for most of the time now, between interrogations.

I found the sensory deprivation strangely comforting. Stripped of perception, all I could do was think, and I needed to do that big-time.

One thing was for sure. I'd been totally wrong about Sundance and Trainers. They did travel beyond the M25.

80

I was shivering, and not just from the cold. My muscles trembled from the effort of maintaining the stress position. I dared not move. I didn't want to find out what the punishment was. My sutured arm was aching severely. There wasn't enough blood working its way up there and I wanted to scratch it to death. The pain in my hands had passed the pins-and-needles stage. I knew they'd ballooned. There was going to be permanent damage unless I could relieve the pressure. I moved my left arm a fraction of an inch.

But even that was too much. A massive kick swept my legs from under me. I dropped, knees first, on to the harshly ridged concrete. Pain shot through me. I could feel my skin being forced open by the sharp edges. Unseen hands hauled me up again and slammed my hands back against the wall. I gritted my teeth, tensed my body, waiting for kicks that didn't come. I could feel the blood leaking down my legs.

Some time later they gripped me and pulled me away. They'd been waiting for the last possible moment before something went seriously wrong.

I was dragged off the concrete and back on to a flat, tiled floor. From the smell of cigarettes and kerosene I guessed we were back in the corridor.

We must have come to a door. One set of arms let me go, and the other shoved me between the shoulder-blades. Then both pushed down on my shoulders. My arse and bollocks hit a cold, hard chair.

This place was damp and musty. I could smell it, and feel it on my skin. The floor beneath my feet was hard and wet.

I kept my head down and gritted my teeth. I didn't want anything loose when the punches came.

Maybe a minute went by. They were fucking about, letting me flap.

Then somebody grabbed a fistful of hair and jerked back my head. The goggles and ear defenders were whipped away.

Now it would begin.

A body shuffled behind me. He bent down and shouted, 'Look up!' He was so close I could feel his breath on my neck.

I blinked uncontrollably. The room was lit as brightly as a TV studio. Strings of bulbs hung along the wall opposite me.

Sundance was walking away from me. I watched his brown leather boots and the bottoms of his jeans.

Trainers sparked up. His voice was surprisingly calm. 'You can make this hard or easy for yourself, son. The choice is yours.'

I tilted my head. He was in the far corner of the room, arranging himself a roll-up. Big chunks of plaster had fallen out of the wall behind him. What little rendering was left was covered with grime and various shades of dried blood.

I was sitting on a stackable plastic chair. Dark puddles had gathered across the pitted concrete floor.

My gaze shifted as he brought out his lighter. The door was covered with a steel plate, and had a little porthole that could be opened from the outside. This was looking horribly familiar.

I glanced up at the ceiling and saw a meat hook that hadn't been in the Yes Man's pictures.

The two of them shared a laugh, then Sundance came right up close. 'That's right, son, you've seen this place before. You've been rendered, son. You're a fucking terrorist now, so we can do whatever we want.' He slapped my face hard. 'Never thought you'd be one of those poor fuckers, eh? Next stop Guantánamo for you, son.'

I had more important things on my mind right now. 'Where's Dom?'

Sundance rolled his eyes. 'Getting more of the same.'

The door crashed open and Mr Sheen and Top Lip thrust themselves into the room. Top Lip had his hair tied back, ready for business. Sweat glistened on his forehead. I wondered if he'd been practising on Dom. He reeked of lemon-scented cologne.

He brought in a wooden stool. I admired the scars on his outstretched forearm as he shoved it down in front of me. He had the look of a man who was about to treat himself to a really good workout.

Mr Sheen was holding a device like a matt grey starship. It had three legs and a speaker suspended in the centre. A lead trailed behind him. It looked like somebody was about to make a conference call.

81

One thing was for sure. The Serbs and the Paddies weren't speaking to each other. Mr Sheen gave Sundance and Trainers a look that said fuck off in any language. Perhaps they didn't like smoking in the workplace.

The Irish both took an extra long drag of their roll-ups.

Mr Sheen put the starship on the stool and hit a button. A small red light blinked on.

The Serbs exchanged a glance and stood back, facing me, with their arms crossed.

We all waited. The smoke was making my eyes water.

After a minute or so the Yes Man's voice boomed out from the speaker. 'Why didn't you do as you were told, Stone? Do you really think I'd just let you wander off and do your own thing?'

'You kept the Predator tasked?'

He would have watched our two glowing bodies stumble down the hill and easily followed the Hiace across the valley.

'I've known you for too long not to. Now, consider your answer very carefully. Where is the film?'

I looked at the four of them and shrugged. 'I don't know.'

They were pleased. This conversation wasn't going to end with the call.

'I will ask you again, Stone. Where is the film? I want every copy.'

'What film? I haven't a clue what you're on about.'

'What did Condratowicz say to you on the way there?'

'Nothing. The fucker could hardly breathe. I think he was trying to say thanks, that's all.'

He sighed. 'Stone, I have a very low boredom threshold. I want to know where the film is. If you can't supply that information, then tell me where he's been hiding in Kabul. Who has he met, and why? You're his friend. He would tell you what's going on.'

'He's told me nothing.'

There was a longer sigh this time. 'I'm going to ask you just one more time. After that, I hand you over to the gentlemen in front of you. You've seen the photographs, you know the form.'

Of course I did. And I was scared. But I wasn't going to show it. I'd hide it for as long as possible.

I leant towards the machine. 'I don't know about any film and I don't know where he's been. I just came and found him, as you asked.'

'Have it your way, Stone. I can hold you both indefinitely. You're the one who told me to think of a reason to task Predator. The official view of Mr Condratowicz is that he's been helping the enemy by buying their drugs. That makes him a terrorist. And you're aiding and abetting. So now – final chance – I want to know.'

I stared down at the wet, crumbling concrete beneath my feet. 'Why would he tell me? It would have been Pete he told, if anyone. He was his mate. He was the one who—'

The Yes Man sighed. 'That's it, Stone. We've reached it – my threshold. You've insulted my intelligence long enough.

'I authorize Phase One.' He wasn't talking to me any more.

I stared at the conference phone. The red light died.

Sundance and Trainers headed for the door. 'We'll go see how your mate's new bruises are colouring up.'

Mr Sheen's desert boots squeaked towards me. He stood to my right, ready to beat the shit out of me if I moved. Fuck that, I wouldn't give him the pleasure. The only thought in my head was that Phase One sounded better than Phase Five and a whole lot better than Phase Ten.

He gobbed off in Serbo-Croat. Top Lip moved behind me and grabbed my wrists for Mr Sheen to plasticuff together. They continued chatting, as if they'd suddenly got some spare time on their hands, and couldn't quite make up their minds how best to use it.

The mouthful of saliva that hit my cheek took me totally by surprise. They reached down, pulled me off the chair and rotated me 180 degrees. I opened my eyes, but I didn't need to. I'd already seen the Yes Man's happy snap.

A tabletop with the legs removed had been bolted to an oil drum to make what looked like a party-size see-saw. Two buckets of water stood next to it, beneath a tap set into the wall. A huge roll of clingfilm lay on a pile of empty hessian sandbags.

The only difference between this and the picture was that a sack was already soaking in one of the buckets, ready for action.

82

I knew all too well how this worked. The gag reflex was an automatic reaction. I knew there was nothing I could do to stop it. All I could hope was that they knew what they were doing. That they'd take me to the edge, not push me right over it.

They shoved me, face up, on to the tabletop, my plasticuffed hands beneath me. They threw a thick webbing strap over my waist and pulled tight. My legs were clamped.

I kept my eyes closed. My chest heaved as I fought to fill my lungs with oxygen.

Water poured from the soaking hessian as Mr Sheen lifted it from the bucket. I managed one last big breath before it was pulled over my head. The wet sacking clung to my nose and mouth.

I fought it. I couldn't help myself. I blew hard

from my mouth to try to get the stuff away from me.

The tabletop tilted and my head went down. A bucket of cold water was tipped over the sacking.

I couldn't breathe.

I told myself to keep calm. *You're not drowning! You're not drowning!*

But water poured into my nose and mouth and my body told me otherwise.

Take it easy! You'll be able to breathe again soon!

The seconds ticked by. I needed so badly to take a big breath. My reflexes took over.

I gagged.

Another bucket . . .

My body went ballistic. I tried to kick and buck. My hands scrabbled frantically at the plasticuffs. I was tearing holes in my own skin.

Another bucket . . .

Neither body nor brain could help me now. I gave in. I tried to breathe, and the more I tried to breathe, the more water I took in. I knew I could swallow it but I didn't; I kept trying to expel it, and then I ran out of air. My body jerked like I was being tasered again.

The tabletop see-sawed the other way and my head swung up. They pulled off the sack. I vomited water and bile and struggled to fill my lungs with air. Water poured out of my nose and mouth and snot streamed down my face. I'd never felt such relief.

They know what they're doing. They won't fuck up. They won't let you die. Everything's a reflex. Control it!

I screamed at them: 'I don't know anything!'

Nobody was listening. One punched my face and the sack went back on.

The table tilted again. And so did the bucket.

I was going to die. I wanted to blow out but I couldn't. I had nothing in my lungs to blow out with.

My strength drained like someone had thrown a switch. I had nothing left to fight with. I knew that death was just seconds away.

The table tilted but the sack didn't come off this time. I coughed and spluttered, puking up water and more bile.

Then, a miracle . . .

The straps were released. I slid off the table on to the floor. More freezing water was thrown over me, but I didn't care. The two of them kicked me against the wall. They didn't talk; they didn't need to. When it came to this kind of performance, the Serbs were best-in-breed.

I curled up with my face to the wall, hands still locked behind me. More water cascaded over me. I screamed into the sack: 'I don't know anything!' I started shivering.

I heard voices. One of them laughed. 'More soon, asshole.'

I was treated to a few more kicks in the

back and the sack was whipped away. The goggles and ear defenders went straight back on.

I was off, I was moving.

I kept my eyes closed and every muscle clenched. I'd happily take a beating, if only they didn't put me back on that fucking thing.

They lifted me to my feet and half dragged, half carried me out of the room. We turned right, back along the corridor. My toes scraped and tore along the rutted concrete.

I was pushed to the floor, and the skin on my knees opened up again. Even that pain was bearable now.

I tried to sit back, and immediately got a kick in the ribs. I had to keep my thighs absolutely vertical and my back ramrod straight. My hands were throbbing again.

I didn't know who else was in there. I didn't know if or when I'd be back in the interrogation room. Another bucket of water was tipped over my head. I shivered uncontrollably. My thighs started to shake. My whole body trembled. My back was hurting after the kicking and with the effort of trying to keep it straight. Something had to give. I bent forward a little from the waist to relieve the pain.

Hands grabbed my shoulders and wrenched me back into the stress position. A couple of seconds later, I was deluged with another bucket of water and the shivers took hold.

83

The concrete ridges dug into my raw knees. I had to relieve the pain. I leant forward, but that just changed the angle of attack. I pretended to collapse.

Kicks rained in and I got hauled back into position.

I must have been there for another ten or fifteen minutes. My hands felt the size of watermelons, and pumped so full of blood they were within seconds of bursting.

I was grabbed under each armpit. A knife blade worked its way between the plasticuffs and my skin.

I was moved immediately. I was relieved to be out of the stress position, but dreading what might come next. The worst fear is the fear of the unknown. The stress positions, the cold water, the cold rooms, the holding area with the gravel,

I knew all this technical stuff was designed to disorient me, get me worried, fuck me up. I knew it all and understood it, but it was still breaking me.

I tried to gauge how far we were moving along what I presumed was a corridor. Was I being taken back to the waterboarding room? If I wasn't, would that be good or bad? A new room might be worse. A new room might mean Phase Two.

The hands on my left let go of me, and the ones on my right pulled me through a doorway. My face banged against the frame.

The floor the other side was slick with water. I was turned and shoved down on a hard plastic chair. My hands were plasticuffed to its front legs.

I stayed hunched for a moment, teeth gritted, every muscle clenched. Then I eased myself forward to try to relieve the pressure on my plasticuffed hands. I'd lost all feeling in them.

My world was dark and silent. I tried to kid myself I felt safer that way. That instead of fearing the unknown, it was better just not to know.

Whatever was in the room with me, I couldn't hear it and I couldn't see it.

I could no longer smell lemon, but I could smell the sulphur of a struck match, then burning tobacco, and that was very bad news. These two knuckle-draggers didn't have the skill to cause pain and keep people alive at the same time.

84

The ear defenders and ski goggles were ripped away once more. The first thing I heard, even through the prison walls, was the sound of a large aircraft landing. I kept my eyes closed and stayed exactly where I was.

When I opened them again, Sundance and Trainers were looking at me from the other side of the cell. The speaker stood on a stool between us, its red light on.

We waited.

Sundance bent closer to it, as if he thought that was how you used these things. 'He's listening.'

He and Trainers stood back and each sucked at a roll-up. They were wearing fleeces to combat the cold. The room held their smoke at chest level.

The Yes Man got down to business. 'Do you know what the American vice-president called waterboarding?'

I couldn't be arsed to answer. It wasn't as if it was going to make my situation any better.

'A "dunk in the water", he said. He doesn't believe it's torture. Rather, a very important tool in the fight against terrorism. Do you know what I find incredible about that?'

Fuck him.

'It's that the Americans gaoled a Japanese officer in 1947 for waterboarding a US civilian during the war. They sentenced him to fifteen years' hard labour.'

He didn't wait for an answer. 'The only difficulty I have with the technique is that anyone will confess eventually – even to things he or she hasn't done. But where we want information, not a confession, I consider it very effective.'

The speaker boomed. He must have leant very close to his microphone. 'Where is the film?'

I stared at the floor. The bottoms of the chair legs had probably once been rubber-tipped. The steel had long since rusted from contact with the wet.

'I keep telling you – I don't know. I don't know what, when, who. I know fuck-all about what Dom's got himself into . . .'

'Of course, the problem we face is that some people get so desperate they begin telling you what they think you want to hear. I hope you won't waste our time by being one of those.'

'Look, I know fuck-all . . .'

'Stone, frankly, I've never liked you. You're arrogant, disrespectful and, even worse, you're disobedient. This is your last chance. My two men wanted to beat the life out of you, even before our Serbian friends began their work. But I said no. I wanted you to have the opportunity to save yourself.'

'Maybe I can find out from Dom. Put us together, give us some time. He trusts me.'

There was no response.

First there was total silence. Then I could make out his voice, but only faintly in the background, like he'd turned to talk to somebody else in his room, or take another call.

When he did speak again, there was an edge of triumph in his voice he couldn't disguise. 'Gentlemen—'

Trainers leant forward. 'Aye?'

'I've got the boy. Everything's changed. Repeat, I've got the boy. The Pole is now neutralized. Go and tell him. He'll take you straight to the film.'

'Stone?' Trainers was almost licking his lips.

'I have no further use for him. Kill him. Repeat, kill him.'

The red light went out. The two of them looked at each other.

I dropped my head.

Trainers laughed. 'You'll be more pissed off than that in a minute, boy.'

He moved behind me. The kick to the back of the chair was so hard I shot forward. My arse came right off the edge of the seat and dropped to the floor. The plasticuffs slid down the chair legs.

Sundance savoured the moment. 'Get on your knees and crawl to the board.'

I could hear them behind me, rocking the tabletop, playing with the straps.

'We're going to take you for a ride on this baby. But you should know, son, you're only getting a one-way ticket . . .'

My wrists strained against the metal. I closed my palms round the bottoms of the legs. I eased first one wrist free and then the other. I struggled to my knees.

'That's right, here, boy – walkies!'

I sprang to my feet and grabbed the seat of the chair. Swinging round, I squared up to them lion-tamer style, the chair positioned like a four-barrelled machine-gun.

Sundance's face hardened. 'Don't fuck about, son. You're only going to—'

It was his turn to be drowned out.

I yelled at the top of my voice and charged.

85

My shoulder sent Sundance flying. He lost his footing and tumbled over the waterboard.

Trainers' eyes widened as I hurtled him back against the wall. The tip of one of the legs dug into his stomach. He bellowed with pain and tried to grab it but I pushed as hard as I could.

His muscles couldn't resist any more. The skin gave suddenly, and the rough, rusty tip jumped forward six inches.

Sundance was struggling to his knees.

I let go of the chair. Trainers slid down the wall with the leg still embedded. His gaze was fixed on the entry wound. He looked puzzled.

I leant down and grabbed the wooden stool by one of its legs. The starship flew into the air as I swung the stool down hard on to the top of Sundance's skull. He dropped like I'd tasered him.

I clubbed him again, this time between the shoulders. The third blow smashed into the back of his neck.

His body convulsed like he was having a fit. Blood poured from his head. I brought it down again, crushing his temple. His hands jerked up momentarily, then dropped. He lay very still.

'Bastard! Bastard!' Trainers' cry was half scream, half groan.

He was slumped against the bottom of the wall like a drunk in a pool of piss. His legs were splayed and he'd kicked one of the buckets over. The chair leg still skewered him.

His eyes glazed as he gripped the leg but made no attempt to pull it out. Perhaps the rusty tip was acting like a barb.

I ran the three or four steps across to him and kicked into the seat where he'd had my bollocks just a few minutes before.

The leg jerked back into his stomach and wedged against something hard; his spine, maybe, or the wall. Fuck him. This one was for Magreb. Dark red, almost brown, deoxygenated blood oozed from his guts. I kicked again and again.

I stood over him for a second, my chest heaving. I knew I had to get moving, had to keep the initiative. But I also needed to stop, catch my breath and think. What was the plan? What the fuck was I going to do?

Get Dom, and get out.

Sundance stirred. He was coming round. I went back to him and brought the stool down once more on his head, then again to make sure he was going to be able to keep Trainers company.

I flipped him over and pulled off his fleece. I didn't feel the cold any more – adrenaline and fear had taken over – but I knew I'd need it soon. I pulled off his desert boots, unbuckled his belt and took off his jeans.

Trainers panted in the corner like a rabid dog. He was trying to suck air but his body didn't know how to any more. He'd lost too much blood. His eyes were empty.

I kicked the chair sideways and he slid slowly to the floor.

86

The hinges were on the right. The handle poked out of a hole drilled into a steel plate that covered the whole door. I put my ear to the metal but couldn't hear anybody on the other side.

I glanced back at the two bodies, then eased it open. Bright light poured in from the corridor. It was a couple of metres wide and fluorescent strip-lights dangled from nails and hooks on each wall. All the doors seemed to be steel-plated. Each had a spyhole, a foot-long bolt, and a puddle of water beneath it. There wasn't a sound.

To the right, about thirty metres away, the corridor led to what I assumed was the holding area.

I closed my door behind me and turned left. Sundance's laces dragged in the puddles. I made a mental note of which cell doors didn't have the bolts thrown. If Mr Sheen or one of his mates appeared, I'd need somewhere to hide.

After about ten metres I came to a pair of steel doors that were clearly newer than the building. I threw the bolts and pulled one open a couple of inches. The first thing I heard was a helicopter in a low hover.

I eased the door open some more, and stuck my head out. Sunlight blinded me. Two white GMC Suburbans were parked about fifteen metres away on the far side of a small compound. Beyond them was a pair of large, rickety gates set into a crumbling block wall.

Birds sang. I looked above me. There weren't any windows. It was a low-level industrial building. The paint was peeling and some of the concrete had crumbled away to reveal the rusty skeleton beneath.

I heard the beat of rotor blades and swung my head to the right. A Puma came into view about two hundred yards away, then disappeared behind the wall. As the engines wound down, I could see the top of a pole and a fluttering flag. I couldn't make out the country, but I'd already seen enough.

We were in ISAFland. Which meant we were comprehensively fucked.

87

I rebolted the door and moved back along the corridor, checking the spyholes left and right.

The first cell held an Arab in an orange jump-suit. He'd only been given a blanket and a plastic bucket to piss in. A fluorescent light burned brightly in the ceiling. He sat cross-legged, reading the Koran.

In the cell opposite was a Pakistani lad. He was naked. Burn marks on his back had turned to weeping sores. His beard was long and ragged. He sobbed as he crouched on his haunches in a pool of his own shit.

The next few cells told much the same story. Some prisoners were naked, some clothed. Some had blankets, some lay shivering. One was chained to the wall by his ankles. Most were cut, swollen and scarred. Different strokes for different folks. The Serbs knew exactly what they were doing.

I didn't feel anything for any of the prisoners. They might have been caught planning to bomb the shit out of London, or have killed and maimed young squaddies out here or in Iraq. If some were innocent, that was tough. I couldn't save the world. I wasn't doing that well trying to save one man.

I carried on past the waterboarding room to where the corridor went off to the right. There were five or six doorways each side. I could hear voices coming from the second cell on the left. The door was ajar. A power lead ran through it from a socket in the corridor. A phone cable headed the other way towards another starship lying outside the last door on the right.

I moved very slowly, my shoulder skimming the wall. I'd come to the right place. As I got closer, the smell of lemon became more powerful. I lowered myself to my knees, then flat on my stomach. I inched my head towards the gap between door and frame.

It looked like the crew room. Two empty sleeping-bags lay on US Army cots. A TV and DVD combo sat on a chair in the corner. The voices came from badly dubbed porn. Beside it, against the wall, was a trestle table upon which two pistols lay in leather holsters, the kind you clipped under the waistband of your trousers.

They were Sigs; I could tell by the grips. There was a pile of spare mags. Two mobile phones were plugged into rechargers connected to the extension lead. Brew kit and US Army MREs (meals ready to eat) sat next to a kettle and a half-empty bottle of Jack Daniel's.

I ran in, grabbed one of the Sigs and stuffed two spare mags into Sundance's jeans. I pulled back the top slide to see a brass casing already in the chamber. I pressed the mag-release catch. It dropped into my hand. The mag was full.

I tucked the bottom of the fleece into my waistband, threw the other weapon, spare mags and the two phones down the front of it, then moved back into the corridor.

88

I stepped over the starship and looked through the spyhole.

Dom was plasticuffed naked to a chair, just like I'd been. His face was drenched with blood. I couldn't hear what he was saying, but I knew it wasn't making Mr Sheen at all happy. He raised an arm and gave him a hard, open-handed slap across the face. Flecks of blood flew like sweat from a boxer's face.

It looked like word hadn't reached them yet that the game was over. Or maybe they couldn't resist dishing out a little bit more punishment.

Behind me, in the crew room, the porn had progressed to the heavy-breathing stage. The air was filled with 'Yeah, baby, yeah' as Mr Sheen gave Dom some more. The force of his next punch tipped the chair on to its side. Top Lip leant down to haul Dom up. Mr Sheen's back was turned momentarily to the door.

I checked the mag was on tight, took a deep breath, and barged straight through.

Mr Sheen spun round. The Sig's foresight was focused on the centre mass of his blurred body. I lowered it and kicked off three rounds.

Top Lip launched himself across the two-metre gap between us. He cannoned into me and smashed me back against the wall. We dropped to the floor together and I kept firing.

The room fell quiet. Dom turned his head. His eyes struggled to focus.

'We're getting out. Can you walk yet?'

'I'll crawl, if that's what it takes.'

I tipped him on to his side and pulled the chair legs away from his plasticuffs. He pushed his aching body into a semi-stoop.

'Come on, let's go!'

I grabbed his hand and dragged him towards the door.

As we passed Mr Sheen, Dom raised a blood-encrusted foot to kick him in the face.

I stopped him short. A plan was taking shape in my head. 'No, mate. We need to keep him looking his best.'

I bent down and hoisted the body into a fireman's lift. I staggered for a moment under its weight.

When we got to the crew room the screen was a blur of writhing flesh.

'Grab the whisky off the table!' I leant against the wall. 'And a sleeping-bag.'

Dom wobbled out of the crew room with the bag round his shoulders. I grabbed his spare hand and hustled him towards the exit.

89

We stumbled as far as the double doors.

'Wait here!' I swung the right one open, blinked in the sunlight and staggered across to the nearest wagon. I dumped Mr Sheen in the front passenger seat and belted him up. I tipped some Jack Daniel's down his front, then laid the bottle on the dash tray.

I moved round and opened the rear doors, then ran back and dragged Dom across the compound. 'Lie down and shut the fuck up.'

He pulled the bag over his head as I slammed the door.

I sat in the driver's seat and changed mags on the used Sig, checked the other was made ready, then slid one under each thigh. Mr Sheen slumped next to me. He looked like he'd pissed himself.

I brushed back my hair with my fingers and

zipped up the fleece, hoping the ISAF boys on the other side of the gates wouldn't look at me too closely. I made sure I had a fresh mag handy and hit the ignition.

I stopped two or three metres short of the gates. There were no quarter-circle scrape marks in the dirt this side. They must open outwards.

I jumped down from the cab and put my ear to the steel but heard nothing close by; no voices, no radio traffic, no guards complaining to each other or listening to Radio Kabul.

I pulled back the bolts and eased it open an inch or two. All I could see was HESCOs, tents and flagpoles. They were about two hundred metres away, the other side of the runway. I pushed the gate some more. It opened directly on to a dirt road. There were no guards.

I pushed it all the way, then did the same with the other and ran back to the GMC.

'Good news, mate – I'm pretty sure this joint isn't official. The ISAF set-up is the other side of the airfield. Keep down and keep quiet – I'll confirm in a second.'

Mr Sheen lolled next to me. I reached inside his coat pocket for his wallet. I pulled out a fistful of dollars and stowed them in my lap.

I drove through the open gates and turned left. The checkpoint was a hundred metres or so down the road. It was manned by a couple of old guys in suits, polo-neck jumpers and pancake hats. The drop-bar was two branches roped together and painted red and white.

We drew level. I grabbed a dollar bill from my lap. The old guy accepted the bribe with a nod.

The other guy began to lift the barrier.

He glanced up as he waved the GMC through, and frowned. He stopped the barrier halfway. There was no point putting my foot down. I lowered the window, tilted my head at Mr Sheen and the bottle on the dash, jiggled my wrist and rolled my eyes.

He looked in and immediately smelt the whisky. He shook his head with disapproval and waved the infidels through.

We drove out past the burnt-out shells of buildings. Wrecked Russian vehicles rusted at the roadside. The MiG in the middle of the roundabout still gleamed in the early-morning light.

90

We turned south on to a dead-straight road. Mr Sheen's head bobbed about beside me like it was on a spring. Dom was lying on the back seat. He'd sparked out straight away.

The dash clock said 10:28.

'Dom, get up here!' I fished in the front of the fleece and pulled out one of the mobile phones. 'Up here, mate. I need your help.'

I flicked open the lid. As it sparked up, a picture of Mr Sheen appeared, with his arm round a woman and two little boys making faces in front of them.

'Dom, for fuck's sake, get up! You've got to call Siobhan! Tell her to get out of the house!'

I saw his head jerk up in the rear-view mirror. 'Up here, mate, I need your help.'

He clambered painfully over to the seats behind me, then leant his head forward until it was more or less level with mine. His wounds were open and weeping.

'Listen, the mobile in your front room, in the drawer. You know the number?'

He looked puzzled. 'Finbar's old one. But why does—'

I passed him a phone. 'Siobhan must go somewhere safe. Where? A place you both know . . .'

He thought for a few moments. 'We had our honeymoon in a little B and B up in Donegal.'

'Think proof of life – tell me something just you two know about the place. Did something happen – unusual, funny, romantic – something you talk about even today?'

A smile flashed across his damaged face. 'The hot water always ran out after one bath. We had to share.'

'Dial whatever number you'd normally use for her, then give me the phone. I need to talk to her first.'

TV Hill appeared in the distance, dead centre of the windscreen. Bleached-out buildings lined both sides of the boulevard. We came to a run of stalls and shops.

He handed the phone to me. It rang three or four times before I got a very sleepy 'Hello?'

'Siobhan? It's Nick.'

'Nick?'

'You saw me Tuesday. I just need you to know Dom is safe.'

'Oh, my God—'

'Listen. This call's being monitored. You're in danger. Do you understand?'

There was silence.

'Listen carefully, Siobhan. I want you to leave the house right away. Get dressed, but don't waste time packing or doing anything else. Just grab that grey mobile from the drawer in the living room and any cash you have in the house. Then go and draw as much money as you can from an ATM. After that, don't use the card any more or pay for anything on credit. Don't phone, don't make contact with anyone. You understand?'

'Yes.'

'Don't say the name, but I want you to go to the place you and Dom had to share a bath every day because the hot water always ran out. Do you understand?'

'Yes.'

'Go there, wait, and keep the grey mobile on. Dom will make contact later. It could be an hour, it could be a few days. Do you understand?'

'Yes, but how is he? Where is he?'

'He's with me, and he's alive. I'm going to pass you over. Don't talk about where you're going and don't call this number afterwards.'

I passed it behind me.

High walls, razor wire and floodlights protected the buildings either side of us. Outside almost every one of them was a plywood guard-house. The guards weren't interested in us. They just sat in the shade and stroked their beards.

Dom sobbed bits of his story to her. There were long silences as he tried to pull himself together.

'Dom, end the call. They could be triangulating. Our drama's not over yet.'

Reluctantly, he said goodbye and closed down. He went to hand the mobile back.

I shook my head. 'Chuck the fucking thing out!'

I thrust my hand into the fleece and passed him the other. 'This too!'

The window powered down and I watched them bounce along the road in the wing mirror.

I took the first available left. If they'd been quick off the mark and were tracking the phones, they'd assume we were still heading south, maybe to the Serena.

Where I really wanted to go was west, to Khushal Mena.

91

We drove down narrow residential streets with crumbling pavements, cars, donkeys and carts parked on each side. Dom bounced each time we hit a pothole.

'Where are we going, Nick?'

'Basma's.'

'We can't put Baz in danger . . .'

'Least of our problems. Predator could be up there now, breathing down our necks. We have to get off the streets. And listen, mate. Bad news.' I turned my head to get eye-to-eye. 'The guy who's tracking us? He has Finbar.' I looked back at the road. 'You've got to tell me everything. About this film, about Pete. Tell me what the fuck's going on.'

He gripped my shoulder. 'You think he'll try to get Siobhan as well?'

'Now he's lost us he'll cover his bases, believe me.'

He slumped across the rear seats. I took a couple more turns until TV Hill was to our left and I knew where we were. The market popped up on our right and we drove past the twisted and burnt-out hulk of the suicide-bomber's wagon.

I pushed past anything in the way, hitting the horn to fuck them off, just like this wagon would have done on a normal day.

It wasn't long before I saw the peak of a wood-stack and the reinforcement rods sticking out of the unfinished buildings either side. There were no vehicles parked on the hard mud in front of the corrugated-iron shacks. Magreb would be on the missing list for another three days, until his brother got back.

A handpainted sign at the roadside announced the polytechnic.

'Nearly there. I need navigation, mate.'

'Left here, Nick.' I could smell him at my right shoulder. A couple of open scabs glistened beneath his stubble.

One more junction and we came to Basma's road. I stopped outside the blue wooden gate and honked the horn twice. When nothing happened I jumped out. I could hear women's voices inside.

The gate opened an inch on the security chain. The mesh of a burqa pressed against the gap.

'Basma – *get Basma*.'

She didn't understand me, but I didn't have time to mess about. I shouldered the gate open. The woman ran shrieking towards the house, her burqa flapping behind her. Fuck it, we'd sort out the small print later.

I jumped back into the wagon and drove through the entrance. There was a parking area to the right. A wriggly-tin roof kept off the sun and snow. Under it was a knackered rusty red estate. I drove towards it and stopped just short.

'What is happening?' Basma was bearing down on me. 'You can't just barge in here like this!'

I ignored her.

I leant inside the estate and released the handbrake. With both feet out on the ground and just one hand on the wheel, I started pushing it out.

'Get out of here! Leave at once!'

The 1980s Datsun estate rolled out in a straight line because the wheel lock was on. It didn't matter. I only needed enough room to get the Suburban past it.

'I've got Dom!' I jabbed a finger. 'Get that gate closed!'

She started running, then stopped in her tracks. She ran back to the Suburban and looked inside. 'Oh, my God.'

Mr Sheen's face was pressed against the window.

'Fuck him. He's dead. Dom's in the back.'

I jumped in and drove the GMC under the wriggly tin. 'I'll get him inside – you get that fucking gate closed!'

92

'Was it Noah James?'

Basma helped me get Dom out of the wagon.

'Yeah – close the gate!'

She looked around but there were no pepper-pots to delegate to. They'd scattered to the main house or outbuildings. Washing hung from lines. Smoke curled from holes in the roofs.

Basma caught up with us again as we staggered up the path. There wasn't a stick of furniture in the entrance hall. The cracked and crumbling walls were bare. A naked bulb hung from the ceiling.

Frightened voices echoed further inside the house. Basma left us. 'Poor girls – I must tell them everything's OK.'

The first door on the right was open. 'In here, Nick.'

The bed in the corner had a lumpy mattress covered by a furry nylon blanket with pictures of lions. The old pillow didn't have a case and was stained yellow and brown. The light was fuzzy. The sun had to fight its way through a thick square of muslin over the window.

Dom dropped to his knees and tried to pull up one of the floorboards. His hands scrabbled but his fingers couldn't grip. I grabbed him, sat him on the bed and draped the green sleeping-bag round his shoulders. 'Just concentrate on keeping warm, mate. This board, yeah?'

I worked my fingers into the gap. The board lifted. Beneath it was a black nylon holdall. I lifted it out and took it to the bed.

I had to unzip it for him.

'The laptop, Nick.'

It was among the clothes and overnight stuff.

Basma struggled in with a bowl of water and rags in one hand, a small suitcase in the other. 'This is all I can do until the girls get some more heated up for a bath. We've got antiseptic cream but no antibiotics. The hospital can't give us any – they ran out weeks ago. The Americans have stopped supplies.'

She tried to dab at Dom's wounds, but he was too busy sparking up the laptop.

'What happened, Dominik? How did Noah find you?'

His eyes never left the screen. 'They set me up.

I thought I was going to meet the Taliban. I fell for it.'

She looked up at me hopefully. 'Is Noah dead?'

'All of them.'

She didn't bother to hide her smile. 'Good.'

I turned to Dom. 'Basma told me you were looking for the guy in the Taliban who supplies the Brits with the gear. But which Brits?'

He fished around and pulled out a washbag. Among the kit was a plastic carrier-bag. 'This one . . .'

He unfolded it and produced a memory stick.

The clip kicked off outside what looked like the front door of 10 Downing Street. A tall, good-looking young guy with long blond hair went in with bags of shopping.

Dom's finger hovered over the image. 'Finbar.' He almost choked as he said the word.

I watched as the camera panned up to the top window. An older man in a white shirt stood with his back to the lens. Finbar walked into the room. The older man held him in his arms and they kissed. A few moments later, they moved out of shot.

Dom pressed the soft screen so hard where the older man had last been that the picture blurred. The film cut and zeroed in again on the large black door. It opened. Both of them stood just back from the threshold, talking. The older one had an overnight bag at his feet.

Dom's voice grated with sadness. 'Finbar had come out to us when he was seventeen. Then, after about a year, he was getting into drugs.'

He looked down. 'We tried to get him to rehab, but he just pushed us away. He took to disappearing for days on end. Eventually he told us he was moving in with a friend.'

My eyes hadn't left the screen. Whoever the older man was, Finbar was kissing him again.

'He wouldn't tell us who the friend was, even where he was living. Siobhan was out of her mind. She needed to know he wasn't killing himself.'

He was breathing heavily. 'We eventually found him.' He pressed the screen again. 'Here, in St Stephen's Green. We just wanted to keep contact, try and help him ... Can you imagine how Siobhan felt? Seeing her son smacked up like that ...'

He pulled at his blood-matted hair. 'Finbar finally said his friend was a businessman who came to the city a couple of times a month. Said he was in property development, a firm from London.' His eyes blazed. 'I wanted to see his face, this arsehole property developer from London who supplies young boys with drugs so he can ... so he can ...' He shook his head helplessly.

'You got Pete to film?'

'Yes. He said he was coming on Friday, for the weekend.'

'And who was it?'

'I don't know. That's the bizarre thing, Nick. I had his photograph, but even with all the resources at my disposal I couldn't get anyone to put a name to the face.'

He pressed pause. 'Nick, if I don't make it out of here, I want you at least to have seen his face. I don't know who he is, but I found out he's an immensely powerful man. Maybe you can trace him. I got started before, well, before . . .'

He bit at a scab on his lip. 'Siobhan's father made his fortune in the property boom. You saw our house? His wedding present to us. There's not much he doesn't know about Dublin property. As one line of enquiry, he got his guys to do some digging. The Land Registry showed the flat was owned by a legit UK company, but then there was all kinds of smoke and mirrors with offshore trusts and stuff in the Caymans, Panama, you name it. Everything was shielded behind nominees and God knows what else. They hit a brick wall.

'I had other irons in the fire. I talked to a contact at the Inland Revenue. He came back promptly and said a very strange thing. They said it was unwise to keep digging, it was a government matter. A government matter? What's the government got to do with offshore trusts and property companies?

'Then the wheels really started to come off.

Moira sent us to Iraq, and I had to do everything by phone and email. We'd only been there a couple of days and I got word that the FCO had something for me. Remember when I thought they were going to give me an interview?

'I went to the compound. Basically, the shit hit the fan. I was told my enquiries in Dublin and Kabul had to stop. The whole drugs thing, off the agenda. Just like that. I told them they had no right to tell me what to do. Next thing I knew, those two Irish bastards were in the room. They told me to do as I was told or else.

'The following day I spoke to Siobhan and she said Finbar had gone walkabout again. She was contacting drug outreach programmes, hospitals. Nothing. He'd vanished into thin air.'

His voice trailed off. He was exhausted. It seemed to take everything he had just to hit play again.

I watched as Finbar and the property developer kissed once more, then the older man picked up his overnight bag and walked out on to the street.

He walked towards the camera, until he nearly filled the screen.

It was then that I realized who he was.

93

So much now made sense, and the little that didn't could wait.

We had to get moving.

'Basma, that red estate of yours – it still work?'

Dom jumped in before she could answer. 'Where are you going? To dump the body?'

'No, mate. The Gandamack.'

He made as if to stand, but the old guys outside the war-victims hospital would have got off their benches quicker. He sat down again and started ransacking his bag for clothes. 'I'm coming with you.'

'No. You're fucked. Look at the state of you.'

'Been past a mirror yourself lately?' He grabbed a pair of brown cargoes and shook them out. Basma pulled them over his feet. 'You going to upload the film to him from there?'

'The film? Why the fuck would I want to do that?'

'In exchange for Finbar's life. It's not such a bad deal . . .'

I shook my head. 'That's not the way it works, mate. It's not just the film that's the problem. It's everything that Finbar, you and Siobhan know. To them, Finbar's just a volatile, unreliable junkie. You're a journalist on a crusade. And Siobhan joins the dots. Will he let any of you, or me, stay alive? Will he fuck. It has to end here. Basma – the keys.'

Dom wetted his hair and tried to push it back. He could have had a full day at Champneys and it wouldn't have made much difference. He wasn't going to be back on the cover of Polish *Hello!* any day soon.

I splashed my face with water and tried to sort myself out. The Gandamack wasn't the Serena, but the way we looked we wouldn't even get past the gate.

I pulled a blue shirt from his bag and dumped the fleece. 'OK, Big Boy, if you're in, you do what I say when I say to do it, OK?'

He looked at me for a long time, then nodded.

I went to the rickety old wardrobe in the corner and opened the door. There weren't any clothes on the two or three wire coat-hangers that hung from the single wooden bar, but I wasn't after a coat.

I had to shield my eyes against the sunlight as I hit the yard. I looked up and gave the Predator the finger.

Dom wasn't too light on his feet but he was moving quicker down the path than he had when we'd come up it. I helped him into the back of the estate as Basma reappeared with an armful of maps. 'I'm coming too. You might need Pashtun. You'll have to drive, though. This country might have a new set of liberators, but we women still can't sit in the driver's seat. The police would pull us over. Everyone would stare. The older ones would throw stones. I'll sit in the back.'

I lifted a hand. 'Basma, you must stay here. I need you to make waves. I need you to put the word round that Dominik Condratowicz is going to expose corruption and drug-trafficking at the highest level. And we need you to keep Dom's laptop safe. We'll take the memory stick, but if anything goes wrong, if you don't hear from one of us within seven days, I want you to contact Kate at Dom's office and get the film to her. Email it, whatever she says. Tell her everything.

'And there's one other thing. The guy in the GMC . . . '

She smiled. 'My girls have already taken care of him. There's no shortage of willing hands round here when it comes to dumping men in holes in the ground.'

'Right here?'

'We have a cemetery round the back. We collect suicide victims from the hospitals and villages and give them a decent burial. We're the only ones who seem to care . . .'

I took the keys from her as two pepper-pots hurtled past us. As they swung the gates open I climbed into the wreck of a car and rolled down the window. 'Basma, thank you. But you're wrong about one thing. You're not the only ones . . .'

She leant in through the window and kissed us both on the cheek. 'May Allah protect you. He always makes sure the tank is full, so that's a good start.'

I fired up the protesting engine. 'Yeah, well, let's just hope the Taliban weren't watching, eh? That peck on the cheek could get you stoned to death.'

We started moving.

'And make sure you dump that wagon somewhere, preferably tonight.'

We rolled out on to the street, turned left and headed for the main.

94

Down by the market, the traffic was still paying no attention to the boys in the drunken-sailor hats, and they were still going berserk.

Dom was fighting the urge to nod off beside me.

We passed the woodstacks. We turned our heads in unison to stare at the little shack where Sundance and Trainers had caught up with us. I knew we were thinking the same thing. Magreb's wife faced a bleak future. In Afghanistan, widows are the lowest of the low. Those medical careers were going to be a long time coming.

Dom sighed heavily, and a tear rolled down his cheek. 'I've been so stupid . . . Peter, Magreb, Finbar . . . God knows who else . . . All because of my stupid bloody personal crusade . . .'

I concentrated hard on the road. 'He was never

going to stop until he had the film. Once he'd destroyed that, it was always going to be your turn next.'

Dom stared miserably ahead. 'I thought it would solve everything. When the Irish guys said they wanted it, I bluffed and Peter played along. I said I didn't have it – not with me, anyway. That was when they dragged us out into the desert and shot Peter dead, right there in front of me.' He turned. 'And I still thought I could steal a march on them. Baz's girls had heard rumours about some big drugs deal going down between the Taliban and some Brits. I knew they must be the same Brits the FCO were trying to stop me investigating. I thought if I could make contact, find proof, whatever, I could put everything right . . .'

'And then Noah and his mate snapped you up and decided to skim themselves a nice little earner on the Dublin property market.' I put a hand on his shoulder.

Gym Tonic was coming up on our left. I took a few more twists and turns until we came to a crossroads. On the far side there was a high wall topped with razor wire. To the right I could see TV Hill.

I negotiated the junction and headed left. Moments later, we were passing the computer shop. I waited for a couple of workmen carrying buckets of rubble to get out of our way, then pulled up outside the pedestrian door to the right of the Gandamack gates.

'Stay here, mate. I won't be long. Ten minutes max. Any longer than that, take the car and get yourself back to Basma's. If I don't show up by tomorrow, get on the first plane out. You'll have to do it all on your own.'

I gave the gate a couple of punches. The slide was pulled back and a set of fiery Afghan eyes wanted to know what the fuck I wanted.

95

I gave Mr Winter Warfare a big smile, and as the door swung open I got a big row of brown teeth back. He was still dressed in the thick black polo-neck jumper, with even thicker stripy tank top. Five or six dusty 4x4s were jammed against each other in the courtyard. I followed the gravel path across the garden to the concrete steps.

I was hoping the reception desk would be unmanned, but the lad in the white shirt was right behind it, all smiles, a model of efficiency. I walked past the rack of Martini-Henrys. 'Hello, mate – everything good?'

'Yes, thank you, sir.'

'I'm looking for a guy I did some business with a few nights ago. Local, mid-thirties, clean-shaven, dresses quite Western – polo shirt and jeans. He was wearing a navy ball cap . . .'

His face lit up. 'Kellogg, Brown and Root?'

'That's the one. Could you do me a favour? Go and check if he's here? I said I'd meet him in the Hare and Hound, but I'm expecting a call and I don't get a signal down there.'

'Certainly, sir. Two minutes.'

'As long as it takes, mate.'

He headed past the weapon racks and back outside towards the steps that led to the basement.

If the fixer really was there, I'd consider taking him with us. A Pashtun speaker might come in handy. If I'd been on my own, I would have driven as close to the border as I could get without having to go through any checkpoints or controls, dumped the car and taken off on foot. I knew these mountains – not as well as the muj or the Taliban, perhaps – because I'd crossed them many times. But I had a semi-cripple in tow, and a seriously ticking clock. We had to get to an airport in Pakistan as quickly as we could. We didn't have any time to play with.

I'd become the world's greatest Martini-Henry admirer all over again. I went to the rack and almost caressed them as I pulled the coat-hanger from my pocket and straightened it out.

I checked the corridor for bodies and CCTV before realizing my bootlaces needed retying. I bent down, slid the wire behind the rack and fished. The slim bundle was where I'd left it. I grabbed my Nick Stone passport and ten hundred-dollar bills.

The young receptionist reappeared, shaking his head. 'He's not in the bar, sir. Can I take a message?'

I gave him the biggest grin I could manage. 'Tell him I was here, but I left early.'

I walked back to Basma's car.

96

Dom hadn't wasted his time. He'd wrapped a *shemag* round his head to hide his blond hair, and was studying the map spread out on his lap. He'd obviously done his stuff. 'Couldn't be easier, Nick. It's east on Jadayi Suhl, then a left when we hit Jadayi Awalimay. It's main road all the way to the Khyber Pass. A hundred miles, tops.'

I gunned the engine. 'It'll be a fucking sight less than a hundred if we've got a Predator over-head.'

I reversed down the alleyway and on to the street.

'How can we tell?'

'We can't. First we'll know about it is either ISAF putting in a flying roadblock up ahead, or a Hellfire missile up our arse.'

'Up the Khyber?' He grinned. 'Either way, nice

knowing you, Nick. And I still haven't thanked you . . .'

'Later, mate, later.'

We passed Flower Street. It was packed.

We drove through the embassy area and past the compound protected by the sangar. I was tempted to stop and ask the big lads hitting the weights inside if they cared to come and ride shotgun.

A couple of Toyota flatbeds screamed past, with four or five police on the back of each, weapons pointing out. None of them gave a fuck about a battered red estate.

We passed the high walls and razor wire that surrounded the British embassy. The barrels of SA80s paraded back and forth behind the sandbags. Nine times out of ten this would have been a safe haven. We could have driven to the barrier, declared ourselves, and the ordeal would have been over. But right now some of the grey men behind those HESCOs wanted us dead. How many? I wondered. How far and how deep had this thing spread?

The estate lurched across a pothole and we bounced in our seats. We came to the main. I turned left, heading north.

Dom tapped the map. 'This parallels the airport road for a while, then veers north-east, then east.'

'About a hundred and sixty K max, right? You

might as well get your head down, mate. Fuck knows, those scabs of yours could do with some beauty sleep. But a few things first. Assuming we get over the border, Islamabad's about the same distance the other side. We'll get flights from there. We'll go separately. You take British Airways, I'll take any other carrier I can. It'll make it harder for the Yes Man to lift us both. He has to do that to control the film, and it'll be easier and cleaner for him if he can do it this side of civilization.'

Dom started to settle. 'The Yes Man? The guy talking to me in the cell or the one with Finbar?'

'Both, mate. They're the same man. Listen, I know him. I knew the two Irish guys too. I don't know his name, never have, but I know he's dangerous, smart and doesn't give a shit about anyone.'

He sat up, ready to question me to death.

'Not now, mate. We've got too much real shit to deal with. Now . . .' I paused as he settled down again. 'Once in Dublin, we'll aim to be at Bertie's Pole at nine a.m. every day for three days. If neither of us turns up in that time, we have to assume the other's been lifted or something's gone wrong. You got that? I'm saying it now in case there's a roadblock round the next corner and we get separated. If we do, then, yeah, it was nice knowing you, too. Who shall I send my invoice to? You or Moira?'

He grinned. 'Moira, definitely. Then me, once she's rejected it.' His grin faded as a new thought came into his mind. 'Nick, there's a real complication to all this. The Yes Man and his team didn't ship their heroin into virgin territory. There's a turf war going on in Dublin, and it's him who sparked it.'

'PIRA won't be liking that one little bit.'

'Haven't you heard, Nick?' He raised an eyebrow. 'PIRA have been disbanded! They've handed in every single weapon they ever had and taken up landscape gardening . . .'

If his aching jaw had let him, he'd have laughed as hard as I did.

'A turf war is the best news I've had all week. It's going to help us get Finbar back. Now grab some kip. I'll wake you when we get to the border and I need your wallet. It's the most corrupt spot on earth. Last time I crossed here it cost a hundred bucks.'

I wasn't sure he'd heard the last bit. His *shemag*-draped head was banging against the window and he was snoring like a chain gun.

I checked the dash. The clock said it was midday. We had a full tank, and that was plenty for the distance we had to cover. We'd be going at a fuel-efficient pace anyway because I didn't want to be conspicuous or get involved in even the slightest accident.

There was nothing much else I could do now but resist the temptation to search for Predator-shaped specks on the horizon.

PART FOUR

97

Herbert Park, Dublin
Tuesday, 13 March
1017 hrs

Dom was standing at the kitchen island. He was on his fourth call and his third coffee since we'd arrived at the house an hour ago.

We'd met up that morning at Bertie's Pole, as arranged, then jumped into a cab and headed straight here to flush out the Yes Man.

We still had our coats on. We weren't staying long. I had a fake leather three-quarter-length number I'd bought in Islamabad, a really good pair of rip-off Levi's and a shirt. The whole lot had come to all of about twenty dollars.

'That's no excuse, David.' Dom was in short, sharp, aggressive, don't-bullshit-me-I'm-the-Polish-Jeremy-Paxman mode. He wanted results.

'He's still missing. You said you'd move heaven and earth. I've been a good friend to you and the police in the past, given you good coverage. Now you've got to start helping me.' He slammed his thumb on to the red button. Inspector David of the Gardai was a golf mate – or had been before this call.

Dom had called in another set of favours all over town. He and Siobhan had already hassled every man and his dog to find Finbar; they'd hit drug outreach programmes, fellow reporters, anybody with influence. Now he was calling them all over again. We wanted those ripples to spread. We wanted to spark up the Yes Man and bring him out into the open. The lines would still be monitored, and there'd probably been a trigger on the house from the moment he'd seen we were flying into town. That was just what we wanted. He knew where we were, and now he thought he knew what we were doing.

The only person Dom didn't call was Siobhan. He'd done that from a call box in the city. She was fine and well holed-up, although if she took more than one bath a day it was cold. She must have left the house as soon as I'd called her. There was half a plate of scrambled egg on the side. It was congealed and rancid, but the flies seemed to like it.

Dom put the phone back into the charger, put

his cup under the espresso spout and threw in another capsule.

'Well done, mate. He'll have followed us since we took off for Islamabad. Now we're back together and searching for Finbar, he'll show his hand.'

The Yes Man would want us dead, but it wasn't going to happen in daylight on a residential street. Drive-by shootings of prominent newsmen or bundling people into vans without anyone noticing were the stuff of bad TV shows. This wasn't Kabul. He would pick his moment, and it would be soon.

'He's like a human Predator, all-seeing, all-hearing. Any time now he'll aim to take us out. But we'll be waiting.'

'Then what?'

'This story can only have one ending, mate. Even if the plan works and we find Finbar alive, he's never going to stop. You, me, your family, we're in the shit – big-time. So we've got to nail the Yes Man, and to do that, we have to bring him to us.'

I unrolled the first of the three twenty-metre extension leads I'd bought in O'Connell Street. I ran it out to the end of the reel, then cut it away so I was left with the plug at one end and three bare wires at the other. 'Where's your broom cupboard, mate?'

He showed me. I grabbed a mop and a couple of long-handled brushes.

I unscrewed the heads and took the sticks over to the roll of gaffer-tape and six forks waiting on the island.

I scored the plastic sheath of the three-core cable with a pair of kitchen scissors, then peeled away about six inches of the plastic. I left the earth wire intact, but exposed about the same amount of the live and the neutral. I twisted each round a fork, and bound them with tape for good measure. By the time I'd repeated the whole procedure with the other two extension leads, each of the three twenty-metre lengths of cable had a pair of forks dangling from its end.

I grabbed a headless broom handle and taped a fork either side of one end, making sure the heads curved outwards. I didn't want current arcing between them; I wanted it zapping into a target and fucking him up big-time.

When all three poles were ready, I picked up my coffee and gulped it back in one. We had to get moving.

He'd watched me fuck about with broom handles and cutlery with a look of deepening gloom. I slapped him on the shoulder, trying to cheer him up a little. 'He might be like a fucking Predator, but we've got some tricks up our sleeves, you and me.' I grinned.

Although we'd have the PIRA weapons, I wouldn't want to risk using them immediately. If we killed the men who came after us, their information would die with them.

We'd have to be a bit careful with my home-made tasers for the same reason. The commercially manufactured ones contain a step-up transformer that produces a short burst of high voltage to catapult a small amount of current. The domestic electricity supply uses a much higher current, pushed by a lower voltage. Tasers aren't designed to kill, but ours easily could. We'd be wiring our targets into the mains.

'A two-second prod will be enough to drop anybody.' I headed for the door. 'Another two seconds and they won't get up. It'll fuck them up worse than a badly earthed fridge.'

Dom hesitated at the island. His knuckles whitened as he gripped the edge of the worktop.

'I know you're worried about Finbar, mate. But that ain't going to get him back. Come on. She's waiting.'

98

We sat in the lobby of Jury's Hotel with three nice frothy cappuccinos. We'd taken a cab back to Bertie's Pole, then continued on foot, doing anti-surveillance all the way. We'd wandered through a shopping precinct and bought two pay-as-you-go mobiles, circled a block, stopped in the middle of a couple of streets and doubled back on ourselves. We'd ended up in a florist's, bought a big bunch of red and white roses, then left by the rear exit. The Yes Man could get his eyes back on us later. For now, we didn't want anyone to see who we were meeting.

Kate was sitting next to Dom on the sofa. She was even more excited to be out of the office doing something secret for him than she had been with her flowers. This was her chance to prove she could make it.

She handed me a folder. 'The file is on

Councillor Connor McNaughten. I called his office first thing, and told them about the new programme.'

'What's it called?'

'*Dublin Let's Go*. That's what I told him, anyway. His office phoned back within the hour saying yes, he'd be delighted to be interviewed. I said one thirty – is that OK?'

She looked at Dom, but I jumped in. 'Great job, Kate. When you get back to the office, could you ring them back and say there won't actually be any filming today? Dom just wants to come over and talk round the idea, get it fixed in everyone's heads. We'll probably bring the cameras along on Friday, at some city location. You know, dramatic backdrop, that sort of thing. Can you do that? I don't want them expecting men with furry microphones and all that shit.'

She nodded and drank the last of her cappuccino.

Dom handed her the flowers. 'Katarzyna, Moira doesn't need to know what's happening yet. It must stay completely secret until we have the foundations of the story. Once that's done, I'm going to make sure you're on my team and not sitting at her beck and call any more.'

She smiled her thanks to us both. The thought of not working for that bitch must have been the best news she'd had in weeks.

I stood and shook her hand. 'Thanks, Kate. You've been fantastic.'

She left and we sat down to finish our brews.

Dom's brow furrowed. 'What's the score if we didn't shake them off? Aren't we putting her in danger?'

'Even if they follow her back to the station, all they'll want to know is what she handed over. They're not going to compromise themselves by lifting and threatening newsroom staff. They're pond-life, mate. They'll want to keep all this down in the weed.'

He took another sip and wiped the froth from his scabby top lip. We still looked like a couple of crash victims but, fuck it, there was nothing we could do about that. And on the upside, it meant Dom wasn't getting recognized every time he turned round.

'What now?'

I flicked through the printouts in Kate's folder. Judging by the number of representatives they had on the city council, Sinn Fein must have pulled out as many stops down here as they had up north. Connor was thinner and greyer than he had been when I'd last seen him. His picture showed him in the classic shoulders-at-forty-five-degrees-to-the-camera pose. He was doing his best to look like everyone's favourite uncle, and his best wasn't good enough.

It was no surprise to me that he'd switched

careers. Former terrorists were turning into statesmen everywhere on the planet. Israeli bombers killed British soldiers on the streets of Jerusalem and were rewarded with invitations to dinner in Downing Street. The ANC was a proscribed terrorist organization, then went on to run South Africa. Even Hamas was now the voters' friend. At this rate, it was only a matter of time before bin Laden became secretary general of the UN.

The Peace Process had produced the same result in Ireland, but that didn't mean everything in the garden was rosy. Even before 9/11, when the Americans had their first really big taste of the realities of terrorism, the IRA hadn't just raised funds in Boston and New York from tenth-generation Irishmen who thought that PIRA were freedom-fighters who played the fiddle in pubs in their spare time. They'd also made a fortune domestically from gambling, extortion, prostitution and bank robbery.

But their biggest earner had always been drugs. The police and the army were too busy getting shot at and bombed, so there had been no one around to stop it. The IRA kneecapped drug-dealers periodically as a public-relations exercise, but only as a punishment for going freelance.

Gerry Adams and Ian Paisley might now be having a kiss and a cuddle at Stormont, and Martin McGuinness might be the Minister of

Education, but deep down in the belly of the island, old habits died hard. There was just too much money at stake and they didn't want anyone else muscling in. Drugs were their big thing. They'd been running the trade for the last thirty-odd years. And it was even easier to cross the border now the army checkpoints had gone.

I closed the folder. 'First you buy me some decent clothes, then we clean ourselves up here, bowl along to City Hall and ask Councillor McNaughten to help us find Finbar.'

'Easy as that? What are you going to ask him? Why don't you tell me, Nick?' Dom's frustration was plain to see. I hadn't told him what I was planning, and I didn't intend to.

I smiled. 'Connor and I go back a long way. He'll help us, believe me.'

'But how?'

I stood up, ready to go. 'Whichever way I want him to. Come on, let's get sorted out. It'll give whoever's following us time to pick us up again.'

99

We were being followed. The green Seat MPV was three behind us, but I couldn't tell Dom yet. If the driver of the cab taking us towards Donovan O'Rossa Bridge was the excitable sort, he'd either drive us off the road or pull up by the first cop he saw.

It was very shoddy surveillance. The two of them bobbed about non-stop, trying to see where we were. They buzzed in and out of our lane to check we were still ahead. They couldn't have been more obvious if they'd tried. In fact, they were so amateur I wondered if they were doing it to scare us. I didn't care: it was good news either way.

I leant towards the driver. 'Tell you what, mate, if we pass a newsagent, could you pull over?'

He stopped almost immediately outside a

Spar. I nudged Dom. 'I'm getting a paper, mate. You coming in?'

I didn't bother to look at the Seat as it passed. Dom was soon up alongside me. 'What's happening?'

'We've got a tail.' We walked into the shop and I pulled a copy of *An Phoblacht*, the Sinn Fein weekly, from the rack. The front page was one big picture of Gerry Adams walking out of a polling station under the headline 'Ready for Government'. I waved it at Dom as I headed for the counter. 'I've been in this a few times myself. Not by name, of course.'

He wasn't sure if I was joking. 'How do you know?'

'We'll soon confirm if they pick us up again. Don't worry, it's a good thing.'

The green Seat soon slipped in behind us once more, and stayed glued to our rear bumper all the way to Wood Quay. As we got out, they moved slowly past us and I made sure they knew I'd pinged them. The driver wore a black nylon bomber jacket, his passenger a green one. Both had dark, very short hair, just one above a crew-cut.

They'd made the wrong choice with the people-carrier: they looked seriously out of place in it. It was a vehicle for mothers with baby chairs and screaming kids off to football practice, not two hard-looking mass murderers packing out the front. But I knew why they needed it. They planned to pack out the back with the two of us.

Dom paid off our cab and it nosed out into the traffic. We walked up to the steps. 'Fuck me, mate, they're either Loyalists or Aryan Brotherhood – not that there's a shitload of difference.'

Concern was etched all over Dom's face. 'Why did you give them the eye?'

'We want to flush out the Yes Man, and we've got no time for finesse. I want him to know that we know he's on to us, so he realizes the clock's ticking.'

We reached the main entrance to the council offices and I tapped Dom's shoulder with the rolled-up paper. 'The Yes Man will be racking his brains trying to work out what we're up to. But he won't leave things to chance indefinitely. As soon as he sees we're alone, and it's quiet, he'll come for us. There's a good chance it will be tonight – so we've got to be ready for them.'

We pushed our way through the glass doors.

'Why do you call him the Yes Man?'

'Because it's the only word he ever wants to hear.'

We were in the foyer of a grey, four-storey 1980s concrete and glass building. The reception area was a sea of disabled access and no-smoking signs and earnest, probation-officer-type faces.

Big posters celebrated the fact that Dublin kids were painting for Africa and that the council were friends of clean air, leading the way in bio-fuels and zero emissions. I felt healthier just standing there.

I read the paper while Dom did his stuff at the desk to a very smiley woman who was on the brink of asking for his autograph. Armed with little laminated passes, we took the stairs to McNaughten's office on the first floor.

'Keep quiet once you've done the intro-ductions and I start waffling, OK? He won't say much.'

A prim, middle-aged woman in a red cardigan sat at her desk outside the room we were aiming for. There was something almost regal about her, even though she'd spent most of her life working in a corridor.

Dom greeted her warmly, and it was all going very well. She'd been expecting us; she ushered us straight in.

The furniture was functional and the windows double-glazed. Pictures along the wall showed Connor shaking hands with Gerry and Martin. A framed Sinn Fein poster hung alongside the Irish flag.

Our boy stood up behind his desk, hand extended. 'Mr Condratowicz, nice to meet you.' His accent was straight out of the Falls Road, even though it had been softened by a few evening classes in democracy and public relations. Most of them had education, these days, now politics was the way ahead.

They shook and Dom introduced me as his producer. We shook too. His brain was already whirring. He knew he'd seen me before; he just didn't know where. He would soon enough. You never forget the faces round you when you think you're going to die.

Dom turned on the small-talk. 'Sorry we're a bit bruised. We were involved in a car crash last week.'

McNaughten lifted his left hand to show off his missing pinkie. 'That's how I got this.'

I smiled at him and he did a double-take. He looked just like his picture on the Sinn Fein web-site. He was dressed straight out of Matalan, with a polyester tie and just enough nylon in the mix of his grey suit for it to shine under the fluorescent light. Dress Sense 101 was obviously one of next term's modules.

He overplayed a desk-tidying routine, then took another glance at me. 'We're proposing new traffic-calming measures at the next meeting. Something really has to be—' He frowned. 'Do I know you?'

I took a step forward. 'Last time we met, you were in the boot of my car on the way up to Castlereagh for the night. Then I read you your horoscope. You came back minus that finger, remember? Car crash, my arse.' I threw the paper across the desk. 'You might be Mr All-green-and-biofuelled-up now, mate, but the old ways are still snapping at your heels, aren't they? I see white-and-above-board Sinn Fein's Seamus Quinn was sent a bullet in the post. What did he do to deserve that? Propose a congestion charge?'

He sat back in his chair, not fazed, not worried, just watching me. 'I'm mistaken. I do not know who you are, and I do not understand what you are talking about. Have you come to threaten me? I would like you to leave.'

I leant forward, my eyes locked on his. 'Connor, mate, I don't give a shit what you'd like. Your only job right now is to listen. This man here, his son is in the shit. You're going to help me get him out of it.'

It was his turn to lean forward. He was about to deliver his enraged-politician bit and fuck us off. He took a deep breath and aimed his right index finger at me.

'Stop.' I stared him out. 'I don't have time to fuck about, so do as you're told or I'll cut that one off as well.'

He looked at his watch and sighed impatiently, trying to make it seem like he was going to give us five minutes of his precious time. But it was a bluff. I knew that, deep down inside, he was flapping.

I pointed at Dom. 'His son has been taken

hostage. We know who's done it, but we don't know where the boy is. You're going to help us – not because I'm going to make you but because when you've heard what I have to say you're going to want to.'

I sat back, letting things calm down a little now I had his full attention. 'This drugs turf war – wouldn't have happened in your day, would it? Not on your own fucking doorstep. But times have changed. The boys that are stepping on everyone's toes are not only Brits but one of them is working for the intelligence service. And he's using UDA dickheads as enforcers.'

I gave it time to sink in. 'You're interested now, aren't you?' I could see it in his eyes. 'You give me what I want, and I'll get rid of them for you. I don't give a shit about who sells what to who – all I want is my friend's boy back.'

I waited for questions but he was too clever for that. He wasn't going to incriminate himself in any way. We might be recording.

'You get me weapons,' I said. 'I want two assault rifles and at least three mags each.'

I reached for his pad of pink Post-its and a pen, then wrote down my new mobile number. 'You sort it, get your people to call me, and I'll collect. Once I'm done, you can have the fucking things back – along with a body or two that can still talk. If you try to fuck me over, make sure you do a good job, because if you don't I'll come back for you.'

He didn't touch the Post-it, or even look at it. He didn't move a muscle. His voice became very clear and very slow, just in case we did have wires. 'I have no connection with anyone involved in drugs, or the now disbanded IRA. I am a councillor of a political party.'

I started walking to the door and Dom followed.

'I don't know any members of the old IRA and I don't know any drug-dealers.'

He was still issuing denials as we closed the door behind us.

Dom said nothing until we'd got out on to the street. 'Tell me about the finger.'

'Let's get a cab to the centre and lose our big green Seat. Then I'll explain while we wait for a call.'

We found our way to a taxi rank.

'By the way,' I said, 'I'm assuming you did national service?'

100

We paid off the cab in O'Connell Street; it was the main drag and there were plenty of shops to get lost in. The Seat was still behind us. It had followed us all the way in. At least the boys in the bomber jackets had learnt not to pass us when we stopped, so we didn't get any more eye-to-eye.

We walked down a little lane and straight into a coffee shop. I checked left as Mr Green jumped out and Mr Black drove off to try to find a parking space. Sundance and Trainers had been brain surgeons compared to these two.

I sent Dom to buy some more cappuccinos and went straight upstairs to grab some seats with a view of the street. It wasn't long before the two of them connected on the pavement below me. Mr Green got on his mobile, eyes darting left, right and centre. He wasn't wearing his happy face; he must have been trying to explain how they'd lost us yet again. Then there was lots of nodding; I guessed they were being told to go back to the house. Dom and I had gone in with bags and come out without. Chances were, we'd go back at some point.

They disappeared as Dom arrived with a tray.

I told him about Connor's pinkie, and about the Yes Man and why I knew him. I told him I'd worked for the Firm and been fucked over so many times by the man that I felt like a relation, which was why I knew what he was planning. I wasn't too certain whether it reassured him or not. But, fuck it, he'd wanted to know.

It only took another forty or so minutes before my mobile kicked off. The voice was from the Falls Road again, but this time without the evening classes. 'I hear you want to pick something up . . .'

'Yeah.'

There was a slight hesitation: he'd pinged – and didn't like – the accent. 'Sheriff Street Estate. Wait outside the Mace mini-market. Someone will pick you up.'

'There's two of us.'

Dom hated being out of the loop. He was straining to listen in, but music was playing, people were gobbing off.

'No fucking way, son. You come alone.' The voice was clipped and abrasive.

'It's two of us or nothing. You know what I'm doing for you cunts. We're both in black jackets and jeans. How far is that from O'Connell?'

'Twenty minutes.'

There was no way we were going to split up now. We had to keep together, and in the open. It was the only way to stay safe.

'Sheriff Street Estate – you know it?'

Dom nodded unenthusiastically. 'Everybody knows it. It's north. I can already smell the burning tyres.'

'Time for another cab, then.'

Five minutes later we were following the route out of town. It was rather nice and clean to start with, but slowly and surely we were getting to the parts the EU subsidies hadn't reached.

The taxi dropped us off at the mini-market and the driver took off like a shot the moment he had his money.

The area was a morass of grimy brown blocks of flats, probably thrown up immediately after the war. They must have seemed like paradise when they were built, but now it was like the Tabard in Bermondsey, a drug-ridden dumping ground.

The Mace store had filthy windows and peeling paint. It was protected by mesh panels and secured with rusty padlocks. According to the poster behind one of the panels, there'd been a drug-related shooting of a schoolgirl there last week and the police were desperate for information.

The burnt-out remains of a Ford Escort stood at the kerb.

Scabby dogs ran along the pavement with scabby kids. Some of them kicked a ball, some just screamed at each other.

Teenagers hung around in threes and fours. They were probably dealing. They looked us up and down like they wanted to know what the fuck we were doing on their turf.

Dom leant against the mesh and tried to make light of it. 'I don't think this'll get much of a look-in on *Dublin Let's Go*, do you?'

'*Dublin Let's Get Fucked*, maybe.'

Two women came out of the shop, gobbing away at a million miles an hour. They stopped and stared. Either they didn't know our faces or they didn't like what they saw. They stood there for several seconds, then walked on without a word, their paper bags full of frozen shit in a tray for their tea.

I felt quite at home there. Maybe that was why I'd always got picked to fuck about in places like the Bogside, running round trying to find ASUs and their weapons.

It wasn't long before two older men rounded a corner and came up the road towards us. They wore black leather coats, gold chains round their necks and cupped cigarettes in their hands. They brought them up in unison to take a drag. If synchronized smoking were on the Olympic roster, those boys would have been going for gold.

The closer they got, the harder they looked. They'd lived fucking grim lives and their expressions said they'd be more than happy to share.

The shorter of the two went straight up to Dom. 'You the one looking for something?' It was the voice on the mobile. He sucked at his cigarette, displaying grimy nails and fingers stained yellow.

'No, it's me.' I took a step forward.

'What the fock do you want them for?'

'What do you think?'

The taller one moved in closer, smoke leaking from his nostrils. His hair was greased back and thinning. 'Don't push your luck, son. You focking Brits don't run this place any more, or hadn't you heard?'

I said nothing. I just wanted the weapons.

Little took another drag and looked up at Dom. Then he turned and we followed.

We went past the burnt-out Escort and down an alleyway between two blocks of flats. It was littered with rubbish and graffiti and it looked like we were hemmed in. There were three other guys waiting, younger guys in hoodies and jeans.

Little turned sharply and shoved me against

the wall. Dom got the same treatment from Large. The other three waded in and man-handled us through a search.

An old woman snapped her kitchen curtains. She'd have seen this stuff too many times before. I could hear kids screaming and shouting, and the rhythmic kicking of a ball against a wall.

They carried on pushing us along the walk-way. Little still led the way; Dom was a step or two behind me, and everybody else followed him.

He was getting a bit chattier. 'I hear this Brit's with British Intelligence and he's got the UDA working for him . . .'

I nodded. 'You got what I asked for?'

Dom appeared at my side, catapulted forward by one of the hoodies. Little stopped, turned, and jabbed me in the chest. He pushed me up against the wall, eyes burning. 'I'll tell you what else I hear . . . I hear you're focking SAS.' That was good for another hard poke. 'Friends of mine were murdered by the SAS. Maybe you pulled the trigger . . .'

It was pointless denying anything. Either way, the guy would do precisely what he wanted.

'Maybe.' I shrugged. 'But right now I'm going to solve a problem for you. It's not like the old days, is it? Gerry says we're one big happy family, these days, and he should know.'

He stopped poking. His skin creased and a

smile played across his cheeks. 'You go down to the end of the alley here, and you'll come to some bins. One of them contains what you want. They're wrapped up in black plastic.'

I turned, making sure Dom was with me. Little pulled me back. 'Those weapons have killed twelve focking Brit soldiers between them. Young lads, they were, in their prime. Well, the four I killed were, anyway.'

He kept hold of me a little bit longer, to let me share his enjoyment of the memory.

When we got to the bins, Dom looked back over my shoulder. 'You never said you were SAS.'

'You just asked how I knew the Yes Man. How the fuck do you think I got to work for the Firm in the first place? Now, get stuck into that bin and have a scavenge.'

101

Herbert Park
Wednesday, 14 March
0128 hrs

I sat well back from the window. The curtains were open but the house was in darkness, and had been since eleven. There had been virtually no traffic for the last half-hour; most of the neighbourhood was tucked up in bed.

They would come for us soon.

Dom sat at the top of the kitchen stairs, gripping the pole of his taser. It was plugged in, but not yet switched on.

Mine leant against the sofa, also ready to go. We both had twenty metres of play.

'Don't forget, mate.' I kept my voice low. 'Just a two-second burst.'

The third taser was on the landing above us, in

case there was a total fuck-up down here and we had to stand our ground upstairs. The two AKs were in Dom and Siobhan's bedroom.

They were our last resort. The Yes Man's guys wouldn't come in guns blazing, and no way did I want to use them inside the house unless the whole thing turned into a gangfuck. We'd wake up the whole street; the police would have the area sealed off within minutes. And that wouldn't get us any closer to Finbar. We wanted to know what was in their heads, but without spraying it all over the walls.

A shiny BMW 5 Series crawled past the house. The couple inside were dressed up for a night out. I wondered what they'd had for dinner. I was on my sixth brew and third packet of Hobnobs since we'd supposedly gone to bed.

They would definitely come tonight. The Yes Man wouldn't risk any more activity from us, any more phone calls or visits – especially since he didn't know exactly what we were up to. He would have to cut it here and now.

There would still have to be some finesse about the lift. I didn't know whether Mr Green and Mr Black could handle that, but I knew the way he'd want it. No gunshots. No noise. Just lift and go.

And I knew the way I wanted it. Whoever came to give us the good news was going to get zapped, then zapped again and again until one of them came up with the goods.

The BMW finally found a parking place and the couple got out. Her body language wasn't encouraging. She wasn't amused with the driver, not one bit. She stormed off towards a house further along the street while the old boy did the business with his key fob. The lights flashed once and he followed subserviently.

I thought about the weapons upstairs, and what they might have done over the years. They were so ancient the wood furniture had been rubbed bare. They were more than old enough to have killed those lads, and now they were going to be killing some UDA, and hopefully even a Brit. About time too. He needed culling.

Vehicle lights splashed across the road. The Seat cruised past from right to left. Both faces peered into the house.

I let them go and kept perfectly still. 'Stand by, mate, they're here.'

'How many?'

'Just the two of them. But they'll be carrying. They're not going to come in empty-handed. Don't fuck about – give them the good news as soon as I shout, OK?'

I stood up and flicked on the socket switch.

They wouldn't just smash their way in, run upstairs and hope to grab us before we knew what was happening. That left only the doors or windows, at the front or back – and even if they had only two brain cells between them, they'd work out that the back was the better option.

The locks on the downstairs toilet window were still undone – I'd made sure of that – and I'd slid open the catch to make it even easier for them. I wanted them to come in together. We needed to zap them both at the same time. Letting either of them do a runner to fuck up the whole plan was not an option.

Another five minutes crawled by. Mr Black walked past the house from left to right, checking everything out. He had a small day sack on his back. Fuck me, was there a third method of entry? Was he going to blow his way in?

He disappeared down the road. Mr Green would surely be working his way round the back, checking the walls to make sure the one they jumped over really was at the back of the correct house.

Mr Black came back the other way, towards the Seat. I waited for him to get out of sight.

'Won't be long now, mate.'

102

We moved into the kitchen. Dom flicked on the power to his taser.

I grabbed the stick with my free hand and put my mouth to his ear. 'With me, with me . . .' We moved slowly back to the island and lowered ourselves behind it.

There was a scraping noise at the window below us.

'When I move, you move. Straight in there before he knows what's happening. And once he's down, give him one for luck.'

Low murmurs drifted up from the garden. The toilet window was given a short, sharp push. They knew it was open now. They'd take their time, ease it up slowly.

I gripped the taser pole in my right hand. The forks would be clearly visible above the island, but by the time they'd spotted it, it would already be too late.

I heard feet touching the floor and the toilet-door hinge squeak. There was a rustle of nylon. I put my hand on Dom's shoulder to stop him jumping the gun.

I heard a low whisper, then the first creak on the stair.

I leant round the side of the island. Light glowed dimly in the stairwell.

Mr Green's head appeared above floor level. He paused and started climbing again, very slowly. Mr Black was right behind him.

I kept a hand on Dom until Mr Green had reached the top step and Mr Black was in view from the waist up.

'Go! Go! Go!' I yelled at the top of my voice, and lunged the four paces to the banister. I was aiming for Mr Black, to make sure their escape route was blocked. Dom had to take his chances with Mr Green.

Both tried their best to react, but Mr Black was too slow. I jabbed the taser forks into his shoulder like I was spear-fishing. He didn't even gasp, just fell forward on to the stairs.

Dom and Mr Green were getting up close and personal. There were a lot of grunts and shouts, and the stools beside the island toppled and fell.

I plunged the forks at the end of my broom-stick into my target's back and left them there.

Dom's taser was on the floor, inches away from

where they grappled. Dom was on top. I grabbed the broom handle as Mr Green arched his back and tried to head-butt him.

I kicked out at Dom. 'Get off him! Get the fuck off!' But Dom was in his own world. He threw a punch at the guy's head. He was well fired up. This guy was about to pay big-time for what Sundance and Trainers had done to Pete.

Fuck it. I touched Dom's back with the forks and he jolted sideways. I pulled him away with one hand and gave the boy on the ground a two-second burst with the other.

'Close the curtains, mate, get the lights on. Go on, go! Go!'

Dom stumbled to his feet.

Mr Green gave an agonized groan. This place smelt like someone had burnt the Sunday roast.

'And turn the power off on mine. I'll use yours to deal with this fucker. Just pull out the plug before we have any more drama, but leave the taser where it is.'

I stood over the guy in the green bomber, ready to give him an extra zap.

Dom tried to orient himself, but he was staggering like a drunk.

'Cancel that, mate – just grab the torch and search this fucker.'

He finally got the message and did as he was told.

I watched as he turned out Mr Green's pockets.

He had a mobile phone and a .38 snub-nosed revolver. There was no need to worry about Mr Black suddenly pulling a weapon. He was toast.

Another minute or so and we had the curtains closed, the lights back on. I gave Mr Green a kick in the ribs. 'Sit up!'

He didn't budge. I didn't blame him. In his position, I wouldn't have cooperated either.

I brushed his leg with the forks. His whole body jolted. He dragged himself on to his arse with his hands behind him. He was bowed, but not beaten. He could smell Mr Black; we all could. 'Fuck it. Get on with it then, boy – fry me.'

I looked at Dom. 'Ask him. Ask him what you need to know.'

'Where is Finbar?' He stooped to Mr Green's level. 'Where is my stepson?'

'Fuck you.'

I touched the forks to his shoulder. He saw them coming and tried to duck, but he went down hard. I gave him a good three seconds and he screamed.

He rolled on to his hands and knees and crawled towards the living room. Dom and I followed him across the floor. 'Fucking switch on, mate. We can do what we want with you here, so what are you holding out for? You'll fucking die – you really going to leave the Brit sitting pretty while you take the punishment? Where is Finbar? And where's the Brit?'

I brushed the back of his calf with the forks and he swivelled like a break-dancer. 'Come on, we can do this all night. Dom here's paid his electric bill. It ain't going to be cut off.'

I sparked up his mobile, a cheap old red and grey thing. He had no call history, no address book. Whoever he needed to call, or whoever was going to call him, they knew each other's numbers.

I gave his arse a jab this time. His body hit the floor like it was trying to melt into it. His breaths came fast and short.

'OK, here's the deal. You tell me who you were going to call once you'd lifted us, and I'll go easy with the cutlery. Let's start from there, yeah?'

His right cheek was pressed to the floor. I brought the forks down level with his left eye.

'What about a jab to the frontal lobe? A couple of seconds of *One Flew Over the Cuckoo's Nest* treatment. You'd end up barking at the moon every Tuesday. Come on, you're not fucking helping yourself. Where is the boy?'

He closed his eye. 'They'd fucking kill me.'

I touched the forks quickly to his skull and he half gurgled, half screamed. I gave him a Timberland in the ribs for good measure. 'Shut the fuck up. That's not what I want to hear.'

Dom grabbed my arm. 'Nick . . .'

If he was suddenly trying to play the good guy,

fuck him. This was the only way we'd get results this side of lunch-time.

'No, mate. If he doesn't tell us, he's going to die.'

Mr Green opened his eye again to see the forks just inches away. 'All right, then, just tell us who you were going to phone. Who were you going to contact to say you'd got us?'

Snot dribbled from his nose and formed a small puddle of slime on the floor. He sniffed hard. 'The Brit . . . I was going to call the Brit . . .'

'And what was the Brit going to do?'

'He was waiting.'

He couldn't control his breathing. The electricity churning through his heart had interfered with the comms system linking his brain and lungs.

'If you don't come up with some answers, the next zap's going to kill you.'

I got down on my knees and leant forward until our faces were level. I wanted to make sure I was close enough to hear if he started to have a heart attack. 'I bet you never thought this would happen when you signed up, eh? Now where's the boy?'

'Dun . . . Dundalk.' It was scarcely more than a whisper.

'Dundalk?'

He nodded like a drunk on a pavement.

'And that's where you were going to take us?'

He nodded again.

'What was going to happen there?'

He didn't need to draw pictures. We both knew. He was probably the one who would have done it.

I stood up.

I wanted him to get his breath back. He still had work to do.

I undid his day sack. 'Right, Dom,' I said. 'Let's have a look at this boy's party bag.'

103

I knew Dundalk well. It was only an hour and a bit up the motorway, and just this side of the border. As a young squaddy in South Armagh's bandit country, I'd often hear PIRA test-firing their homemade mortars down there. It was a sure sign we were going to get zapped within the next couple of days.

Later, when I was in the Regiment, the area still teemed with known PIRA ASU members, until we were told to do something about it. Who knows? Maybe it really was me who'd killed Little's mate. I hoped so.

Dom had all the gear from Mr Green's day sack on the floor. They'd come well prepared. There were foot-long strips of thin rubber to tie us up; gaffer-tape for our mouths; even a couple of black motorbike bags with drawstrings to bung over our heads.

Mr Green had finally managed to control his breathing. I knelt down beside him again. 'I don't want to know, so don't tell me – but if you've got kids and want to see them again, you'll do as you're told. I'm giving you the chance to live, here. You understand?'

He understood.

'In a minute, you're going to give that body of yours a shake and load your mate into the back of the wagon. Then all four of us are driving north. On the way, you're going to do what you're supposed to do and call the Brit. You got a name for him?'

He shook his head. I believed him. The Yes Man was no fool.

'You'll tell him you've lifted us both and you're on your way. Understood?'

'Aye.'

'Which one of you has the keys?'

He jerked his head in the direction of the spiral staircase.

'Here's what's going to happen. You're going to stay exactly where you are until I say to move or you'll get this in your fucking ear.' I looked up. 'Dom, get the keys, bring their wagon round the back, then fetch the weapons and unplug that taser upstairs. Don't want to burn the place down.'

Dom rifled the body on the stairs. The back door opened and closed a moment later.

Mr Green got a bit more confident. 'What do you think you're going to do when we get there? He'll rip your fucking heart out.'

'I'll just have to make sure I rip his out first. How many players has he got there in Dundalk?'

'Fucking loads. Why don't you just let me go? I'll tell you where he is. You can take the car. I don't want any of this shit.'

I touched his head with the forks. He melted into the floor once more.

'How many?'

'Five.'

'Including the Brit?'

'No.'

'Where in Dundalk? Town or outskirts?'

'West. A farm. It's a scrappy now.'

'That's better. Keep doing what I say and you'll still be around for breakfast.'

Dom came back and didn't say a word. He ran upstairs and reappeared with the weapons.

Mr Green's eyes widened. He wanted no part of it.

Dom went down the stairs again. I repacked the day sack and slid it on to my back. I grabbed Mr Green's .38 and pulled out the plug of Dom's taser.

'Come on, move your mate. And you'd better dig that phone number out of your head.'

He got to his feet and made for the stairs. I followed.

Mr Black was in shit state. There was a charred hole in his back where the forks were still embedded. The nylon had melted and burnt. There wasn't any blood, though, just shiny exposed muscle.

There didn't seem to be much love lost between the two of them. Mr Green wasn't exactly in mourning as he lifted the body over his shoulder. He headed for the back door and I turned off the lights.

Dom had the Seat waiting just the other side of the gate.

'Dump him in the back. Then lie on the rear seats, on your stomach, hands behind your back.'

I tied the thin rubber straps round his wrists, pulling so tight the skin whitened. Then I sat on his legs and pulled out the mobile.

Dom closed the gate and jumped into the driver's seat.

The exhaust billowed in the cold air.

'All right, mate. North on the M1, first stop Dundalk.'

He turned the lights on and we rolled out towards the main.

I gave Mr Green a clip across the back of the head. 'Right, what's his number?'

As he recited it, I dialled. 'You might be thinking about being clever and warning him, but remember this. When we get there and the shit hits the fan, he's not going to give a fuck about you. If he wants us dead, he'll think nothing of hosing you down as well. That's if I don't do it first. So think very carefully about what you're going to say.'

I lifted my head. 'Dom, give us a good bit of engine noise and a few gear changes once we're on the main.'

We turned left, and Dom obliged. I hit the button and shoved the phone towards Mr Green's mouth.

'It's me. We've got them . . . We've just left now . . . No trouble, both of them can still talk . . . See you there.'

He nodded and I pressed the red button.

I sat back up, still on his legs. 'Now you're going to tell us everything about this scrappy and who's going to be there, and what you would have done if you'd been in the driving seat.'

104

Dundalk was a big market town whose main claim to fame during the war had been as a safe haven for bad terrorists. Nowadays most people knew it for having spawned the Corrs. As kids they'd probably practised their harmonies in the front room accompanied by the dull crump of PIRA on homemade mortar.

The wet streets were all but deserted. I was fucked. My head bobbed up and down and banged against the window as the street-lights strobed past.

I wasn't the only one. Mr Green had cramp again. I raised my arse a bit so he could fight the spasms, then sat back down on him. With his hands strapped up behind him, about the only other thing he could do was talk.

Half a mile of ruptured old concrete track led towards the farm. He told us he had to make the call immediately before he turned on to it. At the top of the track there was a cattle grid, then a yard full of crushed cars and piles of tyres. As we drove in, we'd see a line of four old artic containers that housed the reclaimed scrap. I stored all these details. If the landscape deviated in the slightest detail, if the track was mud not concrete, if there was a gate instead of a cattle grid, I'd make him very sorry indeed.

Finbar was in the second container along from the right. He was kept tied up most of the time. He slept on a big cushion and had a bucket to piss in. I'd watched Dom's reaction under the street-lights as he listened. He kept the Seat on the road, but he gripped the wheel so tightly his knuckles were as white as thermal imaging.

Dom glanced over his shoulder. 'We're nearly out of town.'

'Start looking for somewhere good and dark to pull in, and we'll get ourselves sorted.'

The street-lights petered out just after a sign had thanked us for visiting Dundalk. Dom slowed about a mile out of town and turned into a lay-by that led to a picnic area. Our headlights picked out tables and seats, and information boards about the local wildlife.

I climbed out and stretched. 'Weapons first, mate.'

Dom went to the back and opened up. I loaded a mag into an AK, pulled back on the cocking handle and released it. It was good to hear the familiar clunk as it rammed a round into the chamber. They'd have heard a lot of those clunks in this part of the world over the past thirty years. Even the cows wouldn't have bothered raising their heads.

Mr Green must have heard it too. He pressed his face a little bit harder into the seat, like he was hoping it would turn into a black hole. He was probably wondering if we'd bin him now he'd described the Yes Man's procedures and the lie of the land.

I handed Dom the weapon as we got out of the wagon, and pulled him to one side. 'You sure you want to do this?'

'It's OK, Nick. I know what I've got to do . . .'

'It's not going to be your best day out. If Fuckface in the back there is telling the truth, there's going to be at least five of them carrying, plus the Yes Man. This might sound corny, but our only hope is to go in with speed, aggression and surprise. You got that?'

He half smiled. 'SAS?'

'We control the fuckers, lift Finbar and get the fuck out. Straight off to Siobhan, and take it from there . . .'

'What about the Yes Man? We can't just kill him, Nick. He's at the heart of all this. We can use him to expose the whole network.'

I ignored him. 'Our mission is to get Finbar,

bung him in the back of the wagon and get the fuck out. We're not trying to change the world. End of story.'

'And the Yes Man?'

I shook my head. 'How many ways are there to tell you this? We've got to kill everyone who tries to stop us – and that means *everyone*. We've just got to crack on with it – step up to the plate, or whatever you Transylvanians say.'

He half smiled and lifted the weapon. 'I've never fired one of these in anger. I did my conscription in the forestry service.'

'Well, we're about to find out how good your basic training was.'

I didn't want him to dwell on it too much. When he was in front of a camera he might have thought he was invincible, but it's a different story when you're doing the firing and anyone with half a brain is firing back.

I walked back to the wagon, loaded and cocked my own AK. 'I'll drive now, mate – you sit on Fuckface. Remember, if we don't get stuck in, we lose – then Finbar and Siobhan lose as well.'

I got in behind the wheel, with the AK across my lap and the two spare mags tucked into my jeans. I waited for him to close the door, then headed on towards Dundalk.

105

'I need to see where the fuck we're going.'

Dom let Mr Green sit up.

'Left at the next junction. It's about two miles down the road. You'll see the sign for Caitriona Farm on the right. I'll need to call before you drive up it.'

I handed Dom the phone. 'Number's still on there, mate.'

We drove on in silence. There was fuck all to say; we just had to do.

Mr Green was getting his voice back. 'Listen, fellas, just drop me off. I'll do the fucking call, but let me go. Come on.'

I didn't bother to reply.

'We're here.' The badly handpainted sign wired to the fence would have looked at home in Kabul. I swung on to the track and stopped.

Dom tapped the keys and shoved the phone to Mr Green's ear.

'Aye, yep, it's me. We're turning in now.' He nodded at Dom, who cut the phone and shoved it into his pocket.

'Dom, shut him up. Use the gaffer-tape and the rubber strapping. Do his legs as well.'

'Hey, come on, please, let me go, fellas – I won't say anything, I won't do—'

Dom rummaged in the day sack.

I drove up a crumbling concrete track on full beam. I flicked on the fancy front fog-lights for good measure. There were no buildings yet, just shiny wet grass.

'You ready, Dom?'

I heard the click of his AK's safety lever.

'You make sure you point that thing at them, not me.'

I wasn't worried about getting shot. That was the business I was in. But getting shot by one of your own side is a bit of a fucker.

I checked my own safety. The arm was still up.

We crested a gentle rise. The farm was spread out below us. Light spilled from the ground floor of what looked like the main house on to a cracked and pitted concrete yard. Wrecked cars were piled haphazardly to the right of it, just as Mr Green had said.

We rattled over the cattle grid.

The concrete hard-standing was about twenty

metres wide and fifty long. The containers were jammed together in a line and padlocked up between the wrecks. The rest of the yard was like any other scrappy – in shit order. Hosepipes led in all directions from wall-mounted taps outside the house. Oily rags had been dropped where they'd been used. Tyres were stacked four or five high in a long line, like the safety wall at a race-track. Dirty water puddled the concrete.

Three guys emerged from the front door and stood waiting. Their cigarettes glowed in the darkness. The full beam and fog-lights hit them and they half turned or shielded their eyes with their hands. They were dressed for Sheriff Street, not the countryside, in jeans, trainers and leather coats. The lights were blinding them and I could see their mouths working as they cursed.

'Dom, you're going to hold them outside here. If they move, don't fuck about. You OK?'

'You can depend on me, Nick. I won't let you down. Or Finbar . . .'

I stopped the wagon with the three still caught in the beam. I left the engine running. I opened the door and got out. Dom was just behind me.

Weapon in the shoulder, safety lever down two clicks to single shot, I took one step to the right of the main beam.

They turned their heads. 'For fuck's sake, turn your lights off, you stupid shite . . .'

I kept my voice low. 'Stand still.' I kept

moving. 'Stand very still.' I spoke like I was trying to coax a child. 'I have a weapon. Stand still.'

I took a couple more steps and they saw what was going on.

'Show your hands! Hands, hands!'

All three were thirty-something. All three had a cigarette cupped in the right hand where their weapon should have been.

'Who's got the keys? Keys for the containers. I want the boy.'

Dom made himself visible on the left. The one in the middle flicked his cigarette to the ground and nodded towards the house.

I had to go straight in. I didn't know when the next lot might be coming through the door. I moved towards it. It was still ajar. Right hand on the pistol grip, pulling the butt into the shoulder, I pushed it gently with my left.

I moved into a tiled hallway. There was a strong smell of cigarette smoke. Voices filtered from a room at the end of the corridor. The beamed ceiling was low. I crouched to present a smaller target as I started along the hall.

The voices got louder. There was a burst of laughter. Cigarette smoke lingered in the doorway.

'On a job well done.' I heard educated Belfast. Glasses clinked. 'Shall we go and sort these shites out now, or let the lads play about for a while?'

I strode into the room, weapon up.

There were three of them sitting in old, floral-patterned armchairs. The Yes Man was in the middle. The two smoking either side of him were older, in their fifties, faces hard as stone.

They weren't fazed to see me. They kept hold of their glasses. A bottle of whisky stood at the Yes Man's feet.

'Playtime's over. Give me the keys for the boy.'

The Yes Man's eyes flicked between his companions. He was out of his depth now.

The one on the right held out his hands. 'Sure, sure. Take him and fuck off. Tell you what, I'm going to stand up and reach into my trouser pocket. The right pocket. I have the keys.'

I nodded.

'Stone! This is ridiculous . . .' The Yes Man was recovering fast.

The guy on the right heaved himself out of his chair. Very slowly, he moved his hand to his trouser pocket; his left was still wrapped round his whisky glass. 'Stay calm, son.'

The Yes Man was feeling feisty. 'Stop this nonsense, Stone. What's this boy to you?'

His companion rounded on him. 'Shut the fuck up!' He held up a set of keys and turned to me. 'Let's keep everything nice and calm now.'

There was a burst of automatic fire outside. The next thing I knew, a whisky glass was flying through the air. All three sprang into action. I had to assume they were going for weapons. I fired a quick double-tap into the one with the keys. A pistol clattered to the floor from his other hand.

I stood my ground, swivelled slightly right. Both eyes open, I fixed centre mass on the second target, who charged at me, head right down like he was making a rugby tackle, as the Yes Man disappeared through one of the doors behind him.

I double-tapped downwards, into his back, and he collapsed on the floor.

A cloud of cordite rose to join the cigarette smoke. It was like being back in the Jock's bar.

I scrabbled round the two bodies and found the ring of keys.

Another burst came from outside.

I charged back down the corridor. 'Dom, I'm coming out! Dom, don't shoot! Dom!'

There was no reply.

I got to the end, gulping for breath. 'Dom, I'm coming out, do you hear me?'

Nothing.

Fuck this. Weapon in the shoulder, I moved into the doorway. Over to the right, against the wall, three bodies lay in a heap. One must have taken a chance on Dom not opening up.

Dom was caught in the Seat's lights. He was frantically kicking and pulling at the lock on the second container. I ran across the yard, past Mr Green, who lay bound and gagged on the greasy concrete. He was moving like a slug, trying to get away.

'Dom! I've got the keys! Dom, calm down!'

He'd tried to blow the lock apart. There were strike marks in the steel all round it. Rust had been blasted away to expose shiny metal. He was lucky a round hadn't ricocheted into his head, or gone straight through and hit Finbar. 'Stop, mate – I've got the key.' I pushed him aside. 'Cover me, mate. I don't know who else is out there.'

I took a deep breath and started trying the keys. The third worked.

I pulled back on the handle. The locking bar creaked and the door swung open. The light from the Seat flooded in.

Dom rushed past me. 'Finbar! Finbar!'

He was just where Mr Green had said, lying on his side, on a large dog cushion. There was a bucket in the corner, surrounded by oily engine parts and wing mirrors. The smell of shit was overpowering.

'Finbar!' He turned back towards me, eyes wild. 'Nick, he's not . . .'

I went over and rolled him on to his back. 'Feel for a pulse . . .'

I lifted an eyelid. The eye was glazed and dull. I looked for an entry or exit wound. There was no blood.

'Finbar!'

He groaned. He tried to say something. A syringe and the rest of his paraphernalia were scattered over the floor.

'Dom, it's OK. The fuckers have kept him smacked up. He's going to be OK.'

Dom looked as if he didn't know whether to laugh or cry. 'It's me, Finbar, it's Dom.' He cradled him in his arms. 'It's OK, we're here.'

I tugged at Dom's arm. 'Come on, let's go, mate. Somebody will have heard that lot and called the police.'

He pulled gently on Finbar's arms and the mass of matted blond hair was moving off the cushion. 'It's OK, Finbar, it's all right, it's Dom. You're OK . . .'

The boy finally realized who it was.

'Dom, for fuck's sake, get him out to the wagon – we've got to go!' My shout echoed round the container.

A vehicle fired up behind me. I ran out as a Mondeo estate screamed past. The wheels lurched over Mr Green's head with two sickening thuds.

There was nothing I could do but fire. It was like someone crashing through a vehicle checkpoint. I stood, got a good position, and kicked off a series of rapid single shots into the fading shape.

Brake-lights came on and off.

I kept firing.

Finally it crashed into a post beside the cattle grid. I was already running.

The Mondeo's rear window was frosted; it had taken five or six strikes.

The Yes Man was crumpled against an airbag. Blood leaked from his neck; he looked like he'd just burst an extra big boil. His eyes were closed but he was breathing.

I wrenched open the door and reached in for the keys. He wasn't going anywhere.

I turned to see Dom staggering to the Seat with Finbar in his arms.

I ran back and helped lift the boy into the front seat, then threw my weapon into the back. I dragged out Mr Black and left his body where it lay.

Finbar was slumped forward against the dash. I helped Dom get a belt round him. I lifted the boy's chin. 'All right, mate?'

He looked, but he didn't see.

I concentrated on Dom. 'Take the weapons, soak them in bleach, get all the DNA off and dump them. Burn this fucking wagon, soon as you can. You ready to go? Turn right on to the main – don't head for the town. Every man and his dog will be heading this way. Go on, get on with it.'

'But, Nick . . .'

'I'm going to stay here, mate. The Yes Man's in that wagon. What's the point of getting the boy out if he can still come back and get us? Go on, fuck off, get Finbar back to his mum. We'll contact each other through Kate, OK?'

He put a hand on my arm. 'I still haven't said thank you.'

He went to hug me and I pushed him away. 'Get off, you soft bastard. If you don't get a move on, you'll be cuddling a five-hundred-pound cellmate, not me.'

He smiled and jumped behind the wheel, and I ran back towards the Mondeo.

The Seat rattled over the cattle grid and was gone.

I tried dragging the Yes Man from the wreckage by his arm, but his legs were trapped and he ended up hanging upside-down, his back arched, blood splattered across his shirt and tie.

His breath rasped through his blood-choked throat. The round hadn't gone all the way through his neck, just nicked him.

I dug out the snub-nosed .38 from my pocket and raked the hard steel fore-sight along his cheek.

He looked at me with no emotion. 'In the boot . . . Four hundred thousand pounds . . . In a diplomatic bag . . . Take it. Just leave me . . .'

I knelt beside him. 'You know what?' I dug the muzzle into his wound. He shuddered with pain. 'I've never known your name, but it doesn't matter, because I've never wanted to invite you round for dinner.' I thought about Pete and Magreb and all the other poor bastards who'd got in the Yes Man's way. 'You once called me arrogant and disrespectful, but you're a whole lot worse than that. You're responsible for a lot of innocent people getting fucked over and killed, and you don't give a shit.'

'And you do, Stone?' He almost spat the words.

I stood up. 'Yes,' I said. 'I do.' I walked across to a nearby stack of tyres. Lying across the top was a rectangle of flowery material that had once been a curtain. I grabbed it and dragged a length of hose across to the cattle grid. Then I went and turned on the tap.

He knew exactly what was going to happen. I didn't need to explain.

I threw the curtain over his face and gave him the good news with a round in each elbow; I didn't want him able to rip it off with his hands. He screamed and jerked left and right, but all that happened was that the blood leaked faster from his neck wound.

I splashed water over the curtain until it hugged the contours of his face. He choked and bucked and tried to kick his trapped legs free. I knew exactly how he felt. I carried on going for thirty seconds before I pulled the cotton aside.

We were both soaking wet. He gulped and wheezed and begged me to stop.

The horizon flashed blue from the direction of the town.

I threw the soaking curtain back over his face and redirected the hose. This time it wasn't coming off. He was never going to have the chance to get at me, or Dom, or Dom's family, ever again.

The gag reflex contorted him. He was drowning, and as his life ebbed from him I felt nothing but relief. No more threats, no more Sundance and Trainers turning up and filling me with dread because I knew there'd be a shit job I had to do.

His body went into spasm, and eventually went limp. I kept the hosepipe there for a while longer, then reached down and felt for a pulse on the side of his neck. There was nothing.

I pulled away the curtain. His face was frozen in a silent scream. I watched it for movement. He'd stopped breathing. His mouth was full of water. More dribbled from his nose.

Headlights bounced through the night sky just the other side of the rise.

I skirted the back of the Mondeo and jumped over the fence. I started to run. Not having soldiers on the border any more wasn't just an advantage to drug-runners.

As I melted into the darkness, brilliant blue flashes lit up the yard.

I carried on running.

Epilogue

I waited at the bottom of the wall as the two flashing blue lights rushed past and turned left, away from me.

The wall wasn't as high as I remembered it. I could probably have managed without the aluminium ladder.

I looked up. There was no security lighting, but the moon was out. There was no sign of razor wire glinting along the top.

I put the ladder against the wall and started to climb. It wasn't long before I was sitting on the coping. I stopped, looked and listened. It was just after two in the morning, and there was just the occasional car or truck, but it would take only one pair of eyes to spot me. There might even be security inside. I didn't know; there hadn't been time to do a proper recce.

I leant down and stretched out my hand. A small one gripped mine. She was light, and it didn't take much effort to lift her up beside me. 'Wait there a minute. Just sit quietly.'

The next one up didn't need help. It wasn't long before we were all sitting in a row. I leant down, grabbed the top of the ladder and hauled it up, then swivelled on my arse and lowered it the other side.

We came down in reverse order.

Moonlight glimmered on a strip of grass, and then we were on concrete. It was only a few steps more to the water's edge.

'Nick, can you hold this a sec? I just want to say something to Ruby.'

Tallulah smiled and handed me the container. She knelt down and gave her stepdaughter a hug. The big shock of hair framed a slightly happier face than she'd worn last time I saw her.

I'd made contact with Dom two days later. They'd gone straight to Siobhan in Donegal and had the great love-fest reunion.

The media coverage was as it should be. The rounds recovered from the bodies confirmed that it was another drugs-related incident, ex-UDA versus ex-PIRA. Forensics revealed that the AKs that had fired them had some previous. They had killed British soldiers in the eighties.

The dead men were discussed at length, but there wasn't a single mention of the Yes Man.

There never would be. Every man and his dog, in both governments, would take his story to their graves.

Siobhan was with Finbar in Arizona now, tinkling bells and chanting. Some kind of trendy New Age rehab woo-woo, Dom said.

He was back in Afghanistan with Kate, his new right-hand girl. Basma had arranged a meet between Dom and the Taliban dealer, who was very pissed off that his British contacts had gone to ground and backed away from their agreement. It would have been worth getting satellite TV just to watch Dom's programme go out. I said I'd pop in and see the three of them in Dublin when it aired, but I knew I wouldn't. I was going to do this one last little thing, and then I'd move on.

'Ruby, remember how we looked at the films of you and Daddy playing at this pool?'

I watched their moonlit reflections on the surface of the water.

'He's mostly in the garden now, so he'll always be with us, in all the places he loved most. But remember how he loved to swim here?'

Too right. In my mind's eye I could see the big stupid grin across Pete's face.

'Nick?'

'Here you are.'

I handed Ruby the urn, and watched as she unscrewed the lid. She had to turn it almost upside down before the tiny handful of ash fell out and spread across the water.

Tallulah put a hand on my arm. 'Nick, thank you. For everything . . .'

One of Dom's first jobs had been to bang four hundred thousand dollars into an account in Kabul, the same amount as I'd invested in Ruby's trust fund. Well, the Yes Man had offered. It had cost five per cent to deposit and move, a bit more than a drug-dealer would pay, but worth every penny.

Basma was going to take a small percentage for her refuge, and administer the rest for Magreb's widow. She'd promised to make sure the four boys received the education the silly fucker had been so passionate about. They'd be doctors one day, maybe.

Everyone's future seemed secure. Except mine. I wasn't sure what I was going to do, but I'd have to get my skates on. My invoice to Moira for helping Dom with his Kabul research was still in dispute, and I was skint.

That $50 million bounty on bin Laden's head was beginning to look awfully fucking tempting.

THE END

SEVEN TROOP

ANDY McNAB

They were like a band of brothers...

In 1983 Andy McNab was assigned to B Squadron, one of the four Sabre Squadrons of the SAS, and within it to Air Troop, otherwise known as Seven Troop.

This is Andy McNab's gripping account of the time he served in the company of a remarkable group of men – from the day, freshly-badged, he joined them in the Malayan jungle, to the day, ten years later, that he handed in his sand-coloured beret and started a new life.

From the pen of the man who invented the modern military memoir comes another storming battering ram of thrill-packed, unforgettable drama. Never before revealed operations and heartbreaking human stories combine to create a new classic of the genre and a book that takes us back to where it all began...

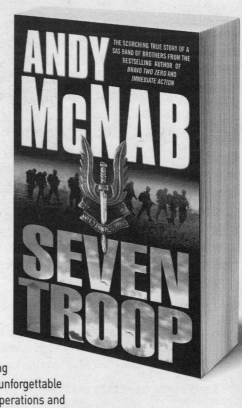

ANDY McNAB

THE SCORCHING TRUE STORY OF A SAS BAND OF BROTHERS FROM THE BESTSELLING AUTHOR OF *BRAVO TWO ZERO* AND *IMMEDIATE ACTION*

SEVEN TROOP

ZEF O HOUF

THE BLISTERING
NEW NICK STONE THRILLER

ANDY McNAB

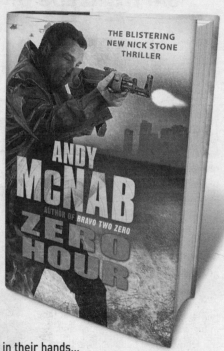

A code that will jam every item of military hardware from Kabul to Washington...

On 5 September 2007, Israeli jets bombed a suspected nuclear installation in north-eastern Syria. Syrian radar – supposedly state of the art – had failed to warn the target of the incoming assault.

A system on the verge of collapse...

Unknown to anyone but the Israelis and the radar's manufacturers, the commercial, off-the-shelf microprocessors within it contained a remotely accessible kill switch.

A terrorist group who nearly have it in their hands...

Now British Intelligence has discovered that the same switches are at the heart of every electronic device in the UK and US arsenal. It will take years to replace the components. So they must deactivate the man who controls them instead.

And a soldier who wants to go down fighting...

Ex-SAS deniable operator Nick Stone is tasked to find and kill him – but this time he's not on 'receive'. For once, his life is under threat for another reason – from within. And now he really is a man with nothing to lose...

SPOKEN FROM THE FRONT

REAL VOICES FROM THE BATTLEFIELDS OF AFGHANISTAN

EDITED BY

ANDY McNAB

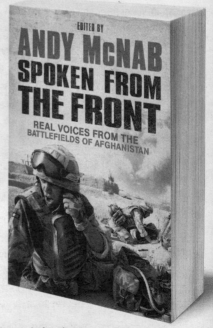

The war in Afghanistan is one of the toughest campaigns the British Army has ever had to fight. Traditionally the graveyard of any invading force, its barren and inhospitable terrain has seen off many comers over its bloody history. When British forces took up their positions in Helmand Province in Summer 2006, they knew what they were getting into. They knew how hard it would be.

Spoken from the Front is the story of the Afghan Campaign, told for the first time in the words of the servicemen and women who have been fighting there. With unprecedented access to soldiers of all ranks and occupations, Andy McNab has assembled a portrait of modern conflict like never before.

From their action-packed, dramatic, moving and often humorous testimonies in interviews, diaries, letters and emails written to family, friends and loved ones, emerges a 360° picture of guerrilla warfare up close and extremely personal. It combines to form a thrilling chronological narrative of events in Helmand and is as close to the real thing as you're going to get.

WAR TORN

ANDY McNAB
& KYM JORDAN

Two tours of Iraq under his belt, Sergeant Dave Henley has seen something of how modern battles are fought. But nothing can prepare him for the posting to Forward Operating Base Senzhiri, Helmand Province, Afghanistan. This is a warzone like even he's never seen before.

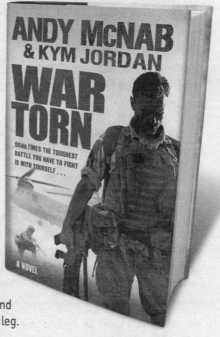

He's in charge of 1 Platoon, a ragbag collection of rookies who he must meld into a fighting force and fast. The Afghanistan conflict is as harsh and unforgiving as the country itself. Their convoy is ambushed before they even reach the FOB, and two of his men are grievously wounded, one scorched beyond recognition, the other left with only one leg.

Back at home, the families of the men – and women – at the front wait anxiously for news. Dave's wife, Jenny, seven months pregnant, must try to hold together the fragile lives of those they left behind, all of whom remain in constant dread of the knock on the door and the visit from the Families Officer, whose job it is to deliver the bad news...

War Torn traces the interwoven stories of one platoon's experience of warfare in the twenty-first century. Packed with the searing danger and high-octane excitement of modern combat, it also explores the impact of its aftershocks upon the soldiers themselves, and upon those who love them. It will take you straight into the heat of battle and the hearts of those who are burned by it.

BRUTE FORCE
ANDY McNAB

BETRAYAL

A cargo ship is apprehended by the authorities off the coast of Spain, packed with enough arms and ammunition to start a war.

REVENGE

Twenty years later, an unknown aggressor seems intent on taking out those responsible for the treachery – one by one. The last victim was brutally tortured with a Black & Decker drill and then shot through the head at point-blank range.

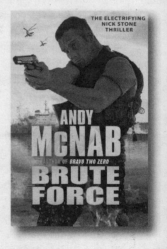

CONFRONTATION

And Nick Stone – ex-SAS, tough, resourceful, ruthless, highly trained – is next on the killer's list. He has only two options – fight or flight – but which do you choose when you don't know who you are up against . . .

'Stunning . . . A first-class action thriller'
The Sun

'Violent and gripping, this is classic McNab'
News of the World